UNCOMMON ASSASSINS

UNCOMMON ASSASSINS

EDITED BY WELDON BURGE

Smart Rhino Publications
www.smartrhino.com

These are works of fiction. All of the characters, organizations, places, and events portrayed in these stories are either products of the authors' imaginations or used fictitiously. Any resemblance to actual persons (living or dead), events, or locales is purely coincidental.

First Edition

ISBN-13: 978-0-9847876-2-3
ISBN-10: 0984787623

DEDICATION

For my wonderful, supportive, and gorgeous wife, Cindy

CONTENTS

NIGHTSHADE   1
STEPHEN ENGLAND

THE PEPPER TYRANT   25
J. GREGORY SMITH

EVERYBODY WINS   37
LISA MANNETTI

FAT LARRY'S NIGHT WITH THE ALLIGATORS   47
KEN GOLDMAN

THYF'S TALE   57
CHRISTINE MORGAN

MISCONCEPTIONS   67
MATT HILTON

SECOND AMENDMENT SOLUTION   75
BILLIE SUE MOSIMAN

KILLER   95
KEN BRUEN

FOR THE LOVE OF BOYS   107
ROB M. MILLER

BLOODSHED FRED   121
MONICA J. O'ROURKE

SLASHER   129
F. PAUL WILSON

FIRE & ICE   147
JOSEPH BADAL

MADAME   169
DOUG BLAKESLEE

THE MAN WHO SHOT HITLER   177
ELLIOTT CAPON

MERCY KILLING   189
LAURA DISILVERIO

SCRUB   199
MICHAEL BAILEY

THE WELLMASTER'S DAUGHTER   205
JAMES S. DORR

WISH I'D NEVER MET YOU   215
JONATHAN TEMPLAR

THE BLUELIGHT SPECIAL   223
J. CARSON BLACK

WELCOME TO THE FOOD CHAIN   235
WELDON BURGE

INSIDE OUT   245
AL BOUDREAU

KATAKIUCHI   255
CHARLES COLYOTT

TAKING CARE OF BUSINESS   265
LYNN MANN

THE WRITERS   269

THE ILLUSTRATOR   279

ACKNOWLEDGMENTS

Thanks go to Nanette O'Neill for her striking cover illustration, to Scott Medina for designing the cover, and to Terri Gillespie for her excellent proofreading skills.

I must also point out here that, although most of the stories are original to this volume, a number are reprints. Lisa Mannetti's story, "Everybody Wins," and Monica J. O'Rourke's story, "Bloodshed Fred," were originally published in the anthology *These Guns for Hire,* edited by J. A. Konrath. Ken Goldman's story, "Fat Larry's Night With the Alligators," first appeared in *Black Moon #2* (September/October 1995). F. Paul Wilson's classic tale, "Slasher," was initially published in the *Predators* anthology, edited by Ed Gorman and Martin H. Greenberg. James Dorr's story, "The Wellmaster's Daughter," was first published in the November 1991 issue of *Alfred Hitchcock's Mystery Magazine.*

NIGHTSHADE

BY STEPHEN ENGLAND

5:23 P.M. Local Time
Ciudad del Este
Paraguay

He wasn't supposed to be here. None of them were. That wasn't unusual—he'd spent well over ten years of his life going places he wasn't supposed to go, doing things he wasn't supposed to do.

The man looked to be in his thirties, tall, at least a couple inches over six feet—his height and dark, close-trimmed beard betraying the fact that he wasn't a local, despite the street clothes. He might have been an Arab, though—there were certainly plenty of them in the Tri-Border Area, the disputed zone between Brazil, Argentina, and Paraguay. The AK-47 assault rifle lying by the man's side was equally common. Ciudad del Este was a nexus for weapons traffickers of all creeds and colors.

The tall man shifted his weight against the sandbags piled on the floor of the third-floor apartment, taking his eyes off the scope of the SVD Dragunov for a moment. The Russian-made Dragunov wasn't a state-of-the-art sniper rifle, but local color was more important.

"Need a break, Harry?" A voice asked from behind him.

He looked down at his Doxa dive watch, then back at the muscular Asian reclining easily on the dingy apartment's bed. "Thirty minutes on the scope, Sammy. Thirty minutes off. You know the drill. We switch in five."

Below them, street noise drifted up through the open window, noise and the smell of rotting garbage.

Two hours.

6:48 P.M. Eastern Time
CIA Headquarters
Langley, Virginia

"Give me some good news, people." For a man with a prosthetic leg, Director Bernard Kranemeyer knew how to make an entrance. He arrived in the operations center of Clandestine Service with all the subtlety of a storm front moving in, dark eyes sweeping across the workstations until his gaze fell upon a short black man. "What's the latest from Alpha Team, Ron?"

Ron Carter plugged the USB cable into the back of his workstation and glanced up at his boss. The director of the Clandestine Service still had all the bedside manner of the Delta Force sergeant major he'd been until an Iraqi IED took off his right leg below the knee.

"Nichols checked in at sixteen hundred local time. Everything's still go-mission."

Kranemeyer moved to the bank of plasma screens filling one wall of the op-center. Screens filled with satellite photos, their timestamps indicating their sequence over the course of the two months of Operation NIGHTSHADE. "How long before the KH-13 closes within range?"

"An hour away," Carter replied, referring to the CIA spy satellite. "The KEYHOLE will be in orbit over the target area for exactly ninety minutes—we'll have full spectrum coverage, thermal imaging if necessary. That's our window."

A rare smile crossed the director's face. "It'll be good to have this over, bring the team back home."

"It would have been so much easier to send in a Predator drone—take him out with a single Hellfire when he leaves the apartment in the morning."

It would have been. But those weren't their orders.

"The president, God bless his soul—isn't about to make the same mistake twice." Kranemeyer shot a sardonic look at his lead analyst. "Relations with Pakistan still haven't stabilized since the bin Laden raid and the administration doesn't need those types of problems south of the border. The whole idea is to make this look like a local job. Total deniability."

That brought a laugh from Carter. "Think the politicos will ever get out of our way and let us do our job?"

5:57 P.M. Local Time
Ciudad del Este
Paraguay

Jean-Claude Manet, aka Ramzi bin Abdullah. Codename: HARROW. At one point the leader of al-Qaeda operations in Europe. Truth be told, the Agency didn't know when or why the French-born Manet had converted to Islam, just that he had become radicalized after moving to Marseilles and coming under the "ministry" of a Salafist imam with connections to bin Laden.

Manet was the perfect recruit. Mid-forties, white, quintessentially French. Even with the thick beard he had grown after conversion, he didn't fit the profile. For five years, the CIA had worked with the French to bring him down, with nothing to show for it.

If Manet's only daughter hadn't started sleeping with a young *khafir* artist from Toulouse—if Manet hadn't then decided to *kill* his daughter ... well, none of them would be here. He was now an SDT (Specially Designated Terrorist) and fair game as far as they were concerned.

Harry Nichols laid his binoculars aside, running a hand over his dark beard. Everything was in place.

A knock came at the apartment door and his hand stole toward the Colt 1911 holstered at his side.

"Answer it, Sammy," he hissed, gesturing to his partner. "I've got your six."

Samuel Han was already on his feet, moving from the bedroom into the living room of the apartment. His suppressed Beretta was clutched in a two-handed Weaver grip, the weapon an extension of himself.

The Asian moved with a grace born of training—he'd been a SEAL once, in a different time.

Harry watched him in the cracked mirror as Han advanced on the door, holding the gun to one side as he opened the door a crack.

"Oh, it's you," were the next words out of Han's mouth as the third member of the team entered the room. Harry slipped the Colt's safety back on and exited the bedroom.

"*Salaam alaikum*, Hamid," he said with a smile, extending his hand. Blessings and peace be upon you.

A light danced in the Arab's blue eyes as he clasped Harry's hand in both of his. "*Alaikum salaam*, my brother."

They'd worked together for so many years, dating back to their time in Iraq. It was Hamid Zakiri's native country, albeit a country he and his family had fled in the '90s.

"Anyone miss me?"

Hardly," was Han's sarcastic response. "Plenty of *great* stuff on the TV."

Hamid favored him with a grin "Latin soap operas may be corny, but they're still better than anything you can buy out there on the street."

That sobered everyone up. They were in the heart of Ciudad del Este's red-light district and pornographic videos were for sale everywhere—many of them locally produced and "featuring" children. It might have seemed a strange place to be hunting the key player of an Islamist terror network, but those were the realities of the war on terror. Nothing was as it seemed.

Harry cleared his throat. "You find anything actionable?"

"I met with SKYWALKER," the Iraqi replied, referring to the Agency's informant. "We talked things over in one of the downtown bars. He says the meet is going down shortly after nineteen hundred local—says bin Abdullah is already in the building, staying under wraps until after the meeting."

"Do you believe him?"

A pause, and Hamid nodded, an expression of distaste crossing his countenance. "He'd had too much alcohol to be lying." A practicing Muslim himself, Zakiri didn't drink. It was the primary reason Harry had chosen him to make the rendezvous.

Harry gestured to the sniper rifle. "We've not been able to pick up much, just an occasional visual on the wife through the window. Thermal's useless, can't penetrate the thick walls. Long and short, we can't independently confirm. Bin Abdullah could be inside. So could a couple dozen Wahhabis."

Hamid walked over to the window. "We have muscle near the door—Libyans by the look of them. Two guys, the big one has a pump gun, but the small one's the leader. You can tell by the way they interact. Little guy's carrying a stainless steel Kimber."

Amateur hour, Harry snorted. You could tell a lot about hired muscle by their hardware. If they chose their weapons based on their "cool" factor, well then—Islamists or not—they'd been watching too many Western music videos.

Time to hold the ball, make the call. Over a decade as a CIA paramilitary operations officer and making these decisions never got any easier. They'd waited two months for this night, for this opportunity. But without independent verification ... they were flying blind.

"Let's do this," he announced finally, looking around at his team. "Sammy, get Langley on the horn. It's time we got the final go-mission."

There was no comment, but he could see it in their faces, his own thoughts reflected in their eyes. They had a bad feeling about this.

7:36 P.M. Eastern Time
CIA Headquarters
Langley, Virginia

"What's the deal?" As soon as Carter turned and saw the look on the face of the DCS, he knew the question had been ill-advised. He didn't even really belong here, the analyst thought. The Intelligence

5

Directorate cut his checks, but with his skill set, he was being increasingly schlepped to the Dark Side—as analysts called the operations side of the house.

"Nichols," Kranemeyer responded, a heavy sigh escaping his lips. "They've been unable to confirm that HARROW is actually in the building."

"That shouldn't be a problem." He didn't see that it was. They'd planned for this. Multiple redundancy. "SKYWALKER's wearing a wire. He confirms HARROW's presence, the team goes in. About as simple as it gets."

An unpleasant smile crossed Kranemeyer's face. "That's what the President thinks too, Carter. This isn't a game. Once you've got men in the field, illegals in a foreign country—there's nothing simple about it. Anything could go wrong. Any one of a thousand things."

6:46 P.M. Local Time
Ciudad del Este
Paraguay

"Roger that, boss. Yeah, I understand. Have Carter monitor the satellite feed—let me know if any problems crop up. We'll give this a whirl."

Harry hit the END button on his TACtical SATellite phone and slipped the TACSAT back in his pocket.

"What's going on?" Hamid asked, glancing over at his team leader.

Harry laughed. "Langley's solved all our problems for us. Or they think they have. We don't *have* to trust him. Once SKYWALKER is in place, they're going to run voiceprint analysis on the conversation to determine whether HARROW is really in the room."

They both knew what that meant. "Five minutes?"

Harry shook his head. "More like ten."

There went the *quick* part of it. Sometimes plans didn't even survive contact with your allies. Forget the enemy. They walked back into the bedroom, where Han lay manning the Dragunov. "The target window opens in twenty minutes with the arrival of SKYWALKER. We need to be ready to strike the minute we have target confirmation, hard and fast. From shots fired we've got thirty minutes to clear the area." He smiled. "The local *policía* may be too corrupt to put in an appearance, but the same thing can't be said of the cartel's muscle. They'll be all over us."

"Tell me again why we couldn't get a camera on the inside?" This from Han.

"Too risky." Harry reached down and picked up a pair of high-powered binoculars, aiming them down the street, watching the pedestrians, the shoppers moving in and out of the myriad of storefronts. Dusk was falling, the dirty, faded buildings casting long shadows in the setting sun. "They're bound to have swept the room before the arrival of bin Abdullah. They find a cam—game over."

"Abdullah," Hamid whispered behind him, uttering an Arabic curse under his breath. "The slave of God. Where do these people get off believing that they speak for Allah?"

Harry didn't take his eyes off the street, but a quiet smile touched his lips. A Christian himself, he and Hamid loved to debate. "It's your religion, my friend. Not mine."

"My religion ..." Zakiri walked over to the window, gently pulling back the shade. "Through history, men have always sought heavenly sanction for their evil deeds. Divine license to kill."

8:06 P.M. Eastern Time
CIA Headquarters
Langley, Virginia

It was a beautiful way to fight a war. Carter leaned back in his desk chair, peeling the rest of the wrapper off a Hershey's bar.

Movement on-screen caught his eye and he keyed his communications headset. "We have the package, EAGLE SIX. SKYWALKER's entering the target area—look for a gray Volvo."

"License number?" Harry's voice, from over four thousand miles away.

The analyst's eyes narrowed as he tapped a command into the keyboard, watching as the satellite image zoomed in on the moving vehicle. "Here we go ... Echo Romeo Zulu oh-niner-seven. He's about four klicks out."

Five million dollars. Cash. Nonsequential Ben Franklins. Carter interlaced his fingers behind his head. It was Agency money, squirreled away from Capitol Hill through a hundred shadow programs. If people only knew ... a lot of government "waste" was simply money siphoned off into the black budgets of the intelligence community. Five million dollars in the back of that gray Volvo. It wasn't by accident that Ciudad del Este was the largest cash economy in the Western hemisphere.

The man codenamed SKYWALKER was a long-time player in the Tri-Border Area, known as a businessman—a middleman willing to deal in most anything. If you wanted enough RPGs to start a small war, enough heroin to send UCLA into orbit, or enough young Thai girls to start an underage escort service, he was your man. A facilitator. It had been five years since the FBI had caught him leaving LAX under an assumed name. Four years since Langley had flipped him, erasing the charges against him in exchange for having a man in Paraguay. Yeah. They'd put a pervert back on the street.

That was the nasty side of the spy business. Carter made a face, throwing the rest of the Hershey's bar into the trash. Lost his appetite. "EAGLE SIX, you should have eyes on SKYWALKER any minute now."

7:15 P.M.
Ciudad del Este
Paraguay

"Boss, we've got a gray Volvo inbound from the north." It was Zakiri, standing well within the shadow of the apartment's window. Harry moved to his side, taking the binoculars from him.

The crowds had dispersed from the street with the setting of the sun—leaving behind the detritus of the red-light district, the neon lights of a distant bar flashing in the gathering darkness. Harry's binoculars picked out the shivering form of a half-naked young prostitute standing beneath the harsh glow of a streetlight. She was doing her best to look seductive, but it came across as desperation. Couldn't have been more than thirteen.

He looked away, re-focusing on his target. Sooner or later, you had to realize you couldn't save the world.

He switched on the night-vision, zoomed in on the Volvo as it pulled into a parking space in front of the target building.

The passenger door opened and a short, balding white man exited, holding a briefcase in his hand. His light jacket did nothing to conceal his growing paunch.

"I have VISDENT on SKYWALKER," Harry announced, more for Langley's benefit than their own. Visual identification.

The Libyan muscle moved from the shadows, advancing on the white man. Not bad, Harry thought, watching them as the big man flattened SKYWALKER against the hood of his car, frisking him.

Head to toe, and back again. James Bond movies aside, there just weren't that many places on the human body from which you could comfortably and quickly draw a weapon. His partner turned his attention to the briefcase, ostensibly checking it for explosives.

Harry aimed the binoculars at SKYWALKER as they hauled him to his feet, adjusting the focus until he could see the sweat on the businessman's cheeks. *Stay calm*, Harry breathed. *Stay calm.*

Stay calm, the man called SKYWALKER told himself. It's what he'd been telling himself ever since this hellish ordeal got started.

He took a look around as they pulled him to his feet. The street was deserted, except for a few drunks and the hooker. She looked familiar—then again, all Asian girls looked alike to him.

Anyone but the Arabs. That's what he'd told them when they'd read him in. He'd do business with anybody but these psycho ragheads. That's what he'd kept telling them—until the leader of the CIA team had laid his choices on the table.

Convey the money to Ramzi bin Abdullah, or be outed as a U.S. government informant. In a city like Ciudad del Este, that would have cut his life expectancy to hours. Three or four of them.

So here he was, working as a courier again. The money was supposed to be from some two-bit Saudi prince—what was his name? Crap.

The little one pushed open the door of the apartment building and waved the Kimber, motioning him inside. He glanced back to see the big guard still standing by the Volvo. Good choice. There were four more identical briefcases in the trunk of the Volvo. A million each.

Enough money to have set him free. Leave, go somewhere in Europe, Eastern Europe preferably, out of reach of the blasted CIA. Eastern Europe, a cash economy with women almost as cheap and desperate as Southeast Asia. To start anew.

Freedom. He licked his lips nervously. It wouldn't work. The Agency was tracking the bills. How, they wouldn't tell him.

Metal on metal behind him, a pistol slide being racked. His heart almost stopped at the sound.

"You don't have to do this," he whispered, instinctively raising his hands. "Please God, don't."

7:23 P.M.

There was no warning. No time to react. The explosion hammered their eardrums, the sound of a pistol being discharged only inches from the microphone. Han ripped off his headset with a curse, throwing it against the wall. "What's going on?"

A second pistol shot followed the first. They could hear SKYWALKER struggling to breathe, hear him cough, a rough, hacking sound. The sound of a man dying.

Harry's face hardened, watching the second sentry, by the Volvo. He hadn't moved, despite the gunshots. He had been *expecting* them.

And in that moment, Harry knew—a disconcerting flash of certainty. A sixth sense, warning of danger. "Scratch this," he announced, "we've been played."

He saw the look of shock on Han's face. "Leave the long gun where it is, it's sterile—nothing to connect it with us. Carter, are you getting this?"

"What's your sitrep, EAGLE SIX?"

"SKYWALKER's dead and I'm calling an abort on NIGHTSHADE. My authority. They have to know we're here."

"Wait one, EAGLE SIX." There was no time. Harry moved to the apartment's dresser, wedging his fingers around the bowed wood, jerking the drawer outward. A small leather attaché case lay inside and he pulled it out, dumping the contents onto the bed. Three envelopes. "Clean passports, Belgian. The entry/exit stamps will be verified by our people if you're questioned. Standard E&E protocols apply." Escape and evade. Last resort.

"Sammy?" The former SEAL looked up from his envelope, his features calm, unruffled.

"Land. Take the *Ponte da Amizada* across the border to Brazil." The Bridge of Friendship. In the Tri-Border Area, the name seemed more ironic than anything.

Hamid had already disposed of the envelope, shoving the passport into his back pocket. "Sea," he said without being asked. "Go to ground until daylight, then take the ferry across the Rio Igacu to Argentina."

That left him, and he knew without looking. Air, Guarani Airport. He'd fly to São Paulo, and then catch a flight for the Caymans. No trail.

Han placed a hand on his arm as they moved toward the door. "If anything goes wrong ..."

He didn't say anything more. He didn't have to. The SEAL was the only married man on the team. Married, with twins.

"You know it," Harry replied, meeting his friend's eyes. "Sherri and the boys—they'll be okay."

Police sirens sounded in the distance, confirming his worst fears. They'd been set up.

"Don't stay together, whatever you do," he admonished, tucking his Colt into the inside of his jacket. "And remember—the cops may be dirty—they're also off-limits. Let's roll!"

8:48 P.M. Eastern Time
CIA Headquarters
Langley, Virginia

Two months. Two months and three days to be exact. He'd been detached to the Clandestine Service for the duration of NIGHTSHADE. In reality, the fun was only starting—the fun of figuring out what had gone wrong. It seemed disturbingly anticlimactic, Ron thought, leaning back in his office chair.

"Nothing like the movies, is it?" He looked up to find Kranemeyer standing behind him, staring at the LCD display of his workstation.

He shook his head. "Has the President been told yet?"

"That's happening now—has the money been moved?"

"That's a negative," Carter replied, bringing up an active window. "There you go. All the trackers are online and stationary."

"Any chance that Abdullah will be able to detect or disable them?"

The analyst shrugged. "Not according to the boys at S&T," he said, referencing the Agency's Directorate of Science & Technology. "The trackers cost almost as much as the cash they're supposed to keep tabs on."

That got a snort from Kranemeyer. "They were meant for the short term—Abdullah's going to get them banked and electronic before too much water goes under the bridge. Kiss the bills goodbye."

"Another five mil in the al-Qaeda war chest, courtesy of the American taxpayer. Of course, any one of our senators on the Hill would see that as a rounding error." Carter was feeling sarcastic, and it showed.

There was silence between the two men for several minutes, and then Kranemeyer cleared his throat. "I know it's tempting, Ron, but never allow yourself to second-guess the man in the field. Leaving three bodies on Paraguayan soil wouldn't have accomplished squat."

At that moment, Kranemeyer's phone rang with the familiar sound of Jon Bon Jovi's *Wanted Dead or Alive* and he stepped away, leaving Carter lost in thought.

Movement on the screen caught his eye and he focused his attention on the trackers. They were moving. He pulled up the streaming feed from the KH-13 on his second monitor, focusing in on the doorway of the apartment.

It was the Libyans, the two heavies from before plus three more. Each of them carrying one of the briefcases. Weapons drawn as they moved out into the street.

Then, behind them. It looked like a woman, the traditional *hijab* draped over her head and shoulders. Carter tapped a command into his keyboard and the resolution cleared up. Two little boys clung to her hands as they followed the armed men toward one of the parked vehicles.

12

No question about it. Ramzi bin Abdullah's wife Noori was known to them as well. And their sons.

The sight was strangely unnerving—to see the family of the man they'd been tasked with killing.

And they were on the move.

Kranemeyer swept back into the cubicle without so much as a greeting, grabbing up a communications headset off the desk. "What's going on?"

"We've been overruled," the DCS announced, his face tense and drawn. "NIGHTSHADE is to proceed at 'all costs'."

Carter shook his head. "Who gave *that* order?"

"The President himself." Kranemeyer sighed. "Not that the man has any clue what 'all costs' means. Probably got it out of some stupid movie. Get me a line to Nichols."

8:07 P.M. Local Time
Westbound on Route 7
Paraguay

The Nissan was at least eighteen years old, more proof the CIA had been neglecting its South American operations for far too long. Harry glanced carefully in the rearview mirror of the Agency vehicle, checking for a tail. Nothing.

He shook his head in disbelief, knowing he was going to have to come up with an answer. Sooner rather than later. He took a deep breath and keyed his headset mike.

"Seems like I remember a day when there was a gentleman's agreement with the White House about *not* micromanaging field ops."

"Different administration, Nichols." Kranemeyer sounded tired, even from four thousand miles away. World weary. "The times they are a-changing. We've located a Saudi-flagged Gulfstream IV on the tarmac at Guarani. Got a flight plan filed for the Windward Islands. Odds on, HARROW's family is headed to meet him there before leaving the country."

"What do you want me to do?" It was perfectly obvious, but protocol demanded that he hear the order. No misunderstandings.

13

"Collect your team. We'll do everything we can from here to keep that Gulfstream on the ground until you can mobilize." There was no indecision in Kranemeyer's voice. Just a cold, calculating certainty. "Once you're in position, eliminate HARROW."

HARROW. It didn't even sound like a man's name. Dehumanize your target. That was always the first rule. Made it easier to carry out the mission.

"It'll need to be close in, there won't be time to set a long-range shot—if they were tipped off, they'll be expecting a team—protocol, not a single man." Harry paused, as if weighing his decision. "I'll do this myself, Han and Zakiri will have enough to do getting out of the country. Have Carter send everything to my phone. I'll need satellite imagery of the Gulfstream and the surrounding area, security arrangements. The works."

There was a long moment before Kranemeyer responded. "We'll do this your way. Just remember—don't get caught."

That went without saying. It was always the way: if he succeeded, no one would ever know. If he failed, no one was coming for him. No glory in this. He closed the phone without saying goodbye.

8:23 P.M.
Guarani International Airport
Paraguay

Ciudad del Este was one place where the Golden Rule was still firmly in effect: *If you have the gold, you make the rules.*

It had been Carter's advice. Go straight in, through the front gate. It saved time, if not money.

Fifteen hundred dollars had gotten him through the security fence, around the metal detector and the scanners. Bribery was a way of life on the triple border. From the look in his eyes, it hadn't been the first bribe that guard had accepted. But it might be the last.

There was a Fokker 1000 bearing the logo of *Sol de Paraguay* taxiing on the runway as Harry strode through the concourse. Probably the biggest plane that could land—Guarani wasn't more than a mid-sized airport. Most any other part of the world, it wouldn't have even been dignified with the *international* designation.

"What's my sitrep?" he asked, turning on his headset. The advent of Bluetooth had made the life of an intelligence officer so much easier. People with electronics attached to their ear no longer raised eyebrows. Or invited questions.

"ETA on HARROW's family is five minutes," Carter replied. "Everything is in readiness for your departure. Once HARROW has been eliminated, give me the code *Firefly*. I'll release the virus."

Harry often wondered if Carter had been a hacker in a previous life. Either way, the Agency was in place to release a computer virus into the Ciudad del Este power grid, focusing on a substation three miles to the south of Guarani. Within ninety seconds of the go-code, the sector would be plunged into darkness.

We own the night. "Be advised, the satellite window closes in fifteen. We'll no longer be able to provide real-time updates when that happens."

"Fine." He'd worked without them before. He could do so again. Three storage containers were lined up near the security fence, a Komatsu forklift parked beside them.

Harry knelt down beside the rear wheel of the forklift, pulling his back-up weapon from its holster. A Kahr PM9, the subcompact semiautomatic was chambered in 9mm Luger. Six shots. Better not be getting into any firefights.

He tucked the pistol back into the left pocket of his jeans after a moment's thought, opting to leave it where it was. It was going to be awkward, a weak-hand draw, but he was counting on surprise. It would be his only ally.

From his crouching position, he could see the Gulfstream parked in front of the hangar. The stairs were pulled up into the fuselage—he could hear the whine of the Rolls-Royce turbofans. This was going to be close—was HARROW going to wait for his family? Was he even onboard?

The uncertainty of field ops. He stayed where he was, staring out toward where the Gulfstream sat beneath the glare of the airport's lights.

Two minutes. Nothing. Harry glanced up to see a pair of cars moving down the access road toward the hangar, with the familiar gray

Volvo in the lead. A calm, slow approach—they weren't looking to draw attention to themselves.

"You should have eyes on the package, EAGLE SIX," the voice in his ear intoned.

"Yeah," Harry replied, staying his crouch. "I can see that."

Forty meters of open ground to cross. No cover. "All you need to do is take out HARROW, do not—I repeat, do *not*—try to recover the money."

He hadn't intended to. What he didn't expect were the next words out of Carter's mouth. "The Paraguayan police have been alerted to the presence of HARROW and the money—he needs to be dead when they arrive."

Harry slammed the palm of his hand against the forklift's tire. "How much time do I have?"

"Probably ten minutes out. Fifteen, tops."

"And you were planning to tell me this when?" he demanded, taking another cautious look around the tire. A bearded man was descending the steps of the Gulfstream, a smile on his face as he approached his family. Ramzi bin Abdullah.

"No choice, EAGLE SIX. There's no way you could retrieve the cash, no way were we going to leave it in the hands of terrorists."

The desk jockeys always knew better. Always. "Time for me to go."

A sound struck his ears—the delighted shriek of a child hoisted in the air by his father. He watched as Abdullah hugged first his sons, then his wife, the black cloth of her *hijab* fluttering in the turbulence of the jet engines.

To kill a man in front of his family ... he'd never done it before. Not like this.

Focus. Dehumanize. *He's not a man, he's a target.* Just a target. That lie never got old, no matter how many times you told it to yourself.

He felt the weight of the Colt in its holster on his right hip, the ice-cold bulge of the Kahr in his pants pocket. To kill a man ... no, *not* a man. Not a father. A target.

Bile rose in his throat and he choked it back, forcing himself to remember.

Standing in a Paris morgue a year before, staring down at the stripped, mutilated body of a young woman, a girl really. Aleena, a beautiful name for a once-beautiful girl. *Silk of heaven*, it meant in the Islamic tradition. They'd found her in the Seine, her body covered with stab wounds, already decomposing.

She'd been raped—by at least five men, according to DNA results. Including her father.

Ramzi bin Abdullah.

Harry ran a hand over his eyes, shuddering at the memory of it. It was like looking into the abyss.

Time to move. *Focus. Think.* He was going to need a diversion if he was to have a prayer of escaping. The blackout wasn't going to be enough, not by itself. He rose from his crouch, spying an oily rag lying on the driver's seat of the forklift. A T-shirt, actually.

Acting on a sudden impulse, he ripped it lengthwise, twisting the soiled fabric into a single long strip. He took another look around the forklift and screwed open the cap of the forklift's gas tank, feeding one end of the rag into the opening.

His target was still in place, in front of the Gulfstream, one of his little boys in his arms, but it was clear. Time was running short.

Kneeling there in the darkness, he pulled his Bic lighter from his pocket and depressed the button. He'd never smoked, but you never knew when you might need a good fire.

A spark and then flame sprang from the tip of the lighter, igniting the cloth. Lighting the fuse.

No more time for hesitation. The moment of truth.

Harry rose to his feet, covering the ground in easy, unhurried strides as he moved toward the Gulfstream.

Thirty-five meters.

The leather jacket hung easily on his tall frame, open, his hands only inches away from his weapons. Last resort.

Twenty-five meters, moving from the shadows now. Two Libyans within the threat matrix, two more near the back of the plane. The fifth had disappeared up the stairs. None of them were *visibly* armed. The Paraguayans might look the other way for many things, but an open display of weaponry?

That was pushing the envelope.

Fifteen meters and he saw HARROW glance his way, concern registering on his face as they made eye contact. The terrorist spoke into the ear of his son, lowering the little boy to the ground.

It was now or never. *"Salaam alaikum,* brother Abdullah," Harry called out, still moving forward, his arms outstretched in greeting. He was painfully vulnerable now.

Fortune favors the audacious.

He could see the bewilderment, the indecision in the eyes of HARROW and the two Libyans. Fatal indecision—every step took him closer to his target.

The little boy peeped out from behind his father's legs, regarding Harry with a childish curiosity. An innocence. "How do you know my name?"

Harry shrugged, watching the Libyans out of the corner of his eye. The big one from the safe house had a hand inside his jacket. His short companion was on a Motorola shortwave, talking to the rest of the team, undoubtedly. Zero hour.

"I come from the base," Harry replied in perfect Arabic. *Al-Qaeda.* "My name is Ibrahim al-Libi. The doctor, may Allah bless him and grant him health, sends his regards."

Dr. Ayman al-Zawahiri.

An expression of pleased surprise broke across HARROW's face. *"Alaikum salaam,* my brother."

Disregarding his bodyguards, he took a step forward, his arms outstretched. Harry glimpsed the little boy standing a couple feet behind his father, his thumb stuck firmly between his lips.

God forgive me, Harry breathed, feeling a tide of emotion, almost panic, wash over him. There was no point—not now. This wasn't a man. This was a target. Yes, a target. *HARROW.*

His left hand slipped down to his pocket as they embraced, kissing on both cheeks in the traditional greeting of the Middle East. No body armor, he could feel that—just flesh beneath the terrorist's shirt.

The Kahr slid smoothly from the polished leather of its holster and he drew Abdullah in close, jamming the gun into his ribs. He could feel the man's body tense against his and he squeezed the trigger once, twice. Point-blank range. Hollow point slugs ripping through muscle and tissue.

Blood and bits of bone sprayed into the air as HARROW staggered toward his son, clutching at the wound. Harry shot him twice more with the Kahr, high in the chest this time. He fell backward, splayed out on the tarmac.

A woman's scream rent the air, shock and sorrow mingling. Time itself seemed to slow down. He glimpsed the bodyguards reacting, the big man coming out of the back of the Volvo five meters away, the pump-action shotgun in his hands. *Primary target.*

The Colt materialized in Harry's right hand, the Libyan's face coming into focus through those straight-eight Heinie sights.

His first shot went wild, the suppressed .45 sounding like a hammer blow—drowned out in the roar of the Gulfstream's turbofans.

Steady, he breathed, hearing the cold, metallic sound of the shotgun being racked. Round in the chamber.

Adrenaline flooding through his body, he threw the nearly empty Kahr away, bringing up his left hand to steady his grip on the .45. Squeezing the trigger with a slow, steady motion.

The heavy slug smashed into the Libyan's throat, sending the man staggering against the side of the car, clutching at his destroyed vocal chords. Out of action.

Next target. A bullet flashed past his ear, the smaller bodyguard standing there, his Kimber blazing fire. Harry threw himself behind the Volvo, taking cover. He rolled over onto his stomach, staring across the tarmac at bin Abdullah's wife.

Tears streaming down her face, she knelt there on the asphalt, cradling HARROW's head in her lap. Her fingers caressed his cheek, coming away stained with blood.

Their son lay across his father's chest, weeping as he tugged at his father's shirt with all of his five-year-old might. The picture of grief. Lives destroyed in the mere seconds since he'd fired those first shots.

It was at that moment that the flame reached the Komatsu's fuel tank. The explosion smote Harry's ears, a fireball boiling into the Paraguayan night.

"Firefly. *Firefly!*" He rose up from behind the Volvo, catching the Libyan distracted and silhouetted against the flames. "Execute, execute, execute!"

The Libyan started to turn, started to react, but it wasn't going to be soon enough.

The two shots resounded as one, the classic double-tap. The small man reeled, crumpling to the tarmac, his legs kicking spasmodically.

Harry looked back, watching as a pair of guards came around the wheel of the Gulfstream, responding to the threat. More than a little late. He squeezed the Colt's trigger, a wild, hasty shot. *The lights.* Why were the lights still working?

In return, automatic weapons fire filled the air around his head. The pair were armed with Kalashnikov assault rifles. Harry dropped to one knee behind the Volvo's engine block, hitting the magazine release and slamming a fresh mag into the butt of the Colt.

This wasn't Hollywood—he was seriously outgunned and he knew it. Time to leave. *The lights.* He needed the distraction to get away.

Sirens split the night, a pair of police cars speeding down the access road toward the hangar. The *policía* were off-limits to him. But not to the Libyans.

He heard the death rattle of Kalashnikovs on full-automatic, saw the windshield of the lead police car explode into a thousand shards of glass.

The car slid off the road and into the embankment. Apparently the Paraguayans had come prepared for an arrest, not a firefight.

Fools. It was going to get them massacred. And he was responsible.

The price of still having a conscience. In that moment, he made his decision, raising himself up over the hood of the Volvo.

Only one of the Libyans was still in sight and he was reloading, having already emptied his Kalashnikov's banana magazine. Less than five meters away. Close enough to see his face, the look of panic in his eyes.

The Colt came up in both hands. Training taking over.

The lights went out suddenly, darkness falling over them like a physical weight. He could have let it go, could have walked away.

He squeezed the trigger a single time, the scream in the night confirming his hit.

The pistol still held ready in his hands, Harry walked forward to where the Libyan lay dying, bleeding out on the asphalt.

He couldn't have been more than twenty-one, twenty-two. A kid. Too young for this.

Harry's face hardened into a pitiless mask. It was the price of war. Nothing more, nothing less.

It would take time for the *policía* to recover from their casualties—time for them to regroup and establish their perimeter.

By that time, he would be long gone. Harry tucked the Colt back into its shoulder holster, zipping up his jacket over it. He set off across the airport runway, walking slowly away from the scene of the crime. Ten meters, and the darkness had swallowed him up.

9:30 A.M. Eastern Time, One day later
CIA Headquarters
Langley, Virginia

"You might want to take a look at this, boss," Carter announced, looking up at the entrance of the DCS.

Kranemeyer took in the peculiarly satisfied smile on his analyst's face and rounded the edge of the cubicle.

CNN was streaming live on Carter's terminal, with *Breaking News* scrolling along the bottom of the screen and a female announcer providing voiceover. "... of this morning, we are reporting on the death of alleged French al-Qaeda leader Jean-Claude Manet, aka Ramzi bin Abdullah. According to Paraguayan authorities, bin Abdullah was killed just outside Ciudad del Este last night, following a brief firefight with the local police, who had attempted to arrest him. Here with us this morning to comment on the impact of the death of yet another senior al-Qaeda leader, I welcome Senator Joe Lieberman ..."

"Are they really fools enough to believe that?"

"The Paraguayans?" Kranemeyer smiled. "Not for a moment—but it's a feather in their cap. And it suits our purposes to give them the credit. What's the status of our field team?"

"They made it out of the country safely, that's all I have for you. From here on out, they'll be off the grid until they re-enter the States."

12:09 P.M. Eastern Time, Seven days following NIGHTSHADE
A playground
Norfolk, Virginia

21

It was a beautiful day, the chill bite of fall just beginning to enter the air. Harry turned off the Suburban's engine, glancing out the tinted windows of the SUV toward the playground. He knew she'd be here. His eyes scanned the crowd, the children running to and fro—the mothers keeping an anxious watch.

There. Blue jeans and a white windbreaker, sitting on a bench near the swings. A playful gust of wind toyed with her blonde hair, revealing the familiar profile. It was her.

He grabbed his shades off the dashboard, pushing the door open with painful reluctance.

The laughing shrieks of kindergartners filled the autumn air as he passed like a ghost through their midst, making his way toward the woman.

This—this was America. He felt like a foreigner in his own land.

The cool air bit at his naked cheek, an unwelcome reminder that he had shaved clean for the first time in two months.

"It's a beautiful day." The woman looked up at his voice, the shadow of dread passing across her features.

"Sammy." Her voice caught. "Is he ..."

"He's just fine, Sherri," he replied, knowing she couldn't finish the question. He took his seat beside Han's wife, leaning back against the hard wood of the bench.

"When will he be home?" she asked, her voice still brittle. Life in the Teams had been hard, but the SEALs had nothing on Langley.

Harry looked over into her eyes. "A couple days, three at the most. He wanted me to check in on you and the twins. Give you his love."

She laughed, wiping away a tear from the corner of her eye. "They're fine—as you can see. They miss their dad, but I'm sure a visit from Uncle Harry will perk them right up."

He followed her glance, just in time to watch five-year-old Lee emerge feet first from a slide. "I forgot to bring them anything," he said, a sheepish smile passing across his face.

The five-year-old straightened, in that split-second staring directly across the playground at the two of them. Eyes filled with that innocence that only a child can know.

A child. Swung high in the arms of his father 'neath airport lights. A child. Standing there on the tarmac, his thumb in his mouth.

A child. Bent over his father's corpse, his little hands bathed in blood, hot tears washing away that innocence forever. Paradise lost.

Harry's throat felt suddenly dry, as though he were trying to swallow and couldn't. He turned to see Sherri looking at him strangely.

"Are you okay?" she asked, putting a hand on his arm. "You're so pale."

Focus. It wasn't working. The adrenaline that had sustained him in Paraguay was gone now, remorse filling its place. He shook off her hand, uttering one final, enormous lie. "Yeah, I'm fine."

He made it back to the Suburban in a daze, leaning back into the seat as he fought the urge to retch. To cleanse himself.

Harry looked down at his hands, and it seemed to him as if they were covered with blood. It wasn't murder, it was war, but it felt no different.

And he knew. He would see that face again, in his dreams. The face of that little boy.

He took a deep breath, fastening his seatbelt as he put the SUV in drive. Toward Langley. Back to work. It *was* war. And there was only one thing certain about this war. It was far from over.

THE PEPPER TYRANT

BY J. GREGORY SMITH

Durango, Mexico

Mike Turcott sat on the plain wood bench in the Tierra del Gato police station and waited for an audience with Chief Vargas. Usually Vargas made house calls to Mike's farm for what amounted to "tribute" in the form of cash, cheese, or whatever else was in season.

"Señor Turcott."

Mike stepped into Vargas's office, a dirty, white-painted room with a simple desk and file cabinets. A few pictures adorned the walls. There were obligatory shots of the governor and the presidente. Mike focused on the portly man in front of him and took a seat.

He wiped his damp palms on his jeans.

"You know me and I have no wish to cause trouble, but Carlos has changed his petty harassment to another level."

"Carlos Tragafuegos?"

Carlos the "Fire Eater."

"Who else?" Mike pinched the bridge of his nose in a vain effort to stem the headache that wormed into his skull. "You know he rarely misses a month to send his people around to issue his challenge."

Vargas nodded and sat back in his chair. His tan uniform shirt bore white salt stains under the armpits. "But you know there is no law against such challenges. Those who accept know his rules."

"Rules? The man's a thug without the balls to run his own business. He does what he wants. And you know what has been happening when he wins the challenges."

"I hear things, but that is not proof."

"Damn it! You grew up in this town. I haven't been here more than ten years and I care more about these people than you do. Didn't you see José Ramírez yesterday? What they did to his face?" Mike knew he was getting out of line. This wasn't what he'd planned, and the chunky cop sat straight in his chair.

"Watch your tone, Señor. If you're not careful, you will attract the wrong kind of attention."

Mike got the message, but he was fed up with threats right about now.

He raised his palms in an effort to show conciliation. "I'm sorry, Senor Vargas, but you must understand. It isn't the way the losers of the challenge are being beaten by Carlos's men; now he's coming after my family."

Vargas leaned forward and Mike felt a spark of hope. "Yes?"

"My wife Carmen was stopped not once but twice by his men and they were quite clear. Then, my Rosa came home with a doll 'some man gave me' when she was at school ..." Mike felt the rage build inside him.

"Why would he care so much?"

Mike took a deep breath. He knew his wife and daughter were in danger every minute now, and the effort to buy into Vargas playing dumb made him want to scream. "Chief Vargas, I'm not blind to the realities of how things work here. I try to keep to myself but I've seen and heard a great deal in the last ten years. I stay out of things that don't concern me. But I know Carlos's brother is a powerful man in Ciudad Juarez." Mike thought "powerful" was a nice euphemism for narco-terrorist. "And apparently he wants to expand his business—or whatever his plans are, it appears his brother is interested in using my farm. That this is about the challenge is just a pretext."

"Perhaps. But why don't you accept his challenge? You beat him before."

"If I could take back one mistake over the last decade, that would be it."

"Is that not where you got the money to buy your farm in the first place?"

He had a point. "I would have found another way."

Now Vargas looked amused. "I have heard you met your wife, Carmen, after the first contest. You were, still are, something of a legend."

"I was a dumb kid with a strong stomach. Now I'm a family man and farmer. It's enough."

"Apparently not."

"Whose side are you on?"

"Sometimes it is about avoiding making the wrong enemies."

Mike needed to refocus the conversation. "Look. My wife and child are being threatened. This isn't about his eating contest, but I think that *has* made it personal with him. Can't we find a way to give him what he wants without me losing my family or my farm, or both?"

Vargas smoothed his mustache. "Señor. I am sorry but our hands are tied."

"But Carlos is no friend of yours." Mike tried to find the most diplomatic phrasing. The man represented his last hope.

"Sí. But he has powerful allies."

Mike had heard the rumors that Carlos didn't even bother bribing Vargas. The implied danger from his brother was sufficient.

"So there's nothing you can do?" Mike began thinking about how much cash he could raise and felt the growing dread that came with the realization that everything he owned was tied up in the farm.

Vargas stared at him. "You believe the threats?"

"Of course."

"Come back in the morning. I need to make a call."

Mike's voice shook while he spoke. He hadn't waited to be summoned, and he ignored the other officer sitting in Vargas's office. "Rosa got a ride home from school yesterday."

"We are having a meeting, Mr. Turcott." Vargas didn't appear surprised to see Mike.

27

"Listen to me, Vargas." Mike looked over to the lanky man dressed in the paramilitary uniform he recognized was from the policía federale. "You, too. My ten-year-old daughter Rosa normally walks home from school with a couple friends. Yesterday, she got a ride from a stranger despite, what we tell her." Mike made a fist to keep his fingers from trembling. "She said the car smelled like smoke and the man said, 'tell your father Uncle Carlos says hola.'"

The federale spoke first. "We have been discussing your situation. It sounds serious."

"You think?"

"My name is Sanchez. I'm afraid due to—how do you gringos say it?—'circumstances beyond our control,' there is little we can do. I promise if anything were to happen, we would open a thorough investigation."

Mike felt a cold wave wash over his body. "After? You're just going to just watch? Look, I get it. Give me some time, I'll sell some of the animals and get you a little something."

Sanchez smirked. "Do I look like I need any goats?"

Now Mike felt desperation smother him. "You want the whole farm, is that it? You can't give me anything to get out of town?"

"We don't want your money."

Vargas spoke. "But perhaps there *is* a way we can help each other."

After a long slog up the dirt road with the strap of his backpack digging into his shoulder, Mike stepped up to the gate. The guards had no compunction about displaying their AK's, telling Mike *they* were the law around here.

Two miles and a lifetime away he'd said a silent prayer for his wife and daughter. He thought about what Carlos had done to force him here, and it put steel in his spine. The guards grinned, no doubt looking forward to the opportunity to put him through the ringer when their boss beat him.

"Open it." They pointed to his bag. Inside there was water, an ice pack, and a tall glass bottle of milk. And a large Tupperware container. They were inside.

Mike tried not to think about his "practice" two nights ago. The first try ended in coughing and puking. A little better the second time with some endorphins kicking, but he still didn't know if he was up to this.

He had to be.

"The scorpions. Tell Carlos I have them and he can't handle them. Or me."

They just laughed, and he heard them relay the message in Spanish.

"Up the hill, pendejo. Don't keep him waiting."

Outside a building that looked more like a cinder-block fortress, Mike saw a wooden table and two benches. It reminded him of a park picnic table.

"Look what the gato brought." Carlos stepped out from the heavy steel door. He wore baggy pants and a loose T-shirt with a print of flames across the front. His brown skin was dark from the sun, and he wore his hair close-cropped and a three-day stubble goatee. Some warlord. Two more guards flanked him, and they wore large-frame revolvers on their hips.

"Still dressing to impress." Mike reminded himself not to get beat up before he even got to the table. He took a sip of water because suddenly his mouth was cotton dry. He knew better than to touch water once they got started.

"You got old since the last time. Are you sure about this?"

And heavier, and probably crazier, Mike thought. He clung to the memory of Rosa and drew strength from her little face. "Maybe you're scared of what I brought?"

"I don't know how you got them before me, but as you have seen, I have been practicing since the last time we met." Carlos crossed the courtyard and a servant brought a tray out to the table. She set a pitcher of water, a bottle of tequila, and a bottle of milk on the table. A boy followed with a pail filled with red and orange peppers.

Mike took out the water and placed the milk next to the other bottle; they were the same thick glass.

Carlos nodded with approval. "You remembered. Do you recall the rest of the rules?"

Mike held up a hand. "Let's be clear. If I win, I get the $10,000 you promise everyone else."

"Of course." Carlos grinned.

"And it ends. You leave me alone."

"All I ever wanted was a chance to prove myself against the only man to beat me. And a filthy gringo, no less. That's hard to live with, my friend."

"You got your wish." Mike spoke through clenched teeth. "But I mean it. You leave all of us alone."

Carlos feigned insult. "And when I win?"

"It's yours."

"It?"

"The farm. You and your brother can do whatever you like with it. Just give me a day to leave town."

"Did you leave an empty tequila bottle on the road to the house?" Carlos put out his hand. "But a deal is a deal, yes?"

They shook and Mike felt the chubby man's grip was stronger than he remembered. He returned the effort knowing farm life had hardened his own muscles, Carmen's cooking notwithstanding.

More men appeared and ringed the table when Mike and Carlos took their spots across the table. It looked like more than twenty and more kept coming. Not that it mattered. One of those thugs with an assault rifle was enough to send him to the next life.

Carlos placed the two milk bottles directly between then. The servant girl set a plate in front of each man. She put on a glove and plunked an orange pepper onto each plate.

"A warm up. We each eat our share and continue until one man surrenders. The first one to grab their milk, spit out a pepper or throw up loses. Clear?"

"Yeah." Mike was sweating already. He forced himself to concentrate on the pepper in front of him.

"We will save yours for last if you make it that far." Carlos pointed at the open Tupperware. He bent down and sniffed the golf ball-sized red peppers. "Dios!"

"Let's get on with it."

30

Carlos held up an orange habanero. The crowd murmured. He popped it into his mouth, chewed and swallowed. He opened his mouth to show it was gone. A slight sheen of perspiration was the only indicator he'd eaten it.

Mike followed suit. He ate these for fun and the burn coated his mouth like a comforting balm.

They each ate one more of those and Mike knew his sweating was pure nerves. The guards murmured and must have mistaken him for a lightweight.

"Enough foreplay. What else do you have?" Mike felt the tingle on his lips.

"Ghosts," Carlos shouted.

He'd asked for it. The Bhut Jolokia, one of the hottest peppers in the world. For the dedicated chili head, this would set his head on fire. He hoped the habaneros woke up enough endorphins.

"Together." Carlos called out. He held up a bright red pepper that looked like a fat, wrinkled pinkie finger.

Mike picked up his and, at a million Scoville heat units, knew pain was on the way.

"Not again, my friend. You won't wear me down this time." Carlos bit to the stem and Mike followed suit.

The heat hit him immediately, but he knew it was a prelude to what was coming.

His tongue burned and the fire seared down his throat and smoldered in his belly. He began to hiccough and the guards leaned closer, hooting.

Mike rode the first waves of pain and thought of Rosa and Carmen. His head erupted in sweat and he felt it break out across his back. His brown hair matted down when he wiped his brow.

"Holy ..."

If this didn't affect Carlos, he was going to lose too quickly.

Mike spared a glance across the table. For an instant he thought his prediction was true. Carlos smiled at him and, other than a slick of sweat all over the man's shaved head, he looked relaxed.

Then Mike looked at the man's arms locked in a death grip on the bench. Carlos's muscles bunched and stood out. The sight of the stress took Mike's mind away from the searing pain he felt, and he tried to draw as much strength as possible.

31

Mike tried to say "Not bad." But his throat felt like it was closing down to a straw and all he did was make a squeak.

The guards roared with laughter and they started to chant "leche, leche," urging him to buckle and take a drink of milk.

Mike knew the moment he did they'd beat him like the others. He hoped by then he'd be in another dimension from the pain.

When he thought the agony was beginning to plateau, he pointed at the container with the Moruga Scorpion peppers. He swallowed and felt his throat open enough to speak. "They call it the brain strain. Maybe it won't work on you."

Carlos looked like he was in a different world. He turned to the servant girl. "Consuela. Medio."

She cut the pepper in half and placed a portion on each plate. A moment after the gold, ball-sized, gnarled red pepper hit the plate, she shook her ungloved hand like it was scalded. "Aiee." She put her fingers in her mouth.

Big mistake.

Seconds later, she waved her hands in front of her mouth and began to hop from one foot to another.

The guards howled and let her suffer. Only when she lunged for Mike's bottle of milk did they grab her. One big guy snatched her up and hauled her away.

That was too close.

"You are next." Carlos popped his piece in and began to chew. "Not as hot as the Ghost Pepper."

"Just wait." Mike ate his and a couple remaining taste buds that weren't already numb registered the flavor. He'd already discovered the other night, this one came on strong but never quit. The burn just built and built.

Carlos was finding that out, Mike saw. Adding this heat on top of the ghost pepper was insanity. When he beat Carlos a decade ago, he'd been a little drunk and they piled on the habaneros. It was all about volume.

"Madre de Dios!" Carlos began to cough and a murmur went up in the crowd. Mike thought Carlos was going to puke. His own hand twitched for the milk.

Not yet. Carlos rallied.

Mike rode the pain to another plateau, then it kicked higher and his stomach wrenched. "Shit!"

The group of guards was whipped into a frenzy; they sounded like animals. Mike fought the stomach cramps and willed himself not to spew.

The guards even looked like hyenas. Literally. Mike realized he was beginning to hallucinate from the endorphin rush that tried to compensate for the warped levels of agony that cooked his frame.

Hold on. For Carmen, for Rosa, for Carosa. Their faces merged in his mind's eye but it still gave him something to focus on.

He felt like he couldn't breathe, but he had to or he'd pass out.

He looked at Carlos. Another illusion. The man's face seemed to be melting like a wax figure in a fire.

Neither spoke. They stared at each other, locked in self-imposed torture. Salvation at arm's length. Not really, but the milk would help.

Which milk, which milk, which milk ran through Mike's brain. Move soon. He could swear Carlos was about to break.

What was he supposed to do? It was getting hard to think. There was the pain and the pain was there.

Mike remembered and, with a big swipe of his arm across his own gushing forehead, grazed his fingers over his eyes.

"Shit, my eyes! Too hot, sonofabitch. Where's the milk?"

But he *could* see. A little. Enough to make sure he grabbed Carlos's milk bottle.

"I'm out!" He ripped the top off and chugged as much as he could before anyone could react. Then he let out a scream and dropped the bottle. "Crap."

The glass shattered and the last of the milk splashed his pants.

Carlos let out a drunken sounding whoop and the guards roared. He jumped up and Mike squinted through his good eye and blinked away the tears from where his finger touched. It felt exactly like when he got pepper-sprayed by a cop one time in college.

He saw Carlos dive on the table and take the remaining milk bottle and drain it like a man possessed.

Carlos belched and Mike's heart stopped when he thought the man was going to vomit.

He tried to will the man to keep it down.

Somehow he did, and Carlos staggered toward him.

33

"You made me earn it, but today *I* am the better man."

Mike fell to his knees. All the strength seemed to have left his legs.

"Don't bother to beg me, gringo. You made a deal and I will put your land to good use." Carlos laughed and the sweat continued to pour off him. His shirt was soaked through like he'd broken a fever.

Carlos leaned over Mike. "You will be gone tomorrow, sí?"

Mike nodded. "You won't see me again."

Carlos held his stomach. "Those were the devil." He kicked Mike in the side and knocked him over.

Mike barely noticed the kick because his entire body felt like a throbbing tooth.

But the kick was a signal and the guards fell on him.

He felt plenty before he passed out.

"Hold still." At the sound of the strange voice Mike woke up again, feeling a bit more clarity than the first time he clawed back to consciousness. Everything was a blur, and he felt like he dreamed the car ride to the hospital.

He opened his eyes and saw a homely nurse apply a fresh bandage to his face. In his confusion he wondered if the nurse was really one of Carlos's guards in disguise and had come to finish him off.

She hissed at him. "You will break your stitches. Hold still."

He did. Where could he go?

"That's enough." Mike recognized the voice of Sanchez. "Leave us."

The nurse disappeared without another word. Mike saw Vargas behind the federale. He closed the door to the small room that Mike realized wasn't a hospital after all. His "bed" was a couch. The color of the wall matched the police station, so maybe he was in a back room somewhere.

"You are awake?" Sanchez said.

Mike blinked and wondered why he'd say that when they were staring at one another.

"You can understand me?" Sanchez's tone grew sharp.

"Yeah." Mike was surprised how weak his voice sounded.

"Well?"

"What?"

"He drank it?"

Oh right. "Yes. But it didn't work."

The cops shared a look. "He threw up?"

"No. That's what I'm saying. He kept it down. I think it was a macho thing even after he won, but he seemed fine. Well, as fine as me, anyway."

The men smiled.

Mike looked for a clock. "How long have I been here?"

"Not long. Just a few hours."

"Why didn't I go to the hospital?"

"We thought it would be safer for you to come here. And you should leave town as soon as possible."

"Why, if it didn't work?"

"Señor. Ricin is not instant and, unfortunately, the ambulances are all broken if some urgent calls come through."

Mike sat up. "So they'll know? I have to get my family."

"You will. As soon as we receive confirmation about an unfortunate reaction to a dangerous game."

Mike felt strange, but then he remembered the whole reason for the challenge. "Are you sure?" He swung his legs off the couch. His entire body felt covered in bruises.

"We will make sure you get to a new town where you can be safe," Sanchez said.

The fog was lifting in Mike's mind. "Where will that be? I need to get back to the states. Even there might not be safe. When they figure out that it was me, they will send hit men all over the world."

"I don't think so." Sanchez shook his head.

"They just got through kidnapping and threatening my family and after our contest Carlos turns up dead? Suspicious, don't you think?"

Sanchez gave a thin smile. "No. And neither will they, because they never threatened your family."

"Of course they did. My daughter—" Mike felt sudden cold. "You bastard."

"Perhaps, Señor. But rest assured that you performed an invaluable service."

Vargas whispered. "And we won't say anything if you don't."

Mike balled his fists but the guns the men carried told him he'd have to ride out a bigger burn than the scorpion's.

EVERYBODY WINS

BY LISA MANNETTI

ANXIOUS? DEPRESSED? THINKING OF SUICIDE?
Now, there's help.
Our 24-hour line connects you
ONE ON ONE
With a New York State Certified Suicide Counselor.

That was as far as Sally Grimshaw read. She punched in the phone number.

"We're here for you," a young woman on the other end said. Sally began explaining, talking faster and faster. Her black moods, her low self-esteem. (And what good did it do to *know* it was low self-esteem? As if knowing could make her feel less like shit.)

"I want to die," Sally finished.

"Mr. Vinny can see you in twenty minutes—"

"See me?"

"Certainly." The woman rattled out an address in the West Eighties. "Can you get here?"

"Yes. Thank you. God bless you, yes—"

"Don't worry about your hair, your clothes—don't worry about a thing. Just get in a cab and come right now."

Sally hung up and rushed into her old trench coat, throwing it on over a flannel nightgown. She snagged an oversized worn black leather pocketbook from the hook inside the closet door.

Five minutes later she walked into a cold, gray day and wishy-washy December flurries. But she had hope, she told herself. Now there was hope.

"I'm forty-seven and I've never even had a date." Sally snuffled into a white Kleenex tissue. "I hate my job. I think they're going to fire me because I call in sick a lot. I can't help it." She twisted the soft paper to shreds, as if it might prevent her from breaking into hysterical sobs. "Four years ago at my high school reunion, not one person remembered me—"

Mr. Vinny ("No last names here, please") held up a pudgy hand. "It's a tough old world, that's God's truth, Sal." Gold pinky ring gleaming, he was paging through the three or four sheets of paper that were Sally's file.

Mr. Vinny's office was painted dark salmon. A huge aquarium built into the wall behind his antique desk added turquoise sparkle. He closed the folder and walked toward her.

"So, Sally, how were ya gonna do it? Huh?" Mr. Vinny sat on the edge of his desk, one loafer dangling. "Pills, a gun, a dive out the window, what?"

"Pills, I guess—"

"Shit, you take pills, maybe you'll get the job done. More likely you'll wake up one morning in Bellevue, and you'll be lucky if you don't end up a vegetable in a wheelchair." He got up and paced a step or two, hands clasped behind his back. "Nope, it's not efficient." He stared at her. "I don't like inefficiency."

Sally wasn't sure what he meant.

"Ya know, nobody can tell you when it's time to check out—I mean look at you." He suddenly whirled around and snatched her file, flapping it in her face. "Overweight, nobody in your life—not even a cat. Your life is a shitpile, and nobody knows it better than you. So whaddya say? Have you had enough, or what?"

38

"I thought—" She stopped. Confusion mounted inside her. She touched her thin brown hair and knew she looked bad. "I hate all of it," she whispered.

"Right. That's my point. But, ya' know, it's not easy to kill yourself. I could show you a dozen files about how tough it is."

"Yes," she said. She had botched everything else—killing herself would be no different. She felt the hot flash of embarrassment and knew her face had turned the ugly purple-scarlet of a wine birthmark.

"Guy holds a gun to his head," he mimed, "but who knows; maybe he chickens out at the last second. Anyway, whammo-slammo. 'Cept he don't die, he just ends up with a dent in his right temple and pissing his pajama bottoms because his fuckin' catheter fell out, only he don't know it, cause there's no feeling from his neck down. Hoo-boy, and he thought he was depressed *before*." Mr. Vinny smiled, his face broadening to a double chin.

This wasn't a place that coddled or pampered; they were going to make her realize what a terrible decision suicide was. "I guess it's a bad idea."

"No it's a great idea! But amateurs ... unless you're, like, channeling Jack Kevorkian, there's no guarantees. You get amateurs involved, it's not efficient. It's bad business."

"Oh," she said. Confused, she clutched her purse a little tighter.

"So what do you say, Sal? Should I pencil you in on my dance card or are you gonna stay miserable?"

"In? You mean like a program?"

He was rustling papers. "I got a guy here needs to be taken out, Sally, and you could—"

"Taken out? I ... I ...What?"

"The bastard's been beatin' the shit out of his wife, the kids. He's lappin' up the booze. He's got millions, and he's still as stingy as a whore's alarm clock. But his wife, she's a woman who understands good business, so she came to us for help. And what I want to know is, are you willing to kill him at the same time you kill yourself?"

"But—"

"We guarantee you go—no messy, half-assed attempts. The lady gets her hit. Everybody wins." He paused. "Sal?"

"You're the Mafia, aren't you?" she said.

He leaned forward, his bulky arms supporting his weight, hands resting on the arms of her club chair, his heavy chin an inch from hers.

"There *is* no more Mafia." He backed away and she breathed easier.

"Between the last three or four asswipe mayors, what we *used* to call a hit man wouldn't touch a contract. Too much risk. There's no loyalty these days. But there are still people who need services. See? This woman needs a service—and you need a service. She paid for it, but, for you it's free. And when it's done there'll be one less creep friggin' up the world."

He paused. "Uh, I was referring to the shit-sucking gentleman. Not you, of course. You're goin' to your heavenly reward."

"I don't know. I mean—" She squirmed in her seat, the thick nightgown wadding into a lump between her fleshy thighs. "How would I ... ?"

"You drive?"

She nodded.

"Smacko." He brought his hands together in a thunderclap. "Head-on collision. We pump you through-and-through with your drug of choice. Guaranteed lights out and you won't feel a thing after the first ten seconds.

"No, I couldn't!" In her mind she saw glass spewing in a slow arc like water droplets from a fountain. She heard the ripping clang of metal, felt the thud of the impact hewing her instantly, saw blood.

"You disappoint me. I thought sure you'd go for the car." He sighed. "You could shoot him. Him and the assholes he hangs with. Have you had target practice? Cause we can arrange lessons at the local shooting range—"

"No guns," Sally said.

"Tough shit. Gun it is."

"I think I should go now."

"I don't think so," he said. "Not unless you want to have a messy accident ... because I got ten lonely guys and five world-weary pre-menopausal ladies like yourself that's gonna call me before the close of business today." His smile was too wide, his teeth too prominent.

She understood at once. One of his other cases, a would-be suicide, would do her in. A small, scritchy noise—the sound of a cornered ferret—pushed its way past Sally's lips. But so what? Death was what she wanted anyway.

"Wouldn't it be better to have time to make your preparations, write your note, call your mother? Get some closure on the mess of your life?"

"No!" She started to get up, but the menacing look on his face told her to sit. She was in a trap, caught under the bell jar of her own neurosis. She was making herself sick and depressed. Was her life so terrible that she couldn't snap herself out of it?

"Cause you can walk right out the door, if you want—but you won't know when the knife's gonna go through your cheek in some cold alley, and there'll be no time to get your shit together. And no guarantees you'd die. Nope, no guarantees. Except the guarantee that you'll suffer."

"Mr. Vinny—" Sally said.

"Just Vinny, now." He smiled. From his desk drawer he removed a plain manila folder and opened it. "Sign here."

A single sheet of white paper with black print like flea dirt came at her. At the bottom was a line marked with a huge blue X.

Sally signed.

A half-hour later, she left with photos of "John Doe," his thinning gray hair offset by a neatly trimmed, silvery mustache. He was wearing a tuxedo in all the pictures.

She hailed a cab back to her apartment.

The contract was totally illegal, she thought,. But she had no doubt Vinny would see she kept her end of the bargain.

The last words he'd said to her were *Happy New Year.*

"Happy New Year," Sally said, sliding the key into the scratched brass of her door lock and letting herself in. "Happy fucking New Year."

Inside the apartment, she opened her black purse and took the greasy towel wrapping off the .22 Ruger. Its serial numbers had been filed off.

Tomorrow she was scheduled for practice at the shooting range at 8 a.m. Sharp.

Vinny told her if she didn't show, he'd begin to have doubts about her intention to honor the contract. And that would be too bad.

Sally picked up the gun and aimed at an age-browned lampshade in her tiny living room. She pretended it was Vinny's double-chinned face.

"Pow," she said, and then she let the hand holding the gun fall to her side. How could she think there was any help for someone like her, or that anyone cared? How stupid could a person be?

"I can't." Sally wept into the phone in her galley kitchen. "This man's never done a thing to me!"

"So what? He's hurt plenty of people. And that's all you need to know. You'll be doing the world a big favor."

"I went to the shooting range." Her tears were coming harder now. "I just know, Vinny, I just know, I mean the minute I take the gun out in the restaurant, someone will see me, I won't be able to shoot, I'll wind up in jail!"

"No you won't, Sally." His voice was ice. "You'll never see the inside of a jail."

"All right," she sighed.

"Good girl. The Moon Over the Tiber Ristorante. 9 p.m. Sharp. Saturday night the 23rd and no later. We don't want to ruin his kids' Christmas Eve. It's a big night with Italians."

The phone came down with a *thunk* in her ear.

It was two days until the end of the world.

She stood outside the restaurant. The crosswinds veered madly around the corners, and she shivered. Garlands of colored Christmas lights sparkled through the fogged glass of the Moon Over the Tiber's red door.

She pushed on the door, and a gust of steamy air scented with garlic assailed her. It was so warm it was almost tropical. Sally shivered again.

A phone call from Vinny this morning had included her final instructions.

She was to take Doe out first, and any baggy gentlemen dining with him were fair game. But no grandmas would get shot because *we're not fuckin' barbarians, capiche?*

Doe, then the linguine-slurpers. And she was told not to worry. Since she refused to use the gun on herself, all she had to do was clamp down on the little yellow capsule she'd been told to keep between her back teeth. A little blood might leak out of her mouth, but, hey, that was it. She'd seen the photos of all those crazy cultists from Guyana, right? Cyanide was a sure bet.

It lay like a dollop of dentist's gel in the gutter between her cheek and her teeth. She'd been afraid she'd inadvertently clamp down on it too soon.

If that happened, the Lifespan Treatment Center was going to bring her mother in for bereavement counseling.

Sally stood in the cramped foyer, hesitating. The gun in her purse felt like an anvil.

Have dinner, Vinny told her. *We want to keep our clients happy. But don't pay for it—you don't want anybody seeing the gun before you yank it out. Stand up like you're gonna use the can, then let 'er rip.*

She'd left no note. Nothing in the dog-eared diary she called a journal about being angry or feeling crazy or having a gun. There would be no clues.

A waiter wearing a long, dark blue apron over his suit showed her to a table. Twenty feet or so away, John Doe was sucking clams from the shells. There was a white napkin tied bib-style around his neck.

"Wine, Signora?"

"Yes. A bottle of Pinot Grigio."

"Bene." He scribbled onto a small pad.

She ordered fried calamari, a Caesar salad, stuffed cannelloni, and tiramisu for dessert.

Sally fingered the empty wine glass on the table in front of her. The wine would taste damn good, she thought. Then she suddenly realized the capsule was in her mouth. How could she eat or drink anything with the capsule in her mouth?

She waggled it out and placed it gently in the under the rim of her bread plate. She would shovel it back in right after the tiramisu, just before the check, just before ... yes, she sighed, that would work out fine.

The waiter brought the wine and uncorked it. "How festive," Sally said, taking a sip and nodding assent.

"Sì," the waiter said, fussing over the glasses, rearranging the tableware, the glowing votive lamp.

The waiter hurried off again.

The condemned woman ate heartily. At least it was a great restaurant. The calamari had been delicious.

Sally was into her second forkful of Caesar salad when she realized the waiter had taken away the bread plate.

The capsule was nowhere on the table.

Panic seized her, and she shifted the short white vase with the single red carnation, the silverware, skimming her finger around the underside of her salad plate. She even lifted the tablecloth and peered at the floor.

It was gone.

It must have disappeared when the waiter cleared the appetizer and dipping oil. Oh hell, did it matter? The capsule was probably already in a big industrial garbage bag, invisible in a soggy mess of half-eaten cream tortes, tossed lemon slices, and limp parsley.

It wasn't like she could ask for it back. *Oh waiter, I'll take the check and my cyanide capsule; I'm afraid of guns, you know.*

Sally stifled a snort, drank some more wine, and ate dripping romaine lettuce, mopping the dressing with the half-eaten slice of crusty bread she'd left perched on the salad dish.

She glanced at John Doe. He was with three other men. They were eating provolone and fruit.

Everybody wins. It was so much like her own dreary, wrecked life.

Everybody else wins, she thought, *but not me.*

And she was tired of it all, tired of being the loser, watching everyone else get what they want. Was she tired enough to do anything about it?

She ate the tiramisu but her appetite was gone, and the food was no more than dust and the steely taste of gunmetal in her mouth.

And Mr. Doe became everything she hated about herself. If he was as disgusting as Vinny claimed—disgusting enough for Doe's wife to want to have him killed—then who was Sally to argue?

44

She pulled the gun out of her purse as she stood, and aimed it at Mr. Doe's face. His startled expression disappeared a moment after she pulled the trigger. His dinner companions never had a chance to react as she easily dispatched them one after the other.

She was a natural at this.

The handful of restaurant patrons had fled, leaving Sally alone with her four victims. Killing them had been shockingly liberating, and she realized she finally had a talent for something in her wretched life. She smiled as she wondered whether or not she could get away with this.

She planned to try. It was incredibly fortunate the cyanide pill had been lost. Perhaps more than fortune. Perhaps fate.

She turned to leave, to begin a new life.

From out of the shadows her waiter approached, his gun drawn.

She could tell he'd been crying.

"I'm sorry, miss," he said. "I have to. I signed a contract."

He pulled the trigger.

FAT LARRY'S NIGHT WITH THE ALLIGATORS

BY KEN GOLDMAN

Sal turned the Cadillac at Homestead toward Flamingo and, heading southwest on Florida 9336, he did not say a word to Danny for the next ten minutes. Instead, he devoted most of his attention to his meatball sandwich until they passed Long Pine Key. He switched to the dimmers as they approached the park ranger station, but so far they had not seen anything that looked like trouble. From the speakers Tony Bennett crooned something about "Nice work if you can get it" as the Caddy sped past the Pineland Trail turnoff.

Finishing the last of his sandwich, Sal stopped at the Pa-Hay-Okee turnstile of the Everglades entrance station and slid a plastic card into the slot without wiping off his thumbprint of tomato sauce. The crossing bar raised to allow the car through. Danny did not bother to ask his partner how he had managed to get the card. You just didn't question Salvatore DiLucca about something like that.

"Past midnight this part of the turnoff's not meant for anything 'cept marsh rabbits or Seminole Indians," Sal finally said. "Guard your cojones, kid. 'Gators ain't vegetarians." Danny did not laugh. He nodded instead and offered a smile that he hoped did not appear weak.

Once the access road turned to dirt, the body in the trunk thumped heavily against the Caddy's hood. It probably would have

47

been easier to haul a Brahma bull into the swamp land, and an hour earlier both Danny and DiLucca had to sit on that hood just to get the damned thing shut. Danny had pumped five bullets into Fat Larry Arnello while the man was still zipping his fly after porking one of Nicky Borelli's whores.

Arnello had made the huge mistake of shaving off a tidy profit from Borelli's Miami cocaine connections while juggling the books he handed to Sal. This put Salvatore DiLucca in a bad place with the old kingpin. Every piece man in Miami knew that no one ever got the chance to piss on Sal a second time.

Danny pumped three .45 slugs into Fat Larry's heart and two into his head just as Sal had instructed, but he did not empty the chamber on him. DiLucca had warned, "You never know when you might need that extra slug." Sal conceded that cutting Arnello's throat may have been more appropriate but why stink up the Cad's trunk? The thought had occurred to Danny to slice off the fat man's pecker and shove it into his mouth just to add a little panache to the job, then figured that might appear a bit hotblooded for a freshie. It was a clean hit, Danny's first, and whacking that lardass proved a lot easier than he had expected. Hell, it even felt good. Nice work if you can get it, just like the man said.

"I'm sure goin' to miss those Arnello dinners. You ever been? No shit, I'd take his wife's lasagna over pussy."

"It's in the meat sauce," Danny agreed absently, still thinking about the swamp alligators and his gonads. He forced himself back into the moment. "Lorraine Arnello does something with the oregano. She wouldn't tell God what's in it if her tits were on fire."

DiLucca nodded, then braked so suddenly that Danny pitched forward and swallowed for air. Sal pulled the Caddy to the side of the road, cutting the engine and headlights in the middle of Bennett's "No, no, they can't take that away from me ..."

The road plunged into darkness. DiLucca looked around and, surveying the area, seemed satisfied.

"Sorry about the jolt, kid. It's easy to miss this trail at night." He reached under the seat, handed Danny one of two high-powered flashlights, and pulled the lever to pop the trunk. Danny followed him to the rear of the car while DiLucca looked under the Caddy's hood.

The younger man covered his mouth and gagged.

48

Fat Larry clearly had seen better days. Arnello's blood had curdled in thick, jelly-like pools of fleshy pulp that smeared the plastic shower curtain with which Sal had lined the cargo area. But this had not caused Danny's stomach to double over on itself. Arnello's spilled guts he had expected. The stench was another matter.

"Christ, the man is a pig even when he's a corpse," Sal said, assessing the damage done to his trunk by Arnello's posthumous shit. Fat Larry had consumed a truckload of pasta and his sphincter could not hold back the Jonestown Flood his bowels had released. DiLucca covered his nose against the hot stew of spilled guts and turds. "Not exactly a death with dignity, huh, kid? Looks like the plastic caught most of it. Phew! What a stink!"

They spread the plastic curtain on the roadside and placed the body on top of it, wrapping Arnello inside like a huge cannoli. Carrying Fat Larry past the saw palmetto and strangler figs along the elevated trail was like trying to haul a piano down a sloping mountain. Although it was not a great distance to the river, the two men found it difficult to manipulate all that blubber while holding their flashlights steady. The hardwood hammocks served as a marker for Sal, who followed the narrowing trail like an Indian scout to the Shark River basin below.

"I know this part of the 'glades better than most of the 'gators. But be careful, kid. The next log you step on might bite your ass clean off."

The two floated the body about a hundred feet into the marsh through the saw grass where the mangroves grew the thickest, leaving Larry Arnello there like a bloated whale that had swum too close to shore. Climbing back to the elevated boardwalk above the basin, they watched the corpse lie face down in the hazy moonlight reflecting off the swamp.

"Okay, fellas," Sal whispered to the dark lumps surrounding Shark River. "Soup's on. Tonight you eat Italian!"

They searched the basin and the tall barbed sedges for movement, their flashlight beams skimming the water-sodden saucer like two lonely beacons.

Nothing moved.

Danny smacked a mosquito off the back of his neck, already sopping with sweat. Swamp crickets rang in his ears, screeching little cooties that did not chirp so much as shriek. A dismal moon crawled behind a dark cloud and winked out, shrouding the river in blackness so total Danny could feel it inside his bones.

"Christ, Sal. He's floating like a bar of Ivory soap. You'd think someone so fucking huge would sink faster than a stone."

"He'll go under when he fills up with some of that marsh water. For now, it's better he don't. 'Gators feed close to the surface where they can smell what they eat. Ol' Larry is about to become one meat-and-potatoes feast, don't you worry 'bout that."

Turning to Danny, his face caught in the flashlight's beam. Danny could see his partner was enjoying this. A smiling Salvatore DiLucca resembled one of those ever-grinning alligators.

Downriver something went *splunk!* Sal aimed his flashlight at the smooth water below the walkway. A dark object that looked like a large tree limb drifted into the beam, barely noticeable in the black ink of the swamp.

Upriver came another splash as a second one, larger than the first, crawled into the water.

The men's flashlight beams circled the basin like searchlights. They sliced through the steamy darkness of Shark River while a galaxy of bugs danced in the glare.

From a small beach about a hundred yards away, another alligator charged the water in an awkward motion that looked like a crawl but was much too fast. It belly flopped into the basin like a clumsy child, vanishing beneath the surface. When it reemerged, its awkwardness disappeared as it slid silently toward the body. Only its twin periscope eyes and the upper portion of its back broke the water's surface.

"Come on, guys ... That's it ... that's it ... There's plenty to go around," Sal whispered. "... just a little midnight snack before callin' it a night, hey?"

Danny gasped, aiming the beam at a fourth alligator drifting toward Arnello, even closer than the other three. "Jesus! I didn't even hear that one go into the water."

This alligator, larger than the others, probably had entered the river just below the walkway where they stood. Aware of its element of surprise, it glided toward its prey faster by keeping mostly underwater.

Four alligators circled the body like a shadowy committee deciding some sort of reptilian pecking order. The large one moved first and fell on Arnello's body so hard that it disappeared beneath the surface. The moment he reemerged the others went for him. There was neither rhythm nor pattern to their attack, just the crunch of bone and a constant cycle of tugging and chewing at whatever flesh they could wrench from the body. The attack became a blood-soaked taffy pull as alligators crawled over Arnello and one another, disappearing beneath him, pushing him under the water then pushing him back up, only to pull him down again. Arnello's arms flailed wildly like a convulsing rag doll, and in the wild thrashing it was impossible to tell if the man was a living or a dead thing.

An alligator tugged at his leg, gnawing it into meaty tatters at the knee. It allowed the limb to drift off, favoring another strike at the man's fleshier torso. Another one took a run directly at Arnello's face and managed to remove everything above his nose but an ear that hung ridiculously from a denuded skull. Much of the frenzied attack became lost behind the constant spray of swamp water, and each time Fat Larry reemerged the twin flashlight beams revealed less of him.

Danny coughed up a taste of his dinner but he chose not to share that information with DiLucca. He snapped off his flashlight and turned away from the scene's bloody denouement.

"In fifteen minutes there won't be enough left of Arnello to spread on a saltine," Sal said, shutting off his flashlight. The thick tangle of slash pines and dwarf cypress swallowed the sky, making the darkness complete.

"Are you okay, kid?"

"I'll be okay once we get out of here."

An awkward silence followed. It lingered in the darkness, forcing Danny to focus on the damp reek of the swamp.

"You haven't seen the second act yet," Sal finally added. His voice, emptied of emotion, seemed measured and rehearsed. Danny could barely make out DiLucca's outline silhouetted against the night sky, although the man stood close to him. In the darkness he somehow sounded distant.

"Second act?"

Danny snapped his flashlight back on, washing the walkway in light. His partner stood in front of him. He held a gun aimed directly at Danny's heart.

"Sal? What the—?"

"Three words for you, Danny. Just three words." He turned on his own flashlight and placed it in front of him to keep a bead on his target.

"Sal, I don't know what you're—"

"You fucked up."

"Sal, what in Christ are you—?"

Danny shut himself up. It was pointless to protest further. Still, he could think of nothing else to do. DiLucca cut him off before he could utter another word.

"—fucked up big time. 'Til tonight, I wasn't sure if Arnello wasn't just tryin' to blow smoke up my ass by fingerin' you as his partner. But when you mentioned Lorraine Arnello's oregano, that sealed it. That asswipe wasn't in the habit of invitin' the freshies over to break bread at his wife's table 'less he planned to talk shop over coffee and cigars."

He stepped closer to Danny, the smile melting from his face like a wax candle. Salvatore DiLucca now was all business.

"Fat Larry pocketed Nick Borelli's profits with an accomplice, Danny, someone the traffickers didn't know. I'd hoped Arnello was just tryin' to save his own sorry ass by namin' names. You broke my heart tonight, kid."

A thought formed so quickly in Danny's brain that he acted on it before it had fully taken shape. Talking Sal out of this was not in the equation. He had understood that much the moment he saw the gun.

You never know when you might need that extra slug, kid ...

Sal had been so right.

He flashed the high-powered beacon into DiLucca's eyes, blinding him long enough to lunge forward and kick the other flashlight off the elevated walkway into the basin below. A bullet tore into his right leg, causing a lightning bolt of pain to flash through the limb. Danny fell to his knees. Going down he tossed his own flashlight over his shoulder, throwing the two men into a darkness devoid even of shadows.

Having no better choice than desperation, Danny rolled off the walkway in an excruciating head-over-heels journey down the embankment to the river's edge. He crawled through a cluster of strangler figs, dragging his shattered leg behind him like a useless pine log.

"I got one bullet left, Sal! Just like you taught me!"

DiLucca fired at the voice coming at him from the darkness below the walkway. The bullet whizzed past Danny's shoulder.

52

Stupid! Stupid!

Dragging himself into a clump of hammocks in the shallows, he clenched his teeth and waded through the cold water of the marsh as far as his agony would allow.

Sal fired again and Danny heard the slug go *plunk!* in the swamp water in front of him.

"I got a whole lot more bullets, kid! A whole lot more!"

DiLucca received no answer. Danny would not be stupid a second time.

"Come on, kid! Take your best shot!"

Still no answer.

A thousand darning needles embedded themselves into Danny's knee. Sal's .45 must have shattered his kneecap and he could not pull himself to his feet without a land mine going off inside his leg. He let the water absorb his weight, and, biting his fist, he tried to muffle the agony he wanted to scream out. Hearing DiLucca step off the walkway, he pushed his way through the hammocks. Maybe Sal was searching for the tossed flashlight. Maybe he was searching for him.

None of this mattered. All Danny needed was one clear shot.

"You're forgetting something, Danny!" DiLucca called out. "You know what it is, don't you? You know what else is out there in that saw grass!"

Danny had not forgotten, but he was a man who had his priorities. Now DiLucca was playing with him, trying to goose him out of the water into the open, trying to get him to say just one word. Sal sloshed through a sea of sedges toward the wounded man concealed by the tall grass in the shallows.

"The alligators, Danny! Hundreds of 'em! They're out there in the dark and you have only one bullet. What you goin' to do, kid? What you goin' to do?"

Danny shoved his knuckles hard into his mouth and bit down on them, trying not to scream. He could not move further if he wanted to. He would not have moved if he could.

"Remember that quiet 'gator, Danny? The big one you couldn't hear go into the water? Remember what he did to Fat Larry? Maybe that sneaky fucker is crawling through the saw grass toward you right now lookin' for some dessert! Can you draw that picture in your mind, Danny? Can you hear him comin' for you?"

Danny could. He held the gun out in front of him with both hands, marine-style, wildly searching to his left, then to his right.

Downriver, Sal shouted out something that sounded as if he had gargled his words, but Danny could not make it out. DiLucca fired another shot, then two more in rapid succession. If he had emptied his chamber he would have to reload right there in the swamp water, much too risky a move for a man who did not hold all the cards. This was not Salvatore DiLucca's style. Unless ...

Unless he was firing at something else!

For several minutes Danny heard thrashing in the water. Then nothing. The stillness surrounding him was worse than anything Sal had screamed out. Danny crouched low in the steamy saw grass waiting for a sound, for something, for anything. His head ached with the riotous chorus of the swamp crickets while a thousand demons did a mad dance inside his brain. In the murky stillness of the Shark River swamp, one demon spoke louder than the others.

Why had Sal stopped calling for him?

The saw grass in front of him rustled like crunched paper.

It was crazy to speak, to utter even one word that might give his position away. But the demons would not let him remain silent.

"Sal?"

There was no answer.

"Listen, Sal. We can work this thing out!"

Nothing.

The tall grass rustled again. Whatever was there, it was moving closer.

Holding the .45 straight out, Danny aimed it toward the sound of crunching sedges and sloshing water. He waited for the grass curtain to part, knowing that in the next moment either a ravenous 'gator or a man with a gun would emerge. He was ready for either. He could do this.

One shot. Just one shot. If he could keep his eyes on the target right in front of him, he could pick it off with one bullet.

"A walk in the park," he whispered to himself. *"Just like a goddamned walk in—"*

The thick saw grass in front of him separated. He held the revolver firm in his grip, one hand steadying the other.

He heard another papery sound, this time from the grass behind him.

... something behind him ...

... and in front of him ...

Danny stared at his hand that held the .45, then slowly dropped his arm to his side. He turned to watch one alligator splash through the grass into the shallows, then two others. They moved in the swamp water in a crawling swim as they circled, watching him, waiting. The grass separated again and two more appeared.

Sal was right. The big one had found him, all right ... and he had brought his friends.

Danny dug one foot into the soft mud while the other floated uselessly in the stinging cold water. One bullet. One shot. A walk in the park. He could do it.

He could do it.

He placed the barrel of the revolver into his mouth and squeezed the trigger.

THYF'S TALE

BY CHRISTINE MORGAN

A wolf's wind howled, winter snow whipping as white drifts piled, the whole world cold and dark as Hel's domain.

Within the longhouse, behind log walls mud-plastered and beneath wet thatch moss-heavy, the folk of Jarl Hodvard's farmstead gathered against the night.

Here around the hearths they sat, upon sleeping-platforms that lined the hall. Here were heaped furs and fleeces, thick cloaks and wool blankets. In stone-ringed pits the fires burned, shedding heat and light while smoke hung thick among the roofbeams.

Bread and cheese and barley beer had been their meal, with a broth of boiled beef and leeks and garlic. Now men passed the mead-bowls hand to hand, that sweet drink, honey-made. Voices rose as spirits did, in merriment and laughter. Children played with hounds on the rush-strewn, hard-earth floor; the women sewed and spun.

And they did not know how Death waited among them.

Ate and drank, spoke and laughed, among them.

Hodvard had at the head of his hall a great chair, oak-carved, antler-adorned, and draped in deer hides and bearskins. A sword, sheathed in leather, rested above it on wooden pegs. To one side of the sword was a shield painted oxblood-red. To the other was a helm, old and much dented.

He had been a warrior once. A hewer of men, a blood-letter, a death-bringer, a cleaver of limbs and skulls. He had plundered rich silver from cities and monasteries. He had won worthy followers to his boar's-head banner.

He was a warrior still, for all that the years might weigh upon him. Though his shoulders might be stooped, his hair and beard gray-streaked, though a softness of paunch rolled over his belt, he would set himself against any number of foes.

He would set himself against them unflinchingly, eager for the battle rage, the red fog that clouded the eyes yet let them see all with an eagle's clarity.

Oh, his youthful times of raids and pillage were done, yes, and they had well served their purpose. How else could he have settled here, wealthy and content? He had fine farmlands, the soil not thin and rough, not rocky and miserly to yield. The fields provided good pasturage, the woods good hunting.

Olrunn, his first wife, had given him six sons. His second wife, young Esja, had already borne him another. Among those of his hall were daughters and in-laws, kinsmen, grandchildren, nephews, bastards, war-brothers, guests and friends. Servants there were too, and slaves, well-treated.

Hodvard was known as a fair and just jarl. His hospitality and generosity were beyond compare. His nature was jovial, his wise judgment often sought in counsel.

Strange, it might seem, that any would wish him ill will.

Or bring violence against him here in the fastness of his own hall.

The mead-bowls passed 'round again.

Men called for music and Erik Deft-Handed fetched down a harp. He played to them a familiar tune, an oar song, one they knew from riding the whale road, Njord's gray waves, in the dragon-headed ships, and they sang along heartily. When it was done, Hodvard acclaimed the harpsman, and threw to him a silver ring.

Then was another song called for, and this time a girl arose, pretty Lundis, Bergulf's sister. Her voice pure as clear water, she sang of Brynnhild's sorrow, the valkyrie maid pining in her love for Sigurd.

The women of the hall found this to their liking, and Hodvard gave the girl a comb of ivory. But the rest wanted next some entertainment more to thrill the nerve and chill the blood, and so turned to Thyf.

"You have traveled far and seen much," they said to him. "Tell us a grim tale!"

So Thyf settled himself near the fire and began to speak.

"This is the Saga of Guldi and Svarti ..."

Once there were two friends known since birth
Babes in arms together, orphaned of mothers
Playmates, they were, and inseparable
Guldi fair-haired as Svarti was dark
The both of them handsome lads, and strong

When they came of age and wished to go to war
Their fathers armored them in mail coats
Gave them swords and shields, helms and horses
And sent them to be trained, to be made battle-ready
Proud sons to bring honor to their names

Guldi proved a bold and fearless warrior
Shrinking from no challenge
Valorous, a true leader of men
Winner of renown and rewards
Gold-girt, with rich rings thick upon his arms

But for Svarti, swift and clever
In the clash of shield walls, the slash of sword blades
The drumming of hoofbeats and the singing of bowstrings
Muster his courage though he would
Time and again it failed him

The others, at first, laughed and jeered
Making much mockery of his plight
Until even Guldi took part
Their brotherhood since boyhood
Their long friendship, forgotten

Soon it was that none would stand beside him
Shoulder-to in the line where lime wood overlaps
Where each man must rely upon his neighbor
Else join the dead upon the corpse-strewn field
Eyes raven-pecked, flesh cold, guts spilled

In fierce battles where men bled and died
His companions would find Svarti
Crouched and cowering, dumbstruck
Unmanned by terror, weeping
Breeches befouled in hot and stinking shame

Until he could withstand no more
Abandoning their war band to slink away
To sell sword and shield, mount and mail
To take up trade in the town, and settle there
Where he prospered, and grew wealthy within its walls

Now, there dwelled in that city the maiden Alfir
Of beauty, wit, and wisdom above all women
Blue-eyed Alfir, daughter of a lord
Whose father, swayed by gold and greed
Consented she would become Svarti's wife

But war kindled in the land, and fanned its flames
Until farms and fields smoldered in black ashes
The folk slain, enslaved, the cattle slaughtered
The city besieged, bereft of mercy
Wracked by famines and the pestilence

Soon Svarti found that all his fortune
Could not stave off sufferings for long
Silver useless 'gainst sickness and starvation
Even emeralds buy no meat or milk
Nor bread when none is to be bought

Just when it seemed hope must be lost
Rescue came, men and horses, over the hills
A sea of shields, spears like tall grain-stalks
Sun glinting on helms, an army
With Guldi's banner flying at its head

They broke the siege and sent foes scattering
For their very lives running in rout and retreat
Cut down as they fled, heads hewn from bodies
The city saved from certain fall
The army welcomed, and Guldi hailed a hero

In the great glad revelry that followed
Alfir looked on Guldi, loved and favored him
Wanting for her husband a brave man, a warrior
Insisting she would wed no other
And Guldi did not disagree

So it was that Svarti, shamed anew
Vowed oaths of vengeance against Guldi
Once his friend, close as a brother
Hated now, his sworn enemy
Heart poisoned against him

Then there came to Svarti's house a traveler
A stranger, a visitor, wolf-cloaked
Bright of eye and sly of smile
Who had heard of Svarti's troubles
And come to make offer of counsel

"For a purse of silver," the stranger said
"Men can be bought, hired swords
Mercenaries loyal-bound to no king
To beset upon Guldi from ambush
Cut him down, and end his life"

But Svarti would not consider this
Saying, "Guldi is too great a warrior

Well-armed and well-armored
Well-accompanied when he rides
He fights as if born of sword and shield

"Whole armies could you throw against him
Like waves against a stone cliff face
Even should by chance some blow strike
To die in Odin's battle glory
Would be Guldi's dearest wish"

"For a purse of gold, then," the stranger said
"I will undertake this task myself
To, by stealth, slay him as he sleeps
Peaceful, unknowing of his fate
No weapon within his grasp

"And so deny him the honorable war death
That would earn him a seat at Odin's table
In high Valhalla, golden-roofed
The feast hall, the mead hall
Of its five hundred and forty doors

"There, men wait, Valkyrie-chosen
For the sounding of Heimdal's Gjallarhorn
To don their war-gear against the giants
In that final battle, the gods' twilight
At the destruction and the drowning of the world"

At this, Svarti let himself be coaxed
Giving the stranger half a purse of gold
For which he would that very night
Go to Guldi, and do mischief upon him
Dooming him forever to Niflheim, Hel's realm

The stranger, whose name was Mord-Vargr
The killer wolf, the murderer
Went forth in darkness from Svarti's house
Stoat-silent and cat-quick

Upon death's errand like a shadow

He donned again his cloak, two-sided
White-furred and black, a gift to him
From the insulter of the Aesir
Mother of Sleipnir, Fenrir's father
The wily one, bringer of Baldr's bane

He went unseen to the place where Guldi slept
Dropping into the hearth embers a sprig of herbs
Troll wife stuff, marsh witchery
Its smoke to lull and cast a pall
Drawing dreamers deeper into dreams

Guldi had by his bedside a broad-bladed axe
On the bedpost his sword belt hung, within reach
A stabbing blade he kept beneath his headrest
A short knife secured to his wrist
All of these, Mord-Vargr slipped from him and took away

The warlord, unarmed and unaware
Defenseless, Guldi slumbered on
He felt nothing as the knotted twine
Looped loosely 'round his neck
Twisting tight and ever tighter

First flush then pallor flooded Guldi's face
Mouth gaping and with lips blue-tinged
He twitched, and gave a thin last gasp
Then strong limbs slackened; he lay dead
Strangled like a stillborn babe upon its own birth cord

Swift and stealthy as he'd come, he left
The wolf-cloaked killer, Mord-Vargr
Returning to the house where Svarti sat waiting
Gut-sick with reproach at his abasement
Even as his heart leaped in wicked joy

"The deed is done," the murderer said; "Guldi lives no more
No seat awaits him among the einherjar, Odin's own
No mead horn and feast of boiled meat
Cut each night from the flesh of Saehrimnir
The immortal boar renewed again each dawn"

Svarti paid what was owed, that terrible perversity of wergild
Yet took but bleak and shallow satisfaction from it
For a coward lives like one half-dead already
And he knew the freezing fogs of Niflheim
Would one day await him as well

But Freya's tears of gold had purchased Alfir's tears of silver
The maiden weeping, grieving for the hero slain
Mourning him, she scorned anew what Svarti offered
So despite his wealth, a dragon's hoard
He grew old and wretched, and died alone

A hush spread as Thyf spoke, and for a span of time it lingered when he finished.

He'd watched the jarl's men grin at the words of war glory and battle carnage, and seen them sneer their disdain for Svarti's cowardice.

And he'd observed how unease seeped into each of them, like groundwater, as Guldi's dishonorable death unfolded. He saw them shiver, and faces go ashen beneath their beards.

Every warrior's innermost creeping fear, dark, gnawing and insidious, was to be denied a glorious death in combat, and be deemed unworthy of Valhalla. To become aged and infirm, crippled, weak, a feeble burden, a frail and useless creature ... or to die of illness, accident ... or worst of all, a low and slinking murder, life not lost but stolen ...

They had asked him for a grim tale, had they not?

Now, gathering themselves, the men uttered bluff and hearty laughter to prove it had not affected them unduly.

"Grim, indeed," Hodvard said to Thyf, "but, well told, well told." And he gave Thyf a brooch of hammered bronze.

The fires had burned low by then, the mead bowls drained, and Hodvard's folk readied themselves for the night.

Some of the men made a joke show of checking that their weapons rested near at hand by their sleeping places. Others peered into the hearths, poking the ash-covered embers as if searching for suspicious sprig bundles, to the amusement of all.

There were none, of course, and the smoke no different than ever.

Neither was it the mead that had been laced with potent herbs.

Soon enough the night noises of the hall became slumbering sounds, rustles and murmurs, snores and slow breaths.

Beyond log walls and thatch roof, wind whistled and snow blew.

Then Thyf, who had lain awake all the while, arose from his furs and blankets.

None stirred at his movement.

He went to Hodvard's great chair. Behind it hung a partition of hides, draping off a smaller chamber where the jarl and his young wife Esja shared a bed.

The dull red glow from the low-burned fires let him make his way unhindered to Hodvard's side. He saw that the old warrior slept with a hand-axe, its iron head leather-sheathed, curled to his chest the way a child might cradle a twig doll.

It was the broth that had been drugged, the broth of boiled beef with leeks and garlic, strong flavored so that the bitterness was masked.

Thyf, with gentle care and caution, lifted the axe to remove it from Hodvard's arms. He put it aside on the floor, where it might easily enough have fallen in the course of normal sleep.

He slid his fingers through thick gray hair, raised up Hodvard's head, and turned it to the side. There was the neck, the nape exposed.

Not the strangling twine this time.

She wanted it done without sign or trace, an undetectable murder.

At the base of the skull where the spine joined with it was a hollow, an indentation of the flesh.

"I bore him six sons," Olrunn had said. "Six strong sons, fine boys."

Thyf withdrew from one of his woolen leg wraps a folded piece of linen, and from it a long sliver of ivory. Its narrow end came to a point, sharp as any needle, while its wider end was blunted. Its edges were honed like those of the thinnest sword blade.

65

Olrunn, the jarl's first wife, was divorced of him and gone away, back to her father's hall. Hodvard's friends and kinsmen said he was well rid of her, for she had been both shrewish, and over coddling of their children.

"He led them all to war, though I begged him not to," she'd said, "and let them all be killed in battle. When I raged at him, furious, he scoffed and said that when he met them again in Odin's feast hall, they would thank him."

He placed the point against the hollow at the base of Hodvard's skull, gripping the blunted end between two knuckles and bracing it with his thumb. In a short, fast jab, he pierced the skin, punching the ivory needle up and deep and at an angle.

"If I must lose my six dear sons, never to see them again in this world or the next, then I would have the same for Hodvard! He will not, must not be reunited with them!" And, so saying, Olrunn had paid Thyf his purse of gold, sending him to do this.

Hodvard grunted, a wet spit bubble escaping his lips.

The slightest sideways gesture sliced the sharp edges in an arc, shearing through the tough and gristly brain-stem, severing it.

The jarl's chest sank, subsiding, on a slow exhalation. A looseness overtook his body and settled him heavy upon the bed.

Thyf pressed the sliver deeper until it had gone fully embedded. Of blood, there was barely a drop. The blunt ivory end, flush against Hodvard's skull, would not be noticed even by the women who would wash and bathe and comb and dress him to be readied for his funeral pyre.

Then he silently returned to lie down again and shut his eyes, and await what despairing outcry the morning's grim discovery would bring.

MISCONCEPTIONS

BY MATT HILTON

I sat in the room, doing the old Sam Spade bit waiting for the femme fatale to knock, and thinking to myself, *There has to be a better way than this.* I couldn't think of anything. A man past forty, whose waist size exceeds his age, needs something kind of sedate to get by on.

The room wasn't a PI's office. In fact it wasn't even much of a room. It was a box at the end of a damp corridor above a pole-dancing club with rusty poles. It was more like a storage closet, plasterboard tacked onto a wooden frame, no paper, no photos or diplomas in frames, just boxes of stacked junk lining the walls and an old Formica-topped table and two plastic chairs. I'd sat in chairs just like them at school back in the '80s. They were uncomfortable then; now that my ass had grown much bigger, they were torture. I was itching like crazy and all I wanted to do was get up and pull the material of my shorts out of my butt-crack. But I held the nonchalant pose of a noir antihero; people kind of expected it when they arrived.

The femme fatale arrived. She didn't knock because there was no door. She just leaned in and scowled at me like I was something filthy. She wasn't far wrong, I suppose. I looked back, and maybe the sour expression on my face told her everything. Femme fatale she wasn't; she'd a face like a hog and the body to match. She was dressed in a floral dress a family could set up camp beneath, a brown overcoat, and dingy training shoes. Bare legs, patchy with dermatitis. Her hair was greasy, tight curls going gray where the black dye had faded. I could see where she'd shaved hair from her chin, the blunt razor leaving a barely healed scar.

"You can't be Ward?" she said by way of introduction.

Well I sure as hell wasn't Sam Spade, but I didn't get what she was meaning.

"Why not?"

She came into the room uninvited and sat on the other chair across the table from me. It squealed in protest, and little wonder. She pressed her hands into the thick rolls of flesh on her upper thighs, giving me a head-to-heels inspection. By the look of things she wasn't impressed. The feeling was mutual.

"I heard you were meant to be something," she said.

I looked down at my gut hanging over my belt. I was more of a man than I used to be, that was for certain. But meant to be *something*? Fair enough, I was no oil painting, but who was she to complain?

"Depends what you want," I said and she snorted.

"Well it's a good job I ain't looking for a wild time."

That pissed me off, but I didn't say. She wasn't exactly my type either, but she was carrying the money I wanted, and like I already said, I was there to make an easy living. Every job has pros and cons. Seeing as I could think of nothing that suited me better, I just took the day-to-day bullshit as a necessary evil.

"When we spoke on the phone, you said that you'd do whatever I asked." She was obviously happy now that I was what she'd expected. She wasn't the least nervous. Maybe it was my lack of response to her sarcasm that reassured her: An undercover cop would have argued his case more, to get her to incriminate herself before pulling out his cuffs.

"Only one thing I don't touch," I reminded her.

"Yes, you said. You never touch kids."

I nodded. "Kids."

"So you do have *some* standards." She was eyeing my rumpled suit, her mouth twisted into a sneer, and I guessed she wasn't confusing standards with morals. That was okay. A body like mine didn't carry a nice suit well, so I just made do with an old one. I didn't dress nice, and I didn't kill children—some legend I'm graced with.

Not that I was squeamish about doing a child, but they carried too much fuss with them. You could kill a man, a woman, and it barely hit the papers these days. But do a kid and there was a national outrage. Doesn't do much for your career chances if the entire country is looking for you, and I had a living to make.

"I don't want you to harm a kid. Not unless you have a limit on mental age?"

I held up the flat of my hand, surprising even myself. "I don't do handicapped people either." I pinched my lips around the politically incorrect term, but I wasn't sure what the acceptable moniker for someone soft in the head was these days. Should have said I'd never killed anyone with mental health issues before, not any in the clinical sense. Plenty of whack jobs and nut cases, mind you, but that's not the same.

The femme grunted and it suited her.

"I was making a joke. My husband still thinks he's a teenager the way he's running around."

I got her this time, but didn't say. So she'd cottoned on that her husband was having a good time, looking elsewhere? Can't say as I blamed him too much. Still, she was the cash cow so I tried to look sympathetic without putting the emphasis on "cow."

"You still sure you want me to kill him?"

"That's what I'm paying you for. I don't want a frigging half-baked job. When you do him, put an extra bullet in his brains to make sure."

"I was just checking. See, maybe after you think about it, you'll have a change of mind."

She shook her head and I caught a whiff of cheap fragrance and sweat. "That bastard is screwing everything in a skirt that he can find. And I've got the proof. The scumbag gave me a sexually transmitted disease and then tried to say he caught it off me!"

I could understand her outrage, I mean, what were the chances of that?

She gave me the beady eye, still didn't care for what she found. "When you've done it, how'd I know you can keep your mouth shut afterwards?"

"I was just going to ask the same thing." We stared at each other, my hard eyes on her limpid ones. When she didn't offer anything, I said, "I'm not in the habit of confessing my sins. I'm taking it that once he's out of the way you want to start a new life. You aren't gonna speak if it means your new life is in a cell not much bigger than this shit-hole."

She looked around the cramped room. Then she shrugged, a roll of fat bulging out of her collar. "I could live with that." She laughed nastily. "If it means getting him out of the way. Really, though, I can't live with him any longer." She placed a pudgy hand over her heart. Her eyes rolled back and I was looking at the vein-marbled whites. "I solemnly promise I won't say a word to anyone," she said in a singsong voice. "So? We have a deal?"

"When I see the cash." I smiled in encouragement.

She dug an envelope out of her overcoat pocket and slapped it down on the Formica. I tried to weigh the contents with my eyes. Couldn't, so reached over and lifted the flap. Plenty of purples, not enough gold notes. "Looks a little light to me."

"Half now, half on completion."

"That isn't the way I work."

"How can I be sure that you'll even do the job? For all I know you could just pick up the cash, walk away, and that's the last I'd ever hear of you."

"Sometimes you have to take things on faith," I told her.

"I'm struggling with that ... you don't look like a professional assassin to me."

"That's because I'm not an assassin. Assassins tend to take out politicians, religious figures, royals ... me, I just do normal, run-of-the-mill people. I'm just a regular ol' hitman."

"You don't look like much of a hitman either. Nothing like the ones you see in the movies."

"Who were you expecting? Matt Damon?"

"I should be so lucky," she snorted. She started picking at the half-healed scab on her chin and I thought, *No one with a face like that has that kind of luck!*

"You've heard my credentials," I said. "You know I'm up to the job."

"I only know what you told me on the telephone. You could've been spinning me a line, just to get your hands on my cash."

"I don't do kids, I don't do handicapped folk, and I don't do lies." My legend was growing.

"By the look of things you don't do much exercise either," she said with a wicked smile, the old kettle and pot argument raging on. "You sure you're fit for your line of work?"

"These days I hardly run for a bus," I acquiesced. "But I don't have to. A bullet's quicker than any man."

"How pat," she smirked. "You still have to catch up with them first, don't you?"

"Nope, I wait until their guard's down. Take them when they're least expecting it. My strategy has served me well, believe me."

"How many people have you killed?"

"You're sure you want to hear?"

"I want to know I'm going to get value for money."

"Thirty-three," I said.

She adjusted her weight on the chair, covering a sniff of disdain with the creaking of the plastic.

"You still doubt me?"

"Can't blame a girl for being nervous with her hard-earned cash, can you?"

"OK. You want proof?"

She patted her opposite coat pocket. I didn't look; I was still watching the disgusting flake of scab hanging off her chin. "I have the rest of the money right here. Show me something that will convince me that you're really up to the task and you've got a deal."

"That's fair," I decided.

I lifted my silenced SIG Sauer from under the table and pointed it at her tremulous gut. I pulled the trigger.

The thud of the bullet pounding her flesh was louder than the gun's retort.

The femme took a moment to realize she was dying. She looked down at the hole I'd just put in her coat, then up at me.

"Will that do it?" I asked.

Her mouth hung open, a string of saliva tethering her tongue to her dentures. She blinked slowly and there was disbelief in her eyes. Maybe it was because I'd shot her, or maybe she still doubted me. That damn flake of scab still waved at me and I used it as a target. Scab and chin disintegrated together.

"So I guess we've got a deal?" I asked. Her head was nodding, her floppy neck riding the ripples still shuddering through her body. The nod was enough to seal it for me.

I jostled myself out of the chair, thankfully unhitched material from the crack of my cheeks, and went over to her. Her arms had fallen to her sides, but her girth pushed them away from her. She reminded me of that spoiled bitch that blew up with juice in Willy Wonka's factory. I dipped a hand in her pocket and pulled out another envelope.

I flicked through the notes. They were all there.

I pushed both envelopes into my pockets and walked along the cramped corridor to the far end, ignoring the pain in my knees. The corridor was long and I was puffing by the time I reached the far end. Maybe the femme was right and I should be in better shape for this game. I dabbed perspiration from my forehead before pushing open a door. I had to look the part. There was another room, not much bigger than the first.

The femme's husband was a little squirt with glasses and a comb-over. His jumper was a market stall special, all diamond patterned down the chest, the two-for-the-price-of-one type you buy on special offer. Black nylon trousers, white socks for frig sake! Couldn't see how someone like him could be living the double life his wife claimed, but she was right in a way. Just shows you that looks can be deceiving. People look at me and don't credit me with much either.

"It's done?" he asked.

I looked down at the little man. His eyes looked huge behind the glasses. He was sitting in the chair where I'd left him earlier, while I prepped for his wife's arrival.

"Just like you asked," I reassured him.

"Did she suffer?"

The malignant gleam in his eye told me the answer he was waiting for.

"Yeah, she suffered."

"Good," he said. "She deserved it. Did she tell you I gave her a sexually transmitted disease?"

"Yeah, you called it right."

"Bitch. It was her who gave me the clap. It was her who was sleeping around."

I didn't comment. It was beginning to sound like I was stuck in the middle of the Jerry Springer show.

"What else did she say?" he asked. "Did she have any idea that—"

"She was certain you were being unfaithful to her, chasing all these young skirts all the time." I laughed at the absurdity of it.

He laughed with me. "You think I'd stand any chance with a young girl?"

Decorum isn't my main strength. "Not a chance."

To his credit, he didn't take any offense. "Crazy bitch has accused me of running after *girls* for years," he said. "She's made my life hell and I think it was all guilt over her own infidelity. Did she admit to having someone else?"

"I didn't ask."

"She must have said something."

"She did. She asked me to kill you."

"What?"

I just smiled at him and he shook his head.

"Isn't that just like the bitch? What a nerve, eh?"

I shrugged. "A job's a job to me, a deal a deal."

"Good job we dealt first, then," he said, blinking mole-like. "I know she despised me, but can't believe she'd actually want me killed. But it does make sense, I suppose. She'd want me out the way so she could sleep around any time she liked. What a bitch!"

I shrugged, held out my hand. "Forget about her; you don't have to take her crap ever again." I snapped my fingers. "Money on completion; just as we agreed."

The man pulled out a thick envelope and I took it from him. Didn't bother counting the notes, because I knew he was good for the fee.

"A deal's a deal," he said, smiling as he mimicked my earlier words.

"Yes," I said. "It is."

I shot him in the head, just like I'd agreed to do for his wife.

But that wasn't the main reason.

The little squirt should have mentioned it when first we met. I wiggled my trousers out of my butt again, exhaling at the chafing pain. I lined up my SIG on his groin. One pull on the trigger and I got payback. "That's for giving *me* the fucking pox."

SECOND AMENDMENT SOLUTION

BY BILLIE SUE MOSIMAN

June recalled her brother's words the day they took away her husband. He had said, "When everything else fails, we have the Second Amendment." The comment burst through her mind like a Roman candle going off in a dark sky. Yet all she could do was ask plaintively, "Where are you taking him?"

The Right to Bear Arms.

June had been bearing arms since she was a kid. Her brother, Lawrence, was three years younger so she was the first to be schooled with weapons. Their father was a hunter, a free spirit, and a firm believer in owning guns and using them. He had only once used a gun against another person and that was because the intruder got all the way through the house to his bedroom, despite the warning he would be shot if he didn't leave *right now*. He didn't listen and he didn't leave. He ended up with a .45 caliber slug in his gut for his failure to take instruction.

June and Lawrence had run from their bedroom, wide-eyed pre-teens, to find the intruder dead on their father's bedroom floor. Though they had seen dead animals before, this scene was enough to set them to shaking and crying. There was a dead man in their house bleeding all over the place.

June's Dad stepped over the corpse and said, "Go back to your rooms. I'm calling the police. You can come out when they get here."

Her Dad was all matter-of-fact about it. Later, when the authorities left, he sat them down at the kitchen table and said, "What I did was a terrible thing, but I was forced to do it. You can't let a man come into your house and either attack you or rob you. I know that was a terrible thing for you to see, but I want both of you to face it and think about it. If you ever in your life have to protect yourself or someone you love, then just do it and don't think about it. If you think about it, you may never get a chance to do it."

Now, twenty years later, with her father dead and her brother living across the country, they had come and taken away her husband. And she had shot no one.

She still didn't understand why it had happened, why they had taken him, and she didn't know really who they were. They wore suits, not uniforms. They knocked politely on the door and when Charles opened it, they stepped inside, took out handcuffs, told Charles to turn around, and within seconds had possession of him. June had stood by, itching to go to the hallway gun rack for the semi-automatic .22, but this wasn't an intruder in the night, this wasn't a marauding force of maniacs swarming through her door. This was government. This was dark, deep, hidden government, and they acted as if they had all the right in the world to walk in and take her Charles from her.

She had protested, as had Charles. "Where are you taking him? Who are you? What's this all about? What's he done? What law has he broken? *Who do you think you are?*"

She was handed a single sheet of paper that mentioned the Homeland Security Act and the governmental right to arrest and sequester a suspected terrorist without recourse to habeus corpus. Before June could get the words read, her eyes swimming with tears and going unfocused, they had quick-stepped Charles out the door and down the walk to a waiting black car.

June stood in the doorway calling, "You can't do this! He's not a terrorist! Are you people crazy? Where are you taking him?"

For all the panic in her voice, for all the tears that spilled down her cheeks, neither of the two men acted as if they had heard a thing. Doors of the car were slammed shut and it abruptly pulled from the curb. It was morning, a bright, sunny Saturday. She and Charles meant to mow the lawn then go to a movie together. Their whole world had come unglued, and it spun around June as she stood helpless in her doorway looking after the disappearing black car as it sped down the quiet neighborhood street.

Inside, she sank onto the sofa, holding the bit of paper in her hand so tightly it was crinkling. She stared down at it and read through the short paragraphs again.

Homeland Security. Suspected terrorist acts. Rights of the government to arrest and sequester. *Sequester.*

The reality of what had just happened left June emptied and as bereft as if her husband had suddenly died before her eyes. She sat back, the tears now turning into streams of fear and worry, her whole body racked with sobs, her breath coming in gasps until she had to bend over her knees and shut her eyes against the world.

An hour later she still sat on the sofa, befuddled and spent. She rose slowly and went to the phone where it hung on the wall in the kitchen. She picked up the cordless receiver and took it to the table to sit in yellow sunlight. She dialed their attorney. When she was told he wasn't available, June lost control and screamed, "PUT HIM ON THE PHONE RIGHT THIS FUCKING MINUTE!"

There was a pause, an intake of breath on the other end of the line, and then a quiet, "Okay, hold on."

Steve Samson came on the line immediately. "June! Why are you cursing and screaming at my secretary?"

"Steve, men came to the house an hour ago and took Charles. They handed me a paper identifying them as Homeland Security officers."

"Uh oh."

"What do you mean, 'uh oh?' This is insane. Charles isn't a terrorist, for God's sake, he sells *insurance!*"

"June? June, calm down. Let me talk to you a minute. I'm not just your attorney, I'm your friend. You and Charles have been to my house for dinner, for parties. And I have to tell you something, sometimes Charles's ideas are ... well, frankly, they're definitely left wing."

"Are you saying because we hold liberal beliefs, the government had a right to come in here and take him? You can't be saying that, Steve."

"I'm just saying maybe that has something to do with it. Has he made any overseas phone calls?"

"Not that I know of," June said, "why would he?"

"Do you think he might have some friends that you don't know about?"

"Steve, you're still talking like Charles has done something wrong and he deserved what just happened to him. Now, I'm going to say this as calmly and plainly as I can ..." She swallowed hard, tears trying to break her down into sobs again. "... Charles is not a terrorist. Charles doesn't know any terrorists. Charles does not advocate the taking over of the U.S. government. He's protested in the city Occupy movement, sure he has, but so have thousands of other people. He contributes money to Independent candidates. He sells insurance, goes to your parties, plays golf, and is my good husband. Now are you going to help me find out where they took him and get him back or aren't you? Because, by God, this is wrong, Steve. A mistake's been made."

Silence over the line lengthened a few seconds longer than June thought it should. Just as Steve began to clear his throat to speak, June said, "Forget it. You know what, Steve, you just fucking forget it, all right? I can tell you're scared to death to get involved."

She hung up the phone and lay her head on her arms on the table. Now what was she going to do? She raised her head, smoothed out the sheet of paper given to her, and scanned it again. In the very bottom right corner in small print was a telephone number with a Washington, D.C. area code. She snatched up the phone and dialed, her hand trembling.

"Hello? Homeland Security. How may I help you?"

It was a woman, sounding as pleasant and cheerful as a greeter at Wal-mart. June said, "My husband was arrested this morning from our home and I want to know why."

"Your name, please?"

"June T. Haver. My husband is Charles Allan Haver. He's an *insurance* salesman." She felt like falling into maniacal laughter. It was ludicrous to think the government feared an insurance salesman.

"Hold please, while I transfer you."

June held the receiver so close to her ear it was causing her pain. She let up the pressure and tried to compose herself. Maybe she could straighten this out and they could laugh about it later, make it a party joke.

The line clicked, then a man's voice said, "Mrs. Haver? My name is Cary Duma. It's true your husband was arrested this morning and I'm sure you were given the statement with this number on it. I'm sorry, but we cannot tell you where your husband was taken."

"You can't? Why can't you?" The panic was back and the world was askew as a leaning telephone pole about to be uprooted by a tornadic wind. "He hasn't done anything! What are you holding him for?"

"Mrs. Haver, I'm sure you understand this is only a precautionary measure, and I'm sure your husband will check out fine and be home again soon. I suggest you be patient and let us do our job. If everything is all right, this will all be over soon."

Now she broke down completely. She hadn't taken a breath since he began talking. She sucked in a noisy lungful of air and said, "This isn't right. You shouldn't be able to take an American citizen out of his home in handcuffs on some presumption of guilt and then not tell his family where he is. This is so wrong it ought to be criminal. I want to visit him. I am his wife. Tell me where he is."

"I'm sorry, Mrs. Haver, I just explained that you need to be patient. You can contact us again in forty-eight hours for an update."

For the second time she hung up, slamming the phone on the table so hard she feared she'd cracked the hard plastic casing. She stood from the table, the chair legs screeching along the floor. She began to pace from the kitchen to the living room, back and forth. She was arguing mentally with herself, arguing with the faceless men who had just disrupted her life.

Can't do this, she thought, balling her fists, her feet scattering staccato sounds across the wood floors as she paced.

But what could she do? This wasn't like fighting city hall. It wasn't even like having a dispute with a state governor or a chief of police or the FBI. This was the hidden, silent arm of the government given great power over the people, taking away their rights to counsel, their rights to let family members know where they were being held, their rights to protest. Charles had simply been swept away into a nether darkness where no one would ever answer questions about him, where anything could be happening to him, where any charges against him weren't being met by an opposing attorney.

June stopped in the hall near the gun rack. There was always the Second Amendment Solution. If someone didn't tell her something soon, if someone didn't allow her to see Charles, there was going to be hell to pay. Hell and damnation following.

It was weeks before she had it all worked out. She had tried finding out what she could of the Homeland Security Act. She had appealed to the attorney general and the governor of her state of Texas. She had found little to help her. Charles was still gone, not a word about him or from him, as if he had vanished on that bright sunny Saturday forever. Finally she contacted one of Charles's oldest friends, Barry Callfirth. The two had grown up together on arid ranches in West Texas and had stayed friends through a lifetime. Not only that, but they both held firm liberal ideas and bemoaned the direction the United States was headed, all predicated on the 9/11 attacks in New York City and on the Pentagon in D.C. The instant that happened, they were on the phone to one another talking about how this didn't seem right, this seemed like some kind of strange event that couldn't happen in America. Then when the President instituted the Homeland Security Act, they both were flabbergasted and alarmed.

Barry still lived in West Texas, not far from Amarillo. June told him on the phone what had happened to Charles. He was instantly furious. "What does your attorney say? What's happened since they took him?"

"My attorney didn't really want to get involved. I think going up against the government worries him. And since they took Charles I've called Washington, D.C. I've appealed to the Texas Attorney General, the governor, and the President of the United States. No one has helped me. Mostly I get shifted from extension to extension until I'm cut off."

"Good Lord, June. This isn't good. Do you think your phone is tapped?"

"I assume that it is."

"Come out here to the ranch where we can talk. You know the way?"

"I'll be there by tomorrow."

Barry sat in a ladder-back chair with a rush seat. He pulled it close to where she sat on his deeply cushioned sofa. "Now let me tell you something," he said.

June frowned and clasped together her hands around the small purse in her lap.

"There's a senator from Texas who's been keeping his guard up and monitoring both me and Charles. He thinks everyone is a suspect, everyone has ulterior motives. His name is Kaden James. Heard of him?"

"Yeah, I know who you mean."

"Well, I found out through the Freedom of Information Act that there's a thick file on us. The name that kept cropping up in the reports was James. Hell, he even collected a copy of an essay Charles wrote in college about the difference between a democracy and a republic. I think this guy is the one who had Charles arrested."

"Oh God. But Charles isn't a terrorist and neither are you!"

"Of course not. This is witch hunting. It was bad back in the Bay of Pigs days, when everyone was suspected of being a pinko Commie if he disagreed with his government. Now it's this overall catch phrase 'suspected terrorist' that gets the nod. Anyone can end up on a list, and anyone does. Including me and Charles because we've been outspoken, independent thinkers since we went to college together. You know we were both on the college newspaper, right?"

June nodded, recalling Charles had told her that.

"Well, I edited and Charles investigated anything that looked suspect to him, any personal right that was being stomped on, whether it was done by the college administration or the U.S. Congress. He was really vocal. I told him one time we were going to get blackballed and end up digging ditches, but Charles just laughed. He was a firebrand. I was his torchbearer. Now it's come to this ..."

"What do you think they want him for? What could they imagine he's done? Barry, you know him. He's got fiery opinions, but he's never advocated anything violent, not once in his whole life."

"I know, but you need to check into Kaden James. He's got it in for Charles. He's been in the senate for thirty-five years. He has plenty enough power to have Charles picked up and locked away. I wouldn't blame the Homeland Security for this, he's just using that as a stick. I'm pretty sure it's James who is behind it."

June sat thinking while Barry made them coffee. She knew already what she was going to do. She was making a trip. She was going to see this senator and confront him on his own doorstep.

Barry saw her off the next morning, admonishing her to be careful or she could wind up in a cell herself. June smiled and gave a sarcastic laugh. "Let them just try," she said. "I know them now; I know how they operate. They won't catch me unaware the way they did Charles."

She would get her husband back. She would spend her life getting him back if that's what it took. No one had a right to treat them this way.

"Mr. James is busy," the housekeeper said at the door. It was a veritable mansion, paid for by taxpayers and lobbyists. The house stood three stories, boasted two wings, and had a wide circular drive that went under a portico framed with white columns.

June stepped inside, brushing past the housekeeper. "I'll wait. Tell him I'm here."

Flustered, the other woman stood holding the open door. She said, "You aren't allowed in here. I didn't invite you inside."

June turned and there was fire in her eyes. "Oh, is that right? Well, I'm in here and if you don't want to make a scene, I suggest you tell Mr. James I'm waiting and I'll keep waiting until I'm either bodily removed—in which case I'll be calling the local TV stations to film it— or he sees me. Now go do your goddamn job."

The housekeeper's eyes rounded and she slowly shut the door. She padded off down the carpeted hall and, without saying a word, left June behind. June knew that perfectly timed curse words coming unexpectedly from a well-dressed woman were extremely effective. It made people jump. It made people listen and follow her commands. She smiled to herself, watching the huge cliffs of the maid's buttocks as they shifted beneath her uniform on her long way down the hall.

An arched opening on the right led into some kind of reception area. June entered and found a chair right across from an ornately carved desk. She sat, not feeling at all nervous. She was over crying and despondency. She was about to take a stand.

It was just minutes before Kaden James appeared. He looked ruffled and out of his element. He wore a dark suit and a light blue shirt, but his tie was askew and the look on his face would have been comical had June been in a humor to think of the man that way. "Mrs. Haver?" he asked, hurrying behind the desk to the chair there. "Could I ask what this urgency is about?"

June paused before speaking. There seemed something about the senator that reminded her of someone from the dim past. It might be the eyes, or the shape of his lips. She mentally shook herself when she realized he was waiting. "Yes, you can. My husband, Charles Haver, was arrested at our home six weeks ago and he's disappeared. I don't have to know where he is, but if he isn't home within one more week, I would say there's going to be hell to pay."

"And why would you bring this matter to my home?"

"I know about you, senator. I did my homework. I know you've kept records on my husband since his college days. I have no idea what your big interest is in him, but I do know you have something to do with his arrest. I want him released. He's innocent of any charge you can think up, dream up, or make up. You are persecuting an innocent man, senator."

He sat back from the blast of her anger. He put up a hand to stop her right there. "I don't know where you get your information, Mrs. Haver, but I have nothing to do with your husband's arrest."

"You were on the committee that helped think up the Homeland Security Act—which, by the way is freaking unconstitutional, and I think if you're only half as well-educated as you claim to be, you already know that—but you helped frame the act. And you've watched my husband for years. Now you think I'm so dull-witted that I can't put two and two together? You think my love and deep belief in my husband would just stand by and let people like you accuse him of some deed and lock him away, maybe forever? Do you people also use torture tactics to get people to confess to things they've never done? Are you into 'waterboarding', Mr. James? Are you going to rush me out of this house knowing I'm going straight to the media to tell them every single thing I know about you? Is that what you really want?" Her voice had risen as she spoke until she ended in shouting.

James flinched and caught hold of the edge of his desk with both hands.

"I ... I'll try to look into your husband's case. I promise that."

Now she stood, her fury at its peak. "You better give me something better than that. You better tell me right now, this minute, that you're going to where he's being held and make sure he's safe. Then you're going to contact the people who are holding him and you're going to get him released. Because if you don't, Mr. James, I assure you I will bring down the mountain on you. You have never seen the backlash of bad publicity like I can brew and dump on your head. I want you to believe that the way you would believe in an oath."

She turned and left the room, her anger still at white hot, blotches blooming on each of her cheeks. She let herself out, slamming the door.

Once outside under the portico where she had parked, the Secret Service men guarding the senator giving her the eye, she heaved a big sigh. As she drove away she wondered if anger was enough. She wondered if by threatening a U. S. senator with bad PR she had broken any law. All the way back to her hotel room she watched the traffic in her rearview mirror to see if she was being followed. She supposed she would know the answer to that when she got to her room. If no one showed up, she was going to be fine for a few hours at least.

Barry sat studying the sheaf of papers on his kitchen table. He had no other clear, open space they would all fit. He had been at it for hours, and now it was after midnight. Outside he could hear doves calling and a soft wind sighing under the eaves of his house. Out here in the western part of the state, he was almost as secluded as he suspected Charles was in his undisclosed jail cell. Barry's closest neighbor was fifteen hundred acres away.

For the past twenty-five years, Barry had sat in these empty rooms of a house he inherited from his father, sat alone with his thoughts that year by year grew more aggrieved. Now his worst fear was realized when they had come to take away Charles. Why they'd arrested him and not Barry was not due to his friend being more liable. It was due to Barry being quieter, more reclusive, and close-mouthed. He had no other friends besides Barry and didn't even really confide in him all his thoughts. He had never married—though he had come close right out of college. But Georgia had taken one look at the ranch house sitting in the center of ten thousand wild, windswept acres of Texas land and had quietly made her way back to Houston and away from his marriage proposal.

He was better off alone. He was able to study and make charts, graphs, and notes on what concerned him most—the disintegration of his country. He was not a madman. Neither was he afflicted with paranoia, bipolar disorder, or any other sort of mental disease. He thought of himself as a good citizen. A citizen on alert. He had been on alert for decades. Charles's arrest was about to move him from red alert to black action.

First he had sent June on a mission. He didn't think it would work, but he had to see if it would. Now it had been an entire month since June had accosted Senator Kaden James at his home in Washington, and June was all over the cable TV news channels. She made a strong plea. She cited her facts and answered the interviewers' questions with a calm verisimilitude that made people listen to her.

Yet Charles was still missing.

Charles was being held against his will and for no other reason than he was sometimes stridently vocal. He hadn't just joined the Occupy Houston group, he had been one of the instigators. He was at every Planned Parenthood clinic when there were protests against them. He sent in editorials to the newspapers. He attended city council meetings where he protested environmental issues and lobbied for affordable housing. He was a good citizen exercising his rights.

Barry thought, of course, the men in the suits would show up at his own door one day. He never imagined they would have a worry about his friend Charles. Charles was vocal, but Barry was more serious. Charles was a lightweight in politics and Barry was an ardent supporter and a ferocious enemy. It was Barry they should have arrested.

Slamming his fist on the stack of papers caused a few to scatter in the air and drift to the kitchen floor. Barry took hold of his fury and tamped it the way one would tamp down a campfire.

Now he had to try to employ the Second Amendment Solution. He wouldn't carry through unless he had to. He wasn't a killer, a political assassin. He just wanted his friend set free and exonerated of all wrongdoing. He just wanted his country to act like a republic and treat its citizens with respect. He just wanted his Bill of Rights back.

It was late fall and Senator Kaden James was on holiday for Thanksgiving. He had come to the cabin early to put in stores and ready this house for his family that would be following soon. The air was redolent of crabapples that grew wild in the woods and the heavy green scent of cedar. He loved this place in New Hampshire. It was small and hidden away from the public. The road leading to it was dirt and rutted, so much so that his Secret Service men always complained about how it was tearing up the cars. It was also not a place where anyone would think a Texas senator might spend a holiday.

He straightened the afghan over the back of the sofa and peered at the roaring fire in the stone fireplace. Perfect. Dolly, his wife, was going to enjoy this respite from the public eye. Over the years that public scrutiny had taken a toll on their long marriage. She early on complained that her life wasn't her own anymore. Everything she did, said, and everywhere she went was cataloged, quoted, noted, and discussed by people who didn't even know her.

He knew her as a former Texas high school sweetheart who became the mother of their five children, and a pretty matron with definite class in the political spotlight. He liked to make her happy when he could. She might even sleep with him again.

He remembered the two bathrooms and went to check if there were toilet paper rolls in them. He had a groundskeeper, but no one to care for the interior of the cabin when he wasn't using it. As he passed a window in the hall, he glanced out to the smaller cabin that sat behind the house and closer to the woods. That's where the men guarding him stayed when he came here. He saw the lights on in there and felt safe again. Dolly didn't like how they were followed around by these men, but they just couldn't live their lives any other way now that he was such a powerful man.

He stepped into the first bathroom and heard a sound that made him halt. He walked a few steps toward the glassed-in shower and saw someone standing there, a gun pointed at him.

"Wha—?"

The enclosure swung open and the man stepped out. He was tall, his face weathered, and James recognized him from official photos in the files he kept in his office. *Barry Callfirth.*

"You're going to make some calls, senator."

"My God, how did you get in here?"

"I've been here a week. Waiting for you. You always have underestimated my investigative powers. I've known about this secret hideaway for years."

James started out of the bathroom and tried to hurry down the hall. A soft pfftting sound arose and wood splinters from the baseboard near his feet flew across the floor. He stopped, turned.

"Why did you pick up Charles Haver? Just because he's got a mouth? How many people do you think listen to him?"

James put up his hand and rubbed hard at his cheek. He wouldn't look the other man in the eye.

"Well? Are we going to have a dialogue like civilized human beings, or am I going to have to take out your kneecaps?"

James's head snapped up at that. He began to stutter, something that happened only when he was under duress. "I don't know why Charles was arrested."

Another shot spat from the handgun and lodged in the wall plaster near James's head. A tiny whiff of white smoke puffed out. "Stop it!"

"I'm not going to stop it, senator. Not unless I have to stop you. And I don't want to do that. Now let's go to the living room where you left your cell phone and make those calls."

Barry walked up to the other man, caught him by the shirt at his shoulder and pushed him down the hall, walking close behind.

"You're going to get in a lot of trouble for this."

Barry laughed. "You won't ever find me to put me into a cell, senator. Not me. So let's not even go there with your useless threats. I'm the one with the gun."

In the living room, Barry pushed him to the end table next to the sofa and indicated the phone with the barrel of the gun. "First, I want you to call your wife. Tell her Washington called you in. You can't make Thanksgiving dinner, it's an emergency and you can't talk about it. Tell her you'll see her at home in four days, give your love to the children."

James hesitated, and Barry thrust the gun to his temple and held it there. "No more warning shots, Bubba. Didn't they used to call you 'Bubba' back in Texas City when you were a shave-tail kid?"

James called his wife and explained just as he'd been instructed. Dolly wasn't happy. So what else was new?

When he finished the call, Barry said, "Now call whoever you have to call and have them bring Charles here. Right here. Tonight."

"When my family doesn't show up in the morning, my men here are going to wonder why and come asking about it." James wasn't cowering; in fact, he was brazenly staring Barry in the eyes now.

"We don't care about tomorrow until tomorrow gets here. Now call and have Charles released and brought here. Immediately."

"What makes you think I have the power to do that?"

Barry lowered the .22 Ruger LR semi-automatic, fitted with a suppressor, and shot Kaden James in the knee. The senator crumpled like a heavy bag dropped from a great height. He let out one scream, but Barry stepped over and placed the bore of the gun in James's open mouth. That mouth filled with silence and sudden fear.

Taking the phone with him, Barry returned to the bathroom, rummaged for the first-aid kit he knew was under the sink counter, and returned with it. He kneeled down and dropped the kit into James's lap. "Here, bandage that before you bleed out, you moron."

James was weeping. Big fat tears rolled down his plump cheeks. "You've crippled me!"

"I've done no such thing. They can fit you with a plate there to replace the kneecap. Of course, they're going to have to replace both of them if you give me any more of your lies and obstructions."

"God, man, what's wrong with you, have you lost your mind?"

"Frankly, I've always wanted to ask you the same question. You helped frame the Homeland Security Act? Really? And that makes you sane? You're kidding me, right? As for my own mind, I assure you my mind is clear as a bell and rings with clarity. Nothing wrong with me but a distaste for how things have been handled in Washington by people like you."

Bandages were wound tight around the knee wound and now James taped it. He grimaced every few seconds when pain hit him, traveling up his knee to his groin.

Barry handed him the cell phone. "I am going to repeat this one more time. Call whoever you have to and make it happen. I want Charles here. And I want him here before morning."

James took the phone and began dialing. It took two hours and a half-dozen lengthy conversations, but he was assured Charles Haver was going to be on the next charter flight to New Hampshire.

While they waited, Barry closely questioned the senator about everything that had ever bothered him. Not just the Homeland Security Act and those behind it, their thinking, but about the reason Kaden James had become such a powerful force within the Senate. And why he thought he could have men waltz into June Haver's living room and handcuff her husband on just the word of one U.S. senator. When James didn't want to answer or when he began to stutter out a partial lie, Barry raised the Ruger and pointed to his healthy knee. It was a difficult way to hold a conversation, but Barry found himself enjoying it.

He discovered James was the head of a group—really more a cult than a group it seemed to his mind—that felt people were about to get out of hand and something had to be erected in the law statues to prevent them from inciting a national crisis. Barry just laughed at that, then waved the gun for James to continue.

After the sun had set and the wind had picked up outside, after Barry closed all the curtains and drapes, he turned on a single lamp near the sofa. There was a knock at the door. Barry glanced through a slit in the curtains. He saw Charles at the door and two men walking back to a waiting, idling car. Once the car was gone, Barry opened the door, ushering his friend inside.

He locked the door and turned to take a frightened, confused Charles into a brief hug. When he stepped back he saw Charles' gaze locked on the gun in his hand. He shrugged and said, "Only way I could get you out, buddy, I'm sorry."

Charles turned to see the senator on the sofa, one leg of his slacks torn open and a bloody bandage around his kneecap. "What's happening, Barry?"

"I had to convince Kaden here to do as I asked. For a little while he wasn't listening. I think he is now, right, senator?"

James kept silent. His sullen face made him look like a wronged child.

"We'll be leaving soon," Barry said. Only then did he see that his old friend looked changed—haunted. His eyes were sunk in their sockets, and blue moons rode beneath. There was a short scar on his right cheek, still red and swollen from stitches. He had lost at least thirty pounds and the clothes he wore hung on him as if he were a scarecrow with all the stuffing leaked out.

"What did they do to you, Charles?" Barry's voice was harsh. He sounded angry enough to slap someone around a while and relish doing it.

Charles said, "What didn't the bastards do. I thought I was in a gulag." He licked his lips, looked over at the senator. "And this prick had his hand in the whole dirty thing. He even visited me on Sundays, just to laugh at my torment."

Barry walked over to the sofa and shot James in the other knee. As James opened his mouth to scream, Barry leaned down and covered his mouth with his hand. He moved in close. "I ought to kill you right now. It might take three shots in the brain to do it with this small caliber, but I think I can get the job done."

James shook his head, his pupils showing whites all around. He grunted behind Barry's hand. Barry sat next to him, slowly removing his hand from the senator's mouth. "What's all this about, senator? Are you just power hungry or are you mad with paranoia or do you just hate your own country? I'd really like to know why you'd target the two of us and torture a good man here—" he waved at Charles with his free hand "—for no reason whatsoever. You broke your own laws, senator. You broke the laws of the land. You let some kind of vendetta against people you don't even know get out of hand, didn't you?"

Barry twisted and, picking up the first aid kit, lobbed it at James, who caught it. He rolled out the bandage, trying to wrap it around his shot knee that was bleeding all down his pants leg. As he worked he said, "Charles took June from me."

"What?!" both Barry and Charles said in unison. Charles circled the sofa and stood before them in his loose-fitting suit and haggard face. "What did you say about June?"

James had the knee wrapped. He tore the bandage, grabbed the tape, and wrapped that all around the bandage to hold it. "I knew June in college, same as you did. Neither of you know it, but I went to UT, too. She was in my political science class. I asked her out. We went on one date and I fell hard. But when I called to ask her out again, she said she had a boyfriend. I was shot down." He giggled nervously. "I followed her a while and found out it was you. I know the day you proposed and saw the engagement ring the next day. I called her again and protested. I tried to make up some stories about you and your newspaper articles and how her future was going to be abysmal if she stuck with you. I told her my father was a senator and I was going to be one, too. I told her I loved her ..." His voice trailed off.

Charles stood with his mouth hanging open. He hadn't even remembered this man back in college at the University of Texas. June had never mentioned she'd dated him.

"Why didn't she recognize your name?" he asked. "Even with just one date, she wouldn't forget such a distinctive name as Kaden."

The senator closed his eyes as if bone weary. "Kaden's my middle name and June never heard it. Back in school I was Marshall. She called me Marsh."

Now it all made sense, but a warped sense, the sense that crazy people made when they told stories about the reasons behind their actions.

"He's crazy as a loon," Charles said finally.

"Crazier," Barry said. "Marshall Kaden James is one obsessed man, aren't you?"

"All this over a lost love from years ago. Crazy." Charles sat down in a chair across from them. "And now you've ruined my life, Kaden. My career is over. I'll end up a man on the run. All because of you and this insane jealousy you've carried for more than twenty years."

"Dolly never loved me." Kaden lifted his chin as if his statement cleared it all up for the other two men.

"Dolly? Your wife, Margaret?" Barry asked.

91

"Yes, Margaret. I've always called her Dolly. She looks a little like June, but she really never cared for me at all. Nothing I've done in our marriage to please her ever does. She gave me two children only because I pleaded. She's a cold bitch and I'm stuck with her. I should have had ... someone better ... I wanted ..."

"We have to get the hell out of here," Charles said, standing quickly and looking around in a panic. "God, I don't know what's happened or how we're going to get out of this."

Barry ignored him. He turned on the sofa until he was facing James. "You're going to come after us, aren't you? You're going to press charges for assault with a deadly weapon, attempted murder, kidnapping, and probably a dozen other charges before you get through with us. We can run, but you're going to make sure we never come back, aren't you? You're one conniving, vengeful son of a bitch, aren't you, senator?"

"Stop calling me that!"

"Come on, Barry, we have to leave. What are we going to do about the Secret Service guys?"

Barry turned his head to look at his friend. "They're probably in bed by now. We'll go out the front. I have a car parked for us not far away under cover. Don't worry. Go on out and wait for me. I'll be right there."

Charles looked from Barry to Kaden James and back again. "You're not going to do anything ... bad ... are you?"

"Not unless I have to. Now get outside."

Once the front door had closed, James tried to pull to his feet. There was a wildness in his eyes that proved he knew how much trouble he was in. Barry pushed him in the chest, back against the sofa. "You'll hunt relentlessly until you find the three of us, won't you? You'll make it your life's goal, the way you made a way, finally, to get hold of Charles to punish him for taking your girl. You're about a buggy cart shy of a load of bricks, you know that? You certainly shouldn't be a senator. It's *you* who needs locking up."

"Fuck you, Barry. I'll do anything I have to do to make your life hell. And, yeah, I'll hound you, I'll find June and I'll ..."

"Stop right there."

"Fuck you."

"Say that again."

"Fuh ..."

The first shot took James in the center of his startled eyes. The second shot entered his right forehead, and the third went in just above his earlobe.

James slumped onto the sofa sideways. Barry checked his wrist for a pulse, found none, and sighed deeply. He hadn't really wanted to kill anyone. He had come here to force this man to release his innocent friend he had loved as a brother since childhood. He always knew it might end this way, but he hadn't really believed it. James was a coward, and it could have ended with his kneecaps had it not been for his bald confession about June. Any man who wielded the kind of power that Senator James enjoyed and who used it to imprison and torture an enemy who didn't even know he was an enemy, was a man surely out of his mind.

Barry looked down at the gun in his hands. He wore latex gloves. He'd take them off once he was outside, not that it really mattered. They knew Charles had been brought here and there was no way Charles had a gun on him. They knew from the copious notes and folders that James kept that Barry was his closest friend. One plus one, and then there were two of them. No one would probably ever know that the whole thing involved June, too.

June. She was waiting for them in the car in the woods. He hadn't told Charles that. He wanted to surprise him. In the car pocket of the rental, he had three tickets for the Bahamas. From the Bahamas he would buy three tickets for Brazil. From Brazil he would buy three more tickets for Lithuania. They needed to disappear, and take new identities. He just hated leaving his family ranch behind. It had been a nice, quiet place for an old bachelor.

Outside he found Charles shivering in the cold night air. He took him by the arm after stripping off the gloves, and bending over in the shadows, they made their way into a copse.

Twenty minutes later they came out on a lumber service road and saw the car. June opened the door and stepped out into a circle of light thrown by the car's interior lights.

Charles hurried toward her, and their embrace and June's happy cry of joy was all that Barry had to see to know what he had done was necessary.

After all, these were his friends. For his friends, he was ready to employ the Second Amendment Solution any day. He would do it again if he had to. He believed in the law and the law gave him that right. It was the one right they hadn't taken away from him yet. Too bad he was going to leave his country with only a faint hope there were no other maniacs running it like Senator James. But a faint hope was better than no hope at all.

"Get in the car, we have to boogie," he said to the couple when he neared them. "We've got some traveling to do."

A hoot owl called after the car as it left the wilderness. It was otherwise a quiet, uneventful night in New Hampshire and Thanksgiving was only a day away.

KILLER

BY KEN BRUEN

He'd written

> *Fail*
>
> *Fail better*
>
> *Fail happiest.*

So ...

So they sent him to the school's social worker.

A very earnest twenty and change young lady.

Gung ho and ready to save the world.

Especially its youth.

She had a photo of Bono on her desk.

Tells you all you need to know, really.

She felt she had buckets of empathy.

Buckets of something.

The young man standing before her was dressed in a long black coat.

She knew

"Duster"

They called them.

She'd read her Columbine stuff.

And he had the requisite scowl.

She checked all her notes.

Combat pants—yes.

Attitude—oh Lord, yes.

Anger—he exuded it.

And she just knew, intuitively she supposed, that he listened to that death metal music.

Wrong.

He loved country and western.

But what the hell, she was way ahead already, knew exactly how to handle him, said,

"John, please be seated."

See?

No chastisement. In fact, a friendly overture, and the use of his first name. She'd learned the value of that in her first year.

He sat, still scowling.

She was thrilled.

Just like her lecturers had promised.

She took a moment to read his essay, the above three lines on failure he'd submitted.

Said,

"John, I've amended your *essay*."

Paused.

Let that hover for a moment, let him know who was the boss, and then moved the paper across the desk.

Asked,

"How does it read now?"

She'd written

Feel

Feel better

Feel happiest.

She's shown it to her roommate, perhaps breaking protocol a tad, but she was so pleased with it, she had to ...

To *share.*

Loved it.

John read it slowly, and then in a very quiet voice, asked,

"May I borrow your pen?"

Took her a little off guard. But she knew, roll with the flow, feel the bonding.

She took out her prized Cross fountain pen, a graduation present from her proud dad.

Handed it over.

John looked at the pen and then he smiled.

It unnerved her a little, but she regrouped. Possibly she should have kept it less personal.

But he was writing, so all was good.

She wasn't entirely sure, her short-range vision had been giving her some trouble, but it looked like he was wearing ...

Latex gloves?

Maybe it was a new fashion trend, and she did try to keep right up there with the young uns.

He finished, pushed the paper back to her.

She thought, if he has dotted his I's with little hearts, she would just die!

She picked up the paper, read

Kill

Kill better

Kill happiest.

She looked up.

Into the barrel of a small-caliber handgun.

He said,

"You're right, I do feel better."

Shot her precisely between her two astonished eyes.

Debated on a second shot—but, no, she was done.

He thought,

"That's all she wrote."

He stood up, debated only briefly if he should return the pen, thought,

"Naw, what would they do? Bury it with her?"

He knew they'd never buy this as a suicide. But, what the hell, worth a shot.

Nearly laughed at his outrageous pun.

Took her right hand, folded the fingers around the still-smoking gun, pushed her head back, and then ruffled her hair, said,

"Good talking with yah."

Any cop worth his badge would see it as a staged scene. But, c'mon, it was Irish cops, get real.

He carefully cut the note to leave her writing, and left that on her desk.

Nice ambiguous note.

He put the remainder in his coat. He didn't need to worry about prints, the gloves took care of that.

He moved round her appointment book and there he was, scheduled to meet her at noon.

High noon for her, as it turned out. He took his razor, the old-style model, and expertly removed the whole page.

He'd been very careful not to be seen entering her office or even the school.

Now, he put on the baseball cap, the dark shades, and took a deep breath.

It was a rush all in itself.

He closed her door gently and put the

DO NOT DISTURB sign

On the glass front, which was about as deep and transparent as she thought she'd been.

She probably needed some *down* time.

He moved unhurriedly down the corridor and his timing was ace—everyone in class and not a soul around.

Out on the street, he moved briskly toward center town, maybe pick up some sounds.

He could, of course, download any shit he liked, but shoplifting was a minor riff and he liked to keep his

Skills honed.

Why pay when you could simply steal them?

Now he just needed to call his chosen partner, have her confirm, if asked, that yes, he'd, as the Americans say, *cut class.*

She'd swear through forty cows that, oh, yes, indeed, he'd been with her all the time.

Was it airtight?

But therein lay the beauty, keep the edge riff going.

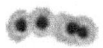

SOME ARE BORN
TO
ENDLESS NIGHT.

Ex-detective Dylan Norton summed up his life in Ds—

Depression

Debilitation

Disgust

He'd been with The Garda for twenty years.

He'd been on the fast track. Having done nigh on ten hard years as a street Guard, he'd managed to gain detective rank and, straightaway, he was assigned to two spectacular cases,

I.e., the ones the papers write about and the TV pundits bleat on.

He was way down the food chain with the hard-bitten detectives, but he solved both cases.

One was a brazen arts theft from the National Museum, and he'd followed his instinct and checked out a young girl whose father had bestowed the precious artifacts.

She confessed as soon as he went to see her.

It didn't make him many friends in the department.

And what should have been glory.

A second major case, the kidnapping of a prominent businessman's daughter, was on the TV constantly.

Paramilitaries were blamed.

Dylan felt different and, purely on a hunch, went to see the man's wife. He was left out by the other detectives as they followed down the leads on dissidents, telling him,

"Wonder boy, man the phones."

Simply put,

"Fuck off."

He'd barely introduced himself to the wife when she started crying, said,

"She's upstairs, I'm so sorry, it was all a stupid mistake."

He was in clover.

Sort of.

Twice he'd delivered, and big. The other guys, they were seriously pissed.

While the papers lauded him, his colleagues ignored him, apart from muttering,

"Bollix"

As they passed him in the corridors.

He took his pension when his twenty were done, and he was still a young forty.

He had no idea what to do next, so he set up as a Private Detective.

Sign of the new Ireland when he checked the yellow pages and saw there were nineteen other P.I.s

In business.

In Galway!

There were, of course, stories of the first P.I.

A drunk named Taylor.

Dylan discarded them as the work of fiction.

Dylan was tall, with a slender frame, and what women called sad eyes.

He called it depression.

Even had it checked out.

The doctor telling him,

"You have clinical depression."

And prescribed various medications.

None worked.

So, he figured,

"Live with the bad bastard."

He always knew when it was about to hit and ensured he'd be busy as a banshee during those episodes.

Business was brisk.

The new Ireland, now in deep recession, had multiple cases of husbands disputing divorces.

Companies going to the wall and wanting scapegoats.

Missing pets.

Mad as that sounds, it paid well and he had to hire a secretary.

A girl in her late twenties with real attitude and a mouth like a fishwife.

Named Kaitlin.

She was a looker, no doubt.

Knew it, too.

A degree in economics.

So why on God's Holy Ground would she want to be a secretary for a P.I.?

Which is what he asked.

She had long dark hair, hazel eyes, a figure she knew you'd kill for, and was dressed like she could give a toss.

In a Clash t-shirt, tight, (very) black skinny jeans, and pink Converse trainers.

She said,

"Do I look like a babe who is going to work for some bollix?"

He thought,

"Jesus wept, of all the women out there looking for work, I get the mouth."

He asked,

"How do you know I'm not ... am ... a ... one of those guys?"

She laughed out loud and, Lord, she had one of those great laughs, didn't care how she looked, just went with the merriment.

She said,

"I could get near most jobs I wanted. I'm smart, look hot ... right?"

Waited for his response.

He hadn't any, least none this side of decency, so she continued,

"I figured it would be fun to be a private dick—sorry, that's you in theory—but I'm the glamorous sidekick you fall secretly in love with but never can have."

The hell was wrong with him? He felt his heart sink when she said *never.*

There and then, he decided not to hire her. Christ, who needed this shite?

She said,

"I'll start Monday. Don't worry about references, you'd be too mortified to read how amazing I am."

She was at the door, added,

"Salary ... you'll do the right thing, you poor thing."

He'd envisaged a Mannix-type gig, where like mostly he shouted,

"Peggy, coffee."

And the poor dumb bitch in that series always brought him his coffee with worship in her eyes.

He cringed even now as he thought, did he actually mention Mannix to her?

He did.

She'd given him the blank stare.

And she'd asked,

"Who?"

Fuck, age was a bastard.

Dylan, unfashionably, didn't have a whole load of baggage or angst or whatever they were calling it.

He had his depression, and that was enough freight on its own self.

One thing he tried not to think about was the time he'd been shot.

Fifteen years in, seen his share of ugly fights, violence, the awful remains of murder victims and worse, the telling of a family about a deceased family member.

He'd never been good at that. But then, how could you?

It wasn't even the weekend, when most of the heavy stuff went down and the drunks went bananas.

It was a quiet Monday.

The call came in about a man behaving strangely in his home in Newcastle.

You had to tread careful there.

The University, the hospital, rich families, old money, and all that nonsense.

He'd gotten the call and took a raw young Ban Garda named Ridge with him.

Upper Newcastle, near where the Franciscan Priory was.

Class.

He'd said to Ridge, who was so eager it damn near broke his heart, and she kept calling him Sir.

He'd cautioned,

"I'll do the talking and just follow my lead."

Her agreement was more than he could actually face.

They knocked on the door; it was answered by a portly man, dressed in silk pajamas.

Dylan had said,

"Sorry to disturb you, sir, but we've had a report of some shouting from your house?"

The man was civility personified, said,

"Please, come in and, oh, it's Professor. I'm at the University."

At least explained the silk pajamas, if ever such could be rationalized.

OK.

They went in.

A large comfortable room lined with books, and the man asked,

"Might you be allowed some refreshments? I know you're on duty, but it's late and we all break protocol sometime, am I correct, Miss? Is that the right PC term? I don't want to break any rules here."

Dylan had nodded at Ridge and she said,

"That would be lovely."

The Professor had that acquired collegiate accent that was loosely termed *West Brit.*

Mainly it said ... you're a peasant and I'm a complete bollix.

Dylan was playing for time, see if maybe the poor bastard's wife was lying dead in the kitchen or something.

The man poured Ridge a dry sherry in a very impressive crystal glass, handed it to her, said,

"Chin chin."

Then added,

"You must excuse me, I've been teaching those morons some Evelyn Waugh, they still think Waugh was a woman."

Dylan should have been more alert, he knew that now but back then, he'd been literally listening to the sounds of the house, and what he heard, was

Nothing.

He was about to ask when the man said,

"Inspector? ... or have you even attained that rank? Did they send the dregs of the barrel to a man of my standing? I have something more belly warming than dry sherry."

And up came the shotgun, both barrels at point-blank range in Dylan's stomach.

He was reloading, muttering about the decline in The Booker Prize quality when Ridge cold-cocked the professor with the dry sherry bottle.

Twice, in fact.

They say nothing on God's Earth hurts more than a gut shot.

They're right.

They had just moved him from the IT unit. He opened his eyes, the morphine giving him a cloud of, if not unknowing, then, unfeeling. A nurse fluffed his pillows, then said,

"You have a visitor."

Ridge, he figured. But his voice wouldn't come. She moved his IV, said,

"It's your son."

Son?

WTF?

Before he could say he'd no family, she ushered in a young man, smirk in place, who greeted,

"Hi, Dad. I killed the school version of Oprah."

FOR THE LOVE OF BOYS

BY ROB M. MILLER

The neighborhood's okay, I guess, for a middle-class series of streets—brightly painted hydrants; split-level homes; the usual assortment of SUVs, soccer-mom wagons, PT Cruisers, and the lemons belonging to all the just-starting-on-the-road teens. But, when it comes to having a playground for the kids, it has one fantastic, magical place—Glendale Park. It's where I can go and do my favorite thing in the world, watch wonderful little boys.

Today was perfect for it—a gorgeous, cloudless Saturday afternoon in June, and the heat perfectly riding that fine knife-edge between just-right hot and oppressive misery. From a distance, the aroma of barbecued ribs wafts over the grass and into the play area—the tantalizing tang pushed along by a perfect breeze.

A fine, park-roaming, boy-watching day.

"Mommy, that scary man's looking at me."

The lad, quite beautiful, sat on a swing, no longer moving, but mother-caught and at a halt.

"It's okay, hon." The smart, protective mommy ruffled her boy's blond curls, and then lifted him off the swing. "Beat mommy over to the teeter-totters."

Mr. Cute-Stuff, perhaps six years old, hurried to the totters, probably having already forgotten about me.

Too bad the mother hasn't.

She walked toward me, a mass of conflicting issues. Her telltale body lingo no mystery, but clear and painful: huffy, nervous, scared, all that. Yet her demeanor's layered with the confidence and haughtiness reserved for those who find safety in daylight, in numbers, and in looking good.

For us monsters, it's different.

"Who in the hell do you think you are?"

The woman stood just a few feet in front of where I sat atop a wooden picnic table layered with graffiti. Pretty brave, considering.

"I'm thorry. Just watchin' your boy. Very handthome." Talking to strangers could be such a pain.

"Stay *away* from my son."

She walked off a bit less haughty, and perhaps a little more fearful, picked up Mr. Cute-Stuff from the teeter-totter, and carried him away. Pretty sad. I could tell the boy was disappointed. He probably blamed me. I was frustrated, too. I wanted to watch him play.

I couldn't blame the woman. How could I? She had no way of knowing I'd never hurt her boy, or any child. She was just a mom who'd probably just moved in. I didn't know her. She didn't know me, hadn't *heard* of me yet—the Mr. Wheat, the face- and body-scarred Quasimodo of Clarksgrove Housing Community. But I knew her son. Reaching into my pocket, I pull out my six-inch clip-it, and with its serrated edge, start carving into the top of the picnic table: *I love you, Elijah.*

A prophet's name. Shame, though, that the woman only seemed to call him that when she wanted his attention; otherwise it was a host of pet endearments. Elijah—not a bad name, at all. Just hope the lad doesn't learn to associate such a grand identifier with being in trouble.

I'm sure the lady will ask around about me, and that's all right. I'm a stellar citizen of our little community.

Strangers never know how to take my appearance, and of a truth, neither do many who know me. But I can't complain. I get along all right. Most of the folks in the community know me, treat me well, and don't even mind me keeping an eye on their kids. At least not when there's plenty of adults around.

It's what monsters like me have to deal with.

I know.

"Mrs. Wheat, I'm sorry." The doctor looked sincere enough, but he talked to mom like I wasn't there.

"Sorry? You say you're sorry?" Mom's eyes flooded with tears. "Look at my son!"

"There are bright sides."

"Bright sides?"

"The reconstruction of his face and jaw are going well. By next year his lips will be functional. And he'll be walking. We're very happy with the spinal surgery. With some speech therapy—"

"Very happy? Look at my boy. MY BOY. How's he ever going to get married, be normal? Have a life?"

"He will have a life, Mrs. Wheat. He will. In the future, with some plastic surgery—"

"My son looks like a monster!"

That's when I knew. I had become a monster. My mommy's little monster. Her little boy no more, little boy long gone.

Mom had been poor, never had a hubby around, and no money ever showed up to fix my pretty face. And there wasn't anything that could ever fix my crooked, ugly, broken back.

What I got, I got for life. But the man that had used me, tortured me? He got twelve years before buying the farm from a shiv in the shower. Far too merciful.

It was okay. Mom had only been partly right. No, there'd never been a marriage, and never would be. No woman wanted a man with only tufts of hair growing out of a burn-scarred scalp, a face that sagged down one side from a shattered cheek-plate, and lips like a fish. But still, I'd managed a life.

Even monsters need a mission.

Even monsters need love. Need *to* love.

And I have that. I have boys. All boys. I love them.

The picnic table was probably a mistake. But I couldn't help it. The table, along with others of its kind across the park, as well as some

109

trees, bear my marks: *I love you, Bobby ... I love you, Anthony ... Tim, Will, Peter, Jamal.* There were perhaps a hundred and fifty such names carved around Glendale Park. There were girl names, too. I saved writing them for days such as this, days when I was going to make a disposal. The writing commemorated such times, acted as an endorsement—a witness.

Thank goodness the day was still young. It was a shame that Elijah was gone, but there were others out and about, playing on the monkey bars, the merry-go-round, out playing tag with their sisters, playing Frisbee.

A great day.

But I was bored sitting on the table with nobody close. For some reason, no one seemed interested in the swings.

Too bad.

I understand, though. I remember. I loved it all, being a boy: playing with my construction set, my Hot Wheels, playing in the park, eating ice cream with the moms—always out of one of those sugar cones, with a mini-marshmallow in the bottom to keep it from leaking—as we'd head toward Frog's Pond to throw slices of bread torn apart to the ducks, my friends (even the girls), adventures, dreams. Oh, *God,* how I loved it.

All of it.

Poor Elijah. Doubt, playing at a park, that I would've wanted a monster looking at me. I *know* I wouldn't have.

I should know better.

Why does a person buy a book, or pass it up to go to a more appealing aisle? The cover. It's *always* about the cover. A nice cover's no guarantee of quality, but it sure as spit gets your foot in the door.

Fortunate for me, familiarity goes a long way in compensating for such an ugly cover.

"'Ey, Donnie!" The boy doesn't notice me. He's way too focused on his deep-sea Captain Nemo escapades, Aquaman fantasies, or his journeys with the *Man from Atlantis.*

Well, maybe not. Those were my fun times, back in my before. Still, the kid was having a blast, far greater than the pool deserved, his imagination surely pushing all his fun-buttons. It was great.

Donnie's mom, Mrs. Spadethrift—a Kathy, if I'm remembering right—maybe it's Kathleen—watched on, face glowing, with a half-eaten Susie-Q cupcake in her hand, as her Donnie-boy played in the pool with his friends: Carlson, age seven; Marcus, six; Mary Beth, an eye-twinkling five-and-a-half; along with who knows how many others in his imagination.

The small pool was designed for young ones, a wading pool, perhaps a quarter-inch in depth along the outer rim of its 25-foot diameter, with the water increasing to maybe two-feet or so, dead-center.

I have to get a closer look, the short walk from my picnic table perch to the pool hardly worth being called a stroll.

I love it, watching Marcus splash, little Ms. MB-Pretty and Carlson, playing their own coded game of water-ball, splash-tag-catch, and Donnie, trying to stay out of the way, in the center of the pool, with as much of his body underwater as possible. That's key when playing in the water by yourself: Getting your whole body underwater. Then you could be anywhere, not just inches under the surface, but anywhere—on a submarine, hard ocean-diving, fighting some monster-shark—and doing anything, from grand escapes of facing and defeating slobbering pools of piranha, too awesomely fun but simple how-long-can-I-hold-my-breath games.

Mary Beth's mom, Sheila, dressed in a casual one-piece summer dress, was there, on the other side of the pool from where I was coming from, talking banalities—like the weather and stuff—with Marcus's dad, Jim. The woman's outfit wasn't too sexy, but did show just enough leg to show she'd been putting extra pressure on herself in some vanity aerobics class. Tramp has been having an affair with Jim for three months now. Her dealings had nothing to do with my first love, or even my second, but cheating on her husband made me despise her. Bill was a good dad. Maybe he'd just have to get an anonymous tip about Sheila's Wednesday one-o'clocks.

Jim was a single parent, which was too bad. Maybe he'd have to settle for some punctured tires or something.

It's a thought.

I won't actually do anything, of course. Not my place.

Not my mission.

I pay attention to what happens in my neighborhood. Nothing's going to surprise me on my watch. I also have an imagination and a right to my own opinions and fantasies. Jim and Tramp could romp all they wanted, but it would be hellfire on my soul before I'd sign off on it.

"What's happening, Mr. Wheat? Enjoying some sun?"

"You kin call me Tim, Mithis Spadethwith. You know that." I liked her. She didn't care about the bad monster cover. And if she did, she *still* didn't. Most in the neighborhood were pretty nice to me. Those that weren't new, but uncomfortable with my looks, they still tended to keep some distance. That was fine. I kept mine, as well. With my second greatest love, it was better that way.

"And deny a gentleman his due title of respect? Never."

"Your boyth having too much fun. Heeth gonna sleep like a bwick t'night."

"Yeah, he probably will."

"Mommy, Mommy, you gotta watch." Donnie stood in the middle of the pool, black hair slicked wet against his head. "Time me!"

"'Ey, DONNIE." I didn't have to yell, but it just came out. Couldn't help it. Seeing young Master Donnie, just standing there, just brought me back to the happy times.

"Hey, Mr. Wheat." Donnie shot his eyes back to his dear mother. "Time me, Mom."

"I will, baby. Do your thing."

"Watch me, Mr. Wheat."

I smiled that I would, knowing he was going to kill it. Boys saved asking their mothers to time them until they were well-practiced and ready to give a star performance, having already timed themselves over and over, readying their lungs for the big parent-brag.

And I was right.

Donnie had done pretty good for a boy his age. Held his own for a bit over a minute before coming up with a victory grin. Not like Frank had back at my house, after I'd poured the bottle of Drano down his throat.

A man's home should be his castle, or so the line goes. I believe it. I've got mine and I'm thankful. It's where I'm most free, maybe not my happiest—there's the park and other places for that—but free. I can sing, not care about my cover, just be myself. Whatever. Plus, there's my second love, and a man's got to have a place to work for that.

My castle's a four-bedroom split-story with a connected two-car garage (though I only own one modest Ford Taurus) and an enormous basement. Front yard isn't much, kind of small, lots of gravel, shrubs and flowers, and a sculpted hedge that doubles as a fence, but a large-walled backyard: patio furniture, a fountain (the kind that has that grinning angel-kid pissing away, not the most flattering representation of childhood), well-maintained grass that costs a bit, marble birdbath, and five or six lawn darts that I just like to toss around in a kind of solo mumbly-peg sort of way.

All mine. Yes, it's plenty of space for one guy, but I need it—a room to sleep, one for guests, an office, a room for trophies, basement to work. What more could one ask?

The bimonthly checks are nice, allowing me to engage in my second love without having to do something as cumbersome as working outside the home. Plus, they allow me to order out so I don't have to do more than minimal cooking.

I hate cooking.

Sitting in my living room, I hit the couch with enthusiasm. It's been a good day—fun at the park, and now back home, with nothing but more fun to come. I got the TV on, watching a recording of one of my favorite *Millennium* episodes, "Somehow, Satan Got Behind Me." Then, I've got my bag of fried chicken, rolls, and beans from MY BROTHER'S BEST, a fast-food place run by some brothers, I guess.

Somehow, Satan Got Behind Me. What an episode. Lance Henriksen is one of my favorite actors, and I love the show. *Loved* it, anyway, seeing as how those bastards took it off the air. But though Lance has such little screen time, this particular show, watching those four bickering demons argue and brag about their techniques for soul-damning, is more than worth it. A real kick in the pants. The demons are funny, informative, and all too evil, and even though the show's fiction, probably all *too* real.

I think so.

I know a bit or two about demons.

Chicken and grub gone, and demon palaver over—time to get to work.

I got up from my seat, cleaned my mess, turned off the tube, and disposed of the trash. It was time to get rid of a few other things, too: Michael's clothes, shoes, and the rest of his shit.

Michael was in my workroom.

I headed downstairs, from my kitchen to the garage, and down, down, and down. The stairs are precisely forty-five steps; I know, because I count them every time I go down. The descent always hurts, and the counting takes my mind off the pain in my back. Sometimes there's just a price to pay for doing what one's been called to do.

Hitting the base of the stairs, I opened the door to the dungeon. I love it down there, can do whatever I need to, and do it without any fear of unwanted interruption, any fear of disturbing the neighbors (sure wouldn't want that), any fear whatsoever. The reinforced and insulated walls and doors make sure of that. Here, I'm in charge, and monster or no, everything goes my way.

I looked at Michael, sitting in the hot seat, butt-naked and scared as hell. Good. I like 'em scared.

The seat rotated and could be locked into any number of positions. I'd set Michael to face the mirrored wall. All the better to have a grand view of what I'd done, of how when he'd fallen unconscious from his fourth beating with rods, I'd taken a Sharpie and drawn a jigsaw pattern all over his face, torso, arms and legs. I wanted him to be able to see my tools, too—the two trays, one with the acetylene torch, the other with the dental picks and probes, the scalpels, scissors, the spreaders.

Was why I'd left Michael an eye.

Before leaving in the morning to go to the park, I told Michael the lines drawn on his body represented the cuts he was going to be butchered into. He hadn't liked that at all. In fact, Michael had looked pretty damned terrified.

The only problem with the chamber was the smell, that filthy aroma of shit-fear-piss-sweat. It all just mixed and coalesced and hovered, like a big nasty air-biscuit, waiting to be gobbled up—again and again and again. It was always present, even after a disposal and a healthy cleaning—though it would be toned down a tad.

On the other hand, the smell helped the torture. That was important.

"Hi, Michael! Are we ready to thtart?" I smiled. He stared back with his one eye, the other now only a leaking, ragged hole. He whimpered under his gag. I admired the hole. It was good work. Had used my special spoon for that one.

Mutilation's a tricky thing. You don't want to do too much. It dispirits the subjects. Makes them want to die. Gets them resigned to it, which isn't good. Even with the rods, I'd been careful to not break any major bones, just a toe or two—maybe a finger. Mostly, I just attacked his muscle groups, turning his meaty portions into purple, swollen masses. And yes, I did do the eye. But that was it—no more. The subject has to be able to exercise his imagination. He has to be able to hope, even as he's overcome with fear. He has to picture himself somehow getting rescued. It's when the subject has hope to cling to— then you've got something to work with.

You also have to freak them out. That's why I always make sure my subjects can see the IV bags hanging on their stands—even though they're outdated and unusable. They don't know that—and, of course, the tools, which are hardly ever used. I've also had great effect with my last fourteen with the marking-pen thing.

That *always* gets the imagination going.

"Leth thtart with dith one." I held up a glistening scalpel, delicately, as if it were made of glass.

Michael stared, eye wide, sweat bathing his head and washing down his front, further streaking the ink on his skin.

RRRRRRiiiiiiinnnnnggggggg

Ah, the buzzer. I'd timed this well.

"Thorry. Be right back." Laying the scalpel on the tray, I picked up a black hood and placed it over Michael's head before leaving to answer the door. Putting the subject in the dark, after leaving him for hours to stare at the tools, is also very effective.

My chamber, the dungeon, is fairly large, encompassing more than forty square feet of prime-time fun space. One door—soundproof, naturally—separates it from the rest of the basement: the laundry area, storage nook, a bathroom, and finally, the door leading upward, approximately forty-five steps. I'd designed the house, but I can't remember why I'd wanted a basement so deep. No matter, everything had worked out fine.

Leaving Michael, I closed the door. He wasn't going anywhere. It was only a short shuffle to the door to the stairs. That door was locked, of course, but only out of habit. A while back, I thought of putting in a peep-hole, but quickly changed my mind—it would've looked weird. Besides, I knew who was calling.

I opened the door. "'Right on time, ath uthual."

"Good to see you, Tim."

Greg looked good—athletic body, chiseled jaw, laugh lines in all the right places, and just enough wrinkles to show he'd grown into the kind of adult that, despite a bit of worn tread, still cared. A touch of late-night peach fuzz had started to grow on him.

"Is he ready to go?"

"Uh-uh. Be juth a minute."

Greg nodded.

Not wanting to see the business at hand, he'd wait here. Greg had always been the sensitive type. That was okay with me. In fact, I thought it wonderful, a trait he'd kept since his boyhood—one, thank God, he'd never lost.

That was the thing that had worried me. I'd saved Greg from the worst of it, ended his victimization with one sure stroke of my blade. But he'd still suffered, poor boy. Thank God his injuries, bad as they were, hadn't ruined his cover.

Greg had also been the first.

I gave my grown boy a friendly pat on the shoulder and went back into the dungeon; the door closed behind me.

Michael had been through the treatment long enough. He'd paid, not enough, I know. For his buggering crimes there could never be enough, not in this life.

The slip noose went around his neck fast. I cinched it tight, tighter—then a bit more.

The man jerked a bit, then stopped. I grabbed my camera.

Greg had been the first, but not the last, thank the Lord.

With him it had been so weird. I was walking down the street, and despite everything, had been enjoying the day. Even with the dark clouds jockeying for best drenching position, the cool wind cutting me

116

with its bite, and my stomach grumbling from being ignored ... none of it, not a bit, had bothered me.

I had felt alive. My nerves on fire, like they'd been touched to some supercharged battery, but with no pain.

And I knew.

Knew.

Walking down that street, and all of a sudden—HIT. My nerves ablaze, and then a glance to my right. An average home: white, large porch, electrician's van in the driveway.

And I knew.

The door was unlocked. I went in. As if by guided by a divine hand, I went upstairs—quiet as a shade ... hit the top of the stairs, then heard a man's demanding voice ... moved closer, and then another demand ... for someone to do it—*to do it*—to kneel down and—

—DO IT.

Though I've no regrets, there are still the nightmares.

I never knew how much Greg might've endured, though it couldn't have been much. In my heart, I'd like to believe not a bit, but I never tried finding out. Instead, what I remember is my body moving on its own, coming behind the man, arm out, then—knife in-hand—swinging in a hook, and unzipping the man's soul, carotid to carotid.

A boy saved. At least most of him.

Michael sat still in the chair, the down payment on his debt paid, the rest, most assuredly, payable in Hell.

I walked back to Greg. "He'th ready."

Greg smiled, a kind of forced affair. He liked these moments, when another piece of trash had paid and stopped breathing under the sun, yet I think every drop-off and pick-up takes him back to the time he'd lost his boyhood.

"I've got a favor to ask, Tim." Greg looked a bit nervous and that surprised me. He could always ask me anything. "It's a little out of your normal line, but I think it's important."

I beckoned him to spill it.

"There's this kid goes to my son's school. Sebastian's his name. Anyway, this kid's apparently hella-clumsy. Lots of absenteeism, black-eyes from doorknobs, that sort of thing—but not quite enough to do anything, officially." Greg paused and looked down, his face barely

117

hiding his shame. "My son's asked me to do something. I've had to tell him I can't."

"Thatth bad, but I not—"

"I'm not saying the dad's gotta be done. But maybe—"

"I underthtand. He'll never hit the boy again."

"Thanks, Tim. You're special—you know that?"

"You're thpethal, Greg. You've alwath been thpethal." Greg gave me a hug, the kind of squeeze that warms the soul. His love for kids—for the boys *and* the girls—was as strong as mine.

Greg broke the embrace. "I'll take care of Michael. Glad the bastard's gone. He'd done four children, all under twelve. Killed one of them." A tear escaped from Greg's left eye. He quickly wiped it away. "Anyway, he's done. And I appreciate it. Hell, we all do. By the way, the mayor wants to know how you like the fountain."

"Tell him ith fine." I didn't really care for it, but it wouldn't have been good form to show ingratitude.

"Good. I will. Also, the statistics are at an all-time low. Right now our county has the lowest case-count of child-related molestation anywhere. You've really cleaned the area up. The guys're saying you'll either have to cast a wider net, or we're gonna have to start shippin' them in."

"Thath OK. I do what I can."

Greg smiled.

I stepped around him, my picture in my hand, soon to join the other hundred-fifty or so in the trophy room. Greg would take the body and put it in his trunk. Then he'd join me for a few hours. We'd make some milk shakes, play some video games, maybe some rounds of I Spy or Twenty Questions. He was my friend, knew the games I liked. I love him.

Greg had been a good boy and had grown into a good man. Now he was a star detective. A man to be proud of. Greg, the other cops, the mayor, and others didn't necessarily like this work, but somebody had to do it, put a stop to the terror. Somebody had to watch out for the children, had to love them.

And that was my mission, my mandate. I don't claim to understand it, or to know whether it's God or fate, or a genetic quirk, but I *have* a gift. I'm that crazy good. The police know it, I know it, and those I catch know it. I'm never wrong. I've directed law enforcement before, told them to check such and such, to search a house, a dump site, and I'm always right. They find the bad trophies, the diaries, the pictures—sometimes bodies. Those I don't catch, the police do, and then they bring them to me. Sometimes the bad guys get processed through the flawed correctional system and end up getting early release, or end up making an easy escape—all so they can be brought to me.

They plead, beg, deny, whine, rage, and cry—but I don't care. I know what happened to me, what turned me into a monster, and I can't be duped. I don't judge a book by its cover. I've been gifted to look much deeper than that.

I see the black and I put it down.

BLOODSHED FRED

BY MONICA J. O'ROURKE

In the envelope his client had forwarded to him, along with his usual 20K fee, was an address followed by a single line of instruction:

150 Beach Road

THURSDAY, 9:00 p.m.

No further instructions, which Fred knew meant a single target. Easy job, ordinarily. Except ...

Fred knew that address all too well. He'd grown up in that house.

Was this some kind of joke?

He needed to know who'd ordered the hit, who the target was.

I'm walking into a trap, he thought as he fixed a cup of instant the following morning. He'd pick up a better cup at Starbucks on his way out of town. For now, taste didn't matter, just caffeine.

But he didn't really believe it was a trap. Besides, who would have set it? His parents? He hadn't seen them in years and couldn't imagine they'd have any reason to betray him—no matter how they might feel about him. He smirked when he thought about his overly indulgent mother and self-righteous prig of a father. Them? Set him up? He imagined the world's most dysfunctional intervention.

He actually hoped his father did have something to do with this. Fred loved the thought of seeing the old man one last time because he imagined his fingers around the old asshole's windpipe. Actually, high-tension wire was much more effective and pretty much untraceable, unlike the telltale signs of prints on someone's crushed neck. Not that it mattered, since the Feds had no clue who Fred was and even less of an idea how to find him.

The rental car, an unassuming Ford something-or-other, rented using fake ID and a fake credit card, brought him "home" in a matter of hours. Once there he drove slowly up and down Beach Road, looking for ... what? Signs of trouble?

Signs of anything, really.

He was surprised the house looked as good as it did. It had been a mess when he was a kid, and his folks had never had the money to fix it. But now, more than twenty years since he'd last set foot in this tiny excuse of a home, they'd clearly made use of their money. Of course, his mother was a Norman Rockwell/Thomas Kinkade fanatic, and it showed. The white picket fence, surrounding a bucolic strip of grass, needed a paint job. They had erected their American Dream, the perfect suburban pukey dream home.

He glanced at the note. Today was Thursday. It was almost nine. He'd run out of reasons to procrastinate. He had an obligation and needed to keep to the timeframe.

He grabbed the bag containing his small arsenal and headed for his car. He wondered again if he was stepping into a trap, but decided he had to take the risk. His parents were assholes, but they weren't more clever than he. He could handle this.

Gun drawn—Glock 19, fitted with the silencer he'd made using a Pepsi can, flex coupling, PVC bushing, and a couple of band clamps—he approached the house from the front, entering through the front gate. There was no need to sneak around the side; no one was on the street, and the closest neighbor lived too far to see the front of the house.

He was about to pass the mailbox when he noticed an oversized red envelope sticking out, the name FRED clearly written across the front. He snatched the envelope and tore it open.

It contained further handwritten instructions:

DOOR'S UNLOCKED.
TARGET IN LIVING ROOM.

WELCOME HOME.

He could still recognize his father's pathetic scribble.

Something Fred had never experienced crept into his stomach: dread. But he couldn't leave now. He'd never failed to complete a hit, and he had a reputation to uphold.

At this point, his approach to the house wasn't even close to stealthy. He sauntered up the path as if he'd just returned home from a date. Not that he'd had many dates. Girls thought he was rather strange and, as one called him, icky.

The front door was unlocked, as the note had said it would be. He stepped inside the foyer and the door snicked shut. By now he was past pretenses or real concern; this had become too bizarre and he wanted answers.

"Welcome home, son," his father called from the living room.

Fred smirked and shook his head, amazed at the casualness of this situation. He stepped into the living room, the gun hanging at his side. He expected to see the old man brandishing a shotgun or rifle. Instead, his father sat empty-handed on the sofa.

"How good to see you," the old man said. Fred immediately recognized where he'd learned his own particular smirk. He'd forgotten how much he emulated his father. And how alike they looked, though he'd imagined that after twenty years things would somehow be different. Not only were their mannerisms similar, so was their receding hairline. Their bodies shared the same lanky lines, same stooped posture. Fred wondered if his father had grown a backbone somewhere along the way but highly doubted it. His passive—and pacifist—father had always disappointed him.

Fred asked, "Care to tell me what the hell's going on?"

"Not much. Same old, same old."

"Answer my fucking question!" He raised the gun and aimed it at his father. "Or I swear to God I'll blow your fucking head off." Then he regretted his impatience. This could be a setup, and he'd just threatened the old man's life.

He waited a few seconds, expecting to see cops explode from their hiding places to arrest him.

No exploding cops.

"So, it's true. You've come to kill me."

Fred lowered the gun. "So it seems. Those are my instructions. But why you? Why did *you* hire me?"

His father sat forward on the edge of the sofa. "Been a long time, Freddie. Miss me?"

Fred smirked. "I never miss."

His father licked his lips and sighed. He held out his hand, as if hoping his son would take it, but quickly lowered it again to his lap. "It's been so long. I've missed you so much. Please, have a seat."

Fred grinned despite the rodent gnawing on his intestines. "A seat. Well sure, what the heck, why don't I have a seat? And maybe you could get me a beer. And hey, while you're at it, maybe you can tell me why I've been brought here to kill you." He sat on the chair near the door.

"You never were patient. Want coffee or something?"

The gun resting against Fred's knee brought him little comfort. "Are you planning to keep making small talk? Or maybe you can give me some answers."

"Is that a no?"

"Well," Fred said, standing. He sniffed once and wiped his palm on his pants. "Anyway, this has been ... surreal. But I have a job to do. You understand."

His father bowed his head. "So it's true."

"What's true? That I'm here to kill you? You hired me, remember?"

His father ignored the question. "I was hoping somehow I'd been wrong. And it took years. You know?"

"No, I don't know. What the hell are you talking about?"

"I hired a private detective to find you. Your mother and I were worried sick and wanted to find out what had happened to you. And finally ... we learned."

"Good for you."

"I learned what you do for a"—he cleared his throat—"living. Your mother died of a heart attack when she found out. So you pretty much killed her, too."

"So that's what this is about?" Fred shook his head and snorted. "Do you understand your stupidity? You *hired* me to kill you. That's one fucked up way to get answers."

"I know," the old man whispered. "And I'm sorry. Somehow I failed you. Somewhere along the way something went bad. But I had to know."

"Yeah, well now you know. And you must know I have to kill you."

"I beg you not to. Not for me, but for yourself. Don't do this, Fred. You still have a chance—"

"Shut up!" He raised the gun and aimed it between his father's eyes. "Don't beg for your life, old man. It won't work."

"I'm not begging for my life. I'm begging for yours. There's still a chance for you. You can change things! Please, Fred, listen to m—"

Fred shoved the gun against his father's temple and shot him in the head. The old man flew back and hit the sofa, the shocked expression on his face now nothing more than a rictus of cracked bone and shattered dentures.

Blood splattered Fred's face and clothing—the reason he rarely fired at such close range. But he wasn't concerned with appearances, and the silencer—though mostly a misnomer—was still quiet enough not to alert the neighbors. Hopefully. But he was prepared for such an event, should someone come along to investigate. The duffel bag he brought and dropped near the front door was his own Magic Bag of Tricks.

"Jesus Christ," he muttered, wiping bits of brain matter off his cheek. "You stupid old fuck." He spat on the corpse. "This was too good for you."

He turned to leave but then stopped. There were still too many unanswered questions. If only he could control his impetuous nature, he thought. That way he could have tortured his father into giving him answers. Fred would have enjoyed that.

A search of the house might reveal something.

He started in the parlor. Searched drawers and shelves, knocking knickknacks and useless framed memories off the bookcase, overturning chairs and cushions. Nothing but dust behind the TV or under the stereo, nothing inside the fake Ming vases his mother had collected.

He glanced at his father's corpse, reluctant to go near it, never mind touch it. Not that Fred was squeamish; he just hated the thought of touching him.

His father was in an almost upright position, and Fred reached inside his robe, separated the lapels. Nothing. He checked the pajamas—also nothing. The body tipped on its side and slumped over, almost falling to the floor.

Taped to his back was a large manila envelope.

On the outside was written, simply, FRED.

He snatched it from his dead father's body.

The unsealed envelope bulged with papers. Fred separated the seams and looked inside. The first set were medical reports indicating his father was terminal, had been given six months to live before the cancer would claim his life. The tests were dated three months ago.

Fred shook his head. Dying?

The next set of papers was his father's will. A quick skim showed the beneficiary was the hospital where his father had been receiving his cancer treatments. They would get the house, the car, any money his father had in savings. Nothing for Fred. He rolled his eyes. How fucking typical.

And the next page showed a nice retirement fund, though it also showed a sizeable amount had been withdrawn just a few weeks ago. The $20,000 he had paid to hire Fred for the hit.

This kept getting better.

But what was Fred's part in this? His father could have swallowed a bottle of pills or stuffed up the car exhaust pipe in the garage. Why involve Fred?

At the bottom of the stack of papers were two envelopes. On one was written OPEN FIRST. He read it.

Dear Fred,

I'm sorry I failed you. Your mother and I were blessed to have a son, and we raised you as best as we could. I guess sometimes that doesn't matter. Sometimes the wiring just gets messed up. We blamed ourselves through the years and wondered what we could have done different.

And then a year ago I found out what you do. How you kill innocent men, women, and kids. Kill them for money. And my whole world ended.

But son, everything you do has a price.

I brought you home because I wanted to save you. But since you're reading this, then that means I'm dead, and I failed you again. I'm sorry. I tried. I wanted to save you. And we could have saved you. We had money. We could have gotten you away in time, gotten you some help, if only we had known. Your mother and I loved you very much and would have helped you. That's what this meeting was about, son—helping you. Saving you.

That was it. Nothing else. Fred read the letter several times, looking for clues, looking for anything to explain why his father had done all of this. If he was trying to save Fred, why would he hire him for the hit? It didn't make sense.

The second envelope had nothing written on it. Fred tore it open.

Dear Special Agent Hobbes,

As we discussed on the phone earlier this week, I believe my son is the killer known as

127

Bloodshed Fred. If I'm right, then I am now dead, because I hired him to kill me.

It breaks my heart to do this, but I can't allow him to kill any more innocent people. If you arrive at my house on Thursday, September 3, at 9:00 p.m., you'll know whether or not I was right. I know you thought I was mistaken, but in my home you'll find the proof you'll need.

And a handwritten note at the bottom:

This letter was sent three days ago, Fred. He got it all by now, including your bank account information. There's nowhere to go now. It's over. Please make peace with that.

Through the thick silence Fred heard his own heartbeat pounding in his ears. But he was still safe, wasn't he? The letter was sent three days ago, so unless his father called the Feds earlier, they still wouldn't know when—

And then he heard the squeal of brakes outside, the slam of car doors, and the heavy and persistent footfalls on the driveway and through the thick weeds and bushes surrounding the house.

His bag of weapons was near the front door where he'd dropped it. Fred grabbed it and bolted up the stairs two and three at a time and reached the top landing.

Eyes wild, Fred ran down the hallway, tripping over the scatter rug, catching himself against the windowsill. He glanced down at the dozens of agents swarming the house.

As the front door burst open and the shouting began, Fred hoped he had enough bullets.

SLASHER

BY F. PAUL WILSON

I saved the rage.

I let them bury my grief with Jessica. It cocooned her in her coffin, cushioned her, pillowed her head. There it would stay, doing what little it could to protect her from the cold, the damp, the conqueror worm.

But I saved the rage. I nurtured it. I honed it until its edge was fine and tough and sharp. Sharp enough to one day cut through the darkness encrusting my soul.

Martha was on the far side of the grave, supported by her mother and father and two brothers—Jessie's grandparents and uncles. I stood alone on my side. A few friends from the office were there, standing behind me, but they weren't really with me. I was alone, in every sense of the word.

I stared at the top of the tiny coffin that had remained closed during the wake and the funeral mass because of the mutilated state of the little body within. I watched it disappear by tiny increments beneath a growing tangle of color as sobbing mourners each took a turn at tossing a flower on it. Jessica, my Jessica. Only five years old, cut to ribbons by some filthy rotten stinking lousy—

"Bastard!"

The grating voice wrenched my gaze from the coffin. I knew that voice. Oh, how I knew that voice. I looked up and met Martha's hate-filled eyes. Her face was pale and drawn, her cheeks were black with eyeliner that had flowed with her tears. A black hat and veil masked her blonde hair.

"It's your fault! She's dead because of you! You had her only every other weekend and you couldn't even pay attention to her! It should be *you* in there!"

"Easy, Martha," one of her brothers told her in a low voice. "You'll only upset yourself more."

But I could see it in his eyes, too—in everybody's eyes. They all agreed with her. Even I agreed with her.

"No!" she screamed, shaking off her brother's hand and pointing at me. "You were a lousy husband and a lousier father. And now Jessie's dead because of you! *You!"*

Then she broke down into uncontrollable sobbing and was led off by her parents and brothers. Embarrassed, the rest of the mourners began to drift away, leaving me alone with my dead Jessie. Alone with my rage. Alone with my guilt.

I hadn't been the best father in the world. But who could be? Either you don't give them enough love or you overindulge them. You can't seem to win. But I do admit there were too many times when something else seemed more important than being with Jessie, some deal, some account that needed attention right away, so Jessie could wait. I'd make it up to her later—that was the promise. I'd play catch-up next week. But there wouldn't be any later. No more next weeks for Jessica Santos. No catching up on the hugs and the playing and the I-love-yous.

If only ...

If only I hadn't left her on the curb to go get her that goddamn ice cream cone.

We'd been watching the Fourth of July fireworks down at the harbor front. Jessie was thrilled and fascinated by the bright flashes blooming and booming in the sky. She'd wanted an ice cream and, being a divorced daddy who didn't get to see her very often, I couldn't say no. So I carried her back to the push cart vendor near the entrance to Crosby's Marina. She couldn't see the fireworks from the end of the line, so I let her stand back by the curb to watch while I queued up. While she kept her eyes on the sky, I kept an eye on her all the time I was on line. I wasn't worried about someone grabbing her—the thought never entered my mind. I just didn't want her wandering into the street for an even better view. The only time I looked away was when I placed the order and paid the guy.

When I turned around, a cone in each hand, Jessie was gone.

No one had seen anything. For two days the police and a horde of volunteers combed all of Monroe and most of northern Nassau County. They found her—what was left of her—on the edge of old man Haskins's marshes.

A manhunt was still on for the killer, but with each passing day, the trail got colder.

So now I stood by my Jessica's grave under the obscenely bright sun, sweating in my dark suit as I fought my guilt and nurtured my hate, praying for the day they caught the scum who had slashed my Jessica to ribbons. I renewed the vow I had made before—the guy was never going to get to trial. I would find a way to get to him while he was out on bail, or even in jail, if it came to that, and I would do to him what he'd done to my Jessica. And then I would dare the courts to find a jury that would convict me.

When everyone was gone, I said my final goodbye to Jessie. I'd wanted to erect a huge angelic monument to her, but Tall Oaks didn't allow that sort of thing. A little plaque would have to suffice. It didn't seem right.

As I turned to go, I noticed a man leaning against a tree a hundred feet or so away. He was watching me. As I started down the grassy slope, he began walking, too. Our paths intersected at my car.

"Mr. Santos?" he said.

I turned. He was a big man, six-two at least, mid-forties, maybe two-fifty, with most of it settled around his gut. He wore a white shirt under a rumpled gray suit. His thinning brown hair was slick with sweat. I looked at him but said nothing. If he was another reporter—

"I'm Gerald Caskie, FBI. Can we talk a minute?"

"You found him?" I said, my spirits readying for a leap. I stepped closer and grabbed two fistfuls of his suit jacket. "You've got him?"

He pulled his jacket free of my grasp.

"We can talk in my car. It's cooler."

I followed about fifty yards along the curving asphalt path to where a monotone Ford two-door sedan waited in the shade of one of the cemetery's eponymous trees. The motor was running. He indicated the passenger side. I joined him in the front seat. The air conditioner was blasting. Damn near freezing inside.

"That's better," he said, adjusting one of the vents to blow directly on his face.

"All right," I said, unable to contain my impatience any longer. "We're here. Tell me: Do you have him?"

He looked at me with basset hound brown eyes.

"What I'm about to tell you is off the record, agreed?"

"What are you—?"

"Agreed? You must never reveal what I'm about to tell you. Do I have your word as a man that what I tell you will never go beyond this car?"

"No. I have to know what it's about, first."

He shifted in his seat and put the Ford in gear.

"Forget it. I'll drive you back to your car."

"No. Wait. All right. I promise. But enough with the games, already."

He threw the gearshift back into Park.

"This isn't a game, Mr. Santos. I could lose my job, even be brought up on criminal charges for what I'm going to tell you. And if you do try to spill it, I'll deny we've ever met."

"What is it, goddamn it?"

"We know who killed your daughter."

The words hit me like a sledge to the gut. I felt almost sick with relief.

"Have you got him? Have you arrested him?"

"No. And we won't be. Not for some time to come."

It took a while for the words to sink in, probably because my mind didn't want to accept them. But when it did, I was ready to go for his throat. I reined in my fury, however. I didn't want to get hit with assault and battery on a federal officer. At least not yet.

"You'd better explain that," I said in a voice that was barely above a whisper.

"The killer is presently a protected witness in an immensely important federal trial. Can't be touched until all the testimony is in and we get our conviction."

"Why the hell not? My daughter's death has nothing to do with your trial."

"The killer's a psycho—that's obvious. Think how a child-killing charge will taint the testimony. The jury will throw it out. We've got to wait."

"How long?"

"Less than a year if we lose the case. If we get a conviction, we'll have to wait out all the appeals. So we could be looking at five years, maybe more."

Cool as it was in the car, I felt a different kind of cold seep through me.

"Who is he?"

"Forget it. I can't tell you that."

I couldn't help it—I went for his throat.

"Tell me, goddamn it!"

He pushed me off. He was a lot bigger than I—I'm just a bantamweight accountant, one-fifty soaking wet.

"Back off, Santos! No way I'm going to give you a name. You'll have it in all the papers within hours."

I folded. I crumpled. I turned away and pressed my head against the cool of the side window. I thought I was going to cry, but I didn't. I'd left all my tears with Jessie.

"Why did you tell me any of this if you're not going to tell me his name?"

"Because I know you're hurting," he said in a soft voice. "I saw what you did to that reporter on TV."

Right. The reporter. Mel Padner. My claim to fame. As I walked out of the morgue after identifying Jessica's tattered body, I was greeted by an array of cameras and reporters. Most of them kept a respectful distance, but not Padner. He stuck a mike in my face and asked me how I felt about my daughter's death. I had the microphone halfway down his throat before they pulled me off him. His own station never ran the footage, but all the others did, including CNN. I was still getting cards and telegrams telling me how I should have shoved it up Padner's other end instead.

"And this is supposed to make me feel better?" I said to Caskie.

"I thought it would. Because otherwise the weeks and months would go on and on with no one finding the killer, and you'd sink deeper and deeper into depression. At least I know I would. I've got a daughter myself, and if anything ever happened to her like ... well, if

133

anything happened to her, that's the way I'd feel. I just thought I'd try to give you some peace of mind. I thought you'd be able to hang in there better knowing that we already have the killer in a custody of sorts, and that, as one father to another, justice will be done."

I turned and stared at him. It's a comment on our age, I suppose, that decency from a stranger is so shocking.

"Thanks," I said. "Maybe that will make a difference later when I think about it some. Right now all I'm thinking is how I want to take the biggest, sharpest carving knife I can find and chop this guy into hamburger."

He raised his right fist with the thumb stuck in the air.

"I hear you, Mr. Santos."

"Call me Pete."

"I'm Gerry. And if the government didn't need the testimony so desperately, I might be tempted to do it myself."

We shook hands, then I got out of the car and walked around to his side. He rolled the window down.

"Thanks again," I said. "You didn't have to do this."

"Yes, I did."

"Sure you won't tell me his name?"

He smiled. "These are some *bad* dudes we want to put away with this trial. But don't you worry. Once all the legal proceedings are over, justice will be done." Again, the thumbs-up sign. "We'll see to it that she gets what's coming to her."

And then he drove away, leaving me standing on the path, gaping. *Her?*

It wasn't working.

The day after Jessica's body was found, I went back to my apartment—Martha got the house, so I've been living in a two-bedroom box at the Soundview condos—and trashed the place. All except Jessica's room. The second bedroom had been reserved exclusively for Jessie. I went in there and with a black Magic Marker drew the outline of a man on one of her walls. Then I took the biggest carving knife I could find and attacked that figure. I slashed at the wallboard, driving the blade through it again and again until I was exhausted. Only then was I able to get some sleep.

I'd done that every night since Jessica's death, but tonight it wasn't working.

Caskie's last words were driving me crazy.

My little Jessica had been slashed to ribbons by a woman? A *woman*? I couldn't believe it. It gnawed at my insides like some monstrous parasite. I couldn't work, couldn't eat, couldn't sleep. The FBI knew who'd killed my Jessica and they weren't telling. I had to know, too. I needed a name. A face. Somewhere to focus this rage that was coloring my blood and poisoning every cell in my body.

A woman! Caskie must have been mistaken. Jessica had been—I retched every time I thought of it—sodomized. A woman couldn't do that.

I lasted two days—and two nights of heartlessly attacking the male figure outlined on her wall. Then I acted.

First thing in the morning, I took a trip to the FBI office on Queens Boulevard in Rigo Park. I knew I'd given agent Caskie my word, but ... my daughter ... her killer ... no one could expect me to hold to that promise. No one.

I was in the lobby of the FBI building, searching the directory, when I heard a voice to my left.

"What the hell are you doing here?"

I turned and saw Caskie. I stepped toward him with my hand extended.

"Just the man I was looking—"

"Don't talk to me!" he hissed, staring across the lobby. "Get out of here!"

"No way, Caskie. Your people know who killed my daughter and they're going to tell me, or I'm going to the papers."

"You trying to ruin me?"

"No. I don't want that. But if I have to, I will."

He was silent for a moment, then he made a noise like a cross between a sigh and a growl.

"Shit! Meet me outside. Around the corner in the alley. Ten minutes."

He walked away without waiting for my reply.

The alley was long and narrow, blocked at the far end by a ten-foot cyclone fence. I waited near its mouth, keeping to the shady side. Mid-morning and already getting hot. Caskie showed up a few minutes later. He walked by as if he hadn't noticed me, but he spoke out of the corner of his mouth.

"Follow me. I don't want to be seen with you."

I followed. He led me all the way back to the rear of the building. When we rounded a rancid-smelling dumpster, he turned, grabbed me by the front of my shirt, and threw me against the wall. I was caught by surprise. The impact knocked the wind out of me.

"What the fuck do you think you're doing here?" he said through tightly clenched teeth.

I was ready to take a shot at his jaw, but the fury in his eyes made me hesitate. He looked ready to kill.

"I told you," I said. "I want to know who killed my daughter. And I'm going to find out."

"No way, Santos."

I looked him in the eye.

"What're you going to do? Kill me?"

He seemed to be considering it, and that made me a little nervous. But then his shoulders slumped.

"I'm so fucking *stupid!*" he said "I should have minded my own business and let you stew for a year or two. But no, I had to try to be Mr. Goodguy."

I felt for him. Actually, I felt like a shit, but I wasn't going to let that stop me. I couldn't let lesser emotions get in the way.

"Hey, look," I said. "I appreciate what you tried to do, but it just didn't work the way you thought it would. Instead of easing my mind, it's done just the opposite. It's made me crazy."

Caskie's expression was bleak as his voice.

"What do you want, Santos?"

"First off, I want to know why you said the killer was a 'she' the other day?"

"When did I say that? I never said that."

"Oh, yes, you did. As you drove off. And don't tell me I misunderstood you, because I didn't. You said, 'We'll see to it that *she* gets what's coming to her.' So how could Jessie's killer have been a woman if they're tracing the killer through DNA analysis of the semen they found in ..." My stomach lurched.

Caskie's smile was grim and sour.

"You think the Bureau can't get a local coroner to change his report for matters of security? Wake up, Santos. That was put in there to make sure that no one ever has the slightest doubt that they're looking for a male."

I wanted to kill him. Here I'd spent nearly a week believing Jessica had been raped before she was slashed up. And it had never happened. But I kept calm.

"I want her name."

"No way."

"Then I go to the *Times*, the *Post*, and the *News*. Right now!"

I turned and began walking up the alley. I'd gone about ten feet when he spoke.

"Ciullo. Regina Ciullo."

I turned.

"Who is she?"

"Bruno Papillardi's ex-girlfriend."

That rocked me. Bruno Papillardi was New York City's number one crime boss. His racketeering trial had been in the papers for months.

"Is she that important to the case?"

"The way the judge is tossing out our evidence left and right, it looks like she's going to be the *whole* case. She may be a psycho, but she's not dumb. She made recordings while she and Bruno were in bed together. Seems that when all the grunting and groaning is done, Bruno tends to brag. There's one particularly juicy night where he talks about how he personally offed a Teamsters local boss who wouldn't play ball. With Regina Ciullo's testimony, we might be able to nail him for more than racketeering. We might get him for murder-one."

I didn't care about Papillardi. I cared about only one person.

"But Jessica ... why?"

Caskie shook his head.

"I don't know. I'm not a shrink. But I know your daughter wasn't the first. Regina Ciullo's done at least two others over the past two years. The others were just never found."

"Then how do you—?"

"She told us. She gave us the slip on the Fourth. She returned the following morning around three a.m. We found the knife in the back seat of the car. We made the connection, put the pressure on her, and she told us. We'd always known she was weird but ..." He shuddered. "We never realized ..."

I wanted to run from the alley, but I had to see this through.

"So you can see our dilemma," Caskie went on. "We can't turn her in. At least not yet. Papillardi's people are combing the whole Northeast for her. If she's arrested, she won't survive her first night in jail. And if by some miracle she does, her lawyer will immediately enter an insanity plea, which will destroy the value of her testimony against Papillardi."

I swallowed. My throat was gritty.

"Where are you keeping her?"

"Are you kidding? I tell you so you can go out there and try to do a Rambo number on her? No way."

"I don't want to kill her."

"That's not what you said the other day at the cemetery."

I smiled. It must have been a hideous grimace because I saw Caskie flinch.

"I was upset then. A little crazy. I couldn't stick a knife in someone. Besides, I already have enough information now to kill her. If I want her dead, I can call Papillardi and tell him she's in Monroe. He'll do the rest. But I don't want that. I just want to know what she looks like. I want to see a picture of her. And I want to know where she lives so I can drive by every once in a while and make sure she's still there. If I can do that, I can survive the wait."

He was studying me. I hoped I'd been convincing. I prayed he'd buy it. But actually, I hadn't left him much choice.

"She's staying on Shore Drive in Monroe."

I couldn't restrain myself.

"In my home town? You brought a child killer to my home town?"

"We didn't know about her then. But believe me, she won't get out of our sight again. She's hurt her last kid."

Damn right, I thought.

"I want to see her file."

"I can't get that—"

"You will," I said, turning. "And by tonight. Or I'll be on the phone. Bring it to my apartment."

I didn't give him my address. I was sure he already had it.

Back in my apartment, I took the Magic Marker and enhanced the drawing on Jessica's wall with a few details. I added a skirt. And long flowing hair styled in a flip. Then I picked up the knife and went to work with renewed vigor.

Caskie showed up around 10 p.m., smelling like a leaky brewery, a buff folder under his arm. He brushed by me and tossed the folder onto the living room table.

"I'm dead!" he said, pulling off his wilted suit jacket and hurling it across the room. "Two more years 'til my pension, and now I might as well kiss it all goodbye!"

"What's the matter?"

"*That's* what's the matter!" he said, pointing at the folder. "When that turns up missing, the Bureau will trace it to me and put my ass in a sling! Nice guys really do finish fucking last!"

"Just a minute, now," I said, approaching him but staying out of reach. He looked *very* upset. "Hold it down. If you return it first thing tomorrow morning, who's going to know it was ever missing?"

He stared at me, a blank look on his face.

"I thought you wanted it."

"I want to *look* at it. That's all. Like I told you: just to know where she lives and what she looks like. If the killer's got a name and a place and a face, I can stay sane until the Papillardi trial is over."

As I was speaking, my body had been gravitating toward the folder. I wasn't aware of my legs moving, but by the time I'd finished, I was standing over it. I reached down and flipped the cover open. An eight-by-ten black-and-white close-up of a woman's face stared back at me.

"That's ... that's her?"

"Yeah. That's Regina Ciullo."

"She so ordinary."

Caskie snickered.

"You think someone with Bruno Papillardi's wealth and power is gonna waste his time with someone 'ordinary?' No way. Good-looking babes are falling all over that guy. But Ciullo's weirdness is one of a kind. She's *anything* but ordinary. That's what attracted him." His voice turned serious. "You really mean that about not wanting to take the file?"

"Of course."

I picked up the photo and stared at it. Her irises were dark, the lashes long. Her hair was wavy, long, and very black. Despite strategic angling of the camera, he nose appeared somewhat on the large side. Her lips were full and pouty. She looked thirty-five or so.

Caskie peered over my shoulder.

"That picture's a few years old, when she was going under the stage name of Bloody Mary. Doesn't show any of her body, which is incredible."

"Stage name?"

"Yeah. She used to be a dancer in a specialty club down in SoHo called The Manacle. She'd do a strip while letting a white rat crawl all over her body, and when she was down to the buff, she'd slice its throat and squeeze its blood down her front as she finished her dance." Caskie's expression was sour. "A real sicko, but she sure as hell got to Papillardi. One show and he was hot for her ass. Say, you got any beer?"

I pointed the way to the kitchen as I continued to stare at the photo.

"In the fridge."

This was the killer of dear Jessica. Regina Ciullo. When she tired of slashing rats, she went out and found a child. I felt my pulse quicken, my palms become moist. The photo trembled in my grasp, as if she knew I'd be coming for her.

"Where on Shore Drive is she staying?"

Caskie popped the top on a can of Bud as he returned to the living room.

"The Jensen place."

"Jensen? How'd you get her in there?"

"You know them?"

"I just know they're rich."

140

He took a long gulp.

"They are. And they're hardly ever home—at least in this home—except in the spring. They're on a world cruise now. And since Mr. Jensen is a friend of the present administration, and a personal friend of the Bureau's director, he's allowed us to stash her in his mansion. It's a perfect cover. She's posing as Mr. Jensen's niece." He shook his head slowly. "What a place. That's the way to live, I tell you."

The woman who murdered my daughter was living in luxury out on Shore Drive, guarded by the FBI. I wanted to scream. But I didn't. I closed the file and handed it back to Caskie.

"I'll keep the picture," I said. "The rest is all yours."

He snatched the folder away from me.

"You mean it?

"Of course. You'll never hear from me again ... *unless*, of course, Papillardi is convicted and she isn't indicted. *Then* you'll hear from me. Believe me, you'll hear from me."

I had put on a performance of Barrymore caliber. And Caskie bought it. He smiled like a death row prisoner who'd just got a last-minute reprieve.

"Don't worry about that, Santos. As soon as Papillardi's case is through, we're on her. Don't you worry about that." He turned at the door and gave me another of his thumps-up gestures. "You can take that to the bank."

And then he was gone.

For a while I stood there in the living room and stared at the picture of Regina Ciullo. Then I took it into Jessica's room and tacked it over the head of the latest outline on the wall. Then I stabbed the figure so hard, so fast, and so many times I had a football-sized hole in the wall in less than a minute.

A week later the walls of Jessica's room were so Swiss-cheesed with holes that I had no space left for new outlines.

Time for the real thing.

I'd been driving by the Jensen place regularly, sometimes three times a day. I always kept the photo on the seat beside me, for quick reference in case I saw someone who resembled Regina Ciullo. I was sure I'd know her anywhere, but it's good to be prepared.

The houses on Shore Drive all qualified as mansions—all huge, all waterfront, facing Connecticut across the Long Island Sound. Although a car or two—a Bentley or a Jag or a Porsche Carrera— always sat in the driveway behind the electric steel gate, I never saw anybody.

Until Thursday. I was in the midst of cruising past when I saw the front gate begin to slide open. I almost slammed on the brakes, but had the presence of mind to keep moving. But slow.

And who pulls out but the bitch herself, the slasher of my daughter, slayer of the last thing in my life that held any real meaning. She was driving the Mercedes. Speeding. She passed me doing at least fifty, and still accelerating. On a residential street. The bitch didn't care. The top was down. No question about it: Regina Ciullo. And she was alone.

Had she given her FBI guardians the slip again? Was she on her way to find another innocent, helpless, trusting child to slaughter?

Not if I could help it.

I followed her to the local Wegmans, trailed her as she dawdled along the cosmetics aisle in the pharmacy department, touching, feeling, sniffing. Probably looking for the means to whore herself up. As ordinary as the photo had been, it had done her a service. In the light of day she was extremely plain. She needed all the help she could get. And her body. Caskie had described it as "incredible." Anything but, from what I could see. I guess there's no accounting for tastes.

I caught up to her in the housewares aisle. That was where they sold the knives. When I saw a stainless steel carving set displayed on a shelf, I got dizzy. Visions of Jessica's mutilated body lying on that cold, steel gurney in the morgue flashed before me. A knife like that had ripped her up. I saw Martha's face, the expressions on her brothers' faces—*Your fault! Your fault!*

That did it.

I ripped the biggest knife from the set and spun her around.

"Remember Jessica Santos?" I screamed.

Shock on her face. Sure! No one was supposed to know.

I pretended she was one of the outlines on Jessica's wall. A deep thrust to the abdomen, feeling the knife point hesitate against the fabric of her dress, and then rip through cloth and skin, into the tender innards. She screamed, but I didn't let that stop me. I tugged the blade free and plunged it in again and again, each time screaming,

"This is for Jessica! This is for Jessica!"

Somebody pulled me free of her and I didn't resist. She'd been slashed like Jessica. The damage was irreparable. I knew my duty was done, knew I'd avenged my daughter.

But as I looked into her dying eyes, so hurt, so shocked, so bewildered, I had the first inkling that I had made a monstrous mistake.

I slammed my fist on the table.

"Call the FBI! Check it out with them!"

They'd had me in this interrogation room for hours. Against my lawyer's advice—who wanted me to plead insanity—I'd given them a full statement. I wasn't going to hide anything. This was an open and shut case of a man taking justifiable revenge against his daughter's murderer. I wasn't going to be coy about it. I did it and that was that. Now they could do their damnedest to convict me. All I needed was the FBI file to prove that she was the killer.

"We *have* called the FBI," said Captain Hall, chief of the Monroe police department. He adjusted his belt around his ample gut for the hundredth time since he'd stuck me in here. "And there's no such agent as Caskie assigned anywhere in New York."

"It's a deep cover thing. That woman posing as a Jensen is Regina Ciullo, a federal witness against Bruno Papillardi!"

"Who told you that?" Captain Hall said.

"Agent Caskie."

"The agent who doesn't exist. How convenient. When did you meet him?"

I described my encounters with Caskie, from the cemetery to my apartment.

"So you were never in his office—if he ever had one. Did anyone see you with him?"

I thought about that. The funeral had been over and everyone was gone when I'd met him in the cemetery. We'd stood side by side for less than a minute in the foyer of the FBI building, and then we'd been together in the alley and my apartment. A cold lump was growing in my gut.

"No. No one that I recall. But what about the picture? It's got to have Caskie's fingerprints on it!"

"We've searched your car three times now, Mr. Santos. No picture. Maybe you *should* plead insane. Maybe this FBI agent is all in your mind."

"I'm not crazy!"

Captain Hall's face got hard as he leaned toward me.

"Well then, maybe you should be. I know you've had a terrible thing happen to your family, but I've known Marla Jensen since she was a girl, back when she was still Marla Wainwright. And that was poor Marla you sliced up."

He had to be wrong. Please God, he had to be! If I did that to the wrong woman—

"No! You got to listen to me!"

A disgusted growl rumbled from Captain Hall.

"Enough of this bullshit. Get him out of here."

"No, wait! Please!"

"Out!"

Two uniformed cops yanked me out of the chair and dragged me into the hall. As they led me upstairs to a holding cell, I spotted Caskie walking in with two other cops.

"Thank God!" I shouted. "Where have you been?"

His face was drawn and haggard. He almost looked as if he had been crying. And he looked different. He looked trimmer and he held himself straighter. The rumpled suit was gone, replaced by white duck slacks, a white linen shirt, open at the collar, and a blue blazer with an emblem on the pocket. He looked like a wealthy yachtsman. He stared at me without the slightest hint of recognition.

One of the cops with him whispered in his ear and suddenly Caskie was bounding toward me, face white with rage, arms outstretched, fingers curved like an eagle's talons, ready to tear me to pieces. The cops managed to haul him back before he reached me.

"What's the matter with him?" I said to anyone who'd listen as my two cops hustled me up the stairs.

My attorney answered from behind me.

"That's Harold Jensen, the husband of the woman you cut up."

I felt my knees buckle.

"Her husband?"

"Yeah. I heard around the club that she started divorce proceedings against him, but I guess that's moot now. Her death leaves him sole heir to the entire Wainwright fortune."

With my insides tying themselves in a thousand tight little knots, I glanced back at the man I'd known as Caskie. He was being ushered through the door that led to the morgue. But on the threshold he turned and stole a look at me. As our eyes met, he winked and gave me a secret little thumbs-up.

for Joe Lansdale

FIRE & ICE

BY JOSEPH BADAL

CHAPTER 1

By an eighth of an inch and one pint of blood, twenty-six-year-old U.S. Army Captain James Brennan missed becoming the 1,301st American to die in Operation Enduring Freedom. Instead, he became the 8,998th to be wounded.

Just released from Landstuhl Army Hospital and on Christmas leave for two weeks, James deplaned at Philadelphia International Airport Gate 23. Into the jetway—December, meat-locker cold. Juking and dodging people waiting to board planes. Down the long corridor toward the front of the terminal. He forced himself to stand ramrod straight, making the most of his six-foot frame, stretching the scar tissue on his leg and the sore muscles in his back and neck. Look strong, he told himself. For Mom, who would notice a limp. For Dad, who would see any sign of weakness. Growing up, he'd hated every time his father had told him, "Stop whining and act like a man." But that mantra had, like a magic carpet, carried him through Basic Training, AIT, Special Warfare School, and twenty-three months in Afghanistan.

Inside the terminal, he searched for his parents; he was certain they would be waiting for him. He grimaced at the thought of his mother greeting him with her usual, shrill, "Jimmy, my sweet boy." But then he smiled. Her greeting always made things seem right.

James had told his parents he was assigned to a staff position in Afghanistan. Hadn't told them he was a killer, the leader of an assassination team. Hadn't told them he'd been wounded. He spotted his father next to a newsstand, but had to do a double-take just to be certain. My God, he thought, Vince Brennan looked much older than his fifty years. He seemed haggard. James put on a smile and walked toward his father, who noted his approach with a wave. The two men met halfway and hugged.

"Hey, Dad," James said. "Good to see you."

Vince pushed away from his son and performed a quick inspection. "You look good," he said.

"Lost some weight, but Mom's cooking will fix that."

"Sounds like a plan," Vince said, but without much enthusiasm.

James looked around. "Where's Mom?"

Vince swallowed, his Adam's apple bobbing. "You got any checked bags?"

"No, Dad. Just my duffel here."

James suddenly felt worried. Something seemed wrong. Mom should be here. And where were his brother, Frank, and his sister, Connie? But he let the patience he had learned in the Army take control. Besides, how wrong could things be?

CHAPTER 2

Vince Brennan expelled a loud breath and said, "I'm glad you're home, son."

James noticed his father gripping the steering wheel.

"What's wrong, Dad?"

Vince glanced quickly at James and then turned back to the road. "Frank's in the hospital. That's where your mother and sister are."

"What happened?" James asked, steeling himself.

"He was attacked a week ago by some guys at a party. They beat him up bad, Jimmy. The doctors put him into a medically induced coma to try to stabilize him. He's on a ventilator."

"He's been in a coma for a week?" James asked. "Is he going to be all right?"

Vince slowly shook his head. "I don't know. Nobody knows."

"Who hurt Frank?" James asked. A wave of heat invaded his gut and icy-cold fingers numbed his brain.

"Don't know," Vince said, shooting James a worried look. "Does it matter?"

James shrugged. "No witnesses?"

"No one saw anything. You know how that goes."

No one saw anything at a party. Hard to believe, James thought.

"Not the homecoming I wanted for you," Vince said.

James reached across the seat and squeezed his father's shoulder.

The fast, heavy traffic of Philadelphia transitioned to the slower, less-congested roadways of Pennsmoor. A former farming area, Pennsmoor was now a bedroom community to Philadelphia and Lancaster. Vince and Frances Brennan moved there from Philadelphia when James was ten, Frank two, and Connie a newborn. Pennsmoor was safe and clean. Its schools were committed to excellence. The Brennans raised their children to work hard, tell the truth, and obey the law. They promoted patriotism and faith in God.

James stared out the window. Christmas decorations adorned the lampposts and garlanded wires hung from one side of the street to the other. Everything seemed surreal after Afghanistan.

At the hospital, they took the elevator to the fifth floor and walked to the intensive care ward. Six glass-fronted rooms formed a semicircle around a pod where two nurses worked. More surrealism: muted-beeping and blinking monitors, funereal quiet, medicinal odors. James spotted his mother talking to a nurse. He walked up behind her and placed a hand on her shoulder.

Frances turned and seemed to experience a kaleidoscope of emotions in an instant. She gasped, then smiled. Tears burst from her pale blue eyes, flowing down her freckled cheeks. Then she exhaled, said, "James, my sweet boy," and grasped her son, burying her head in his chest, sobbing and shaking.

While holding onto his mother, James looked over her head through the window into the room behind her. He didn't recognize the person in the bed there. Bandages, tubes, and medical contraptions overwhelmed the patient. On the far side of the room, fifteen-year-old Connie Brennan slouched in a chair, seemingly staring at nothing.

Connie had always been the beauty of the neighborhood. Now, her usual fair complexion looked almost gray and her blonde hair was tangled and unkempt. The bags under her eyes were purple-gray. She looked old and worn out, as though *she* should be in the hospital bed.

James raised an arm and gave Connie a small wave but got no reaction. He turned his attention back to his mother, who had stopped crying. Frances moved back a half step, blotted her eyes with a tissue, and gave James the once-over.

"You've lost weight," she said.

James made a sweeping gesture, discounting his mother's remark. "I'm fine, Mom. What's up with Frank?"

"The doctor says there's no change. They're still trying to reduce the brain swelling."

James stared again through the window into Frank's room. "Connie's taking it hard, isn't she?"

Vince, now standing next to Frances, rubbed his chin, closed his eyes for a moment. "I can't get a damned thing out of her. She won't talk to anyone but Frank. And all she says to him is, 'I'm sorry.' What's she got to be sorry about?"

Vince and Frances took Connie down to the hospital cafeteria while James spent time with Frank. He held his brother's hand and told him he was there for him, would watch over him. And he said, "I'm going to find the guys who did this to you, Frank."

CHAPTER 3

"I need that Brennan girl tonight, ya hear me?" Nick Carpesi growled. "We got thirty guys coming in from Philly. She was missing in action last night. What happened?"

Terry Blair looked at his twin brother, Howie, and then back at Carpesi. "She's at the damn hospital with her parents."

"That sounds like a fuckin' excuse, Terry."

"No, Nick. But ..."

Overweight but powerfully built, forty-year-old Carpesi glared at the two eighteen-year-olds. The Blairs were man-boys: six-foot four, blond, blue-eyed football hunks. Spoiled punks, Carpesi thought. He jumped to his feet, knocking his chair back against the wall. "You guys are startin' to piss me off. How much money have I given you?"

Howie opened his mouth, but slammed it shut when Carpesi shoved his palm at him.

"Thirty-two grand in less than one year. All you gotta do is recruit high school chippies. Thirty-two grand and all the ass you want. Is that about right?"

"Yeah, Nick," Terry answered. "We appreciate what you've—"

"So the Brennan girl will be there tonight?"

The Blair brothers nodded in unison.

"And she knows what will happen if she doesn't cooperate?" Carpesi asked.

"Of course," Howie said. "Her whole family will pay, like her brother did. And she knows we'll put the videos we have of her on the Net."

"You keeping her supplied with meth?"

"Yep," Terry said, smiling.

Carpesi snatched his chair away from the wall and sat down. "So we got nothin' to worry about." He smirked, grabbed a cigar from his shirt pocket and bit off the end, bending over to spit it into the wastebasket under his desk. He eyed the brothers as he rolled the unlit cigar in his mouth. He finally said, "I need those two new girls you been preppin'."

"They'll be there," Terry said. "They've been on speed daily for two weeks; got pictures of them having sex. Eating out of our hands."

Carpesi laughed. "You boys got your pick of the herd. Girls think they're somethin' special, they spread their legs for you football heroes." He laughed. "Better enjoy it. Won't last forever." He pointed a sausage-sized finger at the Blairs and dropped all semblance of good humor. "Don't disappoint me, boys." Malice dripped from his words.

Terry and Howie Blair got into their fire-engine red, five-year-old Dodge Charger, Howie behind the wheel, and drove away from Carpesi's auto body shop on the outskirts of Pennsmoor. Terry checked the dashboard clock and said, "We should just make it in time."

Howie snapped a look at his brother. "That greaser, Carpesi, as much as told us he'd kneecap us if we let him down, and you're worried about being late for school?"

"Don't be an idiot," Terry said. "We show up late, we get detention, and the school calls Dad. We don't need the aggravation. Besides, it's the last day before the break."

"How are we gonna get Connie Brennan to the party tonight?" Howie asked.

"Just like always. We call her cell and tell her we'll pick her up at midnight. She'll sneak out after her parents are asleep and she'll be back in bed before they're up in the morning. She needs the drugs too much, and she sure as hell doesn't want her ass spread all over the Internet."

"You know it's only a matter of time before she catches the clap, or something worse."

"Yeah, so what? There's plenty of talent to replace her."

CHAPTER 4

James checked his watch: 8:30 a.m. He'd been up since 4:00. Time zone change, worry, and anger conspired to drive him from his bed. He'd gone online on his old computer, trying to get news about his brother's assault. There wasn't much.

James showered, shaved, and dressed in khakis, a blue work shirt, and hiking boots he took from his bedroom closet. Stuff he hadn't worn since college. He picked out a blue ski jacket as well, and found an old pair of leather dress gloves in the pockets. Then he drove Frank's old Honda across town to the hospital. He let the sight of his comatose brother stoke his anger. He sat down next to Frank, talking about things they'd done together, about their friends, about the Eagles and the Phillies.

After two hours, Frances showed up. James was about to let go of Frank's hand and greet his mother when he froze. Frank had squeezed. James jerked his gaze at his brother's face. No change there. Frank's eyes were closed; nothing was moving except his chest, pumped by a mindless machine.

"He squeezed my hand," James excitedly told his mother.

"The doctor said there might be involuntary muscle movement," Frances said.

James placed Frank's hand on the bed and stood. "I have some things to do," he said.

"Can I help you, sir?" a baby-faced, uniformed officer asked as James approached the counter separating the police station lobby from the bullpen and offices.

"My name's James Brennan. I'd like to talk to whoever's handling the investigation into the assault on Frank Brennan."

"Why don't you have a seat over there while I check with the detectives," the officer said. He pointed at a pew-like bench that ran along the building's inside front wall,

Ten minutes later, an early thirty-something woman with short auburn hair, dressed in a conservative blue suit, walked up to him, right arm extended. James shook the woman's hand.

"Detective Joan Summers," she said.

"James Brennan."

"I understand you're asking about the assault on Frank Brennan."

"My brother."

"Let's go get a cup of coffee." She led the way through a door off the lobby, to a break room.

Summers took a dollar bill from her jacket pocket, inserted it into the hot beverage machine, and waited while it disgorged two cups of black coffee. She passed one over to James and said, "Sugar and cream on the counter over there."

"Black is fine. Thanks."

They sat at a table and Summers asked, "How's your brother doing?"

"He's in a coma."

She shook her head. "Bad business. No witnesses. No forensic evidence. We're at a dead end."

"You believe there weren't any witnesses?" he asked.

"Why would you ask that?" Summers asked, squinting at James.

"It happened at a party. People all around. I grew up here. This is a small community. There's only one high school. Everyone knows everyone. Just seems strange to me."

Summers nodded.

"What?" James asked.

She shrugged. "I had the same thought. The kids who were there either didn't want to get involved or were too frightened to say anything. I thought your sister would help, but nothing there either."

"Connie? How could she help?"

Summers gave James a curious look. "You didn't know? Your sister was one of the kids at the party where the assault happened."

CHAPTER 5

James drove back to the hospital and found his sister and mother listening to a man in a white smock. "R. Stafford, M.D." was stitched in red on the left pocket.

The doctor put on a half-smile and said, "Let's try to keep things in perspective. Frank was badly hurt. But the good news is the brain swelling has suddenly and dramatically declined. If he continues to improve, we may be able to take him off the ventilator."

After the doctor left, James watched Connie walk into Frank's room. When he followed her there, she moved away from Frank's bed, over to the window.

James stared at his sister and, in a quiet voice, asked, "What's the matter, Connie?"

Connie hunched her shoulders, still staring out the window.

"Come on, Connie. I know something's on your mind. Let me help you."

Connie turned around, her head bowed, appearing to look at her clasped hands. She finally said in a meek, defeated voice, "No one can help me." Then she rushed from the room, shaking off James's hand as he tried to stop her.

CHAPTER 6

Now that school was over for the Christmas break, Terry and Howie Blair had plenty of time on their hands. With their mother long dead and their father working long hours, they pretty much had the run of their house. This meant they could bring girls home, screw their brains out, and introduce them to drug and alcohol cocktails, turning them into money machines. They'd smooth them out on high-quality marijuana, then get them just a little bit drunk—just enough to break down the rest of their inhibitions. Finally, they'd introduce them to methamphetamines. The speed was the clincher. It turned the girls into sexual Olympic champions. Even with the shame of what they were doing, the girls gave the Blairs all the sex the boys wanted. Sex for drugs. No sex, no drugs. Once they were addicted to meth, everything else was easy. And, of course, there were always the photographs and videos as backup.

"I'm worn out," Howie Blair complained, wearing only boxers in front of the open refrigerator. He pulled out a beer and said, "Nick's going to love these two."

Terry chuckled while he hitched at his sweat pants. "Mimi finally fell asleep."

Howie nodded. "So did little Annie Fannie. Jeez, I've never had a girl as hot as that one. And she's barely fifteen."

Terry laughed. "Speed'll do it every time."

Howie laughed. "They'll be begging for more magic dust by tonight."

"Yep," Terry said. "Their first party. Have to make sure they're ready for action."

"I told them we'd stop by around 11:45. Then we'll pick up Connie Brennan. Should be at Carpesi's party house a little after midnight."

"Carpesi said there'd be thirty or so guys there tonight," Terry said. "Ten guys per girl. At $500 per guy, that's a very profitable night for him."

CHAPTER 7

Forty-eight-year-old Sean Blair opened the front door of his house at 7 p.m. after another twelve-hour day.

"Hey, guys, I'm home," he announced.

No answer.

Blair tried again, shouting this time, but got the same result.

He moved down the hall toward his bedroom, but stopped outside Terry's room. He opened the door and detected the competing odors of sex and marijuana. Blair groaned. The high school girls were throwing their tight little asses at his sons as though they were rock stars. As long as they were careful. But the marijuana was another thing altogether.

He turned around and opened the door to Howie's room and discovered the same pungent aromatic cocktail.

Suddenly feeling twice as tired as he had felt just a minute earlier, he walked to his room, shed his clothes, and put on a bathrobe. He thought about eating something, waiting up for his sons. But he suddenly felt too exhausted to do anything but go to bed.

James had tried unsuccessfully to engage his sister in conversation at the dinner table. He was about to try again when Connie's cell phone rang. She jumped up, grabbed the phone from her sweatshirt pocket, and ran into the living room. She talked in a low, furtive voice. James could see her face flush and then go white. She looked as though she'd been told someone had died. Her free hand jackhammered the air, maybe making a point. Connie saw him staring at her and whipped around, putting her back to him, and rushed from the room and up the stairs.

James glanced from his father, whose face was buried in his hands, to his mother, who had a deer-in-the-headlights look.

"How long's Connie been on drugs?" he asked.

Vince's head came up as his hands became fists in front of him.

"What the hell are you talking about?" Vince demanded.

"Take it easy, Vince," Frances said.

Vince shot a laser beam look at his wife. "What do you mean, 'Take it easy.' We raised our kids to hate drugs. No way Connie—"

James interrupted, "I've seen the symptoms too many times, in the Army. Altered behavior and mood, glassy eyes, drastic change in appearance. She's showing all the symptoms. And look at her hands and arms. She's scratching them and then picking at the scabs. You had to know something was wrong."

"We've known something was wrong for over a month," Frances said. "Your dad and I have talked and talked to her. Yelled even. Tried to get her to go to a doctor. We set up appointments and she runs away. We were going to drag her to the doctor last week, but then Frank ..." Frances paused and then added, "But drugs ... it can't be drugs."

James said, "I'll talk to her."

He stood and walked upstairs. He knocked on his sister's bedroom door.

"Come on, Connie, open up. Let's talk."

"Go away," she said.

James tried again. But, this time, she did not respond.

James stood there in the hall outside his sister's room and finally said, "We'll talk in the morning. You can't put it off forever."

CHAPTER 8

James went to bed late that night and fell asleep as soon as his head hit the pillow. But then something startled him awake. His battle zone nerves were still on high alert. He checked the bedside clock: 12:01 a.m. The rumbling sound of a poor car muffler rose from the street. He got out of bed and looked through his window. A red automobile, passenger side facing the house, was parked there. In the harsh light of a street lamp, James got a glimpse of a long-haired young man in the front passenger seat with what appeared to be a cell phone pressed against his right ear. It looked as though there were a couple girls in the backseat.

The muffled chirping of a cell phone carried to James's bedroom. He moved into the hall and followed the sound to Connie's door. The phone rang six times and then stopped. A minute later, the ringing started up again, but ended as it had before, with no answer.

When the phone didn't ring again, James returned to the window in his room and caught sight of the car speeding away.

James's father left the house at 7 a.m. He would drop by the hospital, be at his job by 9, and return to be with Frank at 6 p.m. He'd return home around 9.

James and his mother had breakfast together at home.

"Why don't you see if Connie's ready to go see Frank?" Frances told James. "I'll clean up the dishes."

James walked upstairs, not excited about confronting his recalcitrant sister, but determined. He knocked on her door and said, "You ready to go?"

No answer.

James tried again. Still no response. He tried the doorknob. Locked.

James slammed his shoulder against the door. That didn't work, so he backed up a step and kicked at the door, crashing the sole of his boot against the doorknob. The lock popped and the door flew open.

"Oh my God!" James groaned. "Call 9-1-1!" he yelled. "Mom, call 9-1-1!"

Connie was hanging from the ceiling fan, her face blue, her neck bent at an impossible angle. A toppled chair lay on the floor. James snatched a pair of scissors from his sister's desk and cut through the pink terrycloth bathrobe belt around her neck. Her body fell into his arms. He lowered her to the floor and started CPR, knowing with absolute certainty it would do no good.

His mother's shuddering sobs coming from behind him, James performed CPR on Connie for ten minutes, until the paramedics arrived. They then worked on Connie and, finally, after another ten minutes, declared her deceased.

One of the paramedics stood and backed off from Connie's body. He looked at James and said, "We've got to wait for a detective to show. Suicide's a violent crime." He shrugged as though in apology. "Don't touch anything."

James nodded while looking at his mother seated on the floor, her back against the side of Connie's bed, her body shaking. He noticed Connie's cell phone on the lamp table next to her bed and remembered it ringing at midnight, at the same time the red car had stopped outside. He glanced back at the paramedics—both preoccupied with repacking their equipment. He pocketed the cell phone and sat next to his mother.

James went downstairs when the doorbell rang. He let in two detectives, including Joan Summers, the one he had talked with the day before, and told them what had happened. He explained that the paramedics and his mother were upstairs in his sister's room.

"Would you mind bringing your mother down here so we can be free to look at your sister's room?" Summers asked.

James went upstairs and brought Frances down to the living room. He sat next to her on the couch. While the other detective went upstairs, Summers sat across from James and Frances and took notes as James again explained what had happened.

"Did either of you hear anything during the night?" Summers asked.

James told her about the car outside the house around midnight. But he decided not to mention the ringing cell phone.

"Can you describe the car?" Summers asked.

"Red. Low slung. Looked like a Dodge Charger. Sounded like a tank out there. Either needs a new muffler or has glass packs. Couldn't see the driver, but the passenger in the front had long blond hair."

James noticed Summers grimace.

"You know this guy?"

She waved a hand at James as though saying no.

"Anything else?" she asked.

"Couple of girls in the back of the car."

"You recognize any of them?"

James shook his head.

The other detective came back downstairs and crooked a finger at Summers, who stood and joined him in the entryway. They whispered for a minute and then Summers returned to the living room and said, "We're finished here. I'm sorry for your loss."

James walked the detectives outside and watched them drive away. Then he heard movement behind him—the paramedics wheeling Connie's body on a gurney to their vehicle. They pulled away just as Vince Brennan screeched to a stop in the driveway.

"How is she?" Vince yelled at James, now standing in the front entry.

Frances ran at Vince and threw herself at him, wrapping her arms around his chest, crying a deluge of tears. "She's gone, Vince. Our baby's gone."

Vince looked at James, his sad eyes wide, eyebrows raised.

"We found her in her room. She—she hung herself."

Vince moaned as though a dagger had pierced his chest.

After Vince and Frances went inside, James removed Connie's cell from his pants pocket and pulled up the record of incoming calls. The last two came from the same number: One at 12:01 p.m.; the other at 12:02. He highlighted the last number and pressed SEND. The phone screen showed the incoming number and the name Howard Blair. James was about to terminate the call when a male voice answered.

"You stupid bitch! You know how much trouble you caused us last night? I'm going to sell your ass on the street until you can't walk straight. You hear me? Then I'm going to kick the crap out of you like we did your spastic brother. You hear me? And we're going to mess up your parents." The guy paused as though he expected a response. When none came, he screamed, "Answer me, bitch!"

James clicked off the phone, barely able to contain the all-familiar rage swelling inside him. The fire and ice of battle. He walked back inside the house, went to the kitchen, and looked at the Pennsmoor telephone directory. He turned to the B's and found three listings for *Blair*, but none for a Howard Blair.

He went upstairs to his room. Sitting on the side of his bed, he forced himself to calm down, to suppress the heat in his gut and the creeping fingers of ice penetrating his brain. He knew what he wanted to do, what he'd been trained to do. But he fought the urge. This wasn't Afghanistan, after all. He'd go see Detective Summers. Tell her about the phone calls in the night. Tell her what the man had said when he called the number on Connie's cell.

CHAPTER 9

James drove to the Pennsmoor Police station. He started up the steps, then stopped and stared at the sign hanging to the left of the building's front door. He hadn't noticed it the last time he was here. It showed the name of Pennsmoor's chief of police. Sean P. Blair. One of the Blair listings in the phone book was for a Sean Blair. Sean Blair. Howard Blair. James didn't believe in coincidences.

What if Howard Blair was related to the police chief? He thought about the reaction Summers had when he described the red car and the long-haired passenger. Something about the description had resonated with her. What if Summers was protecting Howard Blair?

Enraged, James returned to the car and drove to the hospital.

The ICU nurse smiled at him and said, "I just called your folks. We took your brother off the respirator; he's breathing on his own."

James felt a surge of adrenaline rip through him. "Thank God!"

"His brain swelling diminished. He's alert, sort of. Not talking, but looking around and responding."

James entered Frank's room. Although his brother was still hooked up to several tubes, and he looked pale and weak, James felt exhilarated.

He placed a hand on Frank's arm. "Hey there, bro," he said, not expecting a response.

Frank's eyes opened languorously. When his gaze rested on James, he blinked. After a beat, Frank moved his lips and emitted a raspy sound.

James picked up a plastic glass of water with a pink stick-sponge in it. He pressed the sponge on Frank's lips and watched his brother suck at it.

Frank croaked out an indecipherable sound. He gulped and then rasped, "Help ... Connie ... help." Then he closed his eyes and began breathing deeply.

James waited in vain for Frank to wake. After an hour, he went out to the nurses' station and said to the young woman there, "Thanks for everything."

She smiled.

"You live in Pennsmoor?" he asked as an afterthought

"Yes."

"I see we've got a new police chief. When I left for the Army, Glen Schilling was chief."

"Yeah, Chief Schilling retired to Florida. Sean Blair's the chief now."

"Don't know him," James said.

"Wife died of cancer a while back. The chief has two sons who are sure to get big-time football scholarships. Terry and Howie. Real teenage heartthrobs."

Back home, James checked in with his parents and then went upstairs, lowered the retractable ladder in the hallway leading to the attic, and climbed up. Tipping his father's footlocker back, he swept out a padlock key from under the right front corner and unlocked the box. He removed the .45 caliber automatic his father had bought at a garage sale a few years ago, still wrapped in an oily rag, its serial number filed away. He tested the slide and trigger mechanisms and found them in good working order. Then he took out a box of ammunition, two empty magazines, and a cleaning kit from the locker. After climbing down from the attic and replacing the ladder, he went to his room, cleaned the weapon, and then dug an old knapsack out of the closet and placed the pistol and now-loaded magazines in it.

CHAPTER 10

Howie Blair took a beer from the refrigerator and plopped down near his brother on the den couch. Terry zapped the television set with the remote, scrolling through the channels. He clicked on a local channel; a beeping sound came from the set and a news alert scrolled across the bottom of the screen: *Pennsmoor High School coed commits suicide. Constance Brennan hanged herself in her home last night. Tune to Eyewitness News at 6 for the full story.*

"What the hell!" Terry blurted. "Connie Brennan killed herself last night. I thought you said you talked to her this morning?"

"I did," Howie gasped. "She called me."

"What did she say?"

"Uh ... nothing really."

"She didn't say anything?"

"Not a word. But her name showed on my cell when the call came in."

"It wasn't her. She was already dead," Terry shrieked. After a second's pause, he said, "What did you say?"

Howie shrugged. "I don't know. I was really pissed. I shouted. Told her I was going to kick her ass. Like we did—"

"Like we did ... what?"

Howie blew out a blast of air and swallowed. "Like we did to her brother."

"Oh shit! We've got to find out who has that cell phone."

"And do what?" Howie asked.

"Depends on who it is," Terry said.

"I don't like this, Terry. We need to get out of this business now."

Howie stood and started pacing just as the doorbell rang. He looked at his brother and spread his arms in a questioning gesture. "Who the hell's that?"

"How do I know?"

Howie went to the front door and looked through the side light windows. "Some guy," he called to Terry. He opened the door and saw the man had a cell phone to his ear. "Yeah?" he said. But then Howie's phone rang. He snatched the phone from his pocket and looked at the screen: Connie Brennan.

"Hey there, Howie," the guy on the front steps said, as he pocketed his cell phone. "Had to be sure I had the right guy."

James stepped into the Blair house and drove his right fist into the much larger Howard Blair's sternum. Blair fell to the floor as though he'd been poleaxed. James slipped the .45 pistol from the back of his waistband just as a mirror image giant of Howard Blair, fists raised, rushed into the entryway and came at him. But the kid skidded to a stop, the muzzle of the pistol denting his throat.

"Get your piece-of-shit brother off the floor and move into that room," James ordered, pointing toward the den.

When the twins were seated on the couch, James looked from one to the other, his gun hand and gaze moving in synchronous sweeps.

"Okay, guys," he said in a calm, reasonable voice. "I know you put Frank Brennan in the hospital and did something to Connie Brennan. Now you're going to tell me what's going on."

Terry Blair's eyes widened; Howie was groaning with each shallow breath. But neither brother said a word.

"One more chance, fellows."

"I don't know what you're talking about," Terry said. "Who the hell are you?"

James stepped forward and kicked Terry's right shin so hard the kid fell off the couch, clutching his leg and screaming. James grabbed Terry's long blond hair, flipped him onto his stomach, and placed a foot on the back of the kid's thick neck.

James eyed Howie, made sure he was in place on the couch, and then bent over and pressed the muzzle of the .45 into the back of Terry's neck and cocked the hammer.

"Please," Howie rasped, "don't hurt my brother. I'll tell you."

James straightened. He waved his gun hand in a come-hither motion and Howie opened up like a broken faucet. When the kid finished telling his story, James's anger had escalated to a napalm-hot level, icy madness trying to seize control of his mind.

Connie's suffering and shame.

Frank's pain.

His parents' worry and now inconsolable grief.

He forced himself to put a damper on his fury and, a sharp edge to his voice, asked why they beat up Frank.

"He found out Connie was sneaking out at night to meet us. He confronted us at a party later. Threatened to tell his parents. That's when we—"

"How did you keep Connie from saying anything?" James asked.

Howie seemed to go cross-eyed, staring at the pistol in James's hand. His face turned beet-red. "We—we had video of her. Pictures of her ... having sex with men."

"How many men?" James demanded.

The color drained from Howie's face. He swallowed hard. "Lots of men."

"And ..."

"We told her if she talked ... we'd kill her whole family."

"You gave her drugs, too, didn't you?"

Howie nodded, now looking sick enough to puke. "Meth."

James felt blood lust vie with reason. He shook his head to try to clear it. In a husky, feral voice, he said, "I know you geniuses didn't put this thing together yourselves. Who are you working for?"

"Nobody!" Terry said.

James pressed down harder with his boot, causing Terry to moan.

"Nick Carpesi," Howie said. "Mob guy out of Philly."

"And where do I find this Carpesi?"

"You're crazy," Howie moaned. "He'll kill you. Then he'll kill us. The guy's a psycho."

"What do you think *I* am?" James asked.

Howie just shook his head as though confused.

"Where are the pictures and videos you took?" James demanded.

Now looking down at his lap, Howie said, "On the computer on the kitchen counter and on my cell."

"What about your brother? He have a cell?"

"Yeah," Howie said, "but it doesn't take pictures or video."

CHAPTER 11

Nick Carpesi was closing up shop for the day when he saw the Blairs' Dodge pull up outside. The brothers and a third man got out of the car. "Damn! What now?" he muttered as he moved out of his workshop to his office and sat behind his desk. He removed a .9 mm Glock pistol from his desk drawer and placed it on his blotter, beneath a newspaper. He watched the Blairs and the third man, who wore gloves and a knapsack, enter his office. The Blairs looked frightened. The stranger closed the door and turned the lock.

"What's up, boys?" Carpesi asked.

"This guy is—"

The stranger punched Terry in the kidney and growled, "Shut up!" Terry dropped to the floor. His brother, Howie, in front of the stranger, had tears in his eyes.

Carpesi grinned.

The stranger stepped around Howie and pulled a pistol from behind his back, aiming it at Carpesi. He then took a cell phone from his ski jacket pocket and said, "What do you think about me calling the police and telling them about your sex ring?"

"What are you playing at?" Carpesi demanded. "Who are you?"

The stranger just glared at him.

Carpesi knew he couldn't let the cops question the Blair brothers. Even their father couldn't protect them. They'd roll over like two-bit whores. And then there were the drugs hidden in the body shop.

"Let's think this through," he said reasonably. "Why don't you tell me who you are?"

"James Brennan," the stranger said. "Ring a bell?"

Carpesi suddenly knew with absolute certainty the cops were the least of his problems. He swiveled slightly in his chair, hoping to distract the man, and then snatched the Glock from under the newspaper, firing shot after shot after shot.

James felt red-hot heat in his left arm as the cell phone slipped from his hand. He returned fire with the .45, dropping and rolling to his right. As he came back to his feet, he saw a fan of blood and brain matter had painted the wall behind Carpesi. The mobster had reacted exactly as James had expected ... and as he'd hoped he would. The Blairs were lying on the floor. A neat hole had been punched in Terry's forehead; blood seeped from the back of his head, forming an ever-growing pool. Howie was on his side, the left part of his chest covered in blood. Terry couldn't have survived his head wound. James removed a glove and checked for a pulse at Howie's neck. Gone, too.

James replaced the glove and put the .45 in Howie Blair's right hand, raised his arm, and fired a shot in Carpesi's direction, ensuring gunshot residue would be found on the kid. He let the pistol fall to the floor and then picked up Connie's cell phone and put it in his jacket pocket. He left through the office's back door.

CHAPTER 12

James found an alley a couple blocks from the body shop and shrugged out of the pack and his jacket. He ripped a piece from the bottom of his shirt and wrapped it around his left forearm where Carpesi's bullet had knicked him. He removed Howie Blair's laptop computer and cell phone from the knapsack and his sister's cell from his pocket, stomped them to plastic and metal pieces, and dumped the wreckage, along with his gloves and the box of ammunition, in a sewer loudly running with snow melt. He put the jacket and knapsack back on and walked through back alleys toward the vacant lot where he'd left Frank's Honda, two blocks from the Blair home.

The walk took fifteen minutes, allowing time for the heat in James's gut to dissipate and the ice in his brain to melt, coming down from the adrenaline high of battle. The itching of the scar on the inside of his right leg suddenly started again. James tried to ignore it, but the scar tissue was like a spoiled child demanding attention. He rubbed the spot through his pants, feeling the six-inch groove in his flesh so close to his femoral artery.

He drove home and found his father pacing outside in the cold.

"Where you been?" Vince asked.

"Taking care of business, Dad."

MADAME

BY DOUG BLAKESLEE

Now

Patience. Always a matter of patience. All jobs came down to waiting for the right moment, the perfect time to strike. Patience.

Henri looked over the list of names in the dim reflected light from his vantage point. *One hundred guests. Three targets.*

The client had given him the choice of whom to eliminate. None of the guests was innocent, a who's who of the criminal underworld. Henri was to deliver a stark and brutal message.

He stretched his legs with care, avoiding rustling the bushes that concealed his presence. A low fog rolled across the mansion grounds, quickening the guards' pace as they patrolled.

Patience.

Then

"Henri, do you know what day this is?" The portly man ran a hand through his thin, salt-and-pepper hair, then tugged at the neatly waxed mustache.

Henri sat in the straight-backed chair, watching his uncle pace about the small study. The man paused in front of one of the many shelves of books that lined the walls. In the hearth, a small fire crackled and spat, chasing off the edge of the cool, winter's evening that had deposited snow outside the sole window. The young man put down the crystal wine glass before speaking. "It is my eighteenth birthday, Uncle Andre."

The elderly man tugged at his black smoking jacket, smoothing out the wrinkles. He reached up to a large, leather-bound journal. On the spine, in neat gold printing, was embossed *1795*. "You are now officially the Heir. All rights, privileges, and responsibilities of the Deibler family."

"As is expected of me," Henri said, running a pale hand through his short, trimmed black hair. He eyed the book. "Another history lesson?"

"As the Heir, you are entitled to know one last piece of family history." Andre Deibler set the book on a wooden reading stand and gestured to his nephew to join him. He opened the book to a marker and pointed at the reproduction of a woodcut. "This is the first drawing of our family's long and industrious lineage."

The young man followed his uncle's finger. A hooded man with an ax, larger than his body, stood next to a chopping block with a pile of heads on the ground in front of it. Another stack, this one of bodies, sat in the background. The artists had colored in the blood at the base of the block, on the bodies, and on the blade of the ax. A crowd of peasants surrounded the raised executioner's platform.

"Jacques Marc Deibler was named the King's Headsman in 1462 by Louis XI. The family served for over three hundred years as dozens of our sons, and a few daughters, were inducted into the tradition. Our line spread throughout Europe." His uncle carefully flipped the pages as he spoke. "England. Belgium. Italy. Spain. Sometimes with an ax. Other times, with a sword."

"We are no longer the king's headsmen," Henri said. *Not in an age of chemical death.*

"No. The French Revolution saw the last of the Deiblers leave France. By then, the guillotine had become the instrument of choice. Our family had drifted into other professions by then, expanding to become morticians, funeral directors, grave diggers, and ..." He paused and turned to another bookmarked page, "... assassins." The page was a full-sized portrait of a middle-aged man, balding, with a thin and pointed nose, narrow eyes, and a puckered frown. "This is our founder, Daniel Nicholas Deibler."

"His portrait hangs in the front hall, underneath the grand stairs with all the former patriarchs of the family. Why did he leave France?"

"Daniel chose his allies poorly and upon the conclusion of the revolution was forced to flee. He chose the newly created America to settle. That is not the important part of this tale. When he fled, Madame went with him. She was the Deibler family legacy from the very beginning." Andre turned the page.

"That is Madame?" Henri's brows furrowed at the picture. He turned to his uncle.

"She was the first and the last. There is none other like her, before or since. Without such reminders, the Deibler family has no connection to our proud heritage." His face darkened. "Each Heir gains the responsibility for Madame. She was lost for a time, but we have recovered her. She is yours now, Henri. Treat her well and she will always see you through any difficulty."

"She is a useless relic of an older time," said a sharp, female voice.

Now

He observed the couple, laughing drunkenly, exit the basement door. The older man wore a tuxedo, tailored to fit just him. Her dress was a full-length outfit, complete with lace and satin highlights. In the dim lighting, it shone brightly. She pressed close to her companion.

"It is a beastly night. Why do you insist on this walk?"

"The night hides us from prying eyes, my love." The man wrapped a hand around the small of his companion's back, pulling her even closer, as their lips pressed together.

"You're a bad man, Mister King." She giggled. "What would your wife say?"

"She will never know. There's a nice young man who is keeping her attention." He looked around furtively. "They will be busy for some time. Long enough that we can enjoy each other's company thoroughly." The couple moved off toward the back of the house.

Henri smiled to himself, pulled up the hood, and affixed the mask to cover his face. Death with anonymity. He moved across the lawn toward the basement door. A check showed it to be still unlocked. *Patience. Now to get to work.* He would enter like a ghost and leave like the passing of a hurricane.

From above, voices laughing and chatting filtered down through the air vents. Strains of a Mozart waltz competed with chatter, each trying to outdo the other. Wine racks filled the basement proper, bottles of Chardonnay, Syrah, Bordeaux, Champagne, and other vintages. Henri paused to examine one of the racks and bottles. *No dust. Interesting. The stock is recent.* Skulking through the racks, he knew there were no cameras in this section. Security had focused on the exterior and there were gaps in the coverage. *It might be a trap, but that's easily fixed.* On the far wall was a mains box; thick cables extended into the floors above and into the concrete floor below.

Lights flickered and went out as Madame cut the power.

Then

Henri turned to take in the large woman who filled the doorway. A simple, black dress covered her ample figure, the neckline cut low to expose cleavage that strained the fabric to the limit. Her long, black hair was tied into a single braid that hung to her waist. Rouge and eyeliner hid the crow's-feet and frown lines of someone approaching the later years of life.

"Aunt Giselle." Henri bowed.

She nodded and smiled thinly at her husband. "In these modern times, Madame is nothing more than a toy. You have been trained with the proper weapons of the trade. Do not be fooled by sentiment and tradition." Her hand waved at the book dismissively.

"Tradition has kept the family in business for hundreds of years," his uncle said. "Show her some respect!"

"Pointless tradition and training. Contracts can be fulfilled without resorting to antique methods. No hiding or additional work to smuggle in the tools. She is a museum piece that is no longer relevant. Like history, she belongs to the past."

Andre looked at his nephew. "As the Heir, you have the right to choose which tool is required to complete the job. Madame will serve you well in all cases. We are experts, Henri. Not common thugs and

172

criminals that kill indiscriminately. Kill with a purpose and nothing more. No pity. No remorse. Just the contract."

Giselle Deibler snorted. "A gun serves the purpose better and may be disposed." Her eyes focused on the scoped .30-06 resting above the mantel.

"I believe that I will keep Madame. She is not unlovely, nor awkward or clumsy." Henri stood up and raised a glass to his uncle and aunt. "To us. To family. To Madame."

His uncle smiled and raised his glass as well. "To your first contract!"

Now

Henri took the steps two at a time, bursting through the door into the darkened house. Guests yelled and screamed in the dark. He smiled as his low-light lenses illuminated the room. Heavy shutters covered the windows. Another measure that worked in his favor. Chaos reigned in the ballroom. Guns were drawn. Guards fumbled for flashlights, flickering beams of light in desperation across the room.

"Why hasn't the generator started?"

"The windows are all covered."

"Which way to the door?"

His first target hovered near the gas fireplace, silhouetted by the low fire. He was a thin man, balding, with a hook nose and bushy eyebrows, who fidgeted and twitched. On either side were muscle, the kind that scared men hired. Henri smiled, took three steps, hopped on the buffet table, and sprinted. Glassware tinkled into a thousand pieces. Food and drink scattered as he ran, bounced off the table by his footsteps. He lined up on the mark and struck before the muscle could reach for their guns. Blood pooled on the floor as the body collapsed. Proof of the kill obtained, Henri disappeared through the door.

Then

"What is the first rule?" asked his uncle.

"Prepare as if your life depends on it," said Henri.

"The second?"

"There is no room for emotion. The job is never personal."

"The third?"

"Leave no trace. Become a ghost."

"The last?"

"Punish the guilty. Preserve the innocent."

"Good. Keep to those rules and you will always come home."

Now

The second target ran down the hall, pushing aside others. Sweat ran down his face as he huffed and puffed. His collar was undone and shirt half-buttoned, rolls of fat and flesh jiggling under the thin cloth. His pants and undershorts had been left behind. *Almost too easy.* Guests pounded on shuttered windows, with fists and furniture. Women screamed and sobbed. Men cursed and yelled. Guns and knives were drawn and waved in the air. *Amateurs.* The fat man ran right into death's embrace, shrieking in a high-pitched scream one last time as he realized the fatal mistake. His body, arms flailing wildly, crashed through the balcony railing, and landed on the marble floor with a wet thud. Eyes blinked and mouth moved in silent protest to his fate.

Henri grabbed his trophy and jumped down to the floor below, landing on the still warm body of his victim. Blood sprayed from the stump of the man's neck. "Come, Madame, we have one last person to meet." He pushed through the door and into the library. *Empty.* With quick steps, he crossed to a lone bookshelf, reached into the shelf, and undid a hidden latch. The panel swung back, revealing narrow steps that wound upward. *History is important. Those who forget are doomed.*

Then

"The clients have requested to know which of the guests you plan on eliminating." Andre Deibler leaned on the cane as Henri packed the shirts into his suitcase and zipped it closed.

"They will know when it is over."

"There is a concern that you will make this personal. That is forbidden."

"If they have such a concern, the contract should have gone to another family." He walked over and ran a hand over Madame as she lay` on the bed.

"I told them such. It did not reassure them."

"The contract stated I choose the targets for maximum effect. That has been done. Each is marked and the mansion is now a death trap."

"Good. I will see you upon your return."

"Yes, Uncle." Henri picked up Madame and smiled. *Soon. Very soon.*

Now

"It has been a long time, Henri." The wisps of fog drifted across the rooftop. Sharp hawk eyes peered through spectacles at the young assassin. A short brunette cowered behind the man, her high heels tottering on the uneven surface. Slim legs flashed through the slit skirt and her blouse was low cut to accent her bust. His dress was casual; slacks, polo shirt, and loafers. The .45 automatic gripped tightly in his hand was out of place.

Henri nodded in response. "Steven. Fifteen years, five months, and fourteen days."

The man chuckled. "Are you bitter over being abandoned? That you would take my place in the family?"

"No, Father. This is not personal. There is no room for feelings in this matter."

"Yet, you are here. Facing me." Steven Deibler gestured toward Henri. "And you carry that relic and are dressed in that outrageous outfit."

Henri hefted the great ax with a single hand. Blood dripped from the razor-sharp edge, running into the intricate scrollwork etchings on the steel. A plain silver cap and butt sealed either end of the oaken shaft, black with age and stain. "You will show respect for Madame."

"Madame? You named your tool?"

"If you had studied the family history, you would have known her name."

Steven raised the .45 and sneered. "I have killed others that have pursued me. What makes you think you are any different?"

"Because this is not personal." Henri jumped forward, twirling Madame in his hands, light reflecting off the blade. "And you are not the target."

The gun fired too late as Madame took the girl's head.

Later

"A drug runner, a child pornographer, and an arsonist. Heads displayed on pikes for the others to see. Good work." Andre Deibler sipped a glass of Bordeaux. "A very fine vintage."

"Father's cellar was well stocked and I did not think he would miss a few bottles." Henri raised his glass. "A toast. To Madame and another successful contract."

"To Madame." His uncle leaned in. "That was very clever of you to lure Steven out."

"The third target served a dual purpose. Our client is happy. Family honor is served. Everyone wins. The fog made the last act more difficult than I had expected. It was luck that the wind had cleared much of it away."

"Who did you find to act as your second?"

"Really, Andre, you are too focused on the past to see the future in front of you." Giselle Deibler smiled as Henri offered her a glass. She perched on the arm of the chair and kissed the top of her husband's head. "It was not an easy shot and Henri moved too quickly to take the girl's head. He still has much to learn."

Andre laughed. "He will learn with time and make a fine heir." He raised his glass. "To family."

"To family!" Henri's eyes rested on Madame, displayed on the rack, waiting for her next job.

Patience.

THE MAN WHO SHOT HITLER

BY ELLIOTT CAPON

Berlin, June 1943

Gunther Koenig put on an inexpensive suit, a white shirt that had been worn for two or three days without benefit of having been washed, and no tie. He carried a weather-beaten satchel and walked with his head down. In a city of tired, inconspicuous people, he was the most anonymous.

He entered an apartment building on the corner of Potsdamer Strasse and Halpt Strasse, a tall building, at one time one of Berlin's most luxurious addresses. Now the entrance door was unlocked and the concierge was either dead or ... who knew, and who cared. Koenig made a face at the elevator and walked past it to the staircase. He had lots of time, so he very slowly made his way up sixteen floors to the topmost level of apartments. There was a big hole in the south wall of the hallway, the delivery of which had prompted the residents of that floor to vacate for greener climes. Koenig pulled down on the trapdoor in the ceiling and a ladder obligingly, if noisily protesting, came down. He climbed up it to the roof.

All things considered, it was a beautiful day. A few white clouds reflected, rather than hid, the sunshine. Koenig walked to the corner of the roof and looked down at Berlin. He had a clear view of

Charlottenburger Chaussee. He couldn't have thrown a rock from where he was to land on Charlottenburger, but he didn't intend to.

He opened his satchel and took out the rifle components. The barrel, which he had crafted himself, fit perfectly in the stock, which had been removed from an American-made rifle. The trigger mechanism had been modified from a British weapon, and fit perfectly between the other two pieces. This way, when he was done, he would divide the weapon into four components and disperse them in three separate places, forestalling if not completely frustrating any investigators.

It took him moments to put the rifle together, and gently snap in the magazine with eight 5.56mm bullets. He polished both ends of the custom, Swiss-made telescopic sight again, unnecessarily, clipped it to the weapon, and settled down.

There weren't tens of thousands of people lining Charlottenburger Chaussee this afternoon, because it wasn't an official public appearance, but there were certainly more than a few thousand filling the sidewalks, as far as Koenig could see. Any of the Fuhrer's motorcades provided a modicum of entertainment and diversion for people rapidly becoming dissuaded and disappointed; a glimpse at the confident Leader himself was always a good boost for morale. This little expedition from Templehoff Airport to the Chancellery, taking the long, long, out-of-the-way route, was calculated to let the people of Berlin see the Fuhrer, to know that things were going to get better.

There was no roof in the immediate area higher than the one Koenig was on, and he kept himself below the low wall that ran around its perimeter. Security forces—mostly older, post-service-age men and not-yet-service-age boys—along with members of the Berlin garrison of the Wehrmacht and the remaining members of the Berlin municipal police department, were scattered all over the neighborhood, on the street, on balconies, on nearby rooftops. But none of them were at a plane equal to or higher than his; and certainly none of them would have dreamt that his telescopic sight and custom-built rifle would work from such a distance.

Koenig's timing was good; he had only to wait eighteen minutes before be heard the wavelike roar of the crowd, as the Fuhrer's motorcade came closer. Koenig peered over the edge of his little wall.

In the distance, he could see the approaching cars—a Mercedes-Benz W-31, bearing six SS officers; following that the Fuhrer's specially-built Mercedes 770-K; and to the right of the Fuhrer's car and slightly to the rear, its hood even with the 770's rear bumper, another W-31 with six more officers. Koenig slipped the sight off the rifle and used it to study the motorcade. As expected, SS Obersturmbannfuhrer Erich Kempka was driving Hitler's car; next to him sat a Waffen SS General. In the rear seat, in his brown uniform, behind Kempka, sat the Fuhrer himself, and another black-clad SS officer was sitting next to him on Koenig's near side. The car was open, of course, and Hitler was sporadically returning the 'Sieg Heil' salutes of the crowd. Koenig had expected Hitler to be at the far side of the car, from his perspective, and had done his target practice. He had about another forty seconds before the motorcade came parallel to him, and then perhaps, at the slow speed they were driving, another ten seconds' window of opportunity to take his shot.

He carefully put the sight back on the rifle, counted to fifteen, and raised himself up enough to put his elbows on the low wall and brace himself. The small motorcade was approaching slowly. Through the sight, Hitler was as large in his vision as if they were sharing a bed.

The first car passed through the intersection of Halpt Strasse and Charlottenburg Strasse; maybe five seconds later, Kempka drove the car through the same intersection. Now was the ten-second window ... Koenig held his breath and squeezed the trigger.

In that fraction of a second, that hundredth of an inch between the time the trigger was just a piece of dangling metal and the time it sparked a small explosion at the bottom of a bullet, the SS officer sitting next to Hitler shifted himself upward, as if to get a glimpse of a good-looking woman, or pull his underwear out of the crack of his ass.

The bullet caught him between his right eye and ear. He toppled forward, into Hitler's lap.

Koenig did not waste time cursing. It would probably take Kempka a full second to realize what had happened, and then maybe another quarter of a second to floor the gas pedal—too short a time to waste in cursing. Koenig moved the rifle fractionally to his right, as the car continued at its steady pace—but inexorably moving out of range—sighted at his last opportunity, the base of Hitler's neck, and fired.

179

Koenig actually started, afraid (at the speed of thought) that the fountain of blood was going to soak him, so good was the telescopic sight. Hitler slumped forward, and the three cars leaped ahead as fast as their powerful engines could take them. Koenig could hear an incredible wave of sound from the crowd, but he couldn't see them—he was already lying prone, disassembling the rifle and putting the pieces back in his satchel, and crawling back to the trapdoor. He was down the ladder and out of the building as slowly and calmly as his pounding heart and head would let him go.

There was chaos on the streets, though no one seemed to know what was happening. Soldiers of the regular army and the SS, Berlin police officers and firefighters all rushed back and forth on foot and in vehicles, shouting, questioning, apparently giving and receiving all kinds of contradictory orders. Civilians were looking at one another in confusion, most looking at the sky, awaiting the arrival of the British or American bombers, but hearing no air raid sirens, no whistles of descending ordnance. Koenig did not walk resolutely, but just sort of meandered around in confusion, along with everyone else, until he came to the Landwehr Canal. There, surreptitiously and unnoticed by the milling mob of confused people, he dropped the trigger mechanism into the water. He walked over to Kopenicker Strasse, went to the alley behind a row of small stores, and deposited the rifle barrel in a garbage can. Another long walk got him to Frankfurter Strasse, where his beloved telescopic sight was dropped down a sewer grating. The stock was tossed into the remains of a burned-out building on nearby Landsberger Strasse.

Carrying his empty satchel, Gunther Koenig went home. His mouth was drier than the Sahara Desert after a drought and his chest was pounding louder than an antiaircraft battery, but, thanks to practice before a mirror, his face maintained a look of absolute innocence and guilelessness.

Back in his apartment—not the shabbiest one in Berlin, but far from the most luxurious—he had the sudden need to vacate his bowels. He amused himself with the thought that it was a miracle he was managing to hit the toilet, seeing as how he was shaking so much.

He had to flush twice. He changed his clothes, and threw his suit down the building's incinerator shaft. Tomorrow was Burn the Garbage day, which would be fine.

Then he turned on the radio. One could actually hear the tears in the announcer's voice.

"The Fuhrer has been assassinated!" he was saying. "The Fuhrer has been shot and killed! Our beloved Fuhrer was murdered on the streets of Berlin, as he greeted his adoring people!" The announcer actually sobbed, then recovered himself. "This is a terrible day for Deutschland and for the world! Our leader, our savior is no more! Herr Hitler is dead! *Der Fuhrer is todt!*"

Gunther Koenig nodded. *Gut*, he thought. *Alles ging sehr gut.*

Like everyone in Germany, he was glued to his radio for the next twenty-four hours. Information was contradictory, sporadic, often nonexistent. But several facts were incontrovertible. Hitler had been shot and killed. His body had been taken to the nearby Chancellery, where it was being prepared for the most lavish funeral in European history. Two people—one civilian and one military—had apparently been filming the Fuhrer when he was shot, and the films were in the possession of the authorities, and, after editing, would be released in newsreel form within the next few days. General Kurt Zeitzler, Chief of the Army General Staff, had been named as the acting chief of state and had taken over full command of the armed forces.

Unshaven men with their flies buttoned incorrectly and one armpit undeodorized and their ties unmatched to their suits and their medals unpinned to their uniforms *rushed* to meetings in Moscow. And London. And Washington. Hitler was dead. Zeitzler was now in command. The men met, and talked. They sent secret radio messages and heavily-coded cables from London to Moscow to Washington to Lisbon to extremely secretive locations in Paris and Hamburg and Rome. Hitler was dead and Zeitzler was in charge. Dusty intelligence reports were pulled out of basement filing cabinets: Zeitzler was a very good, very average commander. A theoretician and a historian. He was conservative; a thinker; a plodder. One who would wait until the risks were at absolute minimum. He was not a bold striker. He was not, like Waterloo's Austrian commander Blucher, known as "Old Forward." In fact, one uncorroborated report had someone crack that Zeitzler should be known as "Old Wait-and-See."

The men at their meetings in London and Moscow and Washington, and their confreres in Paris and Hamburg and Lisbon and Rome came to a similar conclusion: *Now* was the time to launch the Big Offensive, on both fronts. Now, not in May 1944, but *now*, when the Germans were literally and figuratively knocked for a loop, when they had a hesitant, undoubtedly nervous military commander, when the morale of the soldiers in the field was at its lowest.

But, argued Zeitzler's spiritual conservative military peers on the Allied side, *we are not ready. We are not ready for the offensive. We won't be ready for almost another year.*

Bosh! Stuff! And nonsense! cried the other men at the meetings in London and Washington and Moscow. Strike! While the iron! Is hot! If we're not ready, they're even less ready! An offensive now ends the war *tout suite*, lickety-split, очень быстро!

None of the men at the meetings knew of the existence of Gunther Koenig, though they all, silently and to each other, blessed his mother for having borne him. Then they put the offensive into high gear.

For three days Gunther Koenig sat in his apartment, listening to the radio. He ate a little, more out of a sense of duty than of any hunger. He drank a lot of tea, but abstained from any alcohol. The radio was full of stories of arrests, of investigations by the Berlin police, by the Gestapo, by the Abwehr. Stories of how they were closing in on the suspect(s), how an arrest was imminent. Koenig started every time a door slammed in his building or he heard steps in the hallway, or a black sedan or marked police car slowly cruised past his window. Three days. The only knock at the door came when a neighbor, who was going out to a nearby suburb to get some fresh eggs, wanted to know if Koenig wanted some himself. He had to ask the man to bring him back a dozen, because no one in Berlin turned down fresh eggs.

On the morning of the fourth day, Koenig knew it was time. He was nervous.

Heart pounding, Koenig opened his closet. He pushed aside his suits to clear a space in the back wall. He stepped down on the base moulding with his toe, and a panel slid to the side. In the hidden space behind the wall was a black Waffen SS uniform, with the requisite eagle, death's-head emblem, and the chevrons of a Kapitan. Koenig was shaking as he put the uniform on. He spent more time in front of his mirror than he had ever spent in his life, to make sure he looked perfect. He had something important to do now, something very important.

He called Army HQ and ordered a car. It arrived in due course, and he had the driver take him to the Chancellery. Security there was tighter than he had ever seen it, and his identification cards were not good enough. He had to give a new set of fingerprints and then wait until someone went down to the basement to check them against the fingerprint card on file. It wasn't until the officer in charge of the front lobby was satisfied as to his identity that he was asked what he wanted there.

"I wish to see General Kreutzer," he said. "He is expecting me."

Several phone calls and a ten-minute wait later, an SS Colonel came to the lobby to retrieve Koenig. The Colonel led Koenig into an elevator and down to a second or third sub-basement, then down a heavily guarded corridor. They finally stopped before a heavy door. The Colonel knocked twice and pushed the door open, respectfully nodding Koenig to enter. He shut the door behind Koenig.

There were two Wehrmacht, one Luftwaffe, and one SS General standing in the room. Koenig threw them smart salutes, which they all returned, smiling. The Generals all looked toward a high-backed chair, behind a desk, which was facing away from the doorway. After a moment, the chair swiveled, and Adolf Hitler looked up from it, smiling.

Koenig almost dislocated his arm as he shot it up and out. "Heil Hitler!" he cried.

Hitler chuckled. "Sit down, my boy, sit, relax," he said. Koenig looked around for a chair, found one, and sat, albeit stiffly. The generals assumed relaxed positions. Everyone but Koenig seemed to be having the time of their lives.

"It worked out marvelously, didn't it, Koenig?" Hitler asked.

"Jawohl, Mein Fuhrer," Koenig answered. "Just as you planned."

Hitler chuckled again, and everyone in the room seemed to feel a sudden chill in the air. "Without your superb execution, my boy, the plan would have been for naught."

Koenig hesitated, obviously wanting to say something. "Go ahead, son, out with it!" Hitler prompted.

"I—I'm sorry about the officer who I—who got killed—"

Hitler waved a hand. "Ach! An idiot! He said, out loud, mind you, he said, 'Look, I think that's my mistress over—' and then *phoom!* I have a pocketful of his brains!" Hitler laughed, and this time everyone in the room was *sure* the temperature had dropped.

"... and, sir, I ... I hope I didn't hurt you, when I ..." Koenig stammered.

"Look here, young man," Hitler interrupted, opening a lower draw in the desk. He took out something that looked like a black girdle, or the championship belt awarded in many sports. There was a depression in the belt and several cracks coming from it. "That's where the bullet hit," Hitler said, putting his finger to the depression. He put the object around the back of his neck and turned slightly, to show the assembled how it protected his upper back. "Your marksmanship was incredible, as—" he nodded to one of the generals—"General Kreutzer assured me." The general smiled and bowed slightly. "And," Hitler continued, "those—what do they call them—special effects wizards at UFA, with the blood spurting—*pooosh! pooosh! pooosh!*—all over the place ... ach! The whole thing was brilliantly plotted, magnificently carried out!"

"And ... *mein Fuhrer*, sir ..." Koenig hesitantly offered, "... the ... the plans?"

"Marvelous!" Hitler cried, throwing his hands up in the air. "The Allies are going to launch their offensives ... *too soon*. They are not ready, but they are going ahead, while our counteroffensives are ... perfect?" He raised an eyebrow at Kreutzer.

"More than perfect, *mein Fuhrer*," Kreutzer assured him.

"And then, my dear Koenig," Hitler said, leaning forward, his arms on the desk, "when I make my Lazarus-like return from the dead, and lead our armed forces myself ... can you *imagine* how our own troops will be energized, and how the Allies will be demoralized to the point of defeat, or at least be forced to sue for peace?"

Koenig allowed himself a small smile. "Everything is working out perfectly, *mein Fuhrer,* as you planned it. I'm glad to have been a part of it."

Hitler rose to his feet. Koenig and the generals sprang to attention. Looking at Koenig, Hitler addressed the other officers. "Gentlemen, would you please leave the room? I'd like to be alone with Kapitan Koenig." Each of the generals opened his mouth in question or protest, but Hitler again waved them off. "I am going to embrace this young hero," he went on, "but I don't want any witnesses. Can you believe your Fuhrer is shy, *nein?* I don't think it would serve my reputation well if I were seen hugging another man." He paused. "But this young officer won the war for us, and I just have to hug him."

With perfunctory but polite Nazi salutes, the generals all filed out of the room. There was not one who did not glance at Koenig with a mixture of envy and congratulation.

When they were alone in the room, Hitler came from behind his desk, arms outspread. "Embrace your Fuhrer," he said.

Hugging and kissing between men in Europe is as common as shaking hands is in the United States, and so Koenig unhesitatingly entered Hitler's outstretched arms. Hitler patted him on the back. Koenig was sure he could feel his skin trying to retract into the interior of his body, but he held Hitler's embrace.

After an eternity the Fuhrer broke the connection. "A drink, my boy!" he declared, "Just you and me, two heroes of *der Vaterland* sharing a toast!"

Koenig remembered rumors—quashed, *dangerous* rumors he had heard about young *Obergefreiters* Schickelgruber's activities to ease the burdens of lonely men in World War I trenches—but put them out of his mind. He watched as Hitler prepared two glasses of blackberry schnapps, and handed him one. What was next was more dangerous than taking the shot.

"*Mein Fuhrer,*" Koenig asked, pointing with his chin at the far wall, "isn't that the original National Socialist flag that you had in Munich, at the *putsch?*"

Human nature—even Hitler had some—caused the great leader to turn and look at the object in question, although he had seen it six thousand times. As he turned his head Koenig—almost blind and deaf with terror—twisted the phony ruby on the ring he wore on his right hand and emptied the few grams of white powder hidden there into Hitler's drink. Hitler turned back, smiling, and appreciated Koenig's perspicacity. They toasted, drank, and made small talk for another minute. Then, almost apologetically, Hitler escorted Koenig to the door and graciously ushered him out, letting the generals back in. Koenig gave a textbook-perfect "Heil Hitler!" as the door closed in his face. He looked at his watch: 1423 hours. If ... they ... were right, Hitler would be dead by 2:15 p.m. tomorrow.

Koenig slowly but purposefully left the building and was driven back to his apartment, where he dismissed the driver.

Three hours later, a gray-haired, gray-bearded, slovenly dressed man left the same apartment and got on one of Germany's infrequent trains, and in ten hours found himself in the seaside city of Sylt. The small fishing boat was where it was supposed to be and it stank and rocked like he thought it would, and sometime in the middle of a pitch-black night Koenig was ensconced in the basement of a house in the tiny Danish town of Grasten. The nine men and two women waiting for him almost broke his ribs with hugs and almost drowned him with tears.

"God bless you, it worked," one older man said to him, in accented German.

"Apparently," Koenig replied. Despite repeated doses of medicinal brandy, he was still shaking like a leaf. "They're all set up, waiting, like a primed mousetrap, for the Allies to begin the offensive and then— WHAM! Back from the dead comes Hitler, and the German resurgence carries the day." They all knew the plan, but they also were quite aware that Koenig had a lot of pent-up emotion to get rid of, so they let him tell them what they already knew. "But with the current low morale of the German armed forces, with the inefficient caretakers in charge, when the Allies *do* strike ... the spring on the German mousetrap will be seen to have rusted shut, ah?" Koenig allowed himself a smile, which was repeated on eleven happy faces.

"They'll roll right over those Nazi bastards, the war will be over by January," one of the other men opined.

Koenig raised his empty glass—albeit with a shaky hand—for a refill, which three people attempted to fulfill. "A toast, *meine freunde,* to the geniuses in this room, who outsmarted Hitler ... and Roosevelt, Stalin, and Churchill," he said, with a vibrato of almost uncontrollable emotion in his voice. He drained his glass of brandy with one swallow.

"No," said the older man who had blessed him earlier. "We drink to *you*, Kapitan Koenig."

Koenig smiled. "The mission is over," he said. "I can go back to being called by my real name. From now on, and forever, I am not Marke Koenig ... I am Moishe Cohen."

MERCY KILLING

BY LAURA DISILVERIO

The flesh, barely moist, weighed heavy in Carter's hand. He hefted it. A pound, maybe just over, he thought, laying it on the counter. Its cold stainless steel grazed the back of his fingers as he withdrew them. His hand landed unerringly on his knife, and he slid the blade between the flesh and the skin. They separated with a thin tearing sound. Discarding the scales, he flipped the salmon over and sliced it into even strips. The movements came automatically, soothing in their familiarity, satisfying in their precision. He draped each slice over the steamed rice, then nudged his glasses up with the back of his wrist.

"I don't know how you do it, Carter," the woman who had ordered the sashimi said. Her voice, low-pitched and accent-free, said blond, slim, well-off. Her name was Susan. He'd pegged her as forty, give or take, and looked forward to the days she came into the restaurant. She'd been eating at Little Octopus for about six months now. Sometimes, like today, with a friend over her lunch hour. Rarely, wonderfully, alone. Occasionally, in the evening, with a man Carter assumed was her husband. He spoke to her with the disinterest of someone long married. In the evenings, they took a table; now, she sat not three feet from Carter at the sushi bar, her fingers brushing his as she accepted the tray he handed over the glass display case. She thanked him, and added, "I've never seen—"

"What? A white guy making sushi?" Sam Katsumoto looked up from his station on Carter's right and brayed a laugh. The bamboo rolling mat folded over with a *snick* as his deft fingers trapped the rice, cucumber, and crab into a long, *nori*-covered cylinder.

Carter couldn't decide if it was endearing or irritating that his boss laughed as loudly now as he had the last hundred or so times he'd delivered that same line. He knew what came next and Sam didn't fail him.

"I am an equal opportunity employer," Sam said. *Chunk-chunk-chunk*. He cut the California roll. "I hire the disabled. Ha-ha! Being white is a disability." His donkey laugh cut through the chink of cutlery against plates, conversations, and the sizzle of the grill where the new hire went through his whirling cleaver shtick for a table of tourists.

"Oh, I didn't mean to sound racist," Susan said, flustered.

Carter started to assure her that he knew what she meant, but Susan's friend Erica cut him off. Carter was pretty sure she worked with Susan.

"No one thinks you're racist," Erica said, half-irritated. She lowered her voice and said, "Let your lawyers deal with him, hon. You don't need the aggravation. After what happened ... the TRO—"

Carter missed the rest of what she said, but he knew Susan was in real estate and figured they were talking about the deal that had fallen through. The last time Susan had come in alone, a couple months back, she'd had tears in her voice as she told him about a three-million-dollar deal that the buyer walked out on at the last second. The seller had blamed her, she said, had come by her office to spew obscenities, and thrown a lamp into the wall. She'd eaten her way through the eight-piece chef's choice sampler and then apologized for venting to him. He'd told her not to worry about it, that he liked listening to her, and that he knew someone who could teach the jerk-off a lesson. She'd laughed, thinking he was kidding.

"Come back tomorrow for *fugu*," Sam told the women, interrupting their conversation. "Eight courses. My supplier promises a live shipment first thing tomorrow."

"Not for me," Susan said around a mouthful of sashimi.

"Nothing to worry about," Sam assured her. "I am certified, licensed preparer of *fugu* for thirty-three years. Good Housekeeping Seal of Approval."

Erica said, "I'd like to try it. I hear it has a delicate flavor."

Carter's cell phone vibrated in his pocket. About time. He excused himself and slipped through the swinging door to the kitchen. Shrimp-scented steam dampened his forehead and bare arms as he made his way past the commercial ranges and dishwashers. Something pulpy squished underfoot but he ignored it, like he ignored the "Hey, Carter," from Sam's daughter, Aimi, who waitressed for her father on weekends. He stepped through the back door into the alley that ran behind Little Octopus and its neighbors, a used bookstore and an auto parts shop. The night air settled on his clammy skin, cooling him, and the Dumpster didn't emit its usual stench since it had been emptied that afternoon. The scrabble of claws on metal suggested a rat was searching for an overlooked morsel.

"Batman," he said into the phone, wondering whether this client thought the code name was silly or intimidating. He found the name darkly amusing. He'd been blind as a bat for six years, after all, ever since Syria.

"You should have received confirmation of the deposit this afternoon."

Carter had never met the caller, but from his reedy voice, he imagined a short, middle-aged man with a nervous habit of some kind, maybe rubbing his fingers together or pulling at the ends of a mustache. "I did."

"You got the photo, right? You're ready to move on my wife?"

"As soon as I receive the other item I asked for." Carter always required a photo from his clients, not wanting them to realize he was blind, but it was the personal item that mattered.

"Mailed Monday. It should be there. I can't imagine why you need—"

Carter cut him off. "Her schedule is still the same?"

"Yes." The man was impatient now. "The same as when we last spoke. You'll confirm with me when you've done it." It wasn't a question.

"As we arranged."

After a brief pause that felt to Carter like his client was considering asking for more details, or reassurance, the call ended. He lingered a moment, enjoying the night air, then slipped inside to finish his shift.

When the last customer had left, Carter made his way to Sam's office, where Mercy waited for him. Her tail thumped against the carpet when he came through the door and he bent to let her lick his face. "Let's go home, girl," Carter told the Lab, giving her a pat. His hand slid from her sleek fur to the rough canvas of the guide dog vest.

"G'night," he called to Sam and Aimi as Mercy towed him toward the front door, locked now.

"If you wait a minute, Carter, I could give you a ride home," Aimi offered.

Although she strove to sound offhanded, Carter heard the longing in her voice. An involuntary tightening in his groin made his step falter. For a moment, he was tempted. It had been a long time. Years. But, no. If he gave in to temptation, things would end sooner rather than later, with Aimi disappointed or angry or disillusioned. And he'd be out of a job. It wouldn't go over well with her husband, either. They might be separated, but he'd come by the restaurant two weeks ago, trying to get her to talk to him. They'd argued in Sam's office.

"Carter?" Aimi's voice held a promise, but he made himself keep moving. He needed this job for another half year. Two or three more contracts and his nest egg would be sufficient to allow him to retire to Morocco, as he'd planned since being posted there as an Embassy guard on his first assignment. The clarity of the light, the sky so blue he could drown in it, had sucker-punched him the moment he got off the plane. He'd still be able to absorb that light, he thought, even though he could no longer see it. The fact that the country had no extradition treaty with the U.S. was a plus.

"Thanks," he said over his shoulder, "but Mercy and I like the bus. We like to people watch." With a snort of self-deprecating laughter, he let Mercy lead him through the door. If Aimi was still interested, maybe he'd screw her brains out before he left the country.

Carter inhaled deeply and then blew the air out hard. It was four blocks to the bus stop and he let Mercy take the lead, fishing in his pocket for the pay-as-you-go cell phone. He stripped the sim card from it and crunched it between his teeth, spitting it out when he was satisfied it was mangled. Stopping Mercy with a tug on the halter, he set the rest of the phone down and stomped on it. It splintered beneath his heel. Cheap plastic crap. He kicked at it and a chunk skittered down the sidewalk before falling into the gutter. A car whooshed by. Carter's watch alarm beeped softly and he urged Mercy to pick up the pace, not wanting to miss the bus. The next one wasn't due for forty-eight minutes.

The next morning, Carter and Mercy got off the bus two stops away from Little Octopus so he could check his post office box. Sure enough, the clerk handed him a padded envelope. Mercy nosed it, as if asking him to tear it open, but he said, "Later. When we're home, girl." Waving his thanks to the clerk, he put the envelope in his backpack and headed toward the restaurant, walking despite the drizzle that misted his face and hair. Mercy shook herself vigorously when they arrived, then trotted into Sam's office while Carter washed his hands and put on the paper chef's cap. He exchanged greetings with Sam and the waiters, simultaneously relieved and disappointed that Aimi wasn't working the lunch shift.

Busying himself with preparing tekka maki and California rolls, Carter chatted with the early lunchers already seated at the sushi bar. He was on his own for the lunch rush, since Sam was in the kitchen with the *fugu*, the puffer fish that required great precision in its preparation to avoid spreading the poison in its entrails to the delicate flesh. Carter had tried *fugu* once, on Okinawa, shortly after he became interested in learning to prepare sushi, but hadn't thought it was worth the hype. Still, he'd been fascinated by the preparation process, and by the tetrodotoxin, or TTX, that paralyzed a victim's nervous system so he asphyxiated, fully conscious, if not hooked up to a respirator in time. One of his Navy buddies had died from eating *fugu*. Carter had been with him on leave in Kyoto, although not at the restaurant, and had seen him laid out, naked, on the stainless steel table in the morgue, his eyes staring, his lips blue. It was by no means the first body he'd seen, but it was the least violated, the most clean. No blood, no bullet holes or knife wounds, no abraded hands from trying to fight off death. Carter had stared at the body, fascinated, until the waiting policeman had prodded him for an identification.

His friend's death hadn't put him off wanting to be a sushi chef, and he'd responded to Sam's ad for an apprentice when he settled in the D.C. area after Syria. Sam had spent five years training to prepare *fugu* in Japan, before immigrating in the late 1970s. He had a special area in the kitchen for slitting open the fish and removing its entrails, and special knives he never used for anything else. He double bagged the scales and organs, sealed them, and labeled them "Poison," disposing of them as hazardous waste so no unsuspecting cat or homeless person gleaned them from the rubbish bin. Carter had volunteered early on to transport the baggies to the facility that burned the contents. Sam didn't need to know that some of the baggies never reached the incinerator.

Carter followed Mercy into their small house later that afternoon, plastic baggie of TTX-laden offal and padded envelope in his backpack. He hung the backpack on its hook by the door with Mercy's leash beside it. Since childhood, he'd been a stickler for order, organizing toys and books and clothes by color and size or purpose. His parents used to joke that he was destined for the military, and his habits had come in handy in the ships' cramped quarters. They were even more important now. Carter headed into the small laboratory he had set up in what was meant to be a second bedroom. Closed blinds discouraged peepers and an exhaust system vented any fumes through the roof. He'd told the workman who installed it that he built model airplanes and needed the fan to disperse the fumes from glues and paints. Shutting Mercy out of the room, he stripped, and slipped into the protective coverall he wore when extracting the TTX. The toxin didn't absorb through skin, but he couldn't run the risk of having Mercy lick off any particle that might adhere to his regular clothing.

Gloved, he ran his hand over the smooth glass top of the lixiviating chamber, and poked a finger against the stainless steel filter. Intact. He'd built the extractor himself, before Syria, using a paper he'd read by Chinese scientists about extracting toxins from biological tissues, and lab items he'd bought off the Internet. It was compact, intended to process small batches, but he was proud of it. His vessels, tools, and measuring vials arrayed in front of him, Carter used small tongs to lift a portion of the fish's organs into a Pyrex bowl and mashed them thoroughly. Reaching automatically for the quarter-cup measure and teaspoon, both arranged in ascending height on hooks along the shelves that rose from the counter, he added water and acetic acid to the bowl, wrinkling his nose at the vinegary smell. The solution had to soak for several hours before he could return and heat it to coagulation, add acid to adjust the pH, crystallize and dry it with vacuum pressure, and prepare it as an injectable solution. Not a complicated process, at least not for anyone with the slightest understanding of chemistry, but a long one. It would be almost twenty-four hours before he had the product he wanted.

Removing his coverall, Carter walked naked into the hall, closing the lab door behind him. Fishing in his backpack, he retrieved the envelope and carried it to the kitchen table, Mercy padding beside him, her nails clicking on the wood floors. "Need to get you to the groomer for a nail trim," he told her.

She whined.

Laughing, he patted her, and then tore open the envelope. Its contents slithered into his hands. Aah. All slick silk and spaghetti straps—a camisole. Perfect. He balled the wisp of lingerie in his hand and held it down to Mercy. The dog sniffed at it. "Good girl. You won't have any trouble finding her, will you?"

Mercy barked sharply, once, and Carter laughed again before finding a plastic baggie and sealing the cami inside. "Soon," he promised the dog. "Very soon."

The target's name was Renuart and she was a runner. According to the client, she was forty-six, five-foot-four, a hundred thirty-five pounds, with brown hair and eyes. She lived in a condo in Bethesda, attended Mass on Sunday mornings, and ran daily at six p.m. in a park two blocks from her home. She was most vulnerable during her run, Carter had decided early on, and he'd ridden the Metro to the park four times, walking the path that circumnavigated a small lake, a middle-aged man and his dog out for a little exercise, innocuous, invisible. Now he sat on the bench he had selected, fingering the syringe in his pocket.

Opening the plastic bag containing the camisole, he offered it to Mercy, with the command, "Alert." The dog snuffled at the lingerie, then stood in front of Carter, quivering with excitement. Without her, he wouldn't have been able to continue in this line of work, but her nose was more reliable at identifying targets than anyone's vision; no disguise or change in hair color or weight fooled Mercy's nose. Carter's leg jiggled and he stilled it, only to have it start up again thirty seconds later. Waiting was the hardest. Children's laughs drifted from the jungle gym on the far side of the water. His fingers caressed the slim plastic tube of the syringe, ready to pop the protective cap off as soon as Mercy let him know the woman was approaching.

Even though he was waiting for it, Mercy's sharp bark startled him. She had the woman's scent. "Seek," he told the dog, rising to his feet. He pulled the syringe from his pocket and held it cupped in his hand. The hairs on his arms and the back of his neck prickled.

Mercy pulled him forward, into the path of the woman, and, as trained, jumped playfully at the target. Carter stumbled to his knees, knowing almost everyone would stop to help a blind man up. The woman, already off-balance, thudded into him. Before she could draw back, he drove the syringe into her thigh and depressed the plunger. She gasped and staggered backward.

"Carter? What——?"

Susan's voice, scared, confused, froze him. Oh, God. He'd never known her last name, never connected her to the Susan Renuart whose husband had paid him $75,000 to kill her. He thought briefly, wildly, of phoning 911. Cops, questions, prison. He couldn't bear the thought of having his world curtailed any further. Rising, Carter reached for Susan and brushed her hip before he caught her hand. He guided her gently to the bench and maneuvered her into a sitting position. Her muscles were already stiffening; the TTX worked much faster when injected than ingested. Within a very few minutes, she'd be totally paralyzed, her lungs refusing to inflate or deflate, and she'd die of asphyxiation. The least he could do was be with her until it was over, hold her hand.

"You've killed me, haven't you?" she said. Two harsh breaths, more than the words, revealed her fear. "The last man Jacob sent failed. That damn restraining order wasn't worth the paper it was written on." Bitterness and resignation fought in her voice. "I thought ... I thought you liked me."

"I'm so sorry. I didn't know it was you." He stood in front of her, shielding her from the view of the few passersby. Usually he'd be gone by now, knowing it would be minutes, or even longer, before someone realized there was something wrong with the victim, and frequently a day or more before a doctor or medical examiner identified the cause of death.

"Are you really blind?" She mumbled the words. She shifted and a zipper rasped.

In answer, he raised his dark glasses, letting her gaze on the seared and ridged flesh burned by the acid attack in Syria.

"My God."

An explosion of sound followed her words and the bullet plowed into Carter, who jolted backward, his hands automatically covering the entry wound in his neck. A gun. The client should have told him she'd be armed, that he'd tried to kill her once before and put her on her guard. You couldn't trust anyone, Carter thought, vaguely aware of Mercy barking. He fell to his knees, blood gushing warmly through his fingers as he pitched forward into Susan's lap. Excited voices neared and Mercy whined, her cold, damp nose pushing into his hand.

Suddenly, he could see anew, the painful blue of the Moroccan sky, the glitter of sun on water, a flash of white that might have been a bird. It zipped across his field of vision and was gone. He stared after it, elated, as his blood pulsed over Susan's thigh. When the darkness came, moments later, it extinguished even the memory of seeing.

SCRUB

BY MICHAEL BAILEY

The complex is a maze of endless hallways and all of the doors are the same color, except for mine. The door is painted red, with the numbers 691 etched onto a little plaque above the keyhole. Ethan and I live on the sixth floor in the ninety-first flat. That's how the building works, with even-numbered tenants living on the right and odd ones like me on the left. A folded piece of paper waits for me as I return from work, tucked beneath the door—smashed against the mat—with a copy of a copy of a copy of my lease agreement stapled to it: page three. There's a circled section of small print near the bottom for me to read.

Our even-numbered neighbor anticipates my arrival, as usual, with his robe giving birth to a hairy beer gut. He smiles. Even though he's old enough to be my father, the oily bastard doesn't mind undressing me with his eyes while I fetch the note.

The circled text reads: "Tenants shall not modify exterior walls and/or doors." The note has scribbles telling me to return the door to its original color and provides a paint code I can take to any number of stores: 1325DS#2-66.

This isn't the first time I've come home to this type of notice, but until the stain's gone from my kitchen floor, the front door remains a vibrant, reminding red.

"Can I help you?"

"You a scrub nurse?"

I want to tell him *No, the blue scrubs are a fashion statement*, but I politely nod.

The man grins—only one side of his mouth moves, as if he'd survived a stroke. He scratches himself, turns away and enters his studio. The complex was a hotel at one time, later converted to cheap housing, so his flat's down the hall a bit, across from ours. For two months I've put up with him standing there, waiting for me when I come home from work. He asks a different question every day that doesn't need answering.

After heating a microwave dinner and forcing half of it down, I go to the kitchen floor. It haunts me, calls to me each day more than the last. The kitchen is where he died. Gunshot wound to the head. I find a new brush under the sink—the bristles on the old one are nearly gone—and go to work on removing my husband's death from the cold linoleum.

As I scrub, I see it clearly: Ethan's corpse gazing at the ceiling, a blackish-red hole above his right eyebrow, a pool of blood surrounding his head. The granite countertop and the blender and the toaster and dishes in the sink and even the faucet handle—I cleaned the blood spray from all of it after he was taken out, but his blood on the floor remains a stain.

It lifts a little more each day.

What our neighbor should ask is, "Why don't you move on?"

Not until Ethan's gone, I would say.

I clean until the brush is a light shade of pink and frayed, and then I go out to get the paint.

My job is what keeps me sane following Ethan's murder. During the day, I wear the rubber gloves, the face mask, the fancy blue hairnet, the matching uniform. Everything I do in life involves organization and cleaning messes, it seems.

I come home to the same jerk waiting outside his studio.

My door is still red.

No note this time.

No stupid question.

He wants *me* to ask the question this time, but I don't.

The next day, he's there. He wears a wife-beater and a pair of jeans with a belt trying to bury itself into the chasm of his belly button.

"Got another notice," he says.

It's wedged under my door and I ask if he put it there.

He sips his can of cheap beer with that stupid-looking smile.

"Want me to paint your door?" he says. "I don't mind doing it for you."

It sounds sincere, but I'd then owe *him* a favor.

"Please do not paint my door, and stay away from my apartment."

"Just being nice."

"Thank you, but no thank you."

He stands there as I pick up the note. It's the same message as before—the same copy of a copy of a copy of page three from our lease agreement. Ethan's name is still listed as the primary resident, I notice, as well as the circled small print near the bottom about tenants not modifying exterior walls and/or doors. The scribble tells me to return the door to its original color, like before, and provides a different paint code from before: 451MA-48.

I skip dinner this time and work on the kitchen floor before going out to get the paint.

"Another notice?"

It's another one of his questions that doesn't need answering.

"Please, I don't need this right now."

We lost a patient in the ER, so my day isn't off to a great start. It was an extensive operation involving two surgeons and took most of the day. I was in charge of draping and gloving the team, blood irrigation and monitoring blood loss for the patient, as well as counting needles, sponges and sterilizing instruments. A really long day.

"I asked you to stay away from my apartment."

He points to his door, fewer than ten feet away.

"Don't you ever get tired of seeing them under your door," he says, "those notes?"

I do. I come home to my door each day and am reminded of

Ethan. I want to paint over the red and move on. Instead, I come home to the same red door, the same note, the codes.

The paint codes are really just that: codes.

1325DS#2-66 stands for 1325 D Street, Apt. 2. The number 66 tacked onto the end of it is simply the last two digits of the zip code. Not rocket science. The second address of 451MA-48 translates to 451 Morris Avenue, different part of the city.

My neighbor wants me to talk.

I don't want to. I don't want to talk about the lease agreement and the fake message about painting the door in case someone else reads it. I want to go inside and scrub. I want to forget that Ethan died because I once received a notice wedged under my door with a paint code of 101FR#691-70. This one stood for 101 Feagleship Road, Studio 691: our studio apartment.

I put a bullet through Ethan's head.

It was a lot of money.

The bloodstain on the kitchen floor calls for me.

Soon I'll be able to paint the door and move on, but not until Ethan's gone.

I sign for an overnighted FedEx box that contains fifteen thousand in unmarked messy bills to cover the last two jobs. The package is an Amazon box with a return address of someplace a thousand miles away. I'm not even sure where the money comes from, only that it's never late, and is laundered and shipped from a phony company called ABC Books. Books hide the money well. Inside, I find a stack of hollowed Bibles with the pages cut out to make room for the cash. Sometimes they're Bibles. Sometimes they're encyclopedias. On a Post-it stuck to the inside of the first book is a name to verify against the next coded address waiting for me at my door: JAMES PILCHEN.

The Internet gives me directions to his house, and his Facebook profile is public. He lives seven miles away and I've seen his face. That's all I need—or want—to know about him.

I twist the silencer onto the barrel of my Colt .38 and check the chamber before sliding the gun into my concealment holster.

My neighbor doesn't greet me when I leave.

In less than fifteen minutes my car is parked half a block down from the decoded address for James Pilchen. Surgical gloves wait for me in the glove box. Ten grand for this guy.

I sit in the car reading a Repairman Jack novel on my Kindle and lower the digital book every few pages over the course of several hours. James has a yapping dog in the living room that yaps even louder when a black Mercedes pulls up the driveway. He's got a wife, a trunk full of groceries, a little girl in a paisley dress.

Ethan wanted kids.

I drink at a bar called The Stagger Inn until I shouldn't drive, and then I stagger out.

A text message on my phone from several hours ago reads: "When you're out, you're out" from an unlisted number.

It can only mean one thing.

I should be arrested for driving while intoxicated, or should have at least crashed along the way, but manage to turn onto Feagleship Road and make it to the complex in one piece.

The maze of endless hallways smells like paint, and my door matches all the others in the apartment building. Even over the alcohol, I can smell it. The door is painted eggshell white with the numbers 691 etched onto a little plaque above the keyhole. A folded piece of paper waits for me, tucked beneath the door—smashed against the mat—with a copy of a copy of a copy of my lease agreement stapled to it: page three. Ethan's name is crossed out on this one. There's a circled section of small print near the bottom for me to read, but I already know what it says. I've read it a dozen times. I'm concerned with the paint code, which I've also seen before: 101FR#691-70.

My neighbor is not there to greet me. He has no more rhetorical questions for me to answer and is done sliding notes underneath my door.

I go inside, but not to scrub. I go inside to paint the kitchen floor.

THE WELLMASTER'S DAUGHTER

BY JAMES S. DORR

Touila ... Toufourine ... Oum el Asel. From there, six days journey to Bir Ounane. And who am I, who camps in this wadi, surrounded by the stinking corpses of camels? I am the master of Bir Ounane.

From there, five parched days more to El Mraiti. These are the links that hold the caravan routes together—the wells in the desert within the Great Desert. These are the pearls that Allah has cast in the midst of the furnace, lest men should come to forget His mercy.

I am but a man—a just man, I think. Yet a man who has lived his whole life in the desert.

I have no mercy.

I had a daughter whose name was Zumur'rad, the Jewel of the Desert. I named her myself and, after my wife died, I raised her alone at Bir Ounane. I taught her the values of the oasis and of the desert: About the camel trains that came to us and why, when spring's briefness gave way to summer, most ceased their travel. About Allah's grace that made me a wellmaster, serving at the Caid's pleasure, and made her my daughter.

And always she would have me say more.

"Tell me, Ab'sahib—Lord and Father—about the sands of the Erg Sekkane," she would ask as we sat in the evening, washed in the final light of the sun. "Tell me about the crescent sands, and how they strive to mount even the rock cliffs until all is covered. Tell me as well of the great star dunes, and how they rise to reach the height of two hundred men." We would listen awhile to the far off wind, and I would then tell her about the djinn of the trackless desert, away from even the caravan routings, and how they pleased Allah as I in turn pleased my earthly master, I by doling out water to travelers and they by proclaiming the Lord of All's might.

"And tell me," she would ask yet again, "about the wadis. Tell me about the phantom rain." And again we would listen and I would explain why the desert grows hot—so hot in summer that when storm clouds come, such rain as they carry boils back to the sky before reaching its surface. And how the wadis—the burnt remains of what once had been rivers—thus stay bone dry until a second cloud follows the first, discharging *its* water onto a ground that, even if thirstier now than before, at least has been cooled enough to receive it.

And so we would often continue to sit the entire night through, I speaking, she learning, beneath patterned stars so bright one could touch them.

We spent our time that way until her twelfth spring.

I have met the Caid. He has a palace near the ocean which he departs from only twice every fourteen years. On one of these journeys he visits his cities along the rivers and by the sea, making sure they are garrisoned strongly, while, on the other, he enters the desert.

On this second journey, seven years after the first is completed, he visits the wells. He checks to be sure that his commerce is flowing—to see with his own eyes that what his soldiers, who visit the wells every two or three seasons, have told him is true. It is on this journey that he makes sure that tools and seed, and fresh, healthy camels, and such other things the wellmasters need to tend their oases are being supplied. It was on this journey that he met me.

My daughter had scarcely known five springs when the Caid arrived at Bir Ounane. She does not remember the way he greeted me like a friend. The way he confirmed me as his wellmaster and later, as we drank tea together, told me that when he arrived again, in fourteen more years, he would see that Zumur'rad had a husband.

She does not remember the way we spoke of many things in the perfumed shade of the Caid's pavilion. And so she would ask me, when she became twelve:

"'Sahib," she would say, "tell me about the Caid's palace beyond the desert. Tell me about the cities he visits, and what the ocean is like that he lives by."

And I would tell her what he told me, about the djinn of the ground and the water. I would explain how, in parts of the world, the water lies beneath rock and sand—as it does in our desert—but yet, in other parts, through Allah's mercy, these djinn change position.

"And this is what the Caid called the ocean?" she would ask further. "This changing position. How can such things be?"

"For Allah," I would say, "it is as easy as blinking one's eye." I would have her be silent and we would listen to the earth's murmur beneath the sand, and then I would tell her how rivers of water flowed under the ground, to feed wells such as ours. But elsewhere, such rivers flowed on the surface, and fed not wells, but vast basins of water that stretched as far as a man could see.

I would repeat what the Caid had told me, about dunelike waves that moved through the water, about dust-like ripples that washed on the shore. I would tell of the storms, when the djinn of the air fought those of the water, and how they were feared more than even the storms we knew in the desert—the storms where sand would sweep up to the sky and the sun's face would blacken. And she would weep then.

"Tell me not about storms on the desert," she would say, "nor about an ocean that frightens me more. Tell me instead about the gardens. The cities where the caravans come from and where they go. Tell me about the things of beauty."

At those times I would wipe Zumur'rad's tears away on the hem of my own sleeve. I would then describe, in a gentle voice, how the caravan routes came out of the desert into a land filled with trees and flowers, no matter what season. How birds would sing when the camel drivers arrived at a river, and how that river would flow to the ocean, its waters sweeter than even the honey the caravans' merchants sometimes gave to her when they passed by us. I would describe to her how, where the water was at its sweetest, men built vast cities of emeralds and gold; and how they built palaces out of marble as white as milk, with roofs and domes and turrets so thick the sun couldn't reach through; and how the air within these great halls was at all times as cool as the water of Bir Ounane in the first days of springtime.

Zumur'rad would smile then.

By Allah's grace, the world lies in layers. Layers of sand over layers of water. Layers of heat. Even the phantom rain is a layer—a layer of promise above the dry desert. A promise fulfilled with the second rain.

And so, in this wadi, I bury my camels beneath the sand. I have little strength—my leg has been wounded and even now festers—but I do not have to bury them deeply. A hand's-breadth or two beneath the surface, the ground is cool enough for insects and worms to burrow. A hand's-breadth of sand sprinkled over the corpses protects from the sun.

I work on my knees. When my work is completed, I dig a trench, also, to fit my own body. A place I can lie in relative coolness, conserving the moisture that keeps me alive.

By Allah's grace, thus might I endure forever.

I think about layers—how even a child's growth is patterned in layers. How even trade changes. When Zumur'rad reached her fifteenth spring, the nature of the goods that came by us was different from what it had been in past years.

When once the caravans had carried iron tools from the north, and brought back ivory and spices, many now carried weapons for trading and brought back slaves. And these were larger than most camel trains. As well as the camel and caravan-masters, the boys—apprentices—who swept dung for the evening fires, the cargomaster when one was needed, the slavers' caravans also had guards.

In part for this reason, the slavers were shunned by those who knew more of the ways of the desert. In part they were shunned because slaving is evil—because Allah punishes those who would deal in their fellow men. And yet they continued.

So worried was I about these changes, I did not realize that the nature of Zumur'rad's questions had changed as well.

This time she asked: "Why is slaving evil? Why, if the slavers gain riches from it, do others insist that Allah disdains it?" And I tried to tell her about men's suffering, and death in the desert. About the maltreatment of human cargo by men who sought too great and too fast a profit.

I tried to explain this by telling her stories—unpleasant stories—of Allah's wrath. Of one caravan, in ancient times when they carried slaves too, that was led by inexperienced masters into a sandstorm, cargo and all; and how, unlike the storms of the Caid's ocean, this storm sucked it dry. How it stands to this day in the Erg Iguidi, beyond the well of Oum el Asel, as a silent warning, its camels and slaves and guards and drivers all turned into statues. Their flesh hard as stone.

And I told her that these were the fortunate ones—in Allah's mercy, their deaths were at least swift. That there were other caravans whose masters allowed their camels to sicken until, still days from the nearest well, they could go no farther.

And she interrupted. "Tell me not about death," she said, "but about those who live to enjoy the riches they gain from such cargo. Tell me about the things they buy, the places they live, when they have enough wealth, far away from the desert."

I looked at her when she asked these questions, and saw, for the first time, how much she had grown. I tried to explain how Allah punishes, in the long run, *all* who traffic in evil. She would not listen.

"Tell me," she demanded instead, "why the Caid wishes to stop the slave trade." I had no answer—I had not known.

I asked her how she had heard such things and she answered with yet another question.

"Tell me about men."

Spring had ended. Summer was on us and, because of the heat of the season, all caravans had ceased their travel. And so I told Zumur'rad about men.

I told her of the Caid's promise and how, if she would be patient for only a few years more, a man would be found who would be worthy of her. She would have a husband, and I a partner to help in my old age.

And yet she defied me.

"I will not wait for your Caid's man," she said when I had finished speaking. "I have gotten a lover already. His name is Bes'fariq and he is the leader of one of the largest slave caravans—it was he who told me about the Caid. And when we are married, unlike the man *you* would choose for my husband, he will not force me to stay in the desert."

Spring had ended. The wind had shifted, the burning wind from the south combating the final remnants of air from the north—from the Caid's ocean. This was the time when such clouds that were seen— high, mist-like wraiths above the Hamada, the rock-crowned plateau that separates the Erg Sekkane from Oum el Asel—produced sudden downpours but no lasting rain. When the true water that comes to the desert, through layered rock underneath the dry courses of ancient rivers, had slowed to a trickle.

This was the time when even the sparse green jewels of Allah—the wells that break through the desert's surface—have seen the grass that surrounds them turn yellow, the flowers die and the trees fold their leaves, and so there was little that I could do but pray that one of the Caid's supply trains would come in the fall. I would then send Zumur'rad north to his palace in hopes he could find her a husband right then—even a husband who would not wish to apprentice himself to me at Bir Ounane. But there were no caravans that fall, nor during the winter or early spring of the following year.

Until, finally, Zumur'rad was sixteen.

Again, spring was ending. Again, the winds battled when, out of the north, from Oum el Asel, a caravan came. Zumur'rad ran out with a dipper of water to the lead camel, offering it to the rider who swung down. The water consumed, the rider took Zumur'rad into his arms

210

and kissed her as if they had been long married, then brought her back to me.

"Old man," he said, "my name is Bes'fariq. You may as well know that I deal in slaves."

"I have seen you before," I answered. "In past years I have given you water—that is my job. But is it not too late in the season for seeking slaves? Or do you intend to spend the whole summer south of the desert, and bring your cargo back in the fall?"

The rider turned and conversed with Zumur'rad, speaking in whispers, then motioned to his fellows to dismount. "It is late in the evening, old man," he finally said when he turned back to me. "My men are thirsty and need to be fed. We will leave in the morning."

"To spend the whole summer south of the desert?" I asked again. I looked at my daughter, pressed close to his side, and purposely spoke in mocking tones. "Slavers spend weeks to gather their cargos—even such prosperous slavers as you—and by then it would be too hot to cross back with such a burden."

"Not to spend the summer, old man," Bes'fariq said, his voice rising in anger. "Nor to seek slaves—at least not for this journey." He paused and twisted again for a moment, to ask a question of one of his men, and Zumur'rad continued.

"There has been a war," she said—she did not call me Lord and Father. "Your Caid attempted to put down the slavers and they have revolted. Bes'fariq goes south to join an army that's already gathered at El Mraiti, to bring it back north."

"To bring it back north, with the first heat of summer, and push the Caid into the ocean," Bes'fariq added, again at her side. "We will ride on the edge of the wind, old man. At the very end of the caravan season, stopping only to refill our waterskins, in order to strike when we're least expected." He lowered his gaze and looked at Zumur'rad, then back to me.

"And she will ride with us."

"No!" I shouted. I pushed myself between him and my daughter. Grappled with him. Saw—from the corner of an eye—the hot flash of metal.

I twisted and lunged—felt pain sear my thigh.

And looked at my daughter. Saw how she had stabbed me.

I had no daughter.

I looked at the knife. Looked up at Zumur'rad from where I had fallen.

Watched as the blood—the water and flesh that had bound us together—dripped from her hand.

I wake in the desert, stiff in my trench, my nostrils filled with the odor of half-rotted camels—the three already sickened camels Bes'fariq gave me. I heard him talking when I woke *that* morning at Bir Ounane, discussing the camels with the man he had questioned before. I woke in the hut where I keep summer fodder for my own beasts and heard Zumur'rad join their conversation. It was she who suggested the camels be given to me.

"He fears the desert," she told Bes'fariq. "He fears the slow dying. Therefore let him ride one of these as far as it takes him. Let him have the others as well. You have no need for them."

"That is true," her lover replied. "The ones we have gotten at Oum el Asel, plus the ones we have here, will be more than sufficient. But what if he does not go into the desert? What if he stays here, where there is at least water?"

It was Zumur'rad who kicked the door open and looked down at me where I lay on the ground. She inspected the wound she had given me the night before, looked approvingly at the signs that it had already begun to fester.

She nodded and turned back to Bes'fariq. "Give him a shovel before he sets off—he has several here that he uses to clear the well after sandstorms. Give him a choice. He may go into the desert and dig his own grave, or, if he stays here ..."

Bes'fariq cut her off with a laugh. "Or, if he stays here," he finished for her, "I will kill him when we return, more slowly than even the desert might kill him, and cut his body into pieces. I will then strew them across the desert, so widely that not even Allah will find them to bring them to heaven. If that is your meaning, then you *are* worthy of me, Zumur'rad."

I raised my head. "You would desecrate my corpse?" I asked. "What kind of man are you?"

"Then you have heard what we said, old man—you know what is expected. As for me, I am a strong man. A man who takes from wellmasters like you. Do you understand me?"

"You have taken from *other* wellmasters?" I whispered my horror. *"You would blaspheme Allah by raiding His gardens?"*

"You do understand me. We leave as soon as our camels are saddled. In five days time we will reach El Mraiti and join with my army. We will rest one day, then make our return, arriving back here on the eleventh day after this morning. Do you see those clouds?"

I looked out the hut's door to where he pointed and saw wisps of cloud high above to the north. Empty clouds, but, when one sees the first whiteness, he always hopes that others may follow. I did not speak, but only nodded.

"Good," he said. "Those clouds will have long disappeared when eleven days have passed. You will be like those clouds—do you understand me?"

I nodded again. "You will leave water bags and food—my knife and my clothing—along with a shovel and three dying camels. Enough to allow me to get as far, perhaps, as the Hamada before the beasts perish."

"You do understand me," he said as before. He smiled and put his arm around Zumur'rad's waist, and led her outside to where his men waited.

Ten mornings ago I left Bir Ounane. In two days time I reached this wadi and slaughtered my camels, then made my camp. I buried my camels, the better to let their flesh grow putrescent. Away from the drying rays of the sun.

I dug my own grave.

I lie in it this morning, the stench of my camels—already nearly dead from their sickness before I killed them—assailing my nostrils. It vies with the rot of my own wounded leg, a rot that has long since spread itself into the rest of my body. I lie and wait, gazing north toward the Hamada, where new wisps are forming.

I think about layers. And second rains.

The phantom rain already fell this morning, boiling the stench and the rot into steam. The morning before Bes'fariq's army is due to return, weak with thirst from its own desert journey.

I think about layers—I dreamed of my daughter last night while I slept.

Except I have no daughter.

I look at the sky.

And the second rain hisses above the Hamada—it ends in moments, but this time the ground has been cooled to receive it. To let it puddle and gather and swirl on the rocky plateau. To spill into the wadi ...

I hear a humming, still far in the distance—the sound that water makes moving on sand. A trickle, a flood, that will take my life's spirit—the rot of my body—the stench of my camels—the poison and death that Zumur'rad left to me.

And give it all unto the thirsty djinn who, by Allah's grace, lie under the wadi, jealously guarding the ancient course that feeds the well of Bir Ounane.

WISH I'D NEVER MET YOU

BY JONATHAN TEMPLAR

She'd suggested they meet in a small cafe somewhere away from the main shopping mall in a town he'd never heard of, and Warwick had agreed, quietly impressed by her choice of venue.

It was the sort of nondescript, backwater hole he'd have picked himself, and when he arrived it didn't disappoint. The coffee was served in mugs that had more rings than a Hollywood trophy wife. The special of the day was a tuna sandwich, would always be a tuna sandwich, and it would never, ever be anything remotely special.

Warwick ordered it anyway.

She was out of place here but, to her credit, tried not to let it show *too* much. Her cup had the faint smudge of another's lipstick on the rim, and she dabbed at it with a tissue and swallowed her disgust.

"Are you really sure you understand the implications of this?" Warwick asked her.

She nodded her head. She had a sad face, but one that wasn't naturally sad, had been made so by the events that had brought her to this midday liaison. She would be pretty when she remembered to smile again, or when the things that stopped her smiling had been prevented from happening in the first place.

"Of course," she said, but softly, as if she wasn't sure at all. They never were, in Warwick's experience. They would take the leap, they would contact him, plan to engage his services but they'd never really understand what it was they were considering, what the full effect of their decision would be.

As long as they paid in full, Warwick rarely cared, but he believed that it was always in his own best interests to ensure that his clients knew as much as he could explain to them.

"If you say yes to this, it'll unwind the last five years of your life. This guy, this ..." he struggled for the name, having heard it only the one time and not caring enough to remember it.

"M—Mark," she said with a stammer, a fresh tear in her eye.

"Mark. He'll never meet you. I'll find him and take him out at some point before you were ever due to meet him. You'll never even know there was a Mark, your life will go off in another direction, and you'll never know the difference."

"Okay," she said.

"You sure? Coz you need to remember that I can't guarantee *which* direction your life will go in. Everything that happened to you in the last five years will change. You can't pick and choose; if you decide you want Mark dead before you met him, then you reboot. Everything goes, what replaces it might be better, might be worse, but you can't choose."

She straightened up in her cheap plastic chair, looked at Warwick with a new resolution. "You want to know what he did to me, what he did to my life?"

"I don't want to know *anything*. There's a man out there walking around with a history. You pay me and I'll go back and take him out five years ago, and everything he has done since then will never happen. I'd rather not know too much about what I'm wiping out, thanks all the same."

"He's a bastard, he's a cheat, he's a liar and I can't live one more day without him. I was going to kill myself, you know? I had a bottle of pills and a bottle of vodka and I was all set to end it all. But I couldn't do it and you know why? Because I hate the taste of vodka. If I'd had some rum in the house, I'd be dead by now. And then I heard all about you. And I figured, well, the son of a bitch left *me*, why shouldn't *I* get another chance, why should I be the one to die?"

216

"Look, I really don't care. You pay me what I ask, I don't care if he's the fucking patron saint of sunshine and puppy dogs, he'll have been dead for five long years."

"You're asking for a lot of money," she said. "It's everything I have. More."

"See, this is where you're making me think you don't understand the principles involved in this at all. I take this guy out, then this is all money you've never earned, or borrowed, or stolen, however the fuck you get it. It's money that never existed."

"Then how—"

He raised a hand to silence her. There were tricks of his trade that he was never prepared to discuss with an outsider, even someone who, for all intents and purposes, would no longer exist after he'd completed the job he was being paid to do. The temporal trickery of the bank of Tempus Frugal was something even Warwick couldn't get his head around. All he knew was that any money paid to him for an assassination sat snugly in his account regardless of the continued existence of the person who had paid it in, earning interest from a decade before it had been deposited. 'Off-shore' didn't even begin to cover it. Temporal tax laws were literally being rewritten every day since the breakthrough.

She chewed a few seconds up, pondering it all one last time.

"Do it," she said, and pushed the dirty coffee mug away.

She even paid the bill.

Five years ago

She'd told Warwick, with as little detail as he wanted, that she'd met the man she'd married on April 11 at the marina.

This was all he needed.

He'd submitted it to the Guild and they'd run Mark Scropan's name through the time lines, found nothing that would cause too much damage if he was terminated prematurely, and therefore sanctioned the hit. It had taken little research to track him back from the spot he was due to meet her to a specific hotel and a specific room. He'd been in town for a business deal, the two of them had met by accident after a bird had shit on her shoulder and he stopped to help her clean up the mess, the sort of story that might in other circumstances have sounded charming but felt like more than Warwick would have chosen to know.

It would be an act of kindness the guy would never have the chance to share.

It would have been easy to execute him at the marina; it was a confirmed physical sighting so Warwick knew he would definitely be there, and it was an open area with a variety of vantage points. There was no risk of being apprehended; as soon as the target was executed Warwick would shift back to his contemporaneous moment five years into the future. Any trace evidence, from DNA to shell casings, that was left behind would be of no concern—it technically didn't exist yet.

But Warwick liked to do things quietly and with minimal attention unless he was specifically paid to do otherwise. So he'd decided on one bullet in the back of the head before his target even left the hotel. Clean, swift, merciful.

It was a nice hotel, swanky. But like many swanky things, the surface sheen hid a lot of defects. The guy on the door for one, who Warwick figured he could have skipped past dressed in a tutu at the head of a river dance and not been picked out of a subsequent line up. Lax security was good, a decent elevator service was even better, and wouldn't you know it, he got both. He was carried in an elegance of mirrors and Muzak up to the tenth floor, fingering his concealed Luger all the way like it was a budding erection in his pocket.

Warwick found the right room, opened it with something clever that hadn't been invented yet, and stepped into a yellow gloom created by heavy curtains and soft lighting. He pulled out the Luger, hugged the wall with his back, and slid along the narrow entrance hall into the main room.

Mark Scropan was still in the king-sized bed, facing away and covered by the crisp hotel sheets. Warwick had hoped for this, hoped to reduce any potential drama down to nothing. He crept over to the bed, raised the gun, and put a bullet into the head that dozed beneath.

He knew straight away he'd fouled up.

The sound was wrong, the sad *phut* of the bullet passing through not bone and brain matter but cotton and goose feather. His eyes became more accustomed to the light and he saw that he had been a fucking idiot to ever think this was the shape of a man before him rather than a quickly assembled golem made of pillow and cushion.

218

"Shit," Warwick hissed, and then heard the altogether louder retort of someone else's weapon. The shot took him in the shoulder, reducing the bone to ruin. Warwick spun with the impact, his Luger falling from his compromised hand to the thick weave of the luxury carpet.

There was another man in the room, dressed in sleek black and holding a semi-automatic of a design that Warwick didn't recognize, more advanced than anything he'd ever seen. He could tell from the man's aura that he didn't belong in this time either. He'd come from further forward than even Warwick had.

Warwick's knees felt wobbly, but he was determined to stay upright.

"*He* sent you, didn't he? Scroton? Had the same idea as my client. I didn't think the boy had it in him." His shoulder hurt furiously, but he realized it wouldn't matter for long.

The man with the gun shook his head. "Don't know nothing about no boy, pal. This is all coz of a girl, a girl you ain't never gonna meet no more."

And then Warwick knew what had passed through the minds of everyone he'd assassinated over the course of the last two years, the confusion, the despair, the sudden realization that a future they were supposed to live through, a future that they *had* lived through, was now being shut down at the source.

And then the only thing to pass through his mind was made of hot lead.

Mark Scroton strolled happily onto the marina, enjoying the kiss of the sun on his face, no longer quite so bothered by the palaver at the hotel. He'd been forced to switch rooms at a moment's notice due to some 'unforeseen' problem with the plumbing or some shit; it was all a bit vague. But on a beautiful day, such things never mattered for long. The seagulls were out in force today, circling overhead and threatening to dump on anything that dared to step foot beneath them.

Mark believed that even that would be unlikely to ruin his mood.

Mina watched him pass, thought that he looked far more handsome than she was used to seeing him, minus the five years of a relationship that would break his heart and, ultimately, his wallet.

These moments were always disconcerting, the knowledge that a person you had met, spoken to, come to a business arrangement with, would never recognize you ever again, even though you had grown rich from their purse. She was still quite new to this; she'd only discovered she was Temporally Advantaged a little over a year ago, so the novelty had yet to wear off. She wondered if it ever would, and she certainly hoped so.

Scroton strolled off toward the nearest row of boats, hands in his pockets and a smile on his face. Mina had been here for hours, safe in the knowledge that he wouldn't be meeting his future wife today, that fate had already intervened to make that impossible.

Well, not fate perhaps. The bonnet of Mina's stolen Prius.

Mark's no-longer-future-wife would spend a long few months having her legs carefully pinned back together rather than taking long moonlit walks, but at least she was alive. He had stipulated that. She was a money-grabbing whore, he had told Mina at great and colorful length, and he wished that he had never met the bitch, but he didn't want her dead.

This suited Mina. She always tried to arrange these interventions, these assassinations of the future, without ending a life. The Guild frowned on it at first, she figured because it always meant a little more work to configure alternate time lines that accommodated a living subject rather than the absence of a dead one, but they always sanctioned her jobs eventually.

She'd hung around because of her last visit to the Guild and the impression she'd got from the time clerk that he'd seen the details of this particular job before, that the names and the scenario had been familiar to him. They wouldn't say, never did, but Mina thought that someone else was going to be here today. That the wife had the same idea as the husband, that she too had decided to abort the relationship before it was born. There would be another assassin here, one hired to take down Mark Scroton. She wouldn't interfere, even though Mark was her client. That would be unethical. But she was curious all the same. Wanted to see another of her trade in action, perhaps learn a few tricks for future reference. She rather hoped it was that Warwick guy she'd met one time at the Guild chambers. He had made *quite* the impression.

But Mina had been wrong; for once her instincts had let her down. Mark Scroton went about his business in peace, not meeting any shit-covered women or gun-toting assassins. He even brought himself an ice cream.

Mina got up from the wall she had been perched on and prepared to go home, back to the future, a suddenly richer future thanks to a fortune that Mark Scroton would never know he'd paid her.

And then she had a flash. It happened now and again, was an unwelcome consequence of being Temporally Advantaged. The time lines were shifting, a new future was being mapped and Mina was at its epicenter.

But the images that flashed across the back of her mind were not of Mark Scroton and the girl with the broken legs. It was Mina herself, and the man she'd just been thinking of fondly, Warwick. Meeting here, at this very spot, working on the same couple from different sides. And agreeing to a drink back in their contemporaneous moment.

And then ... it was like a slide show on fast-forward—there was sex, *lots* of sex, and then there were children, and a family, and grandchildren, *so many* grandchildren, and they had children as well, an empire of them and *oh*, the things that they were going to build. Things that so many others would want to break down, would go to any lengths to shatter. Hire anyone that could promise to end it before it started. Hire someone like her.

And it would all start right here, and right now.

Only ...

Then the flash was gone, and she remembered none of it, as it had never existed and was never going to exist. But, for a long time afterwards, Mina found herself poking at the back of her mind as if she had a cavity in her memories, a hole that should have been filled but would always be empty.

And sometimes, just for a moment, she would remember a face. A man's face.

But she had no idea who he was.

THE BLUELIGHT SPECIAL

BY J. CARSON BLACK

Manfred "Mickey" Finn wasn't what you'd call bipolar, except in his vocation of choice: racing thoroughbreds. He made his living not in the middle but in the poles apart—the highest of the high and the lowest of the low. He had strings of claimers all over the Midwest and played the game to perfection, knowing when to claim a horse and when to drop him in class and when to unload him altogether. His horses all looked like a million dollars, but none of them was worth much, except one.

But what a One—the blue-blooded phenom, Avatar. Mickey went in on the horse with some pals as a lark, and the animal turned out to be a world-beater. Better yet, Avatar was great in the sack, siring a dynasty of speedy racehorses with just enough stamina to get them through the lucrative spring prep races before they went lame. After that it was on to the breeding shed, where they passed on their unsoundness to future yearling sales toppers.

Avatar's stud fee was $200,000 a pop. Mickey Finn kept a good-sized chunk of him, which was the smartest thing he ever did.

But he continued to run a platoon of broken-down claiming horses. In sheer numbers, his horses dominated every low-level track in the nation's breadbasket, generating hundreds of thousands of dollars and making him all-time leading money-winning owner at five different tracks. His theory was, you put a thousand monkeys on a thousand typewriters and even if you don't get Shakespeare, you can eventually hit the Pick 6. Plus, Mickey was a ladies' man, and the girls loved hanging off his arm in the winner's circle.

All this Cyril Landry knew as he parked on the cobblestones outside Finn's red-brick colonial-style mansion. Nice day, a postcard of Kentucky in the spring. Blue skies, chestnut trees throwing down dark shawls on a green lawn. Mickey's house was on a hill, of course, overlooking miles of pasture. Landry knew the stallion, Avatar, was not in any of the fields here. He lived just down the road at Stoney Bridge Farm. Even though Stoney Bridge Farm wasn't open to the public, Landry had taken the tour. Avatar didn't look any different from any of the other stallions at the stud farm. He was fat like the rest of them and bay-colored. No markings to distinguish him and not much personality, either.

Mickey Finn answered the bell. Landry knew he would, because Mickey prided himself on running his own show. He had bodyguards, but they were discreet. Had to be, so as not to scare Mickey's girls. Mickey told the blonde who was with him to "go shopping or something," and they sat on the wide veranda overlooking the gamboling mares and foals.

"You said you had a prospect for me," Mickey said.

"Actually, that's not really true."

"It's not? I thought you were a bloodstock agent."

"No, I'm actually not." Landry crossed one knee over the other. "I'm here to talk about Therese Hill."

First, a look of alarm. "What is this? Are you a reporter or something? A blogger? I'm too busy for this kind of thing. You're out of here, bud. Raul!"

"Raul's busy."

Mickey Finn had one thing going for him—a certain animalistic cunning. He figured out pretty quickly that Raul wasn't coming. He knew Teddy wasn't coming, either. Pure instinct—Landry could see it in his eyes.

"What do you want?" Mickey demanded.

"First, let me give you the stakes." Landry switched one knee over the other. Aware of a twinge in his back. For all that money, Mickey

Finn didn't bother with comfortable chairs. "Are you familiar with *The Godfather?*"

"The movie?" Mickey's small eyes flitted around his plump face like goldfish in a bowl. "Are you threatening me?"

Landry said nothing.

"You trying to scare me by threatening my life? Let me tell you, pally, I don't scare."

Landry said nothing.

"Don't you friggin' threaten me. The last person who did that ended up in the hospital."

Landry reminded him, "Therese Hill."

Mickey Finn went quiet. Eyes jiggling right and left.

"Therese," Landry said again, his voice neutral. "Hill."

"Nothing to talk about. I'm not responsible for every spill that happens at Dogwood Park, no matter what you've heard. It's a shame, it really is, and I feel sorry for her and her family. But it has nothing to do with me."

"She has hospital bills."

"I guess she would. These people, they don't have health insurance. They don't think ahead. They just live from hand to mouth, from ride to ride, and all of 'em think they're going to be the next Jerry Bailey. But they won't be. They're a dime a dozen."

"You know she has a little girl?"

Finn's face suffused with red, like mercury climbing up a thermometer. "Plenty of race riders have little girls. So what? She made the wrong move, she gambled and she lost. It happens. You don't see the stewards coming after me. The horse was vet-ready. End of story. Time for you to go, pal."

"I will after you wire $400,000 to Therese Hill."

"Are you nuts? No way I'm doing that! You're crazy to even say such a thing."

"Two hundred thousand dollars. That's how much one mating to Avatar is. Just one. I figure he services about 200 mares here in Kentucky, and then he's shuttled down to the southern hemisphere for another 200. That's a lot of $200,000 checks. I think you can spare just two. One for each hemisphere."

"It's not all my money! Don't you understand finances? I can't lay my hands on that kind of money, and I wouldn't lay my hands on that kind of money. Not for some lowlife girl jockey who got herself into trouble because she tried to go through the wrong hole! Teddy! Get your ass out here! Teddy! Where the hell are you? Come here!" He reached for his cell phone.

Landry pulled a key with a plastic tag on it from his pocket. On the tag was a number and the words LAKELAND STORAGE, Versailles, Kentucky. "If you're looking for Raul and Teddy, you'll need this."

Finn blanched. "They're dead?"

Landry looked at his watch. "It's ten a.m. now. I'll be back sometime tomorrow. By then I'll have the account for the wire transfer—$400,000."

He walked down the cobblestone drive. Finn was stabbing numbers into his phone. He was also looking at the license plate, prominently displayed on the Touareg Landry was driving.

But no one would ever see the Touareg again, nor find its owner, and Mickey Finn could call God himself and it wouldn't get him out of this fix.

"The police are on their way!" Finn yelled as Landry ducked into the Touareg. "You'll be caught before you leave this property!"

"See you tomorrow," Landry said. "Don't forget."

Landry's brother stabled his horses nearest the Horseman's Entrance at Dogwood Park. There was a little swatch of grass where he took his horses out to graze in the afternoons, and a picnic table where Therese Hill—"Terry"—liked to have a smoke while she waited for her little girl to come back from school.

She and Landry were sitting there now. Terry wanted to introduce him to someone she'd met the day before.

The guy's name was Steve. He was an exercise rider at Ellis Park.

"Tell him what you told me," Terry said.

"I heard about the spill," Steve said. "But I didn't know or maybe I just forgot who the horse was. Then when I came here, I realized who it was."

Terry blew smoke, her eyes drifting to the horseman's gate, searching for the school bus. Her daughter, Moira, would be coming any minute. "Tell him how you knew the horse."

Steve flicked an ash from his cigarette and rubbed it into his jeans. "I rode him in the mornings. He was a nice horse. Greg Snipes, the trainer, was also the owner. Horse was on his way up the claiming ranks. He had a nice turn of foot."

Terry nodded. "I liked him. I got on him and he just turned his head around and looked at me, like, 'hello.' I wasn't on him long, but he tried hard and I knew he was honest. I thought we were gonna win."

She stood up. She had to stand up from time to time. Sitting down hurt her. Standing up hurt her, too, so she had to do both to even everything out. Walking hurt her, but that was her living now, walking hots for Landry's brother.

Newcomers to the backside stared at her at first, until they found out what happened. Or they came within cursing distance. She didn't suffer fools gladly, or any other way.

Terry took another drag. "What's keeping them?" she said, looking for the yellow on the street beyond the chain link, looking for the school bus. She jittered with nervous energy, even though her synapses were like tangled wires. She swore she'd get back in the saddle again. Looking at her damaged body, her dragging leg, her lack of basic coordination, Landry didn't think it possible. But if determination could do it …

His brother said she'd improved. Said she didn't lurch as much.

Landry said to Steve, "So you rode him?"

"In the mornings. I'm too heavy to be a jock."

And too old, Landry thought. "Did he win a lot?"

Steve smiled, showed yellow teeth. Baby boomer teeth. Tetracycline from back in the day, a whole generation of people who ended up with yellow teeth. Guy was probably ten years older than Landry. Suffered plenty of wear and tear, but he looked spry as a cricket.

"Oh, he won a few. Last race he ran, back in the fall, was a $65,000 optional claiming. Won it laughing. He was on his way up, all right. Until he was on his way down."

"What happened?"

"Tendon."

"Tendon?" Landry knew that tendon injuries were pernicious.

"Yeah, that was all she wrote. He was off to the farm, just like that."

"Then they tried to bring him back?"

"I dunno. What I heard was, Greg said the horse was so good to him, winning some nice races, he was going to either give him away or retrain him for his son to ride."

"When was this? When did he go to the farm?"

"Last fall. He ran his last race in October, and that was the one where he must've injured it. Or reinjured it."

"It was bad before?"

"Greg's been known to block a joint or two on race day. Never thought he'd do it with a good horse like that, though. But you know how it goes. Run 'em on a wing and a prayer, hold it all together with front wraps, you got a horse going up the ranks and he can make some real money. Denial ain't just a river in Egypt!"

Terry glared at Steve.

He looked defensive. "*I* never felt anything. He went like a Cadillac for me. Never put in a bad work."

"If the horse went to the farm—if he was retired—how come he went down with me in February?" demanded Terry.

"I'm as surprised as you are. I thought he was all done. Stick a fork in him." He winced at his own expression, considering the horse was dead.

Terry looked at Landry, her expression triumphant. "Here's the kicker. Steve, tell him who owned him before Greg Snipes."

"Mickey Finn."

"I knew it!" Terry said, slamming her hand down on the picnic table. Steve had left them by then.

Landry had made the same connection she had.

Why would Snipes bring the horse out of retirement? A horse with a severe tendon injury? In many ways, a soft tissue injury was worse than a clean break. A break could heal, depending on where it was, and a horse could race again. A horse could be absolutely sound. But a tendon, once damaged, was tricky. Connective tissue, the tendon bound muscle to bone. Without good support, a catastrophic injury was likely at some juncture, and that likelihood was enhanced when the injured area was anesthetized before a race. When a twelve-hundred-pound horse puts all his weight on one foot the size of a teacup, and there's nothing there to support the bone, the result can be disastrous.

But you couldn't prove intent. For the bottom-feeders in this game, cutting corners was routine. The track stewards, in their wisdom, didn't bother to test BlueLight Special for drugs after the fact. There was no outside body that could force them to.

"You know they were gunning for me," Terry said. "I was too much trouble, so they set me up. I was the rabble-rouser. It was me who got all the jocks to go on strike. Me and my big damn mouth!" She glared at the horseman's gate as if it had done something to her.

Landry knew what she said was true. He'd had confirmation of that this morning, when Finn said the stewards didn't come after *him*. He said it like he still owned the horse. He said it as if it were common knowledge.

Landry's brother told him the story. Despite the fact that Finn's horses had broken down on the track seven times over a two-week period—three horses dead, two jockeys hurt—he was still the most powerful presence in the Midwest. He had enough horses to fill the races and keep the small tracks going. The jockeys were afraid of injury, sure, but Terry pushed them to the edge when she talked strike. The choice was stark. A jock riding in a low-level claiming race risked his life for $45 a ride—along with ten percent of the purse, *if* he won, placed, or showed. Riding in a $5,000 claiming race wasn't going to make anyone rich.

Terry became the lightning rod.

"You know what really pisses me off?" Terry jabbed her cigarette into the ashtray on the picnic table. "They killed that poor horse to get at me! What did he do to anybody except make them money?" She was up again, like a jack-in-the-box. Seeing her, the fierce way she moved, despite her injuries, despite her awkwardness, Landry began to think she might ride again. Impossible. But miracles happened.

Terry folded her arms tightly to her chest. Fuming. "Minute I got on that horse I knew he was a good one. The way he moved. It was like he trusted me. I could feel it, like he was telling me, I swear to GOD, he would take care of me. We'd win it together!"

She swiped at her eyes, turned away. "He trusted me."

Just then Landry heard the school bus. Terry started toward the horseman's gate.

It happened fast. Moira running through the gate, waving to her mother. Her enormous pink backpack bumping as she ran. Beaming, two green barrettes clipping up her hair on either side, like the little kid in a Dr. Seuss book.

The two big guys behind her, walking through the gate, right past the guard booth. Right past the guard.

One of them grabbing Moira's arm. The other hunkering down to talk to her. Raul. Or was it Teddy?

Mickey must have taken them out of storage.

Something whizzed by him—Terry. She was damn fast for a cripple, homing in on the intruders like a heat-seeking missile. In her hand was a pitchfork from his brother's barn.

Landry caught her in three strides, because he was fast, too. But by then she had one of them—Teddy?—up against the chain link fence, the tines of the pitchfork at his throat.

"You come near my baby and I will *kill* you!" she yelled.

The majority of stud farms are notoriously lax in their security. Landry grew up on the racetrack and knew how most barns did business, which was hardly any business at all.

Instead of criss-cross cameras—one camera sweeping left to right at timed intervals and another camera sweeping right to left—Stoney Bridge Farm had static cameras on the stall interiors themselves. Simple to circumvent.

Landry depended on human nature to do the rest of his work for him. From two previous nights of surveilling the property, Landry knew the guard made rounds every hour on the hour. In between, he sat in a comfy chair in a room off the feed shed and looked at the cameras. Staring at a camera feed is a stultifying job. According to research studies, a person tasked with watching a camera screen maintains his attention span for approximately twenty minutes. After that boredom sets in and the mind strays.

Landry went in at 3:30 a.m. The guard didn't see or hear him. He was reading a magazine. A simple job to grab him from behind, administer a light tranquilizer by hypodermic, and disable the camera feed to Avatar's stall.

Unlike most stallions, Avatar was docile. He didn't try to bite. Didn't snake his head, didn't pin his ears, didn't flash his teeth. Just stood there like the big, overfed hog he was, placidly awaiting his fate. Landry inserted the hypodermic into the jugular and pushed the plunger, then stood back quickly. Most times, horses fall down fast.

The stallion's hind legs folded like a card table and he sat down hard and fell over into the sawdust like a derailed train.

Landry pulled a cruel-looking implement from his back pocket. It looked like the meanest set of pliers in the world.

On the way out, Landry checked the guard. Out cold.

He walked off the farm, straight up the lane to the entrance and down the road to his car. Twenty-five minutes, from start to finish.

The second day Landry went to visit Mickey Finn was almost identical to the first. The same blue sky, the same bluegrass pastures, the identical chestnut trees spreading their shade. The brick colonial house, white columns. Beautiful.

This time he drove a sedan. The Touareg was long gone.

And this time, he had a plastic bag with him.

Earlier, Landry had Googled the expression BlueLight Special. Officially, a BlueLight Special was a discount at K-Mart. But the BlueLight Special was also slang for cops. In this case, the cops weren't interested in what Mickey Finn did on the racetrack. He skated just at the edge of the law and knew the line well. He had the track vets and the stewards in his pocket. So, no help there.

The last definition of a BlueLight Special was a "white trash girl." Landry supposed the term could apply to a single mother on the backside, willing to hop up on the back of any cheap horse and risk her life to keep her kid in shoes and food and cute pink backpacks. It wasn't accurate, but there were plenty of people in the world who thought that way.

A BlueLight Special of a woman with a little kid wasn't going to do anybody any good. And a damaged, broken BlueLight Special of a woman, no matter how feisty and determined, *really* wasn't going to do anybody any good.

Landry had been in a lot of places and seen a great deal of the world. He knew justice was decided on a sliding scale.

When Manfred Finn answered the bell, his two security guys were ranked behind him.

Landry ignored them. "Call your stud manager," he said to Mickey.

"Why should I?"

"Call your stud manager."

Finn stepped back. Uncertainty crossed his features. "If you killed that horse—"

"Call your stud manager. It might be a while before he gets the courage to call you."

Finn punched in the number and listened. His eyes grew wide. He sagged. Sat down on one of the veranda chairs, set the phone down on the table beside it. Aligned the phone neatly with the edge of his cigarette pack. Stared at the table and the objects on it as if he had never seen it before.

Shock.

Landry took a picture of Finn's face with his cell phone. For later.

The extent of the man's distress was such, he didn't even notice.

Time to move this along. "You know what this is?" Landry set the plastic bag on the table and pulled out the cruel-looking implement covered with blood, the one that looked like the meanest set of pliers in the world. Finn blanched. Interesting thing about Mickey Finn; his skin color changed with his emotions, like a mood ring.

"No answer? It's called an emasculator."

"Don't treat me like an idiot, I know what it's for." He stood up.

Raul and Teddy, bruised and battered though they were, closed around him.

Landry ignored them. "I learned to do it as a kid. I was the youngest and so I got the worst job. We had a lot of horses, and most of them weren't good enough to be studs like Avatar was; I got so I

232

could do it in my sleep. First, you put the horse under light anesthesia. You can perform the procedure with the horse standing up or you can do it on the ground."

Could have been the light, but Mickey Finn's face turned a bilious green.

"I prefer the ground method. Pretty simple—you cut the testicular cord, crimp it, and seal off the blood vessels. Make sure the site is good and clean, all the skin tucked neatly back in. A good job takes twenty minutes."

"Shut up!"

"You'll note that the stud manager found him in the paddock. I turned your horse out so he could walk around and keep up his circulation. Wouldn't want any complications to crop up, a valuable animal like that."

"Shut *up*!!!"

Landry said, "But I need to catch you up on where we're at. The price has gone up—$500,000 to Ms. Hill. I now have an account for her, where you can wire it."

"You gelded my stallion!"

A sports car turned from the road and started up the lane toward the house. The top down, a different blonde from the one Landry had seen yesterday at the wheel. Landry said, "Here's the account number. Tomorrow it will be $600,000."

Finn slammed his fist on the table, and the phone and the emasculator and the cigarette pack jumped. "I'm calling the police."

"You can if you want to, but I'll be back tomorrow, or the next day, or the next, for Ms. Hill's money. And every day the price will go up. If I come back tomorrow, it will be $600,000. If I were you I'd lock it in now. Just think of it as the BlueLight Special."

"What are you talking about?"

The man didn't even remember the name of the horse.

Finn said, "She won't get a penny from me. I'll have the police on her like that! You've committed a criminal act—you threatened me and damaged my property! One call to the police and you and she both will be in lockup by lunchtime today."

"I wouldn't do that if I were you."

"You still threatening me?" He spread his arms out from his body. From the sidelines, his bruised-but-hard-looking bodyguards stared impassively from behind dark glasses. "Just try me! One word from me and you'll be in a wheelchair for the rest of your life!"

Landry studied Raul and Teddy. They presented a hard exterior but he could see the cracks. He saw it in the hunching of their shoulders. Behind their dark glasses, they weren't looking at him. They were looking just to the left of him.

They remembered, all right.

Landry heard the sports car's door close. The blonde started up the walk, shopping bags from an upscale boutique dangling from each hand. "Mickey!" she called, "I bought you something!"

Landry looked from the blonde to Mickey. Mickey looked from the blonde to Landry. His expression defiant. A stubborn man.

Landry said, "You might want to rethink your position."

"No way, pally. You're *mine*."

The blonde was almost to the steps. She had the longest legs Landry had ever seen.

Landry leaned up close to Mickey. He cupped his hand over his mouth, and spoke in the man's ear.

"What did you say to him?" Terry asked, after she confirmed that the money was indeed wired to an offshore account in her name.

"I said, 'If I can do it to a twelve-hundred-pound thoroughbred, I can do it to you.'"

WELCOME TO THE FOOD CHAIN

BY WELDON BURGE

"Flash, huh?" The fat man leveled his eyes at the slender man sitting across the table from him. "Why do they call you Flash? Like that comic book guy in the red tights?"

"Something like that. I don't like to waste time," Conwright said. "I was a high school track star. Got the nickname back then. That was in another life, a distant time."

The fat man, Albert Nigroponte, nodded, grabbed another crab from the table. He ate a prodigious amount of steamed crabs and drank his Pabst Blue Ribbon by the keg. His appetite and obsession had impelled him, over the years, to purchase three "all-you-can-eat" seafood joints on the shores of the Chesapeake Bay. The largest and most profitable restaurant, The Magnificent Wharf, was in Annapolis. The restaurant in St. Michael's, The Amber Whale, was the swankiest, for the tourists. The establishment in Havre de Grace, The Hammer & Claw, was a true dive. Nigroponte had chosen the H&C to meet Conwright to arrange their business.

At Nigroponte's request, Conwright had entered the restaurant after hours, long after the restaurant staff had departed for the evening. Nigroponte sat alone at a corner table covered with newspaper. Piled on the newspaper were at least three dozen fiery red, steamed blue crabs. Nigroponte feasted like Neptune. The restaurant reeked of Old Bay seasoning and a distinct, stagnant wharf odor, a foul blend of rotting fish entrails and brine.

"So, can you do the job?"

"In my sleep," Conwright said. "For the right price."

"How much?"

"Fifty thousand."

Nigroponte grumbled and shook his head. "No friggin' way. She ain't worth that. No way."

"No, she's not. But I am. This is a business. I'm a businessman. My reputation speaks for itself or I wouldn't be here. I give you a discount, every slob and his brother wants a discount. My reputation suffers."

"Screw your reputation." Nigroponte pointed an amputated crab claw at him. "I ain't payin' no fifty grand for that bimbo."

Conwright got up from the table.

"Wait a minute! Just one friggin' minute." Nigroponte pasted on a chummy, let's-be-pals smile. "Ya gotta work with me on this. Cut me a break, okay?"

"Yeah, sure. You own the whole marina. That's your yacht in the slip right outside this window. And you can't afford $50,000? Cut *me* a break."

"Listen, I have this cash flow problem, ya see. No thanks to that bloodsuckin' bitch, let me tell ya. Bleedin' me friggin' dry."

"No offense, but I don't need the sob story. Do you want me to off her or not?"

"Yeah. And don't leave nothin' for the medical examiner."

"I'll do it right, don't worry. But I don't come cheap. Take it or leave it."

Nigroponte smashed a crab claw with a wooden mallet, and then gingerly removed the lump of blushing white meat from the split shell. He eyed Conwright, no longer smiling.

"You're one hardass, ain't ya, Conwright? Think you've got the world by the cojones."

Conwright sighed. "You get what you pay for, Mr. Nigroponte."

The fat man grunted. "Twenty-five thousand."

Conwright shook his head. "Fifty thousand, and there's no way they can link it to you. They won't even find the body."

"Thirty thousand. That's my top dollar."

"Fifty thousand. And that's a bargain."

"Screw you." Nigroponte pounded another crab claw with his mallet. "I'll find some other schmuck to do her. A derelict on the street would do it for a bottle of cheap gin."

"And you'd be in jail the next day. Up to you."

Nigroponte popped another morsel of crab in his mouth and washed it down with some Pabst. "I'm not puttin' up more than $30,000," he said. He looked into Conwright's eyes as he spoke. "It's a dog-eat-dog world, Flash. Welcome to the friggin' food chain, ya know? I didn't get here on my good looks or blind luck. Like you, I've done my homework. My contacts, our mutual acquaintances, told me how to deal with you. I know ya need the cash. I know ya owe Solomon Ventura a large chunk of change. You're currently in no position to negotiate."

When Conwright frowned at the mention of Ventura, Nigroponte knew he had him. After a bad run of luck in Atlantic City last week, Conwright was in for 20 Gs—plus interest, of course—with Solly Ventura. Nigroponte knew of Solly from his early days in South Philly, where he still had contacts. Solly was *not* someone you'd want to screw over.

"You trust these people, these contacts of yours?" Conwright asked.

"I trust them. They recommended you highly."

Conwright stared at the fat man, still frowning. Nigroponte cracked open another crab claw, waiting. The silence seemed impenetrable.

"Okay," Conwright finally said, pasting on his own best let's-be-pals smile. "Deal. But, I have expenses. I need $10,000 up front, $20,000 when the job's done."

Nigroponte smiled like a cat with mouse under its paw. "Done," he said. He pulled a wad of bills from somewhere in the folds of his pants and peeled off the cash, six Gs and the rest in C notes—petty cash to the fat man. When Conwright took the money, the bills were damp with Nigroponte's perspiration.

"I need a week, maybe more, to figure out her routines and determine when best to take her out and in what manner. I'll meet you here a week from today to finalize our arrangement."

Nigroponte nodded. "Same time is fine, but I really don't like talkin' here. Never know who might walk in, particularly Sheila. Meet me on the Barnacled Dolphin." He pointed out the window to his yacht. "We'll go out on the bay, more privacy."

"That would be ideal."

For the next hour, Nigroponte told Conwright everything he knew about Sheila's typical day, her favorite haunts, and her friends.

With all the young Navy recruits in Annapolis, Sheila Nigroponte thought it was "strategic" to relocate here after her separation from her toady husband. She was a relatively attractive, tall redhead with manufactured breasts, collagen-pumped lips, and a well-sculpted nose. Why not make the best of her investments? She had no shortage of boyfriends. She still managed The Magnificent Wharf on the waterfront, as she had during her brief marriage, but now only in a cursory manner. Hers was a social life.

Her only true routine was a daily workout at Gold's Gym, only a few blocks from where she lived, from 4:00 to 5:00. Dinner followed this at one of the many restaurants in the area, usually with a different man every night. She ate at The Magnificent Wharf on Friday evenings. When the crowd really hummed, she would flit from table to table talking with prominent local socialites. Her marriage to Nigroponte provided access to a massive bank account and was certainly a step up the social ladder for her, but little else.

Sheila took pride in being a "cougar"—she was always on the prowl for fresh meat. She'd noticed the new guy at the gym last week. Not a meathead with bulging muscles, he was actually quite slender and well-toned—probably a cyclist or a runner, from the build. Not bad looking either, but not Brad Pitt by a long shot. Still, attractive enough. She watched him from afar for a few days. He seemed to be a loner, not interacting often with the other gym patrons.

He was working out on a weight bench when she finally decided to approach him. Sheila stood next to the bench, watching him pump the barbells. When he noticed her, she smiled.

"Hi," he said, returning her smile.

"Need someone to spot you?"

"Nah, but thanks for asking. I'm used to working out alone."

"You new in town?" she purred.

He sat up on the bench, threw a towel over his shoulder. "Just a few weeks. I'm originally from South Jersey."

"I noticed you last Friday, thought I'd introduce myself. I'm Sheila Nigroponte." She moved closer to offer him a better view of her cleavage.

"I'm Jeremy," he said. "Jeremy Irons."

"Like the British actor?"

"A favorite of my Mom's, yes."

Sheila wondered if she was older than his mother. No matter.

"Finding your way around town okay?"

"Pretty much. I really don't know anyone here. My boss sent me here to open a new satellite office, so I'm pretty much on my own. Just me and an empty office right now."

"What do you do?"

"Asian imports, mostly from India. I know, I know! In Annapolis? I guess my boss knows what he's doing." He smiled at her again. "I'm looking for a really good seafood restaurant, a place that knows how to cook mahi-mahi. You'd think in Annapolis I'd be able to find something. Got any suggestions?"

"I certainly do. The Magnificent Wharf." Her smile broadened as well. "Are you asking me to dinner?"

"Depends. Are you going to say yes?"

"If you're paying."

"My pleasure."

No, mine, Sheila thought.

Nigroponte had been drinking before they left the dock in Havre de Grace at the mouth of the Susquehanna. Conwright had to trust his navigational skills, that he could handle the Barnacled Dolphin on a moonlit night.

A large covered pot of steamed crabs waited on deck. Once they'd anchored in the bay, Nigroponte planned to feast again. He already had a table covered with newspaper and assorted mallets, nutcrackers, and skewers ready to fulfill the task. Conwright lifted the lid and looked into the pot.

"Know much about crabs?"Nigroponte asked.

"Not really."

"Nasty little scavengers. They make dead things disappear. They serve their purpose. Kinda like you, huh, Flash? Make dead things disappear?"

Conwright shrugged. "I'm allergic to shellfish."

"Too bad. A keg and a few dozen crabs and I'm a happy man. Didja ever steam crabs, Conwright? Ya throw them in the pot alive, put the lid on, then turn up the heat. Get the steam rollin'. Listen to 'em scramble to get away from the heat. Too bad they can't scream. Can ya imagine being slowly steamed to death?"

"No, I suppose not." But Conwright *could* imagine steaming someone to death, the flesh bubbling and melting. He could easily picture this in his head, and imagined Sheila screaming as she melted to goo.

Conwright loved his work. It was the planning, the fantasizing, the playing out of death scenarios that made it fun and worthwhile—the "hit" was often frustratingly mundane. Reality never lived up to his fantasies. It was always better to go for the clean kill, leaving nothing for the CSI folks, than to actually realize what he could imagine.

Killing for fun—as in his earlier, formative days—had been satisfying.

Killing for *pay* was even more so, even if he did have to sacrifice creativity on occasion.

He could easily imagine killing Sheila Nigroponte using a great variety of entertaining methods. She was a vain woman who treasured her well-styled auburn hair. He would definitely shave her head first. That led him to think of an electric chair, and he wondered if electrocution was an option. Probably not, but it would be fun to watch her fry. So many ways to kill her; he could have fun with her.

Nigroponte anchored the Barnacled Dolphin off the southern tip of Kent Island. Conwright could see the lights of Annapolis to the northwest. There were a few boats to the far south, probably crabbers pulling up their pots.

Conwright joined Nigroponte in the cabin. The fat man retrieved two beers from the fridge, handing one to Conwright.

"So, have ya decided how you're going to do it?"

"The way I normally do it, simple and fast."

"Where?"

"I've been seeing her at the gym, gaining her trust, so to speak."

"Good, good."

"We're going out to dinner this Friday night. When I'm alone with her and the time is right ..."

"Excellent!"

"She won't suspect a thing. She'll probably be in the middle of a conversation with me when I slip the gun out. She won't realize anything until it's too late. It'll happen so fast, she won't feel a thing. Maybe there'll be a look of surprise on her face, but more likely a look of indifference. That's the normal reaction. I always look them in the eye. Sometimes you can see the soul depart from the body, like a vapor."

Nigroponte stared at him like he was a nutcase. "Yeah, yeah. Whatever. As long as ya do it, that's all I care. And don't look for her soul, 'cause she ain't got one."

When they got to the deck, Nigroponte went straight to the pot of crabs. He was slightly drunk.

"Do ya really think you have her fooled?" he asked as he took the lid off the pot. "She's not stupid, ya know. She could be on to ya, settin' you up for somethin' really nasty." He reached into the pot and started yanking out crabs and throwing them on the table.

"She trusts me. She wouldn't turn on me now."

Nigroponte chuckled. "You don't know my wife."

"Oh, I know your wife."

Conwright pulled his Bernadelli, a palm-size Italian .22 automatic, from the holster hidden under his left arm. He loved the slick, warm metal feel of it in his hand, it fit so perfectly in his fingers.

As Nigroponte turned toward him, Conwright looked him straight in the eye. He lifted the gun and pulled the trigger once in a practiced, fluid motion. The bullet perforated Nigroponte's forehead just above his left eye. The single .22 slug ricocheted within his skull like a pinball razor, shredding brain tissue and vital blood vessels. When Conwright could get close enough to his target, the .22 was his favorite means of execution. When Nigroponte's body tumbled to the deck, he stood over him and put another slug in his head, just to be sure.

"I know your wife," Conwright repeated. "And she pays a hell of a lot better than you do."

He put the lid back on the pot of crabs. No feasting tonight.

Conwright turned off all the lights on the yacht save for one below deck. Then he went back to Nigroponte's corpse. He had to get the wedding band off his bloated finger. No wonder Sheila wanted that as evidence that he'd completed the job—she knew he'd have to cut off the finger to get the ring. He couldn't get the ring past the first knuckle. He found a filet knife in a tackle box in the cabin and used that to peel the flesh from the bone. Conwright tossed the bloody pulp off the yacht. With Nigroponte's finger stripped to the bone, he had no trouble removing the ring.

Conwright pulled up the anchor and cut the rope. Using the rope, he lashed Nigroponte's bulk to the anchor, then with great effort tipped him over the side. The fat man went to the bottom like a cannonball.

As he watched Nigroponte disappear into the dark water, he wondered how long it would take the crabs to find the decaying corpse. *Welcome to the food chain, Nigroponte.* He suspected they would come in with the tide and quickly discover the smorgasbord resting on the bottom of the bay. Conwright closed his eyes, imagining hundreds of crabs feasting on the rotting bulk. The larger crabs would come first for the soft tissues of Nigroponte's open mouth and tongue. Several crabs manage to wriggle down his throat for the sweeter meat. In time, the smaller crustaceans would eventually find their way into other orifices, gaining access to the brain. Ah, there was the real prize! The constant pull and tug of their mandibles and claws would come to bear on the tougher optic nerves and muscles. Nigroponte's eyes twitch and turn beneath the closed eyelids, giving the corpse the illusion of REM sleep. The eyes finally collapse into the sockets as the crabs feast from within.

Conwright opened his eyes, looked up at the moon.

Nah, probably couldn't happen that way.

He sighed, turned away from the water.

He then steered the yacht for the mouth of the Chesapeake. Once on the Atlantic, he headed north up the coast to Cape May. He'd already contacted Solly Ventura the night before, who'd agreed to take the yacht in payment for the gambling debt Conwright owed him.

242

The Magnificent Wharf was particularly crowded on Friday night, when Sheila decided to meet Conwright for their final transaction. She'd already ordered dinner before he arrived. He had no intention of staying. She did not know this.

Many men—indeed, most—would find Sheila alluring and irresistible. Albert Nigroponte certainly did, much to his misfortune. But Conwright knew her black heart, knew the ugliness inside. He'd known women like her throughout his life—probably went with the trade, he figured. Femmes fatales. He felt no attraction whatsoever to the recently widowed Mrs. Nigroponte.

"No thanks," he said, responding to her proposal. "I'm sure an evening with you would indeed be pleasurable, in an animal kind of way. But I'm only here for the money."

Her smile instantly dissolved and something darkened in her eyes. He'd seen it a hundred times before.

"Figures," she said with disgust. "You men are all alike. Where's the ring?"

Conwright pulled the wedding band from his shirt pocket and slid it across the table to her.

She picked it up and examined it. "How did you get it off his finger?"

"The hard way."

"I bet." Her grin was the definition of malice.

She pushed the manila envelope across the table to him—$50,000 in laundered $100 bills. "I suppose you want to count it?"

"No, I trust you." If she'd shortchanged him, Conwright could find her. In that circumstance, she would not want to see him again. He imagined her sitting across the table from him with a shaved head. He imagined a car battery, jumper cables, and damp sponges, just to get the party started. Maybe, even if she didn't stiff him, he'd come back for a visit, for a bonus round with her. The fat man paid him 10 Gs, after all—not the full contract, but enough. Conwright smiled.

A young waiter stepped up to the table with a tray. "Crab Imperial?" he asked, looking back and forth between the two.

"Here," she said.

After placing the plate before Sheila, the waiter turned to

243

Conwright.

"Would you like to order now, sir?"

"No, no. I was just leaving."

"The Crab Imperial is superb, sir," the waiter continued. "Sweet lump crab, fresh from the bay this morning."

"No thanks," Conwright said. "I'm allergic to shellfish."

INSIDE OUT

BY AL BOUDREAU

CHAPTER 1

The faint click rousted Graham Pace as though he'd heard a blast from a trucker's air horn. It wasn't the sound that alarmed him; it was the timing. He'd heard it three times a day, seven years running, but never after midnight. The distinct groan of his Stateville cell door soon followed. He rubbed the fading dreamscape from his eyes to focus on two approaching silhouettes.

"Let's go, Pace. Keep quiet and this might not involve any pain." Warden Archer Frankel's usual smirk accompanied the command. He nodded to his guard, who yanked the inmate to his feet. Frankel led the men past cages housing hundreds of criminals who would never again be free.

Pace balked, his nostrils assaulted more intensely than ever before by the fetid stench of incarcerated souls. Omnipresent body odor heightened his queasy unease as bile climbed the ladder of his esophagus. His hesitation earned a violent jab from the guard's polycarbonate billy club. A bitter mix of pain and rage telegraphed vertically through angry vertebrae, causing clenched fists to form at the end of his fencepost forearms.

The march to Frankel's den was all too familiar to Pace. His mind snapped back to the early days just after he'd been processed into the men's penitentiary.

The guards were quick to single him out. At first he thought it was what all incoming convicts faced; beating here, a night in solitary there. The truth eventually came down by way of a snitch that felt sorry for him. Warden Frankel had ordered his guards to administer the biweekly doses of physical abuse. No one would say why, but it became painfully obvious—Frankel loved to watch him suffer.

Pace figured more of the same cruelty was in the offing, though the timing remained a mystery. Maybe the masochistic bastard couldn't sleep and craved an early morning show.

As Pace trailed behind the balding, overweight jail boss, a deep hatred continued to grow, forged by the heavy hand of systemic abuse.

The men walked through the carved mahogany passage to the warden's inner sanctum. "Take a seat, Pace" Frankel said. The guard doled out another violent jab. Pace fell headlong, his chin taking the brunt of Frankel's rising heel. The warden stumbled, and then turned and kicked Pace in the rib cage. "Get this piece of shit up off my oriental."

The guard, who dwarfed Pace's prone five-foot-eight frame, grabbed the wiry inmate and slammed him into an adjacent armchair. Pace fought to control his heavy breathing, to lessen his pain and Frankel's pleasure.

"Today's your lucky day, Pace. You're being granted a furlough." Frankel threw Pace's street clothes and sack of belongings directly at his face. "Don't bother looking for your piece in the bag. It's part of my personal collection now."

Pace failed to react, drawing a subtle frown from Frankel.

"You're going to do a little job for me. You'll be dealing with Jared Jenks while on the outside. Consider him your temporary parole officer. He's waiting for you at the gate. Get your ass dressed and get moving."

CHAPTER 2

The prison access door slammed shut behind Pace. He stopped walking, the reality of being on the outside overwhelming. A double life sentence ensured he would never set foot on the far side of these walls again, yet here he was. The thought of making a run for it crossed his mind.

Two figures approached from the visitors parking area. "Graham Pace?" one of the men inquired.

"You Jenks?"

"That's me. Safe to say you wouldn't turn down a decent breakfast right about now, isn't it?"

"It's a little early, but whatever," Pace said. He glanced at the chrome pistol prominently displayed on the second man's hip.

Jenks chuckled, neglecting to introduce the gun-toting stranger. He headed toward a late model sedan, parking lights ablaze. "Over here." Pace caught up just as Jenks opened the passenger-side door and motioned for him to get in. Mister Pistol climbed in the back behind the driver's seat.

Jenks wheeled onto the highway and headed south as the blown dash speaker rattled out a Dwight Yoakam threefer. No one said a word during the eighteen-mile drive to their first stop: Denny's.

Pace wondered what the hell was going on as they left the vehicle, confident that laws and regulations were being broken. Jenks led them to a table away from other patrons. His associate occupied a separate booth. "Take a load off, Pace. I'm sure you're a bit confused by all of this."

Pace offered no reply.

Jenks, seemingly unaffected by the lack of response, reached inside his jacket and produced three envelopes. He flipped them onto the table one at a time as if he were playing solitaire. "We're not eating," he said to the waitress as she approached. "Just two coffees."

The woman gathered their unused silverware and walked away, no mention of the place setting with a missing fork.

Jenks slid the first envelope across the table. "Round-trip bus ticket to Chicago and a ticket to the Cubs' season opener." He grabbed the second envelope and tossed it in front of Pace. "A hundred bucks in tens and twenties." Jenks took a quick look around before sliding the third one over. "This is a photograph of the guy who'll be sitting next to you at the ball game." He lowered his voice. "Consider him a mark."

Pace felt Jenks eyes on him but gave him nothing, acting as if he were listening to the man blather on about his kid's baseball card collection.

"Frankel and my friend with the gun over there will be seated somewhere behind you, each with a different vantage point. You'll have a familiar audience while conducting your dirty work."

Pace took a long sip of coffee then looked directly into Jenks's eyes. "What's my motivation here?"

Jenks gave a wide smile. "Look, Pace, I don't really give a shit if you do it or not. I've got my marching orders. Archer Frankel has got something on me. I'm doing this to square things with him. He told me to hand the envelopes over, then keep an eye on you. In case you haven't figured it out yet, the guy is off of his tits. Been on meds as long as I've known him. Anyways, he told me to send a slug in your general direction if you become uncooperative or if I see something that doesn't look right. His exact words were 'wound that fake sniper real good,' and that he'd 'take it from there.' And if I know Frankel, he probably hopes you'll try something stupid." Jenks nodded to his associate and both men stood up. "He also said something about your kid sister, but I can't quite remember the details."

Pace remained calm, gathered the envelopes, and rose from his seat.

"Oh, by the way, Pace. The fork you have hidden in your sleeve? Best leave it here. A man could go to jail for something like that."

CHAPTER 3

Jared Jenks turned the radio off and clicked the wipers on low intermittent as a mist ushered in the dawn. "You don't say much, Pace. Any questions before I drop you at the station?"

"Sure, I have a question. Are you gonna give me a weapon or does the warden expect me to carry out his dirty work with Jedi mind tricks?"

"You're not getting a gun. I hit Frankel with the same question. He told me you'd figure something—"

The automatic transmission shifted into passing gear as Pace stomped his boot down atop Jenks's loafer. The man in the back looked confused, his hesitation giving Pace a split second to wreak havoc upon the unsuspecting pair. Though unable to pilfer a makeshift weapon from Denny's, he'd managed to empty a half-full saltshaker into his jacket pocket. Now, using only his peripheral vision, a fist full of the gritty crystals left Pace's hand and hit their mark.

A string of profanity came from the back of the vehicle as the man instinctively rubbed his freshly salted eyes.

Pace dove into the backseat.

"Don't do this, Pace," Jenks shouted as he stomped the brakes and pulled over.

It was too late.

Power had now shifted from two against one to two against eleven—Pace and a ten-round clip.

CHAPTER 4

Graham Pace leaned back against the rear passenger-side door, weapon trained on Jared Jenks's skull. "Change of plans. We're gonna take this little freak show on the road together. Turn around and head toward Chicago. Stay away from the tolls. Back roads only."

Jenks maneuvered his vehicle back into the flow of traffic. "You know you can't—"

"Okay, I don't want to hear you right now, Jenks. Speak when spoken to. That goes for both of you." Pace glanced over at Mister Pistol, who was breathing heavily, looking like a ten-year-old who'd been duped out of his lunch money.

Jenks pulled a quick U-turn.

Pace, caught off guard, lost his balance and reached forward to stabilize his body when a crushing blow to the temple altered his reality. Two strong hands clamped down on his wrist as he tried to shake off the stars that blurred his vision.

All at once, a horrific howl, squealing rubber, and a hot sticky spray filled the air as the firearm was inadvertently discharged in the struggle. Jenks let loose a string of obscenities in a bid to control his vehicle.

Pace wiped a sleeve across his face just in time to see the horizon go vertical through blood-tinted windows. Instinct took over. He pressed his palms tight up against the headliner as flesh and steel performed a synchronized cartwheel. The vehicle made one complete revolution and came to rest on its wheels. The engine continued to run.

Pace took stock of the situation with no time to hesitate. A quick glance at Jenks's associate told of his condition—deceased. The massive amount of blood coating the interior made it obvious; the stray bullet had severed the man's femoral artery. Jenks, though banged up, didn't appear to be critical. Pace reached over and released his seat belt, and then shoved Jenks into the passenger seat so that he could get behind the wheel. He used his sleeve as a makeshift squeegee to remove layers of coagulated blood from the cracked windshield, only to discover the approach of would-be rescuers.

Their jaws dropped in unison as the damaged vehicle sped off.

CHAPTER 5

Pace rolled all four windows down. Chips of safety glass cascaded from the vehicle like a cache of blood diamonds. "Hand me your cell phone, Jenks." Seconds ticked by with no response.

"Jenks!"

The man's head swiveled like an electric Christmas mannequin, with a lifeless expression to match. Pace grabbed a fistful of collar and shook him, adrenalin fueling his aggression. "Yeah, okay," Jenks said, remaining motionless a bit longer before reaching down toward his ankles.

Pace saw leather as Jenks lifted the cuff of his slacks. He lurched toward the passenger side of the car and yanked Jenks's leg up over the center console. Eyes back to the road ahead; he had just enough time to brace for impact as the front fender sideswiped a telephone pole, sending the vehicle into oncoming traffic. He jerked the wheel to correct his course, tore the weapon away from Jenks, and swung the palmed piece directly into the man's forehead. Jenks slumped forward against the dashboard.

Pace needed to find a spot to lay low, to make a call. Signs advertising a multitude of businesses lined both sides of the commercial strip. He spotted an adult bookshop and wheeled into the parking lot. It looked to be closed, judging by the absence of vehicles. He pulled around to the back and positioned the car so he'd be aware of another vehicle's approach. He then searched Jenks's pockets for a cell phone. He found the device and dialed a number.

A weary greeting followed half a dozen rings. "Janine, this is Graham. Listen to me. I need you to get in your car and drive to Stateville. I'm out on a furlough and need your help."

"What? How did you—"

"There's no time to explain. Meet me at Stateville Truck Stop. Leave now. Call this cell when you're about a mile out."

"Okay, okay, I'm on my way."

Pace knew his on-again, off-again girlfriend of seven years was nearly twenty minutes out. He'd stay put until she was close, the rendezvous spot just two miles east. He slapped Jenks's cheek hard a few times, causing him to stir. "Wake up, you stupid prick."

Jenks moaned and brought his hand up to his bruised forehead. "What did you ... why would you—"

"What's Frankel's game, Jenks? You know what's going on and you're going to tell me, right here, right now."

"I ... don't ... know."

Before Jenks could say another word, Pace thrust the barrel of his handgun into the soft hollow just beneath Jenks temple and pinned his head against the jagged remains of the passenger-side windowsill. "You just initiated your own funeral proceedings, Slick." He ground the barrel deep into the man's skull and clicked the safety off.

"All right, wait."

Pace pressed harder.

"He hates the fact you consider yourself a sniper, okay?" Beads of sweat zigzagged down Jenks's cheek as he trembled. "He was an Army Ranger sniper. There's a deep resentment in his gut. Says you've got no honor and that your actions disrespect his military career."

Pace eased the barrel back. "Sit up!"

Jenks closed his eyes and massaged the crater caused by Pace's abuse. "Frankel's wife has cancer. She's got six months, so he's taking an early retirement. Said he wants to end his career with a happy memory. That's why he's doing this. Your pain is his pleasure, Pace."

Pace remained silent for a moment before a smirk appeared. "There's only one way Frankel can avoid being held responsible if this little game goes south. He'll make you take the fall. You had to sign and submit paperwork to take custody of me, right? Did you look it over first?" Pace's smile widened as he watched Jenks's expression turn sour. "Come on, Jenks. You must have kept a copy, right? It's easy enough to check it out. Let's have a look." Pace knew the answer as soon as Jenks turned away, his stare now focused on the highway. "Strange, isn't it? You're headed to jail and I'm going to be a free man."

"That will never happen, Pace. You're delusional."

"Strike a nerve? You're suddenly full of life again. Maybe—"

Pace was interrupted by Jenks's cell phone. Janine's number flashed on the screen. He removed the battery and threw the phone into an adjacent wooded area. He then put the car in gear and headed toward the truck stop.

CHAPTER 6

Graham Pace's girlfriend's eyes widened as he pulled up beside her. Before she could find any words, he said "We need to swap cars right now, Janine. Take this thing straight back to your place and put it in the garage until I come back later on."

"Are you out of your mind? What the hell happened here? And how am I supposed to get to work? I just—"

"Now!" Pace stared her down until she responded. He turned toward Jenks and motioned with the muzzle of his gun for him to get out.

"Oh my god, Graham, there's a dead guy in the back. And there's blood everywhere! There's no way I can drive this thing to my place."

Pace ignored her and stood outside the vehicle until Jenks climbed into the passenger side of their new transportation. A storm of pounding fists rained down on Pace's shoulders, a tirade full of expletives accompanying the assault as he moved to take the wheel. He gave her a shove and drove off, never looking back.

"Class act all the way, Pace," Jenks said.

"That cheating whore gets what she gets. She's lucky to be alive and it's payback time." Pace looked in the center console where his girlfriend usually kept her cell phone. "By the way, you're going to make a phone call. Then you can shut your mouth from here on in, or I'll shut it for you permanently. Your choice." Pace handed over the phone. "Call Frankel. Tell him everything is set."

CHAPTER 7

Graham Pace admired the M24 sniper rifle in his hands. The fact he had located such a weapon inside the span of several hours felt like destiny, though the Internet and Jared Jenks helped make it so. Jenks had proven to be a valuable asset, possessing two things necessary to procure such a weapon on short notice: spotless credentials and deep pockets. On the black market, there are no background checks. However, the process left little time to work out some serious kinks.

Pace's perch inside Huron Terrace, located on the periphery of Wrigley Field, provided a perfect sightline on a particular cluster of bleacher seats inside the ballpark. Upon entering the tower, Pace coerced an elderly woman into letting Jenks and him enter her tenth-floor apartment. Unfortunately, the units had no windows that opened, save a single awning located nine feet above the living room floor.

Pace had a plan. "Drag that dining room table over here, and then take the drawers out of her dresser," he commanded. Jenks gave no resistance, the far end of his own weapon now trained on his chest.

The woman was in for the shock of her life when someone finally came around to remove the gag and ropes now holding her hostage. The living area would soon look much different. The men stacked furniture piece by piece until it formed a platform high enough to reach the windowsill.

Pace stood back and surveyed the structure. He gave Jenks a nod. "That'll work. Head back toward the bedroom. You're going to keep the old lady company. Maybe you two can wink Morse code to one another."

After tying and gagging Jenks, Pace returned to the cobbled tower, satisfied with the job he'd done securing the odd couple. A glance at his watch told him he had about five minutes to spare. He checked the bolt-action rifle again, and then chambered a round.

Pace closed his eyes and slowed his breathing in preparation for the trigger. He thought about Warden Archer Frankel as he said the Army Ranger sniper's motto out loud. "One shot, one kill." A quick scan through a pair of binoculars purchased earlier that day made Pace smile; Frankel had taken his seat at the Cubs game.

Pace picked up the cell phone, placed a call, and hit speaker.

"Jenks? Where the hell are you?" the voice on the other end asked. "I told you to get here ten minutes early."

"Archer Frankel? This is Graham Pace. I need you to shut up and listen very carefully. I'm looking at you through the scope of a weapon you're very familiar with. The M24 is one hell of a rifle in capable hands. Look up toward the building at your one o'clock." Pace took a makeup mirror found in the old lady's bathroom and beamed reflected sunlight in Frankel's direction. "Now say goodbye."

Archer Frankel's jaw fell, his attention fixed on the apartment tower where he'd seen Pace's signal.

The gunshot echoed like thunder across the Chicago skyline as a .300 Winchester Magnum round tore through flesh and bone, in clean and out mean.

Graham Pace was free.

KATAKIUCHI

BY CHARLES COLYOTT

As I'm sure you know by now, lots of people have written about my last job. One of those stupid, melodramatic news shows did a two-hour special about it, too. I heard there was even a made-for-TV movie about it. I honestly wouldn't know. I don't watch that crap, myself.

In any case, nobody got it right. Not really.

You want to hear about it?

Nah, I don't mind telling you. It doesn't matter anymore. What's done is done.

Besides, nobody can touch me now, anyway.

I'm clean.

Let's see. How to start—

I know! I'll tell you a secret: In this game, my game? I'm the best there is. The numbers you've read? The confirmed kill counts? Let's just say that those numbers were pretty conservative. In the past five years, I've managed to earn a little over ten million dollars, which isn't too shabby considering I like to keep my prices reasonable.

By the way, before you start to think that, like, I'm some kind of monster and you start questioning my childhood and all that shit? Let me put all that to rest right now: My childhood was awesome. My parents are great people, and my big brother was a great guy. I am *not* a monster.

I'm a capitalist. And trust me, there's a market for my services. I could've taken ten times as many jobs, if I wasn't so cautious. And if I wasn't so lazy. And if my schedule allowed it.

As it is, though, I'm pretty proud of my record.

Anyway, I digress.

Where was I?

Right. The last job.

So there's this Darknet board I use for getting work. It's called Chiba City.

Hm?

No, not the real Chiba, in Japan. This one's a *Neuromancer* reference. Y'know, the classic William Gibson novel?

Oh.

Oh, right, sorry. Darknet. It's ... uh ... sorta like the Internet's seedy underbelly. It's the stuff that doesn't come up in searches. The stuff you can't get to unless you know somebody. I know a lot of somebodies, let me tell you.

And those somebodies all *think* they know me: O_Kami, the "Great Spirit."

The ghost in the machine.

Back before I even went pro, I started seeding rumors around, from various fake accounts, about a mysterious, steely-eyed assassin of unknown origins. I pretty much just paraphrased my phony bios from old Wolverine comics and spy movies and Repairman Jack novels, but it did the job ... before long, I started get inquiries.

I started to get jobs.

And the way it always worked was like this: At some point, early in the correspondence, I would sneakily infect my client's system with a tiny bit of malware of my own creation. It was a simple piece of identification software, allowing me to determine the who, the where, the why, etc., etc. This allowed me to dodge the occasional law enforcement sting job, but it also gave me a better idea about each client's motives.

Yes, motives. Believe it or not, I'm not so bad. I don't do kids. I haven't done women (not that I wouldn't, necessarily, but there was never a compelling enough reason).

Oh, ha-freaking-ha.

I know what you're thinking, but I have had plenty of dates, thank you very much.

Anyway, dick, my point is that motives fucking matter, y'know? I don't just drop Mjolnir on somebody who doesn't deserve it. With great power comes ... well, y'know.

So anyway, last April. I'm kickin' back on a Friday night, alright, and I'm playing a little World of War-crack, and I get a ping from my laptop. The laptop is what I use for business, so I log off of WoW and switch over. It's a new client. I chat 'em up a little, stick 'em with the malware (I named it M.A.R.K.-13 after the killer robot from the classic 1990 sci-fi movie *Hardware*, which my bro Dennis showed me back in the day), and discover the slightly alarming fact that this particular client—as well as the potential target—is from my 'hood. Or close enough to freak me out a bit, anyway.

Even though they come up clean, my spidey senses are still a-tinglin', so I tell them that I'll get back to them with an answer within a couple of days. This gives me a little time to do some research.

M.A.R.K.-13 tells me that the client—Thomas Dobrowsky—is a forty-nine-year-old insurance salesman from a little town just across the river from where I reside. From that jumping off point, I dig around a little. In under an hour, I find out that he has joint checking and savings accounts with his wife Janice, a forty-seven-year-old nurse. They have two kids: Steven, age ten, and Deena, age twenty-four.

Decent credit rating.

Nice-looking family.

Dude *looks* like an insurance salesman. Wifey's a bottle blonde. A little dumpy-looking now, but I can see where she probably would've been a looker back in her day.

Little Steven is a freckle-faced lad with the distinct look of someone who eats a lot of paste. This kid was definitely taking daily beatings at whatever school he attended, the poor bastard.

And yet, he looked happy in every picture I managed to find.

Big, dopey smile.

A trusting smile.

Unlike his big sis.

Deena Dobrowsky was a slight, pretty thing. Raven hair, pale skin. Something a little Asian-looking about her features (I later figured out that this wasn't quite right; her family is Ukrainian), mostly in the cheekbones, the eyes.

Big, dark eyes. Sad, empty eyes.

There was something about the way she held herself, as if she was trying to disappear.

Seeing that shy sadness in her eyes, I felt my heart break a little. I wanted to find this girl and give her a hug, for god's sake. I wanted to tell her that, whatever was going on, it would get better.

Not that she would've taken me seriously at all, mind you.

Still.

Anyway, after all that, I checked out the target.

Mr. Franklin Alfred Bennington, Jr.

I know who he is now, of course, but at the time I just figured he was some pompous, rich douche bag.

(Spoiler alert: He was.)

Age twenty-five. Classic Aryan looks. In fact, from the pictures I found online (one from an honest to god *polo* match, if you can believe that clichéd shit) he looked disturbingly like Johnny Lawrence, the villain in the 1984 version of *The Karate Kid*.

I was ready to take the job based on that fact alone, to be honest.

But, being a conscientious and diligent little killer, I forced myself to dig deeper.

Hospital records are a little harder to get nowadays, but they still don't give me much trouble. I learned from the best, after all.

My bro, Dennis? I mentioned him, I think. He was the A Number 1, Original Gangsta. The ub3r h4x0r. If you were paying attention, back in the early nineties, he was the guy who hacked the FBI database. What the news media did not tell you was that, that same night, he broke into the D.o.D., the C.I.A., *and* the World Bank ... and not for anything malicious, mind you. He just wanted to show the world that he *could*.

He was fourteen at the time.

And yes, he did some prison time. And yes, he ended up working for a security corporation, locking out other little creeps like himself. And yes, he was (more or less) on the straight and narrow when some drunk asshole in a Miata skipped a curb and splattered the finest brain I've ever known all over the sidewalk of Washington Avenue.

He was engaged. His fiancé was smokin' hot.

He was twenty-seven.

He deserved a shot, y'know?

Anyway, Jesus ... whatever. Am I right?

Back to the front, yo. We got a schedule to keep, after all.

Like I was saying, medical records can get a little tricky ... but not *that* tricky. I would've broken through in no time, except there was a funky kind of lock on Deena Dobrowsky's file. I'd never seen anything like it. Later on, I found out what was up (along with the rest of the world) when it turned out that this Bennington a-hole had it all sealed up.

Because—as you know—it would look real bad for Daddy Bennington if the general public knew what Junior had been up to. Especially since this was an election year and all. Illinois has had its fill of nutbag politicians, that's for sure, but I don't think anybody would vote for a congressman with a firstborn like Mr. Franklin Alfred Bennington, Jr.

You remember the details of the case?

Sure you do.

Deena meets Franklin. They fall in love, right out of high school. Against her parents' wishes, they move in together. After this whole debacle when down, Deena told ABC news that she never would have done it, but Franklin said he wanted to get married. He said they had to do it all in secret because of his daddy.

But that wasn't true.

What was true was that Franklin had a nice little apartment in a nice little neighborhood, and Deena moved in with him. And before you could snap your fingers and say Entitled White Male, he started having little parties. With all of his little polo buddies.

Like I said, there's something about Deena. She's pretty, sure, but it's more than that. There's something there that I hesitate to even name because you'll just laugh at me.

But, fuck it. Laugh all you can, pal.

Hehe.

There's something there, in her eyes, that's pure and good and sweet ... and that's after all the hell he put her through.

Franklin wanted her to entertain his little buddies.

He didn't like it when she refused. Every time she refused.

By the time he took her to the hospital (only out of fear, mind you) she had a concussion, three broken ribs, and severe internal bleeding. That's not counting the damage done by the rape, either. Five guys. Five privileged little bastards who took what they wanted while she cried and screamed for help.

And where were the neighbors, you might ask? They were used to strange sounds coming out of Franklin's place, so they never bothered to ask any questions. Ain't America grand?

I'll be honest with you. When I read her files, the thought occurred to me to unleash a major league hellstorm on every single person involved. I was ready to kill every neighbor, every pedestrian who happened to walk by that night, you name it. But, c'mon ... that's a lot of work. And there's only so much payment, after all.

Like I said, I'm a capitalist.

I gotta be. I'm a major league otaku ... and let's face it: there is some serious truth to that old T-shirt slogan that says "Anime: Drugs Would Be Cheaper." My Japanophilia is yet another thing I inherited from Dennis, of course. He started me on Voltron, the perfect gateway drug for a kid. Of course, before long, you get into Macross and Naruto and Rurouni Kenshi ... and where does it all end?

Oh, I've gone and done it again, haven't I?

Damn.

Well, that tangent derailed my train of thought, but that's okay. You want to know how I do it? This is one of those things that never got mentioned in any of the news stories, you know. They all like to paint me as some cute, harmless little geek, but we both know that's not the full picture, right?

The truth is (and this I learned from Dennis, too. I learned it when he died) that the average person walking around is practically dancing right on the edge of ruin. They want to *think* that everything is peachy keen, but all they really need is a push.

And that's where I come in.

I provide the push, and they do the rest. I get the cash, and they do all the work.

Told ya: Capitalist!

So sometimes it doesn't take much. You hack into their company computer, jack up their work, make them look like a major screw up, and—bang—you got yourself an unemployed mark. Another fifteen minutes fiddling in the bank account and you got yourself a soon-to-be-homeless, dirt-poor mark.

It only takes about an hour to erase someone completely, and then they really start questioning shit. Had one dude so thoroughly cut off that, by the end of a week, he bit through his own wrists because he couldn't even afford a razor blade.

Kinda proud of that one, I gotta say.

But Franklin? I wasn't going to play Magical Vanishing Life with him. First off, it wouldn't work because he was too high profile. Secondly, to paraphrase Pinhead, I wanted to make his suffering legendary, even in hell.

So I did a little Darknet diving.

You know Avenue Q? There's that song "The Internet is for Porn"? Well the Darknet is, too, only it's the kind of stuff that the average person doesn't even want to think about. There's stuff out there that you cannot, and do not, want to imagine.

Crush vids. Rape. Necro. Pedo. Snuff. And then there's the stuff that gives the fans of that other stuff nightmares.

So what I did was this: I waited until I knew that Franklin was home, and, while he was sleeping, I remotely accessed his computer. And, as Mr. Franklin Alfred Bennington, Jr., I—very visibly, very clumsily, very *noticeably*—downloaded a metric crap ton of truly awful, extremely illegal pornography.

(I didn't check the stuff first, mind you. I know enough to know that there are some things you can't un-see, y'know? But I have it on good authority that this stuff was foul.)

Then I sat back and I waited.

And nothing freaking happened.

So, after a week or so, I made a few anonymous (and untraceable) calls to the local authorities.

Still nothing.

Irritating.

So I fixed up a recorded message in a lifelike yet computerized voice (no voiceprints on me, thank you very much) and made another anonymous, untraceable call, this time to the FBI.

As you know, nothing came of it.

Called the local TV stations next.

Nothing.

261

So the kid had way more juice than I ever would have suspected. Or Daddy did.

And that meant that I needed to get a little creative. I siphoned and closed his bank account. I maxed out his credit cards.

I got his country club membership revoked.

Hehe.

And all the while, I was careful. Careful as ever, honestly. Until it occurred to me that maybe being careful wasn't cutting it.

So I decided to start posting some defamatory statements online about Junior. The worst ones—the ones about his predilections for little girls, for instance—disappeared within a few hours. Still, I assumed that people were seeing the stuff while it was up. These things I did from my own account, under my own name, with my IP address easily traceable.

Now you might be thinking that was a risky move, right?

Because Junior could've just hired some guys to pay me a visit, yeah?

Here's the thing, though. When you have a taste for violence, it's not enough to just watch from a distance as someone else gets the job done. When you have a taste for it, nothing else will quench that for you.

Sometimes, you just gotta do it yourself.

And that's how I knew that Bennington would make a run at me.

Oh! Did I tell you? I met Deena Dobrowsky once, did you know that? Yep, the day before Junior came calling. Picture this:

Late May afternoon. Temperature in the mid-90s. Me—all in black, per usual. Her—work uniform. Khaki pants, red shirt. Black apron.

She takes my order: bacon cheeseburger, onion rings, and large Dr Pepper. Before she leaves, she smiles shyly and says that she likes my hair. That made me feel good. I had just dyed the tips, y'know, and they were supposed to come out kinda fuchsia, but they ended up looking pink ... well, you've seen the photos, I'm sure.

That was that. Customer and waitress. Although I like to think about my fingers brushing hers when she handed me the check. Not sure if that actually happened or if it's something I just made up, though.

Right, Junior. Back to Junior.

Are you comfortable, by the way? I mean, relatively?

Alright. I was home alone, that part is true, but the *reason* I was home alone ... well, I suppose by now you realize that it was no big deal to arrange that sweepstakes, the amazing cruise package, all that jazz, right? I mean, obviously I didn't want the folks home.

I hope you'll forgive me for not getting too deeply into the gory details of Junior's visit. It was, well, fairly painful and humiliating, as you and everyone else in the country saw—over and over—for months. What can I say? Sometimes you gotta take one for the team. Of course, the "one" I took involved head trauma, some permanent hearing loss on one side, and an extensive hospital stay. But, as you know, my webcam captured my entire beating. And broadcast it live all over the Internet. Given the buzz already surrounding Junior as a guy who preferred the company of young girls, the authorities frowned on his pretty ruthless assault of a scrawny, helpless, sixteen-year-old anime chick.

So that's the true story of how Franklin Alfred Bennington, Jr. got sent to a magical place where large, tattooed men inflicted vast amounts of karma on his sadistic, preppy anus.

But his death?

His "mysterious" death?

How surprised I was to find that it wasn't me who pulled that job.

At first, I figured Junior got snuffed just for being a dick. But, like I said, I'm diligent. And while I am really slick about hiding my money trails and my online movements and my various computer crimes—

Well, let's just say that you aren't, senator.

I've seen an awful lot of truly heinous shit, doing this job, but I think you probably take the cake. You paid one of my competitors to fake an accident... for your own son... for political reasons.

Classy.

Well anyway, I've told you all of that so I can tell you this: That first question you asked, the last thing you managed to get out of your mouth before everything froze up?

The answer is curare. Maybe you've heard of it? Y'know in those movies where the tribal dudes tag somebody with a blowgun dart and they go all paralyzed and stuff?

Bingo.

I got mine from a relatively reputable source. Darknet, of course. You can't get this stuff from Wal-Mart, you know. Anyway, this stuff paralyzes your muscles. If I left you alone, you'd probably asphyxiate once the toxin freezes your respiratory muscles.

But—

I don't think that's going to be a problem, do you?

I mean, you see the tools I've brought, right?

Sharp, shiny things.

If you're wondering why—well, I already told you. When you get a taste for violence, it's not enough to just watch from a distance anymore.

Sometimes, a gal's just gotta do it herself.

And for the record, sir?

This one's on the house.

TAKING CARE OF BUSINESS

BY LYNN MANN

"Here." She slid the thick envelope across the greasy Formica tabletop. "It's all there. Five now, five when it's done."

My eyes flicked down and back to her face, but my hands remained cupped around my drink. The envelope lay uneasily between us, our own Falkland Island.

"Take it," she hissed, "it's what we agreed."

"I've changed my mind, I want more. Ten now, ten after."

She'd been leaning forward, the better to conduct an intimate conversation amid the diner cacophony. Now she reared back, eyes wide and furious. I could almost see her cobra hood flaring.

"You son of a bitch," she whisper-screamed. "This is what we agreed and this is what I'll pay. It's the easiest ten grand you'll ever make, you asshole. Did you think I came to this lousy ptomaine palace just to bargain with you? Forget it, I'll get someone else. Two-bit hoods like you are easy to find."

Her hand, nails lacquered red like poisonous insects, reached for the envelope, but mine covered it first.

"Tell me again what you want and why."

She regarded me thoughtfully. "I get it," she said. "I watch TV, too. You're afraid this is some kind of sting, right?"

I shrugged, keeping my hand on the envelope. "I just want to know exactly what you want, and when. Then I'll decide whether your money's worth the risk. Start with whom, exactly."

"Fine, for all the listening public: I want you to kill my mother-in-law, Hazel Nesbeth. I want her dead, dead, dead. And I want it done soon. Like in the next five minutes."

I sipped my drink, the amber liquid leaving an oily sheen on the glass.

"Why? You're no spring chicken. Won't the old woman be dead soon enough for you? Or is she leaving you some money you need right away?"

She ignored the insult. "That hag will outlive us all. She's a cockroach; she could survive a nuclear explosion. Ever since I married her spoiled, pampered, mama's-boy son, she's been driving me crazy. Every year it gets worse. I hate her and I want her dead!" She leaned forward again, hissing, "Stop screwing me around. In or out?"

"When?"

"The sooner the better. Make it look like a random crime of opportunity, the kind of thing some punk would do."

"Fine, where?"

"She takes a walk every afternoon. Usually she makes me go with her, not that she wants my company. She just likes controlling my schedule. She always takes the same route: down Laurel, right onto Beech, right into Mapleridge Park. She walks along the shady side of the lake, sits on a bench overlooking the lake for a few minutes, then turns around and heads back, same path both ways. Before she leaves the park she sits on another bench, under some shade trees, for about ten minutes. The park's pretty deserted during the afternoon, do it then."

"You won't be with her?"

She glared, exasperated by my obtuseness. "No, I won't be with her, I'll make something up."

"Wouldn't want to kill the wrong old lady. How'll I recognize her?"

"The old bitch always wears a blue coat and a fake Hermes scarf. She carries a cane and has hot pink sneakers. You can't miss her."

"Huh," I said dubiously. "Them's some of the most dangerous words I've ever heard. Why not stage a robbery at the house?"

"Because I'm not a complete idiot," she answered strongly. "You really think I'm going to tell you where I live, let you into my house? You're too stupid to do this, give me back my money."

I grinned, scooped the envelope up and tucked it into my jacket pocket. "Nope, it's mine now. Don't worry, I'll take care of it tomorrow afternoon. You just practice looking shocked and grieved."

"I'll come back the night after she's dead, with the rest of your money."

She rose but before she could leave I asked, "How do you know I won't just take your money and not do the job?"

She leaned toward me, her expression so fierce I recoiled, a rabbit to her snake. "Because you don't want me to have to find you again, you pissant. I keep my word, you'd better keep yours."

She stalked away; I watched long after she turned the corner.

"How'd it go, Sergeant?" Captain Flannery asked.

"Fine," I answered. "I have it all on tape. Job's set for tomorrow afternoon, in Mapleridge Park. I'm tellin' ya, boss, she's a real piece of work. Tell the guys to be careful she doesn't scratch or bite them—they'd prob'ly die from rabies."

Flannery tendered the expected laugh. "Go on home, we'll wrap it up. Good work."

I half saluted and walked out; all I wanted was to wash off the stench of both the diner and that crazy bitch. Behind me I heard the captain setting up the ambush. I felt sorry for old Mrs. Nesbeth, having to find out that her daughter-in-law wanted her dead. Be ironic if the old thing died from the shock.

"How'd it go?" Lieutenant Michaels asked.

"Slam dunk," Detective Jane Landon answered. "IAD was right, he's as bent as they come. I have it all on tape, he'll be in the park tomorrow, looking for an old woman wearing a blue coat, a fake Hermes scarf, and hot pink sneakers. Just hope that isn't a popular look 'round here."

"We're real grateful for your help on this," Michaels said. "We're a pretty small department and no one local, not even a statie, could have gone undercover."

Jane nodded. "Glad to help. I hate dirty cops. They give us all a bad name."

"You want in on the take down?" he asked.

"Oh yeah," Jane said, "I'll be there. Pink sneakers and all."

THE WRITERS

JOSEPH BADAL

Joseph Badal has had four suspense novels published—*The Pythagorean Solution, Evil Deeds, Terror Cell, and The Nostradamus Secret*. His latest novel, *Shell Game*, was released in June 2012. He is also completing a nonfiction book about Relationship Selling. Joe has had a long career in the banking and financial services industries. Prior to his finance career, he served as a commissioned officer in the U.S. Army in critical, highly classified positions in the U.S. and overseas, including tours of duty in Greece and Vietnam. He earned numerous military decorations. Joe has also written dozens of articles that have been published in a variety of business magazines and trade journals, and is a frequent speaker and instructor at business and writers' events.

MICHAEL BAILEY

Michael Bailey is the author of *Palindrome Hannah*, a nonlinear horror novel and finalist for the Independent Publisher Awards. His follow-up novel, *Phoenix Rose*, was listed for the National Best Book Awards for horror fiction and was a finalist for the International Book Awards. *Scales and Petals*, his short story collection, won the same award for short fiction. *Pellucid Lunacy*, an anthology of psychological horror published under his Written Backward imprint, won for anthologies. His short fiction and poetry can be found in various anthologies and magazines around the world. He is currently working on his third novel, *Psychotropic Dragon*, a new short story collection, *Inkblots and Blood Spots*; and is tossing around ideas for a second themed anthology, as well as rereleasing a special edition of *Palindrome Hannah*. You can visit him online at www.nettirw.com.

J. CARSON BLACK

When a suspected child-killer's plane landed with all the pomp and circumstance of the space shuttle in Boulder, Colorado, J. Carson Black, a political junkie, took note. As it turned out, John Mark Karr did not kill JonBenet Ramsey; he'd merely played the media and fed their insatiable 24/7 appetite. This was the New American Way: celebrity for its own sake. That seed grew into into J. Carson Black's bestselling thriller, *The Shop*. In "The Bluelight Special," Black brings back *The Shop*'s idiosyncratic black ops specialist, Cyril Landry. In addition to being a stickler for good grammar, Landry has a wife and daughter who don't know about his secret life as a killer. When he visits his brother's horseracing operation in the Midwest, Landry finds a cause worth fighting for—and a foe worth taking out.

DOUG BLAKESLEE

Doug Blakeslee lives in Portland, OR and spends his time writing, cooking, gaming, and following the local hockey team. His interest in books started early thanks to his mom, but it wasn't until 2005 that his friend pushed him to participate in NaNoWriMo—that got the writing ball rolling. This is his first published story and he still can't stop smiling. He can be reached at simms.doug@gmail.com and can be found on Facebook.

AL BOUDREAU

Maine-based mystery/thriller author Al Boudreau has traveled the globe in order to gain first-hand knowledge of the various locales and cultures his fictional characters encounter. Boudreau feels this lends an authenticity to his stories unattainable by simple research. He also maintains a keen eye on geopolitical events, pushing the envelope to make his novels come alive. His fiction is based on the real world and the hidden truths buried just beneath the surface.

KEN BRUEN

Ken's bio is:

Ph.D in Metaphysics.

32 books published.

Headstone, the latest book is out now.

A recent spate of acting roles have added a nice slant to his work.

The Web site is www.kenbruen.com

WELDON BURGE

Weldon Burge, a native of Delaware, is a full-time editor, freelance writer, publisher, and creator of Web content. His fiction has appeared in *Suspense Magazine*, *Futures Mysterious Anthology Magazine*, *Grim Graffiti*, *The Edge: Tales of Suspense*, *Alienskin*, *Glassfire Magazine*, and *Out & About* (a Delaware magazine). His stories have also been adapted for podcast presentation by *Drabblecast*, and have appeared in the anthologies *Pellucid Lunacy: An Anthology of Psychological Horror*, *Don't Tread on Me: Tales of Revenge and Retribution*, *Ghosts and Demons*, and *Something at the Door: A Haunted Anthology*. He has a number of projects under way, including a police procedural novel and an illustrated book for children. He also frequently writes book reviews and interviews for *Suspense Magazine*. Check out his Web site at www.weldonburge.com.

ELLIOTT CAPON

Elliott Capon's novel, *The Prince of Horror*, has sold well on Amazon Kindle and other e-book sources. Several of his stories have appeared in *Alfred Hitchcock's Mystery Magazine*, one of which was reprinted as title story of an anthology (*Fun and Games at the Whacks Museum and Other Stories*); one other story was reprinted in Signet's *Mystery for Halloween* and was read onto books-on-cassette. His stories have also been published in *Amazing Stories*, *Fantastic Science Fiction*, *The Horror Show*, and *American Accent Short Stories*.

CHARLES COLYOTT

Charles Colyott lives on a farm in the middle of nowhere (Southern Illinois) with his wife, daughters, cats, and a herd of llamas and alpacas. He is surrounded by so much cuteness it's very difficult for him to develop any street cred as a dark and gritty horror writer. Nevertheless, he has appeared in *Read by Dawn II*, Dark Recesses Press, *Withersin* magazine, *Terrible Beauty Fearful Symmetry*, and *Horror Library* Volumes III, IV, and V. You can contact him on Facebook, and, unlike his llamas, he does not spit.

LAURA DiSILVERIO

The author of nine mystery novels and counting, Laura DiSilverio is a former Air Force intelligence officer. She writes the Mall Cop series (Berkley Prime Crime) and the Swift Investigations humorous private investigator series (St. Martin's Minotaur). The third book in that series, *Swift Run*, hits bookshelves in Dec 2012. As Ella Barrick, she is the author of the Ballroom Dancing mysteries for Obsidian. Her articles have appeared in *The Writer* and *Writer's Digest* and she is a faculty member of Mystery University, sponsored by Mystery Writers of America, and serves as secretary for the national board of Sisters in Crime. She lives in Colorado where she spends her mornings plotting murder and her afternoons parenting her teen and tween, and tries to keep the two tasks separate. Find her at www.lauradisilverio.com or friend her at www.facebook.com/lauradisilverio.

JAMES S. DORR

James Dorr has two collections from Dark Regions Press, *Strange Mistresses: Tales of Wonder and Romance* and *Darker Loves: Tales of Mystery and Regret*, while his all-poetry *Vamps (A Retrospective)* came out last August (2011) from Sam's Dot Publishing. An active member of SFWA and HWA with nearly four hundred appearances in venues from *Alfred Hitchcock's Mystery Magazine* to *Xenophilia*, Dorr invites readers to visit his site at http://jamesdorrwriter.wordpress.com for the latest information.

STEPHEN ENGLAND

A resident of rural Maryland, Stephen England is the author of the bestselling political/spy thriller *Pandora's Grave*. As a lifelong connoisseur of the written word, the transition from reading into writing was a natural one, and England's first novel, *Sword of Neamha*, was published in 2009. Set in pre-Roman Britain and told through the eyes of a young Celtic warrior, this coming-of-age adventure enjoyed moderate success and was heralded by reviewers as "epic" and "visceral." Released in the summer of 2011, *Pandora's Grave* represented the culmination of nearly a decade of writing and research into the Middle East, Islam, and covert operations. As the first volume of the *Shadow Warriors* series, the novel quickly won acclaim from reviewers as "a cross between Clancy and *24*." *New York Times* bestselling novelist Brad Thor called it "A terrific read from a great new author." The book was selected by GuysCanRead.com as the winner of their 2011 Independent Novel Contest. England blogs on current events and takes on the state of the publishing world on his Web site, www.stephenwrites.com. His story in this anthology, "Nightshade," forms a prequel to the *Shadow Warriors* series, and work is underway on the second book of the series, *Day of Reckoning*, with a release expected later this year.

KEN GOLDMAN

Ken Goldman, an affiliate member of the Horror Writers Association, has homes on the Main Line in Pennsylvania and at the Jersey shore, depending upon his mood and his need for a tan. His stories appear in over 645 independent press publications in the U.S., Canada, the UK, and Australia. More than thirty of Ken's tales are due for publication in 2012, and he is currently putting the finishing touches on his novel, *...Of A Feather*. Since 1993, his tales have received seven honorable mentions in The Year's Best Fantasy & Horror. His book of short stories, *You Had Me At ARRGH!! : Five Uneasy Pieces* (Sam's Dot Publishers), had been an all-time top-ten best seller at the former Genre Mall, and his novella, *Desiree*, is available in eBook downloadable format on the Damnation Books Web site and on

Amazon.com in Kindle and print format. Ken isn't famous yet; he expects that to happen posthumously.

MATT HILTON

Matt Hilton quit his career as a police officer with Cumbria Constabulary to pursue his love of writing tight, cinematic American-style thrillers. He is the author of the high-octane Joe Hunter thriller series, including his most recent novel *No Going Back*, published in February 2012 by Hodder and Stoughton. His first book, *Dead Men's Dust*, was shortlisted for the International Thriller Writers' Debut Book of 2009 award, and was a Sunday Times bestseller. Matt is a high-ranking martial artist and has been a detective and private security specialist, all of which lend an authenticity to the action scenes in his books. Check out his Web site at www.matthiltonbooks.com.

LYNN MANN

Lynn Mann lives in Maryland with two rescue cats and a supportive husband. Her writing reflects her eclectic reading, unusual education. and far-flung travels. Several of Lynn's stories have been published online and in small magazines, and her short story collection, *Mr. Smith's Errand*, available on Amazon. Her awards include 1ˢᵗ Prize in the 2011 Maryland Writers Association New Novel Contest (*Do You Do Murders*) and 3ʳᵈ Prize in the Windmill Women's Writers annual Short Story Contest. Along with her full-time job, she writes, raises orchids, and sails on the Chesapeake Bay whenever possible. For further information or to contact her, visit lynnmannauthor.com.

LISA MANNETTI

Lisa Mannetti's debut novel, *The Gentling Box*, garnered a Bram Stoker Award and she was nominated in 2010 both for her novella, "Dissolution," and a short story, "1925: A Fall River Halloween." She has also authored The *New Adventures of Tom Sawyer and Huck Finn* (2011); *Deathwatch*, a compilation of novellas—including "Dissolution" ; a macabre gag book, *51 Fiendish Ways to Leave Your Lover* (2010); two nonfiction books; and numerous articles and short stories in newspapers, magazines, and anthologies. Her story in this anthology, "Everybody Wins," was made into a short film by director Paul Leyden, starring Malin Akerman and released under the title *Bye-Bye Sally*; the film has been posted on YouTube. Lisa lives in New York. Visit her author Web site at www.lisamannetti.com, as well as her virtual haunted house at www.thechanceryhouse.com.

ROB M. MILLER

Born and raised in the hood of Portland, Oregon, over the years, Rob M. Miller has been victimized by violent attackers; thrashed violent attackers; enlisted in and honorably mustered out from the U.S. Army; taught martial arts; and worked in security, video store clerking, window washing, tire retreading, and store stocking. After two years of freelance stringer work and a number of publishing credits, he tired of nonfiction and turned to use his love of the dark, his personal terrors, and talent to do something more beneficial for his fellow man—*scare the hell out of him*! His work can be found online at the TheHarrow.com, as well as in American and British horror anthologies. He moderates a writer's site at www.writers-in-action-spruz.com, and his own Web site can be found at www.robthepen.pigboatrecording.com.

CHRISTINE MORGAN

Christine Morgan divides her writing time among many genres, from horror to historical, from superheroes to smut, anything in between and combinations thereof. She's a wife, a mom, a future crazy-cat-lady and a longtime gamer, who enjoys British television, cheesy action/disaster movies, cooking and crafts. Her stories have appeared in maby publications, including *The Book of All Flesh*, *The Book of Final Flesh*, *The Best of All Flesh*, *History is Dead*, *The World is Dead*, *Strange Stories of Sand and Sea*, *Fear of the Unknown*, *Hell Hath No Fury*, *Dreaded Pall*, *Path of the Bold*, *Cthulhu Sex Magazine* and its best-of volume *Horror Between the Sheets*, *Closet Desire IV*, and *Leather, Lace and Lust*. She's also a contributor to *The Horror Fiction Review*, a former member of the HWA, a regular at local conventions, and an ambitious self-publisher (six fantasy novels, four horror novels, six children's fantasy books, and two role-playing supplements). Her work has appeared in *Pyramid Magazine*, *GURPS Villains*, been nominated for Origins Awards, and given Honorable Mention in two volumes of Year's Best Fantasy and Horror. Her romantic suspense novel, *The Widows Walk*, was recently released from Lachesis Publishing; her horror novel, *The Horned Ones*, is due out from Belfire in 2012; and her thriller *Murder Girls* was just accepted by Skullvines. She's currently delving into steampunk, making progress on an urban paranormal series, and greatly enjoying her bloodthirsty Viking stories.

BILLIE SUE MOSIMAN

Billie Sue Mosiman's *Night Cruise* was nominated for the Edgar Award and her novel, *Widow*, was nominated for the Bram Stoker Award for Superior Novel. She's the author of fourteen novels and has published more than 160 short stories in various magazines and anthologies. A suspense thriller novelist, she often writes horror short stories. Her latest works include *Frankenstein: Return From the Wastelands*, continuing the saga of Robert Morton from Mary Shelley's classic, and *Prison Planet*, a near-future dystopian novella. She's been a columnist, reviewer, and writing instructor. She lives in Texas where the sun is too hot for humankind. All of her available works are at Amazon.com. Check out her blog, "The Life of a Peculiar Writer," at www.peculiarwriter.blogspot.com.

MONICA O'ROURKE

Monica J. O'Rourke has published more than seventy-five short stories in magazines such as *Postscripts*, *Nasty Piece of Work*, *Fangoria*, *Flesh & Blood*, *Nemonymous*, and *Brutarian* and anthologies such as *Horror for Good* (for charity), *The Mammoth Book of the Kama Sutra*, *The Best of Horrorfind*, and *Darkness Rising*. She is the author of *Poisoning Eros*, written with Wrath James White, *Suffer the Flesh*, and the collection *Experiments in Human Nature*. Watch for her new novel later this year from Sinister Grin Press! She works as a freelance editor, proofreader, and book coach. Her Web site is an ongoing and seemingly endless work in progress, so in the meantime find her on www.facebook.com/MonicaJORourke.

J. GREGORY SMITH

Prior to writing fiction full-time, Greg Smith worked in public relations in Washington, D.C., Philadelphia, and Wilmington, Delaware. He has an MBA from the College of William & Mary and a BA in English from Skidmore College. His first published novel, *Final Price*, was originally self-published, before being signed by AmazonEncore, and released in November 2010. He is also the author of the psychological thriller *A Noble Cause*, published by Thomas & Mercer, January 2012.

JONATHAN TEMPLAR

Jonathan Templar has written a large body of acclaimed dark and speculative fiction, much of which has been published in anthologies and compilations from a range of publishers. Jonathan's recent work includes the story "The Meat Man" in the charity collection *Horror for Good* and "Basher" for the shared world anthology *World's Collider*. His novella *The Angel of Shadwell*, the first in a series of stories for steam-punk detective Inspector Noridel, is to be published by Nightscape Press in September 2012 and his first collection of stories, *The Geometry of Hell*, is due later in the year. Jonathan has an author site with a full bibliography at www.jonathantemplar.com.

F. PAUL WILSON

F. Paul Wilson is the author of forty-plus books and numerous short stories spanning science fiction, horror, adventure, medical thrillers, and virtually everything between. His novels regularly appear on the New York *Times* Bestsellers List. He has received the Lifetime Achievement Award from the Horror Writers of America, the Stoker Award, the Porgie Award, the Prometheus and Prometheus Hall of Fame Awards, the Pioneer Award from the RT Booklovers Convention, the Inkpot Award from ComiCon, and was voted Grand

Master by the World Horror Convention. He is listed in the 50th anniversary edition of *Who's Who in America*. Millions of his books are in print in twenty-four languages. He also has written for the stage, screen, and interactive media. His latest thrillers, *Nightworld* and *Cold City* feature his urban mercenary, Repairman Jack. Paul resides at the Jersey Shore and can be found on the Web at www.repairmanjack.com.

THE ILLUSTRATOR

Nanette O'Neill _____

From Dublin, Ireland, Nanette O'Neill was born in 1984. She has a slight obsession with finding as many different ways to express herself visually as possible, and she adores painting ladies in particular. Nanette has a Higher National Diploma in Graphic Design and Media from BCFE Dublin and has worked on various projects from sculpting set props for TV to designing fascinators for professional dancing troops. Her other hobbies include smoking excessively (while trying to quit in particular), being snobby about (as well as drinking) whiskey, and going to gigs with friends (or moaning about not going to enough gigs with friends). To see more of her excellent work, visit www.the-nanette-o.deviantart.com.

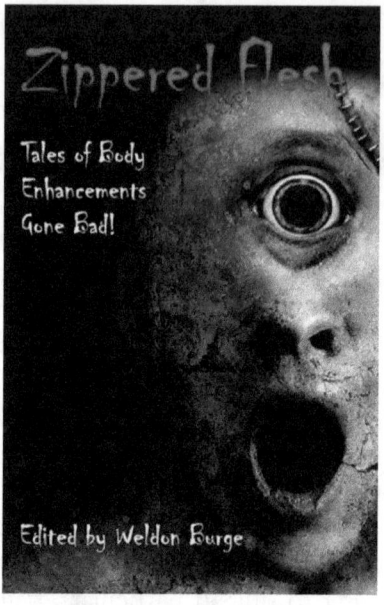

www.ingramcontent.com/pod-product-compliance
Lightning Source LLC
Chambersburg PA
CBHW071307170626
46809CB00001B/357